Trout Kill
a novel

Hope you enjoy the story!

Paul

Paul Dage

outskirtspress
DENVER, COLORADO

This is a work of fiction. The events and characters described herein are imaginary and are not intended to refer to specific places or living persons. The opinions expressed in this manuscript are solely the opinions of the author and do not represent the opinions or thoughts of the publisher. The author has represented and warranted full ownership and/or legal right to publish all the materials in this book.

Trout Kill
A Novel
All Rights Reserved.
Copyright © 2013 Paul Dage
v4.0 r1.0

Cover design by John Turley. All rights reserved - used with permission.

This book may not be reproduced, transmitted, or stored in whole or in part by any means, including graphic, electronic, or mechanical without the express written consent of the publisher except in the case of brief quotations embodied in critical articles and reviews.

Outskirts Press, Inc.
http://www.outskirtspress.com

ISBN: 978-1-4787-1709-6

Library of Congress Control Number: 2012920293

Outskirts Press and the "OP" logo are trademarks belonging to Outskirts Press, Inc.

PRINTED IN THE UNITED STATES OF AMERICA

Acknowledgments

For Kassia and Kelly ....

To Chris, whose bold dreams helped to inspire ... may your castle grow. Mick, who believes I can play with the Varsity. Patrice, whose friendship and wise counsel are invaluable. The '05 Dangerous Writing cohort at Cannon Beach, who helped rekindle the spark. The Emotive Gang, led by the irrepressible Ricardo. Jessica and Joanna, such gifted teachers. Leah and Daniel, who know how to do stuff I don't. John, the talented art guy. And especially to Debra, whose grace, wisdom and boundless love helped to keep this novel alive; and Bev, for her love and our common history.

Prologue

Despite his heavy winter coat, his long johns and the wool cap he had pulled to the lobes of his ears, he felt chilled. His hands trembled on the wheel. The toothpick between his lips shook. The car's blasting heater did not help. The center of what remained of his life—his god dot—felt frozen.

He hunched deeper into his coat and slowed the car. Anymore, to navigate a curve he had to *direct* his hands to move, *demand* that his right foot ease its pressure on the pedal and *instruct* his eyes to mind the road. Anymore, his body functioned by stern command, not instinct. Hell, even the rare straightaways along the winding coast highway demanded his fullest concentration.

A mile farther, he pulled over at a vista point and parked. The car's headlights shot into the dark void beyond the guardrail. He killed the lights, then thought better of it and turned them on again. He got out and stood beside the open door—an exertion that triggered yet another cough. It wracked him, and the toothpick shot out like a dart. He spit a lump—streaked with red, most likely. He shuffled forward to the guardrail. He leaned against it, resting, and then he lifted one complaining leg over the rail and thought *Anymore, climbing is a bitch.*

From where he stood behind the guardrail he could sense, but not see, the plunge of the cliff. The edge was well beyond the thin fog of his breath, and the meager throw of the headlights. He walked forward into the thickening darkness and then halted. He could not see his feet. The ground ahead, he knew, was uneven and covered with hummocks of grass and low brush. He shuffled on, feeling his way. There was just blackness and the growing ocean roar. When he sensed the closeness of the edge—perhaps just another step beyond—he stopped. The ocean surged against the rocks far below, and salty gusts blasted up the face of the cliff, and he breathed in as deeply as his one lung allowed. It embraced him, his love for the ocean. For the past forty-seven years, it had nourished him and cursed him.

He welcomed the vision of what awaited him: Doris, entrusted to carry out the stipulations of his final will, would bring his ashes to this point of land, stand where he now stood, and scatter his gray remains to the sea's peaceful deep, the heaving swells and the vast, underwater beds of swaying kelp. The vision, somehow, warmed his feet and helped to mend a rent in his life.

The feeling was short lived, and he was troubled once again by the chilling thought there were some things that a will could never settle up.

He returned to his car—a slow, exhausting struggle—and then pulled back onto the highway. Driving south, he retraced the same winding stretch he had just traveled. Anymore, the road was just a road. The countless other times he'd driven this stretch of the coastline—always leaving his home at midnight, always stopping at the vista and standing at the cliff's edge, and then driving back home—the illuminating sweep of his car's headlights had never failed to summon the voices of his stories. His fingers had tapped them out on the steering wheel, but now the voices did not speak anymore.

He turned the radio on, and the hiss of static filled the car. "Sheeit!"

It surprised him, the unbidden impulse that had compelled his hand to reach and push the knob. He had forgotten the car had a radio. He fiddled with another knob, trying to shut the damn noise off. Then, as clear as the stars that shined in the sky, Bing Crosby emerged from the static. He was singing "I'll Be Home for Christmas."

"Goddamn."

Christmas was ... when? Still a couple of weeks down the road, as best as he could recall. The chances were he would not live to see it, so there would be no need for Doris to fret about his gift, or to cut a fir from the woods, haul it into the house and stand it beside the fireplace. The boy, though, Raymond, had been pestering him for a certain gift—the Underwood.

Bing's croon was more than tolerable, honey-coated, and even enjoyable. He had to admit, Bing had a damned fine set of lungs.

He knew better than to sing along: a coughing fit might haul up another scrap of lung. His voice, like the days he had left, was of limited supply. The song took him back to such different times they belonged not to him but another man, it seemed. A wife, a little girl, a log house on a gravel road. He began to mouth the words—"I'll be home for Christmas ..."—and then, his voice gruff and shallow, he tried to sing aloud.

A dry fist seized his throat and cut his air; his eyes watered, blurring the road ahead. He coughed violently. His hands jerked and the headlights canted toward the ditch. Half blinded, he cranked the wheel back, trying to correct. A jolt raced through his chest. It was terror. He gasped and got air.

Somehow, the car was now ambling down the road, between the lines and doing forty.

"Sheeit!" Singing might kill him first, before he had a chance to die by other means.

He listened to Bing and kept his mouth shut. The terror, though, had warmed his bones.

Ahead, as he approached yet another curve, a doe ran onto the highway. She was no surprise. Since October, he had seen her along this same stretch nearly every night. He slowed the car. She was a black-tail, a dark-eyed beauty with her head held high. She bounded across the road, leapt the ditch and a few yards farther on she halted at the edge of the woods and waited, looking back the way she'd come. Her ears leaned that way. Two nimble fawns, twins, their spots almost identical, came frisking out of the darkness. He stopped for them. When they crossed through the headlights, their tiny hooves shined against the pavement and their eyes gleamed yellow. They ran to their mother, who led them into the woods where they disappeared in the underbrush.

Bing was singing like an angel, and the old memory came like it always did, sharp and piercing, and he tried to turn it aside before it stabbed too deeply, and he did, but not before he wondered what might have been, if Rose and their sons had lived, and not before his eyes had blurred with tears again.

A mile farther south, he turned off the highway and headed up a gravel road. It cut through a dense stand of mossy spruce, cedar and fir. There was a fork; he turned left. Beyond, the road emerged from the woods and crossed a wide meadow where, on the far side of it, the windows of his home glowed. He parked in front of the house, and when he shut the engine off the music died. Already, he missed it. He got out and began staggering along a footpath toward the porch. Stunted, frostbitten hydrangeas flanked the path. There was a trellis, the roses gone wild. He climbed a step, rested, and then climbed another. He stood on the porch. It slanted to the north. Forty years ago, he had built the porch footings too small. They had sunk, causing the posts and beams to sink, causing the deck to slope. The porch, though, was not the worst of what ailed the house. There was the wind-damaged roof, the crumbling foundation .... *The whole damned place is going belly-up.* It was the grindstone of time and his recent indifference. He crossed the porch, opened the door and braced himself against the jamb, gasping.

Inside, he hung his wool cap on the hall tree. Earlier, Doris had built a ripping good fire in the fireplace, and Raymond had stacked an armload of fir on the hearth. The fire's warmth graced the log walls of the living room, the fir-clad staircase, and the chairs, tables and bookcases he had built with his own hands. The cases stood empty, their shelves barren. *Good,* he thought. *Raymond has carried the last of the books to the loft.* He was sorely tempted to cross the living room and hold his hands to the fire's dancing warmth. Its heat, he knew, would seep deeper than the car's.

Anymore, warmth was his only inspiration.

He shuffled over to the stairs, grabbed the newel post, set his foot on the first tread and looked up. There was a gauntlet of risers and treads. He had heard that every step a man climbed added a bit of time to his life.

Nonsense, he hoped.

He climbed toward the loft, a struggle, shutting exhaustion from his mind. At the top, he stepped forward to the wide-open door. The padlock, un-clasped, hung on the hasp. Earlier in the day, he had left the door unlocked, for Raymond, and so that the heat rising from down below would enter the loft. He flipped the light switch, and one bare bulb lit; the second bulb did not. At the far end of the room, moonlight filtered through the only window.

Stacks of books covered nearly the entire floor, a narrow aisle passing between them. He hobbled down it. Food had never tasted good unless his nose was in a book; the books were a lifetime of breakfasts, lunches and dinners. He had never thrown or given one away. For this, he owed his mother Susanna a great debt. But the love she had instilled was, like his love for the ocean, a mix of curse and boon. She had inspired *his* imagination, but he could never forgive *her* imagination, which, he felt sure, had exhorted her to leave Jeremiah, her husband, and run off with Harold Weeb. Infidelity, like reading, required an imagination.

Midway along the aisle, he halted and turned to his left. He faced the log wall, a few feet away from where he stood, and blew a silent kiss at the painting hanging in the shadows there.

He went to his desk and turned on the lamp. His ancient Underwood sat there, a Model No. 5, a relic from the Thirties. It had been Jeremiah's. Its balky *q* angered him, how it smacks the paper and, instead of recoiling to its nest and joining its fellow letters, hangs there like an undecided cock. Now, the *q* was hanging there again. Raymond, he figured. The boy loved the old machine's rat-a-tat clack, and was always pestering to bang out stories about invisible flying dragons or wizardknockers or turdhouses or catapults that flung flaming hay bales at hordes of ogres.

During a rash moment, he had promised the boy the machine for Christmas. He had changed his mind. Like an old dog, the damned machine needed shot. It was worn-out and, at least for *him*, it would never write another story. Besides, *Underwood* was a name better suited for a coffin. Funny how a man can ignore regret and shoot what he once loved.

He would make it up to the boy, or his will would. Maybe Raymond would buy one of those fancy electrics, or a new-fangled computer.

He pushed the stuck *q* down to its nesting place.

His legs ached and trembled; he eyed the chair. *To hell with it. Stand and suffer, you old coot. Eat a shit-pot full of pain and lick the spoon clean.*

He would make it quick: one slug through the platen. But how in the hell, he wondered, could he ever explain shooting the typewriter to the nine-year-old?

He collapsed into the chair and sat there, facing the machine. He lifted one hand to the keys, and then the other hand, and let his fingers rest on the home row. Three fingers pressed down three keys, one after the other, and each of the steel arms swung in crisp arcs and smacked the platen. It was such a simple word—*the.* It still intoxicated him, like a double-shot of Hennessy. It beckoned other words and, in turn, those words summoned others that eventually shaped a story.

He pulled his hands to his lap. He had better get on with it, before his strength pissed away, or sentiment got the best of him. He unlocked a desk drawer and lifted the pistol out, a Browning .45. It too had once belonged to Jeremiah. Tiny spots of rust bloomed on the steel. *It could use a good oiling*—and that painful thought led to memories as deep as the wrinkles in his face: the smell of fresh-baked apple pie; and the gagging, unctuous tang of Hoppes #9 gun oil.

He thumbed the hammer back, lifted the gun and aimed at the platen, just above the V-notched typeguide—where countless times before the words had swung up and pounded out the voices in his head, those from his night drives. He had loved writing, and hated it. He tried to pull the trigger, but his hand started shaking. Then the tickle, the constriction, and yet another ragged cough bent him double.

The attack passed, as they now did with growing reluctance. He sat back in the chair and breathed as deeply as he dared.

A cardboard box sat in the corner.

"Sheeit!"

He had told Raymond to carry all the books from downstairs up to the loft, and then to haul off every damned and dusty box, filled with who-knew-what from who-knew-when. He had paid the boy five good dollars. *Take the damn things to the garden and burn them.* But Raymond had probably forgotten this last box and, instead, plunked away on the Underwood, or he'd seen a squirrel out the window and gone traipsing after it.

The box looked heavy. He got up from the chair and hefted it. *Not so heavy after all.* He set it on the desk and pulled a flap loose. Dust rose in the lamplight.

In the shadowy bottom of the box, he saw a child's pale face. A little girl with—he bent closer—yes, her eyes shut. She had blond hair. He swallowed down an itch in his throat, and moved the box closer to the lamp.

She wore a red-and-white gingham dress and one white stocking on her foot. The other foot was bare.

She smiled up at him, and she held her arms up and giggled in her rippling sweet way.

He blinked—not believing what his eyes remembered. He staggered back; his breath emptied out and his vision blurred in the backward rush of years. Pain shot through his chest and down his arm; his knees buckled and he grabbed the chair to brace himself.

No! Not now, not yet!

He could breathe again.

He reached into the box, lifted the doll out and held her stiffly, at arm's length. Her eyes remained closed; their lashes were impossibly long.

He had forgotten the color of her eyes.

Over her left ear, a barrette pinned her hair back.

The dress was soiled, a black smear of Cat grease. His own hand, he knew, had put it there. Again, a memory gutted him, nearly drove him to his knees: the doll lying in the pathway ... the antiseptic stench of ether ... on the mattress, his wife splayed and bloodied ... his daughter, asleep, sucking on her thumb ... the crack of the .45 ... the bounce of Redbow's stethoscope.

He shook the doll, trying to jostle open her eyes. *Blue ... or are they green?*

Her eyes stayed shut. He shook her again, harder. Then the lashes fluttered up.

Like March moss.

The green stabbed him, piercing to the center of his god dot.

Chapter 1

The yellow sign with the bent black arrow said to slow down, there's a curve ahead, but I knew the corner well enough—a blind and banked twenty-five—and the tires on my pickup had a fair bit of tread.

The headlights cut through a night heavy with the ocean's scent, with sweeter traces of the winter woods, spruce and cedar, mostly. The trees crowded thick to the shoulders, their boughs overreaching, and it seemed we were driving down a ragged tunnel. A steady mist fell.

Beth's hands lifted from her lap and grasped her seatbelt: Her way of saying *Eddy, slow down, you're speeding; I'm afraid; please slow down.* She was bundled in a coat and sweater against the draft shooting cold through the hole in the floorboard.

I eased off the gas; the needle dropped toward forty, maybe forty-five and we entered the curve.

A doe stood at the edge of the pavement. She was stiff-legged, tail up, neck graceful, alert and beautiful, caught full in the sweep of lights. Her eyes gleamed yellow and she snorted fog. Maybe that was when I fell in love with her.

But a startled deer, I knew, might do anything. She might just stand there and, glassy-eyed, watch us pass, or she might turn and bound away into the woods, or she might trot straight ahead onto the road. I shifted down a gear and to give her more space, veered left and across the yellow line.

Beth gasped.

All the doe had to do was nothing. Just stand there.

She spun on her rear legs and bolted—a dun-brown flash that struck the right front fender. The steering wheel shuddered; the jolt of impact shot into my hands, up my arms and into my chest.

Beth screamed—maybe. In that crystalline moment, it could have been me.

The doe flipped into the air, banged off the windshield directly in front of Beth and disappeared over the cab.

The pickup slewed across the highway, crossed the centerline, spun a one-eighty and came to rest in the far shoulder of the southbound lane.

The engine idled smooth, indifferent, as if something hadn't just died. A headlight pierced the night. The doe, I knew, had busted out the other one. I held onto the wheel with both hands, scared, afraid to let go, knowing it had been me, not Beth, who'd screamed. Or maybe it had been both of us. I took my foot off the brake.

Beth sobbed—a great shiver that came through the bench seat. Her face was pasty white, her hands tight around her seatbelt.

I said, "Are you okay?"

One hand fluttered away from her seatbelt, stalled in midair, fell to her lap and curled up. "Oh, Jesus, Jesus!"

I said, "She just came out of nowhere."

Beth said, louder than the rough idle of the engine, "You bastard! Oh, Jesus! You bastard!"

"I didn't have time."

"You were speeding!"

"I didn't—"

"Speeding!"

The cab got real quiet. The windshield on Beth's side was a spider's web of cracks, a smear of red. Beth drew away from it, pressing her back into the seat.

I keyed the motor off.

She sobbed, some part of her fear letting go, and then she took a deep breath. Her next sob seemed choked off, an incomplete release, as if she were holding back the bulk of it, the most anguished part—not yet, not in the cab, not with me sitting there so close. When I reached for her hand, it jerked away.

Beyond the gravel shoulder, beyond the grassy ditch that ran parallel to the road, the conifers stood dark and thick. I said, "It's okay. You're okay. It's just an accident."

"It's bigger than that! Things like this happen for a bigger reason than we can ever know. You could have killed us, Eddy. Don't you see that?"

She didn't believe in "accidents," but rather the mysterious workings of God's obscure will. "The doe spooked. You can't ever tell what a deer will do."

Beth twisted away and faced the side window, her nose close to the glass. "You should go and see."

"Yeah, the fender. Okay, I'll check it out." In my haste to escape, I fumbled the handle of the door.

"I meant the deer, too. See about him, too. The poor thing."

"She's a doe. But, yeah. We can't just leave her on the road."

"Hurry. We're already late."

We had reservations at the Edgecrest, an ocean-view room with HBO and pillow mints, still another hour's drive north in Glass Point. Beth had packed a special pair of Wal-Mart panties, pink, embroidered with Rudolph the Red-nosed Reindeer. As soon as we got there, I'd toss her on the bed and make love to her. Then I would prop myself up against the headboard and down a stiff shot of Jack. Beth didn't drink. Maybe I'd have two shots. We'd sing "Rudolph the Red-nosed Reindeer," and I'd make her laugh. With the roar of the surf lulling us asleep, the things weighing on us would slip away. In the morning, I'd tell her all about Dr. Lund and Uncle Silas. I would tell her everything.

Beth said, "Be careful, for cars."

"Yeah, okay. I'll be careful."

"And turn the blinking lights on."

"The hazards?"

"Yes."

I pulled the knob on the dash and the hazards blinked yellow a few times and then quit. I pushed the knob in, pulled it out again. Like other things, the hazards didn't work. "Shit."

Beth shook her head.

I could feel her growing anger. It was festering. The fester would sink deep and then crystallize into memory. In the months and years ahead, she'd remind me over and over again. She had a way of making diamonds out of shit like this. I set the emergency brake and reached for the door handle again.

"Shouldn't we move farther off the highway?"

"I'll check the damage first. It'll just take a sec."

She jabbed open the glove box and rummaged through the Dairy Queen napkins. I was glad the weed wasn't there. I'd stashed it in my travel bag. She found the flashlight. Its beam swept across the splintered windshield and into my eyes.

I blinked, turned my head away, saw a swirl of bright dots.

"Here," she said, "so you can see."

I took it and got out. The wet chill seeped through my Army field jacket. Mist swirled through the beam of the flashlight and the shine of the one good headlight. Around front on the right side, the fender was buckled—not too bad, though. A strip of chrome ripped from the body, dangling. Deer blood and shit pellets and hair smeared across the hood. A wisp of steam hissed from underneath the hood. On Beth's side, the arm of the wiper was sticking upright. I pushed it back down.

She watched through the busted windshield. Her fear, I think, ran a lot deeper than mine, and wider, too, like a spreading-out river after heavy rains. I couldn't point a finger at anyone. It was just an accident. I could do something, like walk around and check the fender, assess the damage. Beth couldn't. This kind of damage wasn't something in her realm. She didn't know what to do, anymore than I knew how to bake a cake or teach a kid how to read. For her, accidents didn't just happen. She was a long way from Milo, from her comforting Jesus mug of steaming tea, her frayed bathrobe and slippers, from the safety of the home she thought would never hurt her. But nothing was the doe's fault. A lot of *ifs* popped into my head about speed and time and luck, and *if* any one of those things had been just a little different then the doe would still be alive, and Beth and me would be cruising along, miles closer to the pillow mints, to making love and confessions.

She rolled her window down a couple of inches. "Are we okay? Can we drive?"

I stood there, the flashlight trained on the fender. "Yeah. It's just the fender, mostly." And because I was feeling lucky that things weren't worse: "The insurance will cover it."

She shook her head. "You increased the deductible. Remember? From five hundred to a thousand dollars."

I did remember.

We'd had a big fight over it. Who's gonna need a low deductible for a piece-of-crap pickup? Maybe Dr. Lund was right: I was a risk junkie, a guy balanced high atop a greased tight rope and asking for a blindfold, wishing I were higher yet, someplace in the stratosphere over the Grand Canyon. Sure, I can do forty around a kiss-your-ass corner. I should've taken that job selling used cars for Beth's dad, a no-fucking-risk opportunity, with health insurance and coffee breaks. I'd turned it down years ago. Then the owls shut the woods down, and I'd lost my job felling trees. Beth's father was a good man, but for me wearing a white shirt was a far cry from a roaring chainsaw spitting sawdust at my boots in the woods. So, I'd gotten a part-time job at Sparky's place.

I kicked the tire. It was solid. "Jimmy'll bang the dents out, fix the windshield. And firewood's as good as money."

She just sat there looking at me through the side window, like she was thinking Jimmy was a half-blind perv with a greasy beard that hung to his zipper, with worn out wrenches and no hoist. Or maybe she was hoping that he'd Bondo my dents too, smooth them out till they hardly showed. But mostly it was the money. Even if Jimmy just charged me for the parts, the dough wasn't in the budget. Beth ran the checkbook and bought the groceries—always on sale and with coupons. She'd taught the girls how to save their pennies and nickels and, beyond that, polite ways to talk and how to dress, what spoon and fork goes where, and don't flush your tampons down the crapper and into the septic tank.

Even then and there, with a doe dead and Beth upset with me, I felt that soft squeeze of my heart and knew I still loved her.

We just feel things different sometimes.

I tilted back my head and looked up. The black sky felt good on my face, and then out of that black I heard a scream … from the south, from this side of the curve we'd just come around. I aimed the flashlight that way and saw nothing except the sheen of wet pavement.

And then another eerie shriek, but weaker than before.

Beth heard it too. She leaned forward and peered through the windshield. "What was that?"

"The doe, I think." I'd heard something like it before, years ago when I'd gut-shot a forked-horn. When I walked up on it, it screamed like a woman giving birth to an axe.

Beth squared her shoulders, hugged herself. "It sounded so …?"

It didn't surprise me, how she couldn't finish that thought, how it had turned into a question. Death rattles are so far beyond her familiar, she could never begin to imagine one.

I said, "She's hurt bad."

"The poor thing."

I nodded and thought about our—no, my—sick and dying dog.

She said, "You'd better go and see. And be careful. We're already late." She rolled her window up, pulled her coat tighter.

I started walking, feeling as if every step was pulling me farther away from what needed fixed. The headlight helped me see for a little ways. Beyond its reach, the flashlight led me about fifty yards farther to the doe.

The doe, stretched out across the yellow line, held her head up and turned toward the woods. Her ears aimed at the woods. One feeble hoof scraped against the pavement. The other front leg—on her left side, where the fender had struck—had snapped below the knee; the shinbone gleamed. A scrap of hide held it on. Her back legs twisted in a way that meant she had a broken back. Her stomach had busted open and vapors lifted from her guts. Fog huffed from her nose.

I fell in love with her again—or maybe for the first time—a sweet nausea rising from my gut to the center of my chest. And, then, an unclenching that allowed a ragged gulp of air. Her musky scent buckled my knees. I felt hope, or something of the sort, mysterious and beyond me. The tears just started pouring, and seemed to wash away any need to confess.

She kept her head up and turned away, eyes always toward the woods. To her, I wasn't even there. Only the woods were. I was just a scent dampened by the mist.

Her good front leg scraped the pavement again. Her head wavered but didn't drop.

I shined the flashlight into the woods, saw only a dim swath of dripping trees, all else black. Beyond the woods, the ocean was a low rumble, unseen. I went looking for a rock, off the highway, beyond the shallow ditch. Several larger stones lay half-buried in the dead grass. I stuck the flashlight under my arm and knelt over a rock about the size of a cantaloupe. It needed both of my hands to lift, fingers laced beneath, and then carry toward the road.

To the north, my pickup's faint headlight winked once, twice, three times: Beth signaling, impatient for the pillow mints and HBO, for me to tidy up the mess I'd made. From where she sat in the pickup, as seen through the veil of mist and darkness, I'd be invisible, and the flashlight would be a distant firefly.

Back at the highway, I halted a step away from the doe, so close my boots were in her blood. Still, she kept looking into the woods. The rock was cold in my hands. I knelt and laid the flashlight on the pavement, its beam full upon her. It cast her shadow far. I told myself *Make the rock quick and sure. Not like before, with Silas.*

I lifted the rock above my head, aimed between her ears and heaved it down quick. Her head snapped down and the rock tumbled away. Off balance, I lurched forward and nearly tripped over her, fought to keep my feet under me. I staggered back. My heel kicked the flashlight in a strobbing circle. It blinked out. Standing there in the darkness, I heard the soft huffing of the doe.

I found the flashlight and shook it back alive.

The doe was at my feet. Her eyes were glazed thick, her lower jaw slack. Pink froth bubbled from her nose. But her head was up.

"I can't kill anything right."

A rush of sound and light swept around the corner and hurtled toward us. I just stood there scared shitless, too dumb to even wave the flashlight or move. The car swerved around and sped past, missing me by a few feet, and its road spray cast a shroud. I dropped to my hands and knees beside the doe and puked, first lasagna, then bitter fear and bile.

Beyond my pickup, the car had stopped. It was idling quiet there, its exhaust glowing red in its taillights.

I stood. My legs were unsure. The bright rush of the car's lights had frozen me. Always before, I'd never been so afraid that I couldn't run away.

Still shaky, I walked back to the pickup. Beth rolled her window down again, not far, just those same few inches as before. She was gripping her seatbelt with one hand, the other braced against the dash. She nodded over her shoulder at the car, still idling about twenty yards behind her. "What's happening? We should leave. Come on, please."

She didn't know about the rock, or the still-suffering doe, how close I'd come to getting run over. I nodded toward the car. "Maybe he wants to help."

"He?"

"I thought I saw a man."

"Help? With what?"

"I'll go see."

"Eddy, don't. Let's just go."

She meant go *now*. She meant the shitfuck I'd created was already bad enough, and if things got shitfucked up anymore, then Christ would have a fit, and if He had a fit so would she. She meant I'd ignored the road sign that screamed *Slow down!* She meant if I'd just get in the damn pickup and drive sanely up the highway to Glass Point then Christ might think of forgiving me, and if He found it in His heart to do so, she would too. There was still a chance of making love.

I said, "She's still alive, the doe."

"Eddy, please. For God's sake."

"Lock the doors."

The car was a black Ford, an older model, its trunk secured by a length of wire looped to the rear bumper. I walked up slow to the driver's side. The man was looking down at something in his lap, his face half hidden by the collar of his coat. He wore a red cap and had a white beard. The radio was playing a Christmas song. A book lay beside him on the seat. The heater pushed warm air out the open window.

I said, "Hey, thanks for stopping."

He never looked up.

"There's been an accident."

The Ford's wipers glassed back and forth. The dash lights glowed. Then he reached for the radio, turned it off, lifted his head real slow and looked out at me. Underneath the brim of his cap, his eyes were dark hollows in a lean, tired and old face. He had a toothpick in his mouth. Wispy white hair that straggled down from the cap to his collar. He said, "You okay, Son?"

"Yeah, sure. I'm fine."

"Seeing you there, it surprised the heck out of me. Came close to killing you. I'm real sorry."

His voice was gravel, rough and dry. I nodded back toward the pickup. "The wife's pretty shook up."

"Can't blame her for that, not one bit."

"I shouldn't've been standing there. It's a wicked blind corner. I hit the doe. She's real bad off."

"An accident, like you said."

"She panicked, ran right into me."

He reached his right hand out the window. "Name's Spencer."

His hand was soft, with big, loose bones. "I'm Eddy."

He nodded twice. "How's your rig?"

"A little banged up, but okay to drive."

Spencer spit the toothpick from his mouth, grabbed a handkerchief from his lap and coughed into it, a series of hawking rasps. His shoulders hunched. He folded the hanky and set it back on his lap. He cleared his throat. "Have you seen any fawns anywhere near here?"

I looked off into the dark. "Fawns? It's pretty late in the year for fawns."

"They're twins, cute as hell."

"You think this doe …?" My voice caught. Fawns without their mother wouldn't stand a chance. Not with the hard winter and coyotes around. I swallowed down the bile taste.

He looked up at me. "Take it easy on yourself, Eddy."

"Goddamn it."

"These things happen. A man never knows." He reached down for something on the floorboard between his legs. He brought it up and handed it out the window slow. It was a gun, a pistol.

It scared me, its sudden, unexpected appearance, and I backed away a quick step.

He said, "You say she's bad off. Well then, maybe she needs a little help. Go ahead and take it."

His hand and arm started shaking, maybe from the weight of the gun. It was lying flat in his open hand, the grip toward me, the barrel pointing at his coat sleeve.

He was right: A gun is surer than a rock. I took it. The pistol was an older Browning .45, the barrel rusty. The grip felt warm, from the car's heater, I supposed. I double-checked the safety.

"She's cocked and loaded for bear. Clip's full. Just thumb the safety off when you're ready."

"It's rusty, could use a little oil."

"She works fine, if that's what you're getting at. True, she needs a little TLC but, hell, lately, a lot of things do."

Trout Kill

I nodded, shrugged.

He gestured toward the pistol. "You know guns, I see."

"Yeah, a little."

He looked off into the woods for a long time while the wipers swept back and forth. "Do me a real big favor, Son."

"What's that?"

"After you shoot her, lay her down in a good place."

I pegged him as a softhearted nut, a guy who'd carry a shovel in his trunk to bury the roadkill he chanced upon. Maybe that is what he'd been doing, cruising for road kill. The gun was to end any suffering. But what he'd just said about a *good place* made me swallow hard again. It fit with the way I felt about the doe. You can't just drag what you love to a ditch and leave it there. I nodded. "Okay, I'll find her a good place."

My pickup's horn blared. For Beth, things were spinning outward in an ever-widening storm.

Spencer startled. His hands fumbled for the steering wheel, gripped it. He stared straight ahead, the tip of his beard brushing the top button of his coat. "You'd better get on with it."

I just stood there. "We're on our way to Glass Point. A sort of vacation, me and the wife. Beth. Her name is Beth."

He kept his grip on the steering wheel.

Funny, I thought, *how I just open up to strangers. And why should he give a damn?*

Walking back toward the pickup, I dropped the gun into the pocket of my jacket, told myself *Let Beth know what's going on, that things are going okay, that Spencer's a real nice guy who's helping out, that I've gotta find a good place to lay the doe.* But Beth had her window up and her stare glued on the busted windshield, so I walked past her and the pickup and headed for the doe.

We'd gotten a late start from home because it had been a busy night at Sparky's—Ladies' Night, two-for-one drinks—and Sparky'd asked me to tend the bar for an extra hour. The place was hopping: *Wheel of Fortune* was playing on the big screen, the pool tables were clattering, the jukebox was juking, and the Rogue ales were flowing like horse piss. The hour slipped into two hours, and I'd forgotten to call Beth to let her know I'd be late. When I got home, she was sitting at the kitchen table stewing. It was after ten o'clock. She'd made lasagna. A candle nub guttered beside two glasses and a bottle of Ernst's wine. Licker got up from his favorite spot by the wood stove and hobbled over to greet me. I scratched his neck underneath his blue nylon collar. The walnut-sized lump on his neck had grown to a baseball. I told Beth I was sorry, that I should've called to let her know. Her stare was as hard as the lump. She said, "You never call." I told her about Ladies' Night, how busy Sparky's was. "Sparky paid me," I said, showing her the two hundred dollars. She said, "We have reservations. We have a ten-percent-off coupon." I'd forgotten about the reservations, maybe because the motel, the Edgecrest, had been an idea I'd gotten from Dr. Lund, not my own idea. I wanted real bad to grab the wine and drink the whole damned bottle. But I reached across the table, took her hand and said, "We can leave now. It's not too late." She shook her head, pulled her hand away, plated a slab of the lasagna and almost threw it at me. I smiled and ate. Food was how she'd sometimes forgive me. Licker wagged and sniffed; his appetite wasn't near what it used to be. Beth ate small bites and kept her chin aimed at her plate. I had a glass of wine, then two. In the living room, the angel glowed on top of the tree. Tinsel and ornaments hanging off every branch, and Beth's Jesus mug hanging on the kitchen rack. She'd already called BJ and Kate, our twin daughters, and told them we'd be gone for a couple of days. They were at college, both freshmen, but they'd be coming home for Christmas. She'd arranged for a neighbor to take care of Licker, give him his chow and pain pills. Beth's packed suitcase was sitting by the kitchen door. I'd gotten up from my chair, stepped around the kitchen table to where she sat in her chair, cupped her left breast in my hand and said, "I'll drive slow. I promise."

The doe's chin was flat on the pavement. She was barely alive, the froth red now, not pink, and I could've just stood there and watched her die. But she was a mother of twins, like Beth was. I remembered the vision of her standing beside the road with such wild grace and beauty.

I lifted the pistol, thumbed off the safety and pulled the trigger. The night flashed; my hand bucked and the mist swallowed the retort. A spat of pavement exploded. From five feet away, I'd missed her head and shot the road.

Beth screamed; the distance between us muffled it. She hated guns, and hated that I knew them. I waved the flashlight, hoping to reassure her that things were going okay.

Then the doe lifted her head again, maybe out of some primal instinct, and looked off into the woods, still taking no notice of me, her eyes now, again, unglazed and fiercely wild. Then her head dropped; a frothy red wheeze escaped from her, and she died with her eyes wide open.

The gun felt obscene, its cold steel heft. I safetied it,

slipped it into a pocket, then knelt down, picked her up in my arms and staggered to my feet. She felt broken and her guts slumped. I turned in a slow, dazed circle in the middle of the highway. A *good place*, Spencer had said. I carried her across the shoulder, beyond the shallow ditch and into the woods. There were no stars or moon, just the black, looming shapes of trees. It wasn't far to a big cedar. Of all the trees in the woods, cedars are the best, their fragrance and russet grain, the swoop of their graceful limbs. I shouldered through the wet branches and stood beside the thick-barked trunk. Dry duff covered the ground. I laid her there, beside the wide trunk on the bed of duff.

The coyotes will come soon, or the crows. They'll say words for you.

I returned to the highway. Beth saw me coming and rolled her window down a little bit. She looked scared and mad. I nodded toward the Ford. "This man, Spencer, he lent me a gun, for the doe, for helping her."

"God, Eddy. I can't believe this!"

"It needed done."

"That man, he could be ... he could have ...!"

She meant Spencer could be an unChristian guy who'd shoot me and rape her, or some such wickedness. "I put her down someplace nice, underneath a big cedar."

She shook her head and rolled the window up.

The Ford was still idling quiet, the radio playing another Christmas song, the heater billowing heat. Spencer seemed to have gotten older. He sat with his head slumped, his beard flattened on his chest.

I said, lying, pointing the flashlight at my feet, "It went okay." I handed over the gun, holding it out for him.

He lifted his head, but he never reached for the gun. "Is there anything else?"

"No, I took care of her."

He nodded, reached for the gun, took it and fumbled it in his stiff fingers as he drew it back inside the car. He laid it on the seat. "You found a good place to lay her down?"

"Yeah, underneath a cedar."

"That's a fine place. Damned fine."

"Yeah."

"Looks like she bloodied you."

He was looking at my field jacket. It was blood-soaked, and red gouts clung to the olive drab. "That's okay. It'll wash out."

"Blood can be a stubborn thing."

The mist was thinning; the low, rising quarter moon was now a blurred halo. I switched the flashlight off. "I've gotta get going. Thanks for stopping and helping out."

"A man does what he's got to do, eventually." He stuck out his hand and we shook again. He held on longer than before, his grip clinging, and underneath his cap his eyes glistened. "It was real nice to meet you, Eddy."

"Yeah, same here." I turned and hurried back to the pickup.

Beth was standing beside the cab, her door open, as if she were undecided about what to do next: run away or get back in, cry for fear or scream with rage. She'd wrapped herself in a blanket and she was shaking. The moon made her pale skin milky. She looked beautiful.

I said, "Everything's okay. We can leave now."

She pulled the blanket tighter. "Take me home!"

"Home?"

"I can't stand this, Eddy."

"What?"

"You. Everything. Just not knowing what you'll do next." Her anger broke and she began to sob.

"But we'll be there in an hour. I'll drive slower."

Her shoulders heaved underneath the blanket.

I stepped close to hug her. The door was in the way. I turned her toward me. In my awkward embrace, she felt unyielding, just a cold and damp blanket. "It's not too late, Beth. We have reservations. Come on. Get back in."

She shook her head, shrugged me off, got in the pickup and sat there stone-faced. I closed her door and walked around to my side. Up the highway, Spencer's Ford hadn't moved. Maybe he was waiting, watching us in his rearview mirror, seeing if the pickup would still run okay. I slid behind the wheel and Beth shrank away. And then she saw the blood on the blanket, and on her hands—from my jacket when I'd hugged her. She grimaced, got the box of wet-wipes from the glove box and rubbed at her hands frantically, tossing one wipe after another onto the floorboard at her feet.

"It's hers," I said, meaning the doe's. "I'm sorry."

"Just take me home now."

I started the pickup, put it into gear and pulled ahead slow, passing by where I'd thrown up in the doe's blood. Behind, Spencer's taillights disappeared in the rearview mirror. Safely past the blind corner, I sped up, but kept it under fifty. Beth gathered the wipes from the floorboard, stuffed them into the folds of the bloody blanket and shoved the blanket behind the seat. I listened hard to the engine's hum, and kept an eye on the temperature gauge. For a mile or two, the pickup ran fine.

Trout Kill

Then the needle of the gauge shot into the red. Twenty-seven miles north of Milo, I slowed down and pulled over to the side of the highway.

Beth saw the needle and moaned. For her, the miles home must've seemed like a million.

I said, "We're running a little hot. I'll check the radiator. We'll be okay."

She just handed me the flashlight.

I got out and walked to the front of the pickup. Steam rose from underneath the hood, and a hissing stream shot from the bottom of the radiator. I popped the hood, muttered, "Shitfuck!" and then went looking for an empty can along the highway. I found one—a goddamned Budweiser. I filled it with water from the ditch. It took ten trips to the ditch and back to cool down the radiator. I kept the can, just in case. When I got back in the pickup Beth had folded her hands together and was mumbling a silent prayer. I started the engine and pulled back onto the highway. After a few miles, the needle began its climb north again. Beth's hands gripped her knees, and as the pointer crept toward the red, and then entered the red and kept on climbing—now having reached a *bad place* far beyond the sway of her mute prayer—she started praying aloud.

It was not a good time to confess about Dr. Lund or Uncle Silas, or a few other minor sins, but at least I'd had the foresight to keep the Bud can. I pulled over and filled the radiator again.

And miles farther south, to cool things down, again; and more miles south, again.

A mile north of Milo, as we approached the bridge that crossed the wide mouth of the Tyee River, midnight had come and gone. Fog had set in. The needle was married to the red, and the radiator's hot stink filled the cab. Beth's prayers were louder than the whining engine.

But like I always did whenever I had to cross that shitfucked bridge—the needle and the prayers be damned—I shoved the gas pedal to the floor.

Chapter 2

We were on our second pipe, Sparky and me. We stood beside the Dumpster. He toked and passed the pipe to me. I toked, held, released.

The fog was thick. It seemed to have settled over us with different smells. There was the salty ocean, just across the highway from the parking lot of Sparky's Bar and Grill; there was the Dumpster stench of rotting vegetables; there was the stale stink of cigarettes and griddle grease that clung to Sparky's suit; and there was the weed we smoked.

From where we stood, the roadhouse was a dark, low-slung shape barely visible. The Sparky's Bar and Grill sign blinked on and off. A smaller sign said "Spaghetti Night!"

Spartacus Alfonso Jefferson—Sparky—was black-on-black: his black skin against the black night. His breath shot out white, and mine shot out white, and the pipe we smoked shot out white. The fog made a yellow halo around a streetlight. The moon and stars were invisible, but that was something Sparky never noticed. He was from LA, where neon blotted out the night. He was a short man, hardly as tall as the Dumpster. Dressed in a three-piece suit that looked like a lizard skin. About the homeliest man I knew, an ugly from well beyond the harbor, close to that of a pug-nosed mutt. But after two pipes, his face had ironed itself out and become human. He had pretty teeth. I loved him like a brother.

And his pipe was pretty, too, with a long stem that cooled the smoke, a hand-blown bowl of swirly colored glass. Ernst grew the weed in his barn—good, biodynamic shit, sticky with potent resin. It would kick your ass and take names. After just a couple of hits, stupid had its fingers down your throat.

It was somewhere around two-thirty and—unusual for the coast—close to freezing. Except for a few dim storefront lights, the fog had swallowed Milo. Across the coast highway, the unseen, muffled ocean beat against the rocks.

Sparky said, "Feelin' better yet, darlin'?"

I laughed.

He laughed.

I'd told him about the deer, about Beth being pissed off. He was a good listener, the best I knew, a far better listener than Ernst. Sparky owned a bar, so he had to be. Even through my hazy story, he could see Beth's point of view real clear. Sometimes I thought Sparky was half woman. I loved that half, too.

Beth was home in bed, sleeping. She could sleep regardless, no matter how fierce a shit storm blew. No matter she hadn't said a word beyond the Tyee Bridge, then when we got home her going over to the neighbors—waking them in the dead of night, telling them I wasn't feeling well and we'd aborted the overnighter—and bringing Licker home. No matter she was hotter than the radiator. She could just turn it all off and sleep, and that is what she did. I, though, hadn't been one bit tired. I soaked my jacket and the blanket in the tub to sluice out the doe's gore. I walked around the house four times. I finally went back inside, shed my clothes on the bedroom floor, climbed into bed beside Beth and laid there buzz-eyed, seeing that doe, feeling her thump in the steering wheel. I felt sick in love with her. I got out of bed real quiet, went back to the tub and scrubbed the jacket with a brush. I hung it over the tub to drip dry. The cuff on a sleeve was singed black, from a bonfire years ago—a reminder of Nura and our adultery. Still juiced and wide-eyed, I'd gotten dressed and walked the mile to Sparky's place. Sure enough, he was smoking out at the Dumpster, his nightly habit after swabbing out the bar and scraping off the grill, before crashing in his wifeless, kidless, doublewide trailer at the far end of the parking lot.

He said, "You gettin' lots of lovin' from Beth?"

"Yeah, lots."

"She's a fine, fine woman. Ooo-ee!"

Sparky was always saying he'd never met a woman he couldn't understand or love. I said, "You ever feel trapped?"

He threw his hands out wide. "Not anymore, honey. Can't see it happenin'. Ooo-ee! I've got my cages, too, just like everyone else. All mine got doors. When life gives you lemons, put doors on 'em."

That was Sparky, always seeing tulips in the graveyard, always turning chicken shit into chicken soup—especially after two pipes. The Dumpster, he'd said, reminded him of his old neighborhood in L.A.

Back in '92, he'd left Watts after the Rodney King riots and come to Milo to start a new business. He'd figured Oregon was like the state's license plates said, a Pacific Wonderland. Milo was a backwater filled with unemployed rednecks, and when they judged him by the local standards, Sparky was seen as a very odd duck, a mallard in a bowling alley. The yokels called him a queer Californicator. Back then, I'd just lost my job in the woods, was on unemployment, and when I met Sparky he was looking for someone who knew a hammer from a chalk line, so he hired me to help build the roadhouse, Sparky's Bar and Grill. Now I was his part-time bartender.

I said, "You gonna need me tomorrow?"

"Billy's coming in, remember?"

I nodded. Billy was the other bartender. I'd told Sparky I'd be gone for a couple of days with Beth to Glass Point.

"That pool table I ordered, they're delivering it tomorrow. Ooo-ee! A spanking-new Wrangler, slot-operated, with fancy-dancy Italian slate. And she's got felt as smooth as a baby's butt!"

I visualized the next day's swing shift. The usuals would start drifting in after five o'clock, bitch about the channel on the big screen, play cribbage, or get up a game of pinochle, maybe down a cold one or a mixed drink, maybe eat dinner—fish and chips, probably, or whatever Sparky's special was. The gamblers would exercise their bad luck on video poker. I said, "There's hardly room for another pool table."

"We'll make the necessary room, darlin'. We'll just have to scoot the juke into the corner. Say, I've been thinking about a salad bar. What do you think of adding a salad bar?"

"Milo doesn't eat salads. Milo eats red meat."

He laughed. "That's what you said about jo-jos and ranch dressing."

"So, this guy walks into a salad bar . . . ."

"And says let us turn up and pee." He chortled, handed me the pipe. The smoke was cool going down my throat. I blew another halo at the streetlight, at the quarter moon and stars I couldn't see—just sort of feel.

He said, "You're a lucky fellow, E.T."

"Damn right."

"You've got everything a man could want. Mercy! Beth's an angel, and those girls of yours! Ooo-ee! Cute as cute can be. Yes, indeed! Everything!"

I nodded.

"And that great big beautiful home you're going to build! There's another way you're lucky. You can build something as grand as a house. Imagine that! A whole house! That hammer of yours pounds pure magic."

I didn't even nod.

And then the weather fooled me. A frozen drizzle started falling out of the fog. The sifting crystals were so feathery they landed on the plastic lid of the Dumpster without a sound. That close to the ocean, snow never happened. Except it wasn't snow, more like downy fuzz. Sparky tipped his ugly face up and started chasing ice with his tongue, a giggling kid, arms thrown wide, dancing around the Dumpster.

I stood there and watched Sparky turn white, the shoulders of his lizard suit and his kinky black hair.

Chapter 3

I am a bug trapped in whitewater, my wings soaking wet, being whirled around and around in an eddy on the downriver side of a big rock. Below, lurking on the gravel bottom, is a monster trout—a lunker. It's Uncle Silas. It's always him. His cold black eyes swivel upward and see me, a drowning bug, and then he fins up to where I'm spinning and he swallows me, Eddy.

Heart pounding, I sat up in bed.

Goddamn shitfuck!

Beside me in the still darkness of our bedroom, Beth snored.

I reached out for her and let my hand rest on her unmoving hip till my breathing slowed and my heart felt the warm squeeze. There was no use pretending to sleep now. I sat up in the bed. The bedside clock said the sun would rise later.

I swung my feet out from underneath the covers and brought them down on Licker's tail. He yelped soft. "Sorry," I whispered. He crawled from beneath the bed, his claws clicking on the hardwood, his Lab bones hurting. He stood and shook as best as he could, wagged, wedged his hot nose between my knees. I scratched his ears and wished his nose were cold. I loved him for how he never held a grudge. He lay back down beside the bed.

I got dressed—jeans and denim shirt, boots—and eased the bedroom door almost shut on my way out.

In the dark hallway, the girls' bedroom door was open. I flipped their light on. Their twin beds were empty: BJ's with the green quilt, Kate's with the orange. It still astonished me, how BJ and Kate had suddenly become old enough to leave home and go off to college and, even more amazing, claim poli-sci majors. Not in the least like their old man had done. More like their mother, who always had her eye on the future. Their hope chests, which I'd built for their sixth birthdays— and that looked as identical as they were—sat at the foot of their respective beds. I lifted the lid on Kate's. Inside the chest, my old infielder's glove lay beside her prom dress. The leather was cold, stiff and hairline-cracked; it needed a good rubbing with Rawlings oil. I fisted the pocket, a satisfying smack. When the girls were five or six, I'd found the glove buried in an attic box. By then, my fierce love for baseball had simmered into nothing more than watching games on TV, so I'd tossed the glove in the trashcan. Beth pulled it out and said, "Don't ever throw away what you used to love." And then, "You can teach the girls how to play."

So I kept it and bought gloves for Kate and BJ, and I taught them how to crow hop and throw, and the harder the grounder comes at you the softer your hands have to be. They played softball all the way through high school and were good enough to get college scholarships that paid for tuition and books. Playing ball was paying for their poli-sci.

I tossed the mitt back onto a bed, turned out the light and stepped across the hall into the bathroom. I stood there pissing, eyeing my still-damp jacket, drying out over the tub. I loved the jacket for its big pockets, and the burnt sleeve, but not especially for how it conjured up the Nam. Despite the scrubbing I'd given it, the stain of blood was still there. Once it sets, blood endures.

I flushed the toilet and it started running. Jiggling didn't help. I lifted the top off the tank, adjusted the ballcock and muttered, "Fucking owls." For many years, I'd called myself a logger, and setting chokers had paid a decent wage. We'd saved a little money, bought the empty lot across the street from our rental, drawn up floor plans and got a building permit. I'd built the foundation, then figured out what I'd need for the framing and bought a lumber package. If we just kept renting, we'd figured, it was just pouring money down a rat hole. So I'd build our new home with my own hammer. Sweat equity, they call it. But things started going belly-up: to save the spotted owl habitat, the Feds shut down the woods, so I had to do odd jobs and collect unemployment, and then years ago the building permit expired. Since then, other things had, too.

But what the hell. Owls need a home, too.

I jiggled harder and the toilet still ran, but slower.

In the kitchen, Mr. Coffee sputtered on at 6:40, and the window above the sink was too dark to tell if the ice had stopped falling.

The wood stove stood between the kitchen and the living room. I grabbed a *Watchtower* off the kitchen counter, wadded it up and stuffed it in the cold firebox. Beth was touchy about the magazines, especially around Christmas, which Witnesses weren't supposed to celebrate, much less get a tree or buy gifts, much less decorate the hell out of the house. I tossed in sticks of dry kindling, lay on bigger chucks of fir and then struck a match. It spurted blue. The magazine caught, then the kindling pitch sizzled and the smoke roiled black.

Trout Kill

The empty kettle sat on the stove. *Fill it up for her* I told myself; *get it boiling for her morning tea, the way she loves it, so hot her lips will barely graze the mug as she sips tea and steam.* Doing even one little thing for Beth would maybe help to lighten her mood.

I filled the kettle, set it on the counter, lifted down her mug from the rack. Jesus was painted on it. He wore a kind of spacey smile and had droopy eyes, like He was drugged with empathy or Prozac, or like He'd pulled off a big miracle and was feeling smug. A smug mug.

Somewhere between when I lifted the mug off the rack and swung it over the sink, it slipped from my hand and fell. The sink was cast iron. What happened next was biblical: the cast iron rent the mug asunder and, lo, the iron begat a mighty host of shards, and each shard did disperse upon the iron plain unto its resting place, yea, verily, the shards of Jesus did settle.

I gathered up the mess, tossed it in the trashcan, filled my own favorite coffee cup—it had a frog painted on it. The coffee was bitter, only lukewarm. Mr. Coffee never made coffee taste as good as the smell. Not even close. Every sip and sniff was an unfulfilled promise. I went to the pantry, got a full bottle of Jack, poured a shot into the frog and put the bottle back. The sweet jolt of bad coffee and good booze warmed me quicker than the stove.

Okay.

My notebook lay on the top shelf, an old three-ringer, from when Mr. Willis made us take notes in Senior English at Oak Creek High. In the fall of '67, Beth sat right in front of me, and her shiny chestnut hair was stark against the backdrop of the dull green chalkboard. One day Mr. Willis read a poem about a guy who wore his trousers rolled and dared to eat a peach. Beth got it—the part about the peach—and I didn't. She tittered, turned red, wouldn't tell me what was what. Even Ernst got it; he made a wise-ass remark, something about hot fruit. After class that day, love-struck by Beth's chestnut hair and her brains and how she'd blushed, and enchanted by the ghost of her bra strap underneath her thin blouse, I asked her to the homecoming dance. She'd half-smiled and said, "So, you dare to eat a peach?"

I sat down at the kitchen table with the notebook. It was thick with paper. Flipped the notebook open to the page of my most recent nightmares, skipped a line, penciled in the number 193 and dated it.

A smudge of sunrise slanted through the sink window.

Licker came limping down the hall and curled up between the stove and the wall. I loved that, too, his curl. He'd had a good life, had chased his share of rabbits and squirrels, gotten a few ticks and fleas and dug up a flowerbed or two. He laid his muzzle on his paws and shut his rheumy, glossed eyes.

I whispered soft, "Hey, bud."

He looked up.

"Good boy."

He laid his head down again.

I wrote about the nightmare, exactly as I remembered it and Dr. Lund said I should. Uncle Silas had named me Eddy, as in the whirlpools you see behind rocks sticking up in fast rivers. In some nightmares, I felt like a bug must feel when it's caught spinning around and around, only I spin around in my first name, and then get eaten by my last name: Trout.

I wrote this in the notebook: "Trout kill … Trout run … Trout love."

Each of them seemed, somehow, like the centermost point in the heartwood of a tree, the first ring of growth—the god dot—and that scared the hell out of me. I tore the page out, took it to the stove and burned it.

I went to the refrigerator, opened a package of hamburger, pinched off a gob and went back to my chair at the kitchen table. I rolled the meat into a ball, hid it in my right fist and rested both fists on my knees. "Hey, bud."

Licker raised his head and looked over.

"Come here, bud."

He got up slow and hobbled to me. His nose twitched, an inch away from my right fist. He wagged once. "Good boy." I let him take the meat off my palm and he mouthed—not wolfed—it. The haze cleared from his eyes. I patted his head. He shambled back to the stove and lay down again.

When he couldn't smell the meat anymore, I'd have to do something.

The phone in the living room rang. It'd be Ernst, telling me *Daylight's burning and there's a castle to build so get your sorry ass out here pronto.* I hustled over and picked up before the third ring.

A woman's voice said, "Eddy?"

I stepped into the kitchen and quick-looked down the hallway; the bedroom door was shut, Beth wasn't up yet. I lowered my voice. "Dr. Lund?"

"Yes, Eddy. I wasn't sure you'd answer."

"What the heck's going on?"

"Is this an appropriate time for us to talk?"

I kept my eye on the bedroom door. "You're not supposed to call me here."

"This is very important. Em has been arrested, and she's being detained in the county jail."

That was hardly news, so I figured there had to be more to Dr. Lund's urgency, or maybe Jesus was pulling an eye-for-a-mug, biblical revenge thing. Em hated jails as much as I did but, in her case, her hate could further damage her. "She's okay, isn't she? I mean, the cops didn't beat her up or anything."

"She's fine, for now. I saw her yesterday. We talked in her cell, briefly."

I could hear the worry in her crisp words. "What'd she do this time?"

"Do you know St. John's Hospital?"

I said I did. It was one of Em's favorite nests, a sort of R-'n'-R place in the Big City where she could check into the ER to escape the cold, find a warm respite from the biochemical storms that jerked her brain into deep black holes or, contrariwise, sent her mood rocketing to Happyville. For a couple of years, Dr. Lund had been treating her with meds and therapy sessions.

She said, "Last night, at 3:17 A.M., Em walked into the ER and demanded to see a physician, because her medications had been stolen, she said, and she needed something to help stabilize her. The police report says her behavior was 'extremely agitated, threatening.'"

"Uh-huh."

"The ER refused to admit her. It's their policy now ... very misguided and wrong-headed, in my opinion, because it targets certain individuals who have been tagged 'abusers' of the system. Em's on their list. I'm afraid all the ER's in the city have adopted the same policy. Sometimes, people like Em don't know where else to turn."

"So why was she arrested?"

"The police report says she pulled a knife. If the admitting nurse didn't let her see a physician right away, she threatened to cut herself."

"Goddamn it. And did she?"

"She tried to, apparently. There was a scuffle with a police officer, but no, the officer managed to wrestle the knife away. She has a few bruises, but nothing for you to worry about."

She'd never pulled a knife to hurt herself before. It scared me. All her past attempts, three that I remembered, had been with pills—never enough of them to do a permanent job, just enough to get her stomach pumped and Vaughn's full attention. He was her ex, dead for about a year—and good riddance. The knife, I figured, was a louder cry for help. Still, she hadn't called and let me know how she was feeling, and that surprised me, almost as much as the knife did. "What are the charges?"

"In the scuffle, she hit the officer with an umbrella and broke his nose. The officer's name is Korduski. She has been charged with assault, resisting arrest and disorderly conduct."

She'd never hit a cop before either. I was proud of her for that. But the shit storm she was riding was beginning to sound like a hurricane. Something had set her off, lit her fuse. "Look, all she wanted was some meds, maybe a good night's rest, a chance to get her head on straight. Christ, what's an ER for, anyway?"

"Since Vaughn's death, as you know, her life on the street and sleeping in temporary shelters has exhausted her. She needs a safe place to rest for a while."

"I've asked her a hundred times to come and stay with us."

Dr. Lund was silent.

Licker came over and nosed my hand. As best he could, he smiled up at me. The tumor high on his neck had spread to his brain but, so far, it hadn't entirely messed up his sense of smell. He could smell the worry in me. Goddamn. My dying dog was trying to comfort me. After Vaughn killed himself, I took Licker to the city to see Em. Through her tears and crying, she rubbed his belly and scratched behind his ears. She loved all animals, and was the kind of person who gets upset whenever a robin's egg falls from its nest—seeing the crushed, speckled-blue shell. Vaughn had been a mean-fisted, schizo crack hustler, but he and Em had always shared a desperate, needy closeness. Maybe she saw him as a rabid mutt that needed loved. On a dare with Em, hopped up on meth, he'd drunk about a pint of charcoal lighter fluid. There was no funeral. I never saw the body, or wanted to. Two months after Vaughn died Em got evicted by her landlord. She was jobless and broke.

Dr. Lund said, "The county has placed her on a suicide watch, per my recommendation. Given her history, it is necessary. I have sedated her and, due to her increased anxiety, I doubled her Lamictal. A guard checks on her every fifteen minutes. Eddy, she may be entering another delusionary phase."

I glanced toward the bedroom hallway again. "Look, Em needs out of there fast. She doesn't like walls."

"I talked to Officer Korduski and filled him in about her background and circumstances."

"Maybe I could talk him into dropping the charges."

"No, Eddy. I'm advising you against that."

She was right about that. Me talking to any cop was a dumb idea.

Trout Kill

"There's something else, Eddy, I feel I must share with you. I have Em's permission to do so." She paused, and I could sense another, bigger boot about to kick me in the ass. "A few days ago, Em told me, a man came to see her. He was old and sick. He claimed to be her father."

I snorted my disbelief—she might just as well have told me I'd won the lottery, and I never buy a ticket. I made a fist and threw a roundhouse at the air. Father? We had none. Em sometimes dreamed crazy dreams about a "father" who was *taller than a tree* and had *one blue eye and one green eye*. "That's bullshit, Dr. Lund, and Em knows it. She's jerking you around."

"Yes, possibly."

"It's like you said. She's delusional. She's seeing things that aren't really there. You know that for a fact, right?"

"Nothing is for certain, Eddy, including most of what one believes to be true."

"I try not believing half of everything I think." I stepped over to the Christmas tree; it was flocked, snowed and ornamented, with hardly any green showing. The reflection in a glassy red ball curved my face and warped my nose into a zucchini. An ache began to pulse between my eyes, about an inch deep behind my skull, and I wanted to beat it out with the phone, or any blunt instrument. "Look, tell her I'm coming up to see her today. Tell her I'll bring licorice. Will you do that for me, Dr. Lund?"

"That's nice, Eddy. She will love seeing you, I am sure. I will see her later this morning, and I'll inform County that you will be arriving later today."

"I should get there around two-thirty, three o'clock. Can I, uh, drop by afterwards and see you?"

"I'd like that very much. It has been a while, hasn't it? But just a moment and I'll check my appointments." She set down the phone—on her desk I imagined, which sat in the middle of her office, which reminded me of a rain forest. She was a green-thumbed plant nut. She picked up, spoke again. "I have a four o'clock cancellation. Will that work for you?"

"Yeah, Doc, and thanks for calling, for helping Em. I owe you, again." The "Doc" was an accidental slip. Dr. Lund preferred keeping our relationship on a "professional level," as she called it.

She said I didn't owe her a thing, and that she'd try not to call my home again, and then we hung up.

I went to the stove; its welds were hot and popping, stretching out their molecules. At my feet, Licker grinned up at me with a stupid look, slack-eyed and slack-tongued, and I thought *Maybe that's what love looks like*. After hearing about Em, I needed another splash of Jack. Or a blow of weed. My hands shook. Jack or weed, it didn't matter which, just something to settle me, and to hold onto, a glass bottle or a glass pipe.

I remembered when Em and me lived together on Whetstone Road. Uncle Silas had been dead about three years. Em was twenty-one, had a job in Oak Creek at Ender's Second Hand Store, working for Marge Gooding, the owner. During the last few months of my senior year, Em would drive me to Beth's house every morning and drop me off. I'd get there right after Beth's parents left for work, about an hour before first period Modern Problems. Her parents had a Chevy dealership in Rosewood, fifteen miles away. On those mornings in Beth's bedroom, the two of us alone, her bed sheets smelled exactly like she did. That's when Beth taught me about peaches. Em knew what was going on. All those mornings when she dropped me off, she'd grin and say, "Have a peachy day, Brother."

I'd always thought of Em as a sort of canary, because of her yellow hair and light bones and flighty ways. The thing about canaries is that hurricanes can kick their tails and blast them out of the sky.

Chapter 4

Beth was still asleep, cocooned in her blankets, her peaceful face hiding absolutely nothing. Her eyes were gently shut, her mouth a lax smile.

I stood beside the bed, reached down to nudge her awake and explain I was driving to the Big City to talk some sense into Em, to help her not hurt herself anymore, to keep her meds regular, to ask her again if, after she got out of jail, she'd come live with Beth and me in Milo.

Beth's hair fanned across her face and the pillowcase, and each soft breath she released fluttered a strand lying across her cheek. I loved her chestnut hair.

We got married in the summer of '68, right after high school, and Beth moved in with Em and me on Whetstone Road. I loved Beth the only way I knew how: I built things, like a new bed and flowerboxes, and I shot pheasants and deer for supper. Till I got a steady job in the woods, we didn't have much money. Beth's parents tried to help us out but I said no, we'd make do. We never slept in Uncle Silas' old bedroom, but in the other bedroom with one tiny window that, it seemed, was too small to let escape the big memories that haunted me. During our first married night together, after we made love and then fell asleep, I had a nightmare and woke up screaming. Beth held me tight. I told her about when I was eight years old and Uncle Silas shot a doe from the kitchen window with a .22; he handed me a skinning knife and said *Gut her*. The knife was dumb in my hand; I stuck her belly and the visceral stink mixed with the sweetness of his Old Spice, gagging me; he took the knife and cut out her heart; he lifted it at the moon, and then he took a bite of it.

Beth cried and held me close against her breasts and her chestnut hair was comforting. She kept saying *It's just a bad dream; it's just a bad dream.*

A week after that nightmare, the Army gave me a one-way Greyhound ticket to Fort Lewis for basic training. When Beth saw me off at the bus station she slipped a pair of white-lace panties into my hand, the pair she'd worn on our wedding night, and she said *So you'll keep loving me, and to bring good dreams.*

The Army made me a sniper because I scored Expert on the rifle range and I could play dead in the mud for a long time, but mostly because of my good night vision. My hitch in the Army was for three years, and I never had a single nightmare, not even after sniping Cong in the Nam. While I was gone, Beth went to school and got certified to teach grade school. After my hitch, I moved back into the Whetstone house with Beth, and the dreams about Uncle Silas started right up again. Funny how the shit that happens when you're a kid sometimes fucks with your head worse than a war does.

I stood there in our quiet, dark bedroom looking down at Beth. We'd been married for twenty-nine years, and she'd never had the chance to teach grade school. I felt sorry for what I'd done to Jesus, wanted to Super Glue Him back into a mug again, wanted to resurrect the *Watchtower* from the ashes in the stove. I loved Beth the most right then—looking down at her, her asleep in the quiet of our bedroom, when regret had its warm embrace around my good intentions.

I left the bedroom, went to the kitchen and wrote a note: *Went to see Em. She's in jail again. Be home for supper late. Sorry about the mug, an accident. And sorry for last night, too, the accident. I'll see Jimmy tomorrow about the repairs. Love, Eddy.*

I grabbed the notebook, the bottle of Jack, threw on my still-damp fatigue jacket and got a bottle of Ernst's wine from a case in the pantry.

Outside, the world was frosty and glittery. More frozen rain had fallen during the night, and ice coated everything. We lived a few hundred yards from the ocean, at the foot of a hill crowded with Doug fir, maples and a few hemlocks, with undergrowth of ferns, azaleas and rhodies. The hillside looked like a silvery Christmas postcard, every sagging branch and bush beautiful with ice.

A limb cracked like a gunshot and fell with a glassy shatter. Too much beauty breaks things.

The house, gray as the sky was low, needed painting. To me, it had never felt like a home; it was a dwelling that belonged to the landlord, just an address where the rent went.

Our *home* used to be a set of drawings in my notebook, a two-story with lots of big windows and smooth, Sheetrocked walls, and skylights that let the sun shaft in. But our *home* was now the moldering, tarped-over framing package sitting beside the garage: two-by-fours and sixes, four-bys and six-bys; a twenty-foot-long laminated beam; a unit of plywood patinaed with black mildew. And on the lot across the street from where I stood, our *home* was now the grown-over foundation I'd built years ago; the lot was closer to the ocean and perched on higher land, where I could feel the ocean's power and see the low-flying gulls skimming over whitecaps. A spectacular view, though, does not make a home. A blackberry thicket had overgrown the site, and I thought of it as my blackberry house. Inside the foundation walls, the winter rains had made a foot-deep pond. It was frozen.

On clear summer days, I liked to sit up on the roof of our rented house, look west across the road, over the foundation and the blackberries, far beyond the highway, all the way to the horizon where the sky and the ocean meet.

My pickup was a beater, a white Datsun, its belly salt-rusted, the fender dented from the doe. The ice had coated over the cracks in the windshield. I scraped the windshield clear, popped the hood and drained a can of Heavy Duty Stop Leak into the radiator. I topped off the radiator and, just in case, filled two plastic gallon jugs with extra water.

Then I got a shovel, dug up a sword fern at the edge of the woods, set the fern in a box, threw some dirt around the roots and then set the box in the back of the pickup.

I peeled out, fishtailing around the potholes in the road, trying to get a feel for how slick the ice was, and took the shortest route to the highway, then headed north for about two hundred yards and drove into Milo.

The town straddled the coast highway like a small rag on a clothesline, and the beauty of the ice couldn't hide its homeliness: the beat-up gas station, the worn grocery store, the Church of the Holy Redeemer where Father Mullen preached, the weather-beaten houses, Jimmy's Wrecking Yard and, where I bartended, Sparky's Bar and Grill. The Milo Elementary School, where Beth spent her days working as a volunteer, where years earlier they'd offered her a full-time job because she was so damned good with the kids. I'd talked her out of it, saying BJ and Kate needed a stay-at-home mom, saying we didn't need the extra money, saying I'd get a better job someday. And the Milo General Store, good for a few groceries but not much else. And a boarded-up restaurant, The Sea Hag, where a flock of gulls squatted on a roof, the shingles peeled by a winter howler. The gulls reminded everyone that two birds had pretty much killed Milo: First, the owls had shut the woods down and tossed half of everybody out of work; then an oil tanker, the *Avian Wing*, ran aground and gummed up the beach with tar balls. After that, the tourists stayed away in flocks, not that they'd ever considered Milo as an idyllic roost.

The town didn't have its own cops; a County Mounty might swing by every few days or so.

The Good 'Nough Inn looked like a pumpkin on a bluff that overlooked the sea. The owner was Denis Gastineau who, like Sparky, was a bit eccentric. I'd recently helped him convert the Old Milo House into an inn: rewire, replumb and reroof—no payment, just his good company, his booze and fine cooking. He'd painted the inn bright orange, and it was due to open for business any day.

I stopped at the General Store and bought a yard-long rope of licorice—black, Em's favorite. Stuffed it in a pocket and hit the road for the Big City, about a three-hour drive.

I had a plan: I'd get loaded on the way there; after I got there I'd talk some sense into Em; after that I'd see Dr. Lund; then I'd hit the road south and be home by suppertime, just like my note to Beth said I would.

I drove fast out of town on the coast highway, still trying to get a fix on how fast was too fast. The ice wasn't that thick.

The temperature gauge, so far, was holding about normal, the Stop Leak doing its job.

About a mile north of town I crossed the bridge over the Tyee. Icicles hung from the girders. I tried hard not to look anywhere but straight ahead, not to turn my head and look about forty feet down, where the gaping mouth of the river was pushing out into the ocean. But how can you not look at what swallows you?

I looked.

The river, swollen from the heavy rains over the Coast Range, roiled and spread out in the gray ocean like a brown fan. *Down there*, I thought, *Uncle Silas is the lunker; and up here, I am the bug.* It happened sixty miles upriver, south and west of Oak Creek at our Tyee swimming hole. They dragged the river for him but never found his body. *Em and me put him there.* I'd always imagined he'd washed down the river where he was now, at its mouth, waiting underneath the bridge to swallow me.

I tipped up the bottle of Jack, and by the time I reached the end of the bridge, I'd drunk it down to the bottom of the label.

Past the bridge a quarter mile, I turned off the coast highway and headed east, following the river. The icy hills rolled past. I cranked down the window, held my arm out. The cold wind numbed it. The Jack was sweet. Steering with one knee, fishing out a joint from a stash in my jacket and lighting it, the red coils of the lighter just underneath my nose glowing and warm. All the way to the freeway, about an hour drive, the weed smoke swirled out the window. When I hit the freeway, I pushed it to eighty. No ice now ... just overcast skies and eighteen-wheelers. The pickup's tires hummed on the black ribbon. A Rod Stewart love song came on the radio and Beth popped into my head, a clear vision: Us holding each other at arm's length and dancing slow—our arms so unbelievably long that she was a distant speck, just a dress with hair, and the current flowing through our arms was softer than a volt, and fading.

I welled up.

I'd forgotten to put the kettle on the stove for her tea.

In the suburbs of the Big City, the county slam was a red-bricked building on steroids. Medium-security, two hundred beds, cop cars everywhere. The visitor parking lot was mostly empty. I was drunk and stoned; things glowed around their edges, the clouds and such. A crew of glowing orange-suited inmates spread glowing bark dust in the glowing rhody beds.

I emptied the joints out of my jacket, stuck them underneath the seat, then got out and stretched my legs. I quick-chewed a stick of Doublemint and did a brisk walk around the pickup, flapping my arms to air out the smell of weed smoke.

A helicopter flew by, invisible above the clouds. Its thumping rotors reminded me of LBJ, the Long Binh Jail, on the dusty road to Bien Hoa, just outside of Saigon. I'd been court-martialed, sentenced to six months for insubordination, disregarding a direct order to off a water buffalo, supposedly a means of VC transport. From four hundred yards away, through the lens of my Leatherwood scope, the buff had looked docile: sunk to its knees in paddy muck, tail swatting, cud chewing, giant brown eyes gazing right at me. I told the butter bar the buff looked friendly, very unlike a VC. He said to shoot it. I said to fuck off, that I knew a VC from a friendly. When the MPs in-processed me at LBJ, one of them searched my duffle bag, found the wedding-night panties Beth had given me. He

Trout Kill

held them up between his thumb and forefinger, fixed me with a leer, grabbed his crotch and moaned loud. I just grinned, then came over the table between us and swung a roundhouse aimed at his head. He sidestepped the punch, arm-barred me to the floor and pinned me down till his MP buddies cuffed and hammered me. For the first few weeks after that, I beat off at night underneath the mosquito netting. After those weeks, Beth's face began to fade away in my head till, without those panties, she disappeared. The pictures she kept sending to me didn't work the same.

The chopper's thump died away, the gray sky was just the gray sky again, and I headed across the parking lot. A sign at the entrance to the jail said Happy Holidays, told visitors where to report. I unwrapped another stick of Doublemint and stuck it in my mouth with the first stick. Inside the building, a rush of warm, institutional air that made me feel like I was being processed and filtered. A security guy directed me through a metal detector, then handed me a form. I filled it out, a Service Request Form, and took it to a glassed-off desk, the check-in for inmate visitations. A sergeant with an acned face gave me her bored look, asked for my driver's license. I said, "I'm here to see Emily Trout."

She nodded, not bothering to check the license. "You must be her brother."

I nodded.

"Dr. Lund said you'd be coming." She pointed to a list of visitation rules.

RULE 1 said inmate visitors should not be under the influence of any drugs or alcohol. I just chewed my gum and emptied out my keys and wallet.

Another cop frisked me, pulled the yard of licorice out of my jacket pocket.

I said, "A rope, for climbing the walls."

"Wise ass." He stuffed it back into the pocket.

A female guard—her nametag said Wallace—escorted me from the check-in. Her khaki shirt was ironed stiff. We walked across a commons area with round tables and green walls, turned a corner and went down a corridor. For a big woman, Officer Wallace moved fast and loose, her arms swinging, her head bobbing like she had a happy song stuck there. When she'd given me her quick-glance once-over, I'd felt her profiling me: *male Caucasian, mid-forties, six-footish, graying hair and—hard to say in this light—either blue or green eyes that look sleepy.* She said, "Mr. Trout, ain't this weather we're having terrible?"

"It's December."

She laughed. "December: month that lasts a year, it seems to me. Christmas is coming, though. That's the nicest time of the year."

"Hey, if Santa can deliver all those presents, why can't you guys fix my crazy sister?"

She shook her head. "Mr. Trout, she ain't crazy. Crazies don't cry like she cries."

"How's that?"

"Oh, that's hard to say exactly. But if I were to say, I'd say she cries so wide open the tears just flow. You know what I mean?"

Officer Wallace was okay. "Yeah, I think I do know. Thanks. That's great. Thanks. I owe you. Thanks."

"What you thanking me for?"

"My sane sister."

"What you owing me for?"

"It's what I do best."

"You've heard about what she did at the St. John's ER. Well, she might have broken Korduski's nose. If I knew him well enough, I'd be sure to give him a bad time about that." She laughed again. "Hey, don't get your hopes up, but word is he's thinking about dropping the charges. He's got his pride to consider. And don't you worry about your sister. I'm checking up on her every fifteen minutes. She ain't gonna hurt herself on my watch."

We passed down another corridor with cells on either side, with low voices seeping through the walls and doors. I felt eyes on me, a stranger who'd come for a visit. We stopped in front of a narrow door with a small window. Officer Wallace looked in and knocked soft. "Miz Trout, you have a visitor, your brother."

Officer Wallace turned and faced me. Her eyes were smart. They'd done a lot of measuring, of sizing up. She'd noticed the blood stain on my jacket, the singed sleeve cuff, the patches on my faded jeans, my uncombed hair, the wad of chewing gum. She'd probably smelled right off that I'd violated Rule 1. She could have breathalyzed me and made me walk a line.

She unlocked the cell door, said, "I'll be right outside, Mr. Trout. Have a nice visit."

Chapter 5

The cell was a gray cage with cement-block walls, a narrow bunk, a stainless-steel toilet, a small sink and no windows except for the door.

Em sat on her bunk with her head down. Her dirty yellow hair hung in greasy ropes. Her rough street hands were in her lap, one clenched in a fist. She wore a bulky blue smock with no collar or sleeves, made with some kind of quilted nylon, too stiff to fashion a noose. It fit her body like an extra-large shell fits a small turtle, with wide gaps around her arms and neck. The laces were gone from her tennis shoes.

I said, "Hi, Em."

Her head came up real slow, and then her eyes found my eyes. Whatever sedative Dr. Lund had given her that morning, it had taken hold. Her eyes weren't spring moss, more like dusted lichens. She smiled at me, a tardy, lopsided grimace that froze and went nowhere. She tried to stand but only got halfway off her ass before slumping back to the bunk. She held up her thin arms, keeping that fist closed, and said, "Hi, Brother."

I lifted her up to her feet and wrapped her in a big hug. She loved hugs. She laid her head against my chest. Arms hung at her sides, and even inside the turtle's armor, she felt limp and puny. Her oily hair was more brown than yellow, matted to her skull.

She said, "You smell like gum and Mary-Jack."

Trout Kill

That's what she called my sedatives. "I smuggled in some weed and booze. So you can get loaded."

"I missed you."

I swallowed the lump of gum. "How you doing, Em?"

She finally raised her arms and hugged me back, buried her nose in my field jacket. "Is my hair pretty?"

Her words were slow and spaced-out, and when I didn't say anything she took my hand and pressed it against her head. It felt like a tough nut. What looked like iodine stained one ear. The ear had a small cut, from the tussle with the cop, I guessed. She asked me again, talking into my chest real slow, "Is ... it ... pretty?"

"Yeah, sure, okay. It's pretty."

She shoved away, spun around and stepped over to the wall. It didn't surprise me, how she'd speak slow and then move fast, turn a change-up into a fastball. Whenever she'd gone off her meds, and then got back onto them, for a day or two quick and slow came and went. Her blood was uneven. So was mine, from the pot and Jack. She knew I'd lied about her hair. For as long as we'd been brother and sister, she could read me like a pop-up book.

She said, "This place needs a damned window. You can't see the sky or nothing."

The one in the door was about a foot square. I went along. "Someday I'll build you a big place with lots of windows."

"Big as the sky?"

"Bigger."

"With no rough walls that give you splinters?"

"Smooth as butter."

"Like the pictures you've drawn? Those kind of walls?"

"Just like."

"And the outside walls made out of rocks?"

"Yeah, sure, periwinkle rocks."

"And pets. A dog and cat and rabbits."

"Sure."

Then, her voice a whisper, her back still to me, her face up against that wall, "Do you still believe in them?"

She'd lost me. "What?"

She turned around and faced me. "Periwinkles."

I nodded. "You bet I do."

Her eyes were slow blanks. Then her gaze drifted to the scar on my forehead, just below my hairline, a white jag of skin shaped like a minnow. I thought of it as a birthmark, but Em had always sworn it was a scar. She said, "I don't anymore."

We both got real quiet. When we were kids, we'd go down to the creek below the Whetstone house and play in the shallows with the periwinkles, caddis fly larvae. They built their tiny, tube-shaped houses out of real small pebbles. Fish ate them. Fishermen used them for bait. Their rock houses, though, helped to keep them safe.

She asked about Licker, said she missed him and asked if I'd brought him with me. I said he was home, doing real good, still chasing rabbits and digging holes in the yard.

She shook her hair, like women do, and the oily ropes whipped around her skinny neck and flailed her. Her eyes were sly now, with glances that shot sideways. She twined a finger in her hair. "Florence said my hair's the prettiest hair she's ever seen."

She'd lost me. "Who's Florence?"

"You know." She nodded at the door.

She meant the guard, Officer Wallace. Em was looking fishy; she was yanking me around for the fun of it. Or maybe another delusion had taken hold. I didn't believe her. "Why didn't you call me?"

"Cause you wouldn't have believed me. Just like you don't now."

"Tell me what happened at the ER."

She pushed away, sat on her bunk and stared at the wall. "Guess what else Florence said."

"Come on, Em. Maybe that cop'll drop the charges. Officer Wallace said—"

"Guess, Brother!" She held that closed fist above one knee and dared me with her eyes. They were April now, sparkling with spring rain.

I said, "Hey, take it easy. We don't play that game anymore, remember?"

"It's okay this one time. I allow it!" Her fist pounded down on her knee.

I grabbed her arms and jerked her up from the bed. "Okay. Don't do that." Her whole body was stiff like the smock. I let go of her. "I'll play, but just this one time."

She smiled—all teeth and lips, her kick-ass smile. She reached up and put a finger where my hair ends and my face begins, on that scar. "Good for you. Start guessing away."

I screwed my face up, like I was thinking up a good guess, and she kept her finger pressing on the scar. I said, "She said that your hair's pretty."

She jerked her finger away, but I could still feel where it had been. "You lose! You're not even close. She said she'd like to kiss me."

I spun away and punched my hand. I'd never been very good at jousting with her, at figuring out what was riffing through her head.

Em looked triumphant. "Now, guess what *he* said?"

"He?"

"Dad."

"Goddamn, Em. That's not funny." I should have seen it coming, so right down the middle I never even got the bat off my shoulder. That's the way it is sometimes, not ready for the fat ones. But she had a coiled-up way of thinking, and I was mad at her about the guessing game, one we'd sworn not to play anymore. She'd set me up with one delusion—Florence—and then served up a fatter one.

She sat on the bunk again. "Dad's exactly like I remember him. His face, I mean. Only different, you know? All gray and old and wrinkled. He looked really, really sick."

I faced her again. Her eyes were wide and bright and focused. I needed to steer her back to where she was—in a cell for busting a cop's nose. I had to be tough with her. "Did you hit that cop?"

"He was all friendly and stuff, and he even offered me some money. I didn't take it. I didn't think it was Dad—at first, I mean. He just all of a sudden showed up."

"Jesus, Em. An umbrella? And what's with the knife? What the hell were you thinking?"

"But it *was* him."

"We've gotta hope that damned cop drops the charges."

"When I knew it was him, really him, I got mad. Really, really, really mad. I wanted to piss all over him for what he did. I said, 'Go away.' I said, 'There's nothing I want to say to you. And Eddy doesn't, either.' He said he understood how we felt. I said we would never ever forgive him. I said I burned the house down. I said we killed his brother. I said we'd done just fine without him around for all these years. I told him to go fuck himself. With a mop handle. That's what I said, 'Just go fuck yourself with a mop handle.' And I said he could die. 'You can do Eddy and me a big favor and go die.'"

I was the turtle now. All her mad words just bounced off of me. "I'm gonna get you out of here real soon."

"I said you hate him too. I said 'Why don't you just hurry up and die?' That's what I told him."

"Just hang in there. I'm seeing Dr. Lund. We'll talk to that cop. We'll make him understand. We'll bust you outta here."

"He knows you."

"Dr. Lund doubled your dosage. That'll help."

"He knows where you live."

"You're taking the pills, right? Every day, right?"

"He's going away soon. He said so."

"The pills, damn it!"

"You know what, Brother? Even *adopted* kids have a real dad and a real mom."

Em had faint memories of a woman she called Mom. I didn't. Growing up, sometimes we'd go into town with Silas when he bought groceries or something, and one of Em's favorite ways to pester me was to point to some woman walking down the street and say *See that lady over there? She's got Mom's red hair.* Or, *See that lady with the black purse—she's got Mom's exact green eyes.* Or, *I wonder if that lady in the yellow car paints pictures as good as Mom's.* And growing up, Em half-remembered a *tall-as-a-tree* man who always had *his nose in a book.* I didn't.

She talked about him like a ghost. For all of my life, not having those memories was a hole I'd sometimes try to fill with a woman who had red hair and green eyes, or some tall man.

I said, "Dr. Lund, she'll come again and see you soon. I'll make her."

"Guess what I told him. Guess!"

I sighed—loud—to make it clear I was ticked off, ready to take another wild swing at something. She just looked at me, hopeful, like I'd jump on board her crazy train. All I could do was try to derail it. "Em, no more guessing games, okay?"

"I told him about the river." She laughed like a kid, a rippling giggle. "He said he didn't even know about that. How could he not know? Huh? He's such a liar."

"Em, come on." I was pleading.

"His eyes aren't so blue anymore." She got a puzzled look. "Or green?"

"We've gotta get you a lawyer. Don't talk to anyone, okay?"

Her eyes pinched together with a question: "And then what? I mean, if I get out of here, then what?"

"You can come and stay with Beth and me. I'll find you a job."

"In Milo?" She laughed, bitter this time. "There's only one bridge in Milo, and I can't live under it. Besides, I've got friends here."

Since Vaughn died, Em had hung out in the city with a loose crowd of Streeters, few of whom I'd ever met. Two names came to mind: Sister Ruth, a homeless junkie, and Village, a schizophrenic guy who hated questions. I wanted to be Em's good brother so bad I couldn't think straight. She needed a brother, not street friends. I wondered if her hands remembered how to do normal things, like water a plant or make a grocery list or fold a bed sheet off the clothesline.

Just that quick, Em got cheerful—the fake kind with a motor mouth. "Guess what? Florence said she likes me. She touches me when no one's looking. You know…" She pressed her hands against her smock-covered breasts, moaned and rolled her eyes.

I glanced at the door and wondered if Officer Wallace could hear us. "Come on. She's a good cop. She checks up on you."

"Yes, she sure does." Em got up, stepped to the wall and punched it, hard, with the fist she'd kept balled up. The wall peeled the skin off her knuckles.

"Damn, Em!"

"I miss Vaughn. He's really, really good to me."

Sometimes she talked as if Vaughn was still in the room.

She was glaring at the wall. We were five feet apart—her facing that wall, me standing between her and the sink—but she was long gone to a place where Vaughn was still alive and a good guy who'd never beat her up for her food stamps. I said, "Look at me, Em. We've gotta figure out things."

She kept turned away. "But you'll be leaving me, won't you, Brother?"

"Come on. That's not fair."

"Florence said I could stay with her for as long as I want. She said she'd love me."

"Em, come on."

"She promised she'd love me for a quarter."

"No. Don't say that." I went to the door and pounded on it twice. It opened quick.

Officer Wallace looked worried. She said, "Everything okay?"

I stepped outside and she closed the door behind me. "I need a big favor, Officer Wallace."

Her nostrils sucked in. "What's up, Mr. Trout?"

I walked in a slow circle, and then another slower one. Florence folded her heavy arms across her broad chest. I kept walking. Circles, I told myself, are good things to walk. I said, "Shampoo."

"Oh?"

I kept walking. "Yeah. Some shampoo and a towel and a hair brush."

She nodded. "That's it? No hacksaw or file?"

"Yeah, those too."

She looked at the cell door. It was open about an inch. "I'll be back in a minute." She headed down the corridor and disappeared around the corner.

I stood there alone. The window in Em's cell door was two feet away, but I couldn't look through it. If I did, I'd see a scared bird beating her wings against a cage. I'd see how bleak and empty the mile was between her and me. All I could think was how to make it shrink down and let her fly free.

Officer Wallace came hustling back. She gave me a towel with the stuff folded inside of it. I wanted to hug her, make love to her right there on the cement floor in the way that trusting strangers do: a gentle gift given and received, from one to another, with no questions asked or strings attached. "Thanks. I owe you another one."

Even underneath her black skin, I could see the blush. She said, "You don't owe me anything."

"It's good to owe people."

She smiled and pulled the cell door open.

Em was still standing where I'd left her, sucking on her bleeding knuckles.

I set the towel on the bunk and unfolded it—a bottle of VO5 shampoo and a hair brush, one of those cheap kinds with plastic bristles. I led Em to the sink and turned the water on. "I want to wash your hair. Okay?"

"I hate him as much as you do. He wouldn't tell me his name."

"Lean down, over the sink."

She did, stiff, because of that smock. I splashed her hair, soaking it with warm water, getting my jeans and the floor wet.

The shampoo came out of the bottle thick as honey. I poured a gob right onto her head and worked it around and down to her scalp. Her neck was tight. "Take it easy," I said. "It's okay." I kept working in the lather, and after a little while her head began to droop a bit, and then droop some more, and then her shoulders sagged toward the sink. She moaned and it trembled through my fingertips. I kept doing that, working up a frothy crown, getting the dirt loose and massaging her head, being careful with her ear. I washed all the shampoo out, poured a new gob on and did the whole lather-rinse thing again. "Okay. Nice and clean now."

For a minute, she stayed right where she was, slumped over the sink, letting the water drip off. I led her to the bunk and she sat down. I toweled her hair, rubbing hard, feeling her skull under my fingers, its hard nut shape, wishing the towel could reach inside and rub out all the bad memories. Like Licker leaned into an ear rub, she leaned into the towel.

The towel made rats' nests. I raked the tangles with the brush but the bristles kept snagging. She winced, clamped her eyes shut. I raked easier. Lots of hair came out. The snarls were tough bastards.

And then she reached up and caught the brush mid-stroke and took it from my hand. She held it right under her nose and breathed in the smell of her own clean hair. "It smells pretty." She began working the brush, making short, downward jerks. It finally broke through but she kept right on till the brush passed through like the wind. She looked so happy right then.

She didn't stop. She kept right on with the brush, working it faster and faster and then spanking it hard against her scalp; her face pinched into a sour scowl, and the brush became a mad rasp going at her.

I caught her hand and stopped it.

Her eyes jerked onto me. She said, "I want to go all the way away. I want to be nothing."

I looked straight into her and smiled as big as I knew how. Her eyes were so goddamn sad. I took her hair between my fingers and let it slide through. "Okay, now it's pretty." When I let it go, her hair fell across her face.

She frowned and stood up from the bunk. "If I had a quarter, guess what I'd do with it."

I shook my head. "No, Em." I turned away. Quarters were her lunkers. When she fixates on them, she's being swallowed by a bad memory of Uncle Silas, who used to give her a quarter for every time she "won" a lunch pail guessing game.

"I'd drop it down the wishing well." She started humming a childhood song. She stopped halfway through. "Are you seeing Dr. Lund today?"

Trout Kill

I faced her again. I nodded. "She's gonna help get you out of here."

She grinned. Her eyes went sexy. She crossed her legs just the same as Dr. Lund crosses hers, ladylike, with not much ankle showing. "'So, Eddy, what's in your notebook for me today? Anything juicy and Jungian?'"

She thought I had a thing for Dr. Lund, and I did. "Em, we don't have a father. We never did."

She turned away and faced the wall and put her toes right up against it and began banging her head on the blocks, not hard. The shine in her hair bounced. "I saw him. I saw him. I saw him."

I put my arm around her waist. I beat my head, too. The wall was tough. We did that for a while, our heads knocking. She took my hand in hers—the one she'd kept in a fist—and slipped something into it. I didn't look, just kept knocking. It was something small.

She stopped first and stood there watching me beat my head. Then I stopped and looked in my hand. She'd given me a plastic blue butterfly with its wings spread out. It was a barrette. I thought she wanted me to clip it in her hair. I reached for her hair.

She stepped back. "It's Dolly's."

"Dolly's?"

"Dad gave it to me."

I shook my head. "No, Em. Don't."

"He said Dolly had it in her hair."

She'd talked about the doll before—Dolly—how she'd played with it when she was two or three years old, but then somehow lost it. She couldn't remember how. I remembered her carrying a doll around, too. I figured she'd bought the barrette and had it pinned in her hair when she got arrested; she'd stashed it, maybe in her bra.

She took my hand. Her fingers were dry wishbones. She was looking at the block wall as if gazing through a clear window, her eyes focused far beyond. "He said it made him cry."

"What?"

"When he found Dolly."

I threw her hands away and the barrette fell to the floor. I pounded my head against that wall again, harder than before, to knock some sense into her, to make her see what a fucking stupid thing it was to beat your head against a wall.

She picked the barrette up and made another fist around it. "How are you doing, Brother?"

I kept pounding. "I'm good. And you?"

She laughed brightly. "We have lots of secrets, don't we?"

"A few."

"Or maybe they have us."

She was sinking farther into some half-true memory, and as fast as she was sinking into it I was getting madder, and no matter how hard I beat my brains against the blocks, nothing was going to change. So I quit. I faced her. "Anything you want me to say to Dr. Lund?"

She just threw her arms around me and squeezed tight. "Thanks for coming, Brother. I love you."

"I love you, too."

I went to the door and opened it. Officer Wallace stepped inside and said to Em, "Your hair is beautiful, Miz Trout."

Em turned away, fell onto her bunk and curled up. Officer Wallace looked at me and shook her head slow, her eyes sorrowful.

Trout Kill

I pulled the rope of licorice out of my pocket and laid it on the bunk. Em didn't move. Her hair shined yellow, but not like a canary. Canaries fly and sing songs. She was that skinny turtle inside its shell, and a speeding car had just come along and run over her.

Then she reached out, took the licorice and smiled. "You remembered."

Chapter 6

I hurried down the steps of the county jail, ran to my pickup and headed to the freeway. The gray sky had dissolved into thin blue, and the weak sun sank toward the western hills. The freeway into the city was a slow stampede of cars, big rigs, pickups and SUVs. The slow drive, though, gave me time to think.

Em was right about one big thing: Even adopted kids have real mothers and fathers. And if our mother or father had deserted us, or if either of them had known what Uncle Silas was doing to us and hadn't stopped him, then I'd want to kill them. I'd kill anyone who'd known and done nothing.

My earliest memory was the game of Walls. Em and me played it together after Uncle Silas left for work. We'd go to the drawer in the kitchen and get a black twist of licorice to eat. Em always carried a doll. We'd each hold one of the doll's hands, clamp our eyes shut and, chewing on the licorice, we'd walk around the house blind, touching the log walls; they had adz scars and rough chinking. We'd count the branch collars, those bumps where the limbs had once grown. Sometimes we got splinters that we tweezered out. We'd feel our way up the stairs to the loft, where we'd go and sit at the small window that overlooked Whetstone Road. One winter day after a foot of snow had fallen, a bird landed right below us on the porch roof. Em pointed and smiled, her teeth black with licorice. The bird had bright red feathers. The doll in Em's arms had red hair and a white, fish-shaped barrette. The bird was red against the white snow, and the fish was white against the red hair.

Red on white, white on red.

The barrette she'd shown me in her cell was blue, not white; and it was a butterfly, not a fish.

The old man Em thought was our father was not. He couldn't be. Em's street world swarmed with drunken, whacked-out Streeters who swore they were Jesus or Abraham Lincoln or Jimi Hendrix. The old man was just another boozehound who'd staggered underneath Em's bridge, or Jesus with the tremors.

The sun was almost down by the time I got into the city and found a place to park. The buildings reminded me of canyon walls, and the pedestrians were a rippling river. I got the fern I'd dug up from the back of the pickup, dropped the bottle of Ernst's wine and my notebook into the box with the fern, then started walking toward Dr. Lund's office.

It was a couple of blocks away on the brow of a hill, in an older part of the city, a mix of coffee shops, apartments and small businesses. I entered a ten-story brownstone with bright windows, and the elevator groaned up to the eighth floor.

Dr. Lund's receptionist, Martha—pierced eyelids, heavy black makeup—smiled when I entered the waiting area. "Go right in, Mr. Trout. The doctor is expecting you."

I soft-knocked twice, entered the room and stood between a lush philodendron and a big Wandering Jew, breathed in the moist rain forest smells, earthy and musty. Flowers exploded: their splashes of yellow, red and pink; their fronds and waxy leaves so green you almost winced. Stacks of clay pots stood against a wall; bags of potting soil and fertilizers lay behind her desk, which sat in the middle of the room like a huge toadstool. Flanked by pots filled with gaudy orchids, two Morris chairs faced each other.

She was standing in front of a big window, her back to me. She was a twig of a woman, barely five feet tall, about fifty, with short red and curly hair. She was fussing with a plant that had a lot of nodding flowers. She said—to the plant, I guessed—"What's this world coming to, MS Barkeria palmerii?"

She called her plants by their Latin names. "Hello, Dr. Lund. Sorry I'm late."

She turned, and seemed a bit surprised to see me there, as if the plant she'd been talking to had held her complete attention. Her eyes, gray like the north side of old concrete, crinkled into a smile. "Oh, Eddy. Please come in. Tell me how you've been."

"Traffic's pretty bad." Her round glasses made her eyes look bigger. She wore jeans, a sweatshirt and a scarf.

She eyed the box I was carrying. "It's the rush hour. Busy, busy."

"And the happy hour." I grinned, carried the box to a corner, set it down beside seven other ferns that were growing there—one for each of my previous visits. Their fronds were lush. I lifted the wine and the notebook from the box and took them over to one of the Morris chairs.

She stepped to her desk. It was wooden relic, with a patch of moss growing out of one of its rotting corners. The moss looked happy; she kept it well watered and shaded. A thick file lay beside a pair of gardening gloves. She picked up a yellow legal pad, walked over to me in brisk strides. We shook hands. Her firm grip never failed to surprise me.

She gestured to the chair at my side, and I held the bottle of wine out for her. She raised an eyebrow, said, "Eddy, you know better. But I appreciate the thought. Thank you, but no thank you."

I grinned. "Come on, Doc, be an outlaw."

"The fern is quite nice enough. Thank you. Very thoughtful of you."

I shrugged, set the wine down beside an orchid. Some professional code forbade her from accepting it. Ferns, yes; wine, no. She had to draw a line somewhere, I figured. But the thing was, I wasn't her client. We'd never talked about money or kept regular appointments. She was trying to keep Em's head straight, not mine, and the state paid her for it. I owed her for helping Em, but the ferns weren't payment enough.

She motioned to the chair again. We sat. She crossed her legs—exactly like Em had crossed hers, prim and casual. She placed the pad on her lap and asked about Beth, BJ and Kate. I said the girls were coming home for Christmas, and we'd open presents, have a nice dinner, hang out, play catch, hit a few grounders, go beachcombing. The orchids around my chair made a perfumy cloud that smelled like angel food cake. Behind Dr. Lund, the windows faced east over the darkening city. I settled my notebook in my lap. She penciled something down on the pad, maybe the date.

I wanted to just sit there and look at her. Her smooth knee shined through a hole in her jeans; dirt stains on her Reed sweatshirt and her Hush Puppy shoes. Her loud-purple scarf argued with her red hair. I don't pretend to know anything about what women wear, especially smart city women who write thick books, but her Goodwill clothes looked pretty native to her, like the leaves gracing a willow tree. A million times in my head I'd made love to her on her desk, her skin white, her ass sweet, her Goodwill scattered across the floor.

She said, "Let's begin, shall we."

I always started with a weather report. "It's icy down south, freezing rain. Weird stuff."

The foot of her crossed leg bobbed once.

I looked out the window. Mount Hood stood sixty miles to the east; its snowy flank caught the day's last reddish light and the bottoms of the clouds caught the reflection. A pink cloud seemed to wink at me; it was exactly how, when she'd crossed her legs a moment before, the pale skin of Dr. Lund's knee had winked through the tear in her jeans.

She reached down beside her chair and stroked an orchid, a light-pink petal that fused into blood red.

I leaned toward her, gripped the arms of the chair, and told her all about the night before, the doe and how I loved her, Spencer's gun and Beth freaking out, crossing the Tyee Bridge doing sixty, the radiator, then how I couldn't fall asleep, and walking down to the bar and grill and getting wasted with Sparky. It came out in a rush of words that wouldn't stop till it did.

She nodded and didn't write anything down. "Glass Point, the motel, a little get-away—you tried to do something nice for Beth, for the two of you."

"Those were your ideas. Remember?"

She just looked at me, then nodded. She'd mentioned them at our last meeting a few months earlier. "Still, you made a big effort. That is important. It's progress. You can build on it."

"I called the doe an accident."

"I'm sure it was."

"I was speeding. Beth wanted me to slow down. Maybe I just wanted something bad to happen."

"That's possibly insightful. Please, go on."

I shrugged, thought *Maybe all I need is to fall in love with anything*. I said, "Em has this goddamned fantasy thing in her head, and so she runs into the ER, tries to knife herself, breaks a cop's nose. And now she's making up sick lies about her guard."

She jotted something on the pad—maybe that I'd just changed the subject, from me to Em. She held the pencil in a way that made the eraser almost motionless. Behind her, the mountain was turning from red to purple, the color of her scarf, and the pink clouds were now gray. She said, "Tell me about the guard, Florence."

I did.

"So, you think of Florence as an ally, someone you can trust?"

"Yeah, I guess so."

"When I saw Em, she acted distraught, withdrawn and pre-occupied. Did she receive you warmly?"

"How could she? They'd put her in a goddamn smock."

"I am the one who ordered it. It is for her protection. She has a history with which we're both very familiar."

I nodded, and felt oppressed by the weight of that history. "Some birds, wild ones, thrash against their fucking cage till they die." I sat back and took a deep breath. Beneath her rough surface, Em wanted normalcy. Death scared the hell out of her. During my visit in her cell, I'd gotten the sense she was hiding something new, and that something both scared and gave her hope.

Dr. Lund stood up, set the pad down and got a watering can from over by the window. She said, "I called an attorney. He owes me a favor or two. Maybe he can help with Em's release. But for now, let's keep the faith, okay?" She walked past me and over to the fern in the box. She waved the can over the fern, and the pattering shower made the fronds bounce. "Eddy, please: no more ferns. I dearly love them, as you know. They're truly beautiful. But no more such gifts, please."

She'd just drawn another line. I wanted to run over it, scream out her first name—Patricia!—and hear the roar of my lust bounce off the windows. "Okay, no more ferns. Or wine."

She put the can down, returned to her chair, picked up the pad again and sat, crossing her legs—the other way, right leg over left. "Okay, what are you sharing with me today?"

I opened the notebook to Number 190. "This one's from October 23rd."

"Wonderful."

A few years ago, Em mentioned to Dr. Lund that I'd been writing down my nightmares. Dr. Lund was real interested. She called me, said she was looking for case studies for a new book, something about archetypes, something about "confronting the unconscious" and Jung's *Red Book*. I agreed to see her, thinking that, somehow, it might help Em. My nightmares were Em's, too, but she never wrote hers down. When I drove up to meet with Dr. Lund that first time, I'd told Beth I was seeing Em, and that's what I had kept telling her—not exactly lying about Dr. Lund, but rather not revealing her. I wasn't fooling myself: If Beth ever found out about Dr. Lund, she'd be hurt and angry. Just another example of speeding around corners, I guess. But I've come to see Dr. Lund different than I used to, like how a tree's roots feed it. I'm the tree; Dr. Lund's my roots. She has ways of probing deep into ground I've never thought of, and drawing from it the nourishment that gives me hope.

Anyway, at that first meeting with Dr. Lund she said she'd love to see all my nightmares, and talk to me about them. Everything would be kept in strictest confidentiality: In her book, I'd be Mr. X from Town Y.

I took a deep, ragged breath and began reading 190, verbatim, the way Dr. Lund preferred.

A big big river so wide I can't see across brown and mad water rolling real fast. The current's got a tree in its grip. A fir. Its bole mostly sunk underneath the water and no limbs sticking up. All the branches are gone. There are faces growing in the bark and they might be a man or woman or maybe both. The bole rolls over and there're more of the same faces underneath.

When I looked up from the notebook Dr. Lund was looking right at me, her eyes calm and not measuring. Her hand, though, was quietly filling up the pad, the pencil gliding, writing down some kind of shorthand or gibberish—whatever shrinks write down when they hear the babble of idiots.

I said, "That's it."

"And you woke up sweating?"

"Yes."

She nodded. Her pencil relaxed. "What frightened you the most?"

"The faces. I don't know them. And trees have branches."

She wrote some more.

I dropped the notebook on the floor, walked over to the

ferns, picked up the watering can and waved it back and forth. A dribble leaked out. "Beth and me, we haven't made love for a long time. I can't remember when. Last summer, maybe. No. It was in the fall, late October. The maples were turning orange. It was just something I did one morning waiting for Mr. Coffee."

The only sound in the room was her pencil scratching. Maybe she was noting the time proximities, my story of love-making close on the heels of my nightmare, or something about sex when the leaves are falling. "Please, Eddy, go on."

I set the can down and returned to my chair. "How's the book coming?"

She stopped writing again, adjusted her scarf, pulling one end down a bit, her wrist supple. "It's coming along fine, thank you. Of course, there's never enough time for it. I'm currently working on a chapter about souls."

"Yeah? Interesting." I wanted to pull a joint out and smoke it with her, get every flower in the room stoned. Souls lived in her world, not mine, just like Jesus lived in Beth's. Ernst, too, was big on souls, even in his cows and pinot noir. And Sparky. Sometimes after work when we smoked at the Dumpster, Sparky would assure me I had a soul, and that I unconsciously believed in invisible spirits both within and outside of my-self—like how I sensed Dr. Lund was my roots. Faith takes a soul, Sparky said. But it was just so much hocus-pocus psy-chobabble New Age shit. For me, it was good enough that Dr. Lund needed me for her book. In that regard, Mr. X had her bent over a barrel, if not her desk.

She turned to a fresh sheet of yellow paper. "What you mentioned earlier, about the accident. I find it interesting that you might think it otherwise. That is, hitting the doe was not strictly an accident, in that you ignored Beth's pleas for greater caution."

Somehow, she could say accusatory things without a hint of allegation. "I don't know. I've been around that corner a hundred times. My tires are pretty-damned good, the tread. The road was wet, sure, but the doe just bolted right into me. If I'd slowed down a little earlier, who knows …?"

"Why did you disregard Beth?"

"Her warnings don't register."

She nodded. "We've been through this scenario before, Eddy. Is it beginning to sound familiar to you?"

I just looked at her.

"You may recall when we last met we talked about—how shall I say?—your persistent enthusiasm for inducing stressful situations."

"As in I intentionally sped around that blind corner looking for an adrenaline fix?" It was one of her very first theories—that I was a stress junkie—and it had absolutely nailed me. In fact, my tires were bald, and their lack of traction excited me. But there was more to me than that, and Dr. Lund knew it, so she was always probing deeper into my ground, what she called *the soup of my psyche*. Bringing the right theory to light, she'd told me, would help me figure out myself.

"There's a whole physiology involved, a feedback loop of adrenaline and dopamine, of stress and good feelings, of sustaining a high."

"You called it stress homeostasis, right?"

That morning I'd deliberately broken Beth's mug, then lied about it on the note, calling it another *accident*. I'd gotten drunk and high on weed, fishtailed on ice, driven eighty on the freeway, then strolled into a jailhouse filled with cops. I'd given Dr. Lund a bottle of wine that I knew would piss her off.

She said, "Your friend, Ernst, you've said he writes poetry."

I frowned, nodded. I'd often talked to her about Ernst, his wine and farm, mostly.

"There's a long tradition of poetry as, shall we say, a form of self-help therapy."

Bingo! I smiled, feeling better, now that I saw where she was heading. "So who needs self-help?"

"Cowper, Byron, Plath—they all tried to exorcise their various demons."

"So who has demons?"

"Don't we all?"

"Didn't Plath kill herself?" Funny, the factoids that stick with you from high school.

Her eyebrows lifted. "Yes, that's right. She'd suffered a miscarriage, among other tragedies. And she was bipolar."

"Yeah, just like Em is."

"Why does Ernst write poetry?"

"He's a dreamer. And he's got demons." I was thinking of his black moods, the vortexes that sucked him into soulful despair. I crossed my legs like she had hers crossed. "I don't really know, exactly."

"Does he show them around to other people?"

"Hell, no. Only to me."

"And?"

"His verse is a bit purple."

"And?"

"He jabs a vein and writes a poem. Reading his stuff, sometimes it's like entering a slaughterhouse, and he's the side of beef. And sometimes it's like he's a cloud that never rains. It all depends on his mood."

She laughed—a sudden fork's ring against a thin glass. She leaned forward over her crossed legs. "Then perhaps you can see my point."

I did. She had connected the dots: demons to poets, poets to Ernst, Ernst to me, me to demons. A perfect circle, almost. I shook my head. "Come on, Doc. Poems are just another way for Ernst to suffer."

"Humor me more." She smiled and leaned back in her chair. "What's your favorite place to think about?"

Places are important, so I thought hard, wanting to give her the right answer. I stood and walked over to a window. Down below, the streets were yellow streaks of headlights. To the east, the mountain was a black cone. I said, "A desk."

"Oh?"

Her reflection was in the window, and I could see her head turn toward her own desk, then back to me.

"Yeah, back in high school. It fit my ass perfect, and its armrest fit my arm perfect."

"Mr. Willis' class?"

"He was a real joker. Called the guys 'dolts' because we didn't know how poems can woo a woman. He said dumb things, you know, like 'Brush up your Bard/Start quoting him do/ Brush up your Bard/And the girls you will woo.' He loved that word: *woo*."

She laughed again, a sort of gift.

I kept watching her reflection, and I wanted her to laugh again. "Anyway, my desk was in the back of the classroom, where I could turn around, look out the window and see the baseball field. I'd sit there and dream about baseball."

"That's a lovely memory, Eddy."

"And I'd stare at Beth, too, or at least her back. She sat right in front of me."

"What did Mr. Willis ask you to write about?"

She was leading me in another circle; I felt like that lost guy in the snowy woods who thinks he's walking out till he comes full loop and stumbles on his own footprints. "I don't know. Stuff. He had this poster above his desk: Question Reality."

"Oh?"

"So I wrote a story about a deer that hunted me. It had a gun and I had four legs and a four-point rack. You know, twisting reality around. He gave me a C, but it was a lot worse than that."

She wrote down some more notes, a page or two, her hand a bee now, as if something had excited it, and then she looked up again from her pad and stared at me, at my back. Her reflected image was sharp off the clean glass. She said, "Have you ever considered poetry for the fun of it?"

I just stood there pretending to look down at the traffic, wondering what her hidden thoughts really were, the ones she'd never show to me. Then I spun around fast, hoping to catch her off guard, get her to look away and be embarrassed, reveal something, or at least prod her to change the goddamn subject. But she just kept appraising me with her steady gaze, not quite analytical, certainly not mortified in the least. I said, "I'm worried about Em. She could do something real crazy. Can you see her again, maybe tomorrow?"

"Of course, Eddy. Tomorrow. And don't worry. Florence is looking after her, and she's safe for now."

I walked over to my chair, knelt and grabbed my notebook. She stood. I snapped open the rings and removed several sheets of paper—my most recent lunkers, the bad nightmares she hadn't seen yet. I handed them to her. "I've gotta go. I promised Beth I'd be home for dinner."

She smiled, took the papers and thanked me. "Perhaps we can chat more about poetry next time, all right?"

"Sure, next time."

She stepped to the door, opened it, called Martha into her office. Martha entered, took the papers and left to make copies of them.

Dr. Lund knelt, got the bottle of wine I'd left by the orchid, handed it to me. "Tell Ernst I'd love to see his vineyard some day."

I nodded. "Please, don't call me at home again. I'll call you."

On the drive back home, the needle climbed toward the red, then deep into it, and the radiator began to steam, so I pulled over and poured in a gallon of water.

Chapter 7

The throbbing ache woke me from a deep sleep. It hurt pleasantly. What Sparky called a Texas blue-veiner, a diamond-cutter, a dick so hard a cat couldn't scratch it.

I slid my hand underneath the sheet, squeezed and felt the steady thumping of my heart. The hurt spread upward to my stomach, then downward to my curling toes. My hips arched till the sheet pulled tight.

Next to me, Beth was breathing quiet, dead to everything—a knack she had for utterly dreamless sleep. I rolled over against her, rested my hand on the sweep of her hip and pulled her butt closer.

She rolled away.

It was my fault, too.

I thought about Dr. Lund—Patricia—her topography of wet valleys and soft hills.

Beth's body was not dissimilar. She was a good-looking woman, even after two kids and putting up with me. I hated comparing her to Dr. Lund. It wasn't fair. But their two bodies just popped side-by-side into my head, and then just as quick, out.

I slipped from of bed and dressed: socks first, feet dancing on the freezing floor. Licker crawled out from underneath the bed, shook a kink out of his spine and followed me into the kitchen. A new Jesus mug was hanging on the hook. Beth must've had a spare. I built a fire, leaving the door of the stove open to create a nice draft. I filled the teakettle, sat it on the stovetop, then went to the pantry and downed three jolts of warming Jack. Got my notebook, took it to the stove and stood close to its wafting heat.

Poetry?

I'd have to ask Ernst what he saw in it. But then again, maybe not. Ernst was a guy who didn't care to be examined. We had that flaw in common, among others.

In the back of the notebook, the old article from the *Oak Creek Tribune* was Scotch-taped to a sheet of paper. The tape, like the article, had turned yellow. *Don't read it again*, I told myself. *Just burn the damned thing.*

I read it.

Local Resident Drowns

Silas Doelger Trout, 38 years of age, a lifelong Oak Creek resident, drowned in the Tyee River last Sunday afternoon. His body has not been recovered. According to his adopted son, Eddie, 15, the accident occurred as Mr. Trout rescued Eddie from the rapids at a favorite swimming spot on the river. Mr. Trout was overcome by the strong current. No service is planned. Mr. Trout was employed by the L & R Lumber Company and resided at his home on Whetstone Road. He is survived by his mother, Susanna, address unknown; his two adopted children, Emily, 18, and Eddie; and his twin brother, Pence, address unknown. Pence is still being sought by authorities for questioning in the murder of Dr. Lawrence Redbow, who died of a single gunshot wound July 15, 1950, at the Trout residence on Whetstone Road.

They misspelled *Eddy* three different times.

They said Em and me had been *adopted*.

They said Uncle Silas had a twin brother named Pence, and Pence was a murderer.

August 25, 1965, a Wednesday, the day the paper was delivered to our mailbox at the house on Whetstone. When Em and me read it, we just looked at each other, stunned.

That word *adopted* was a sucker punch. It knocked us for a loop. No one had ever told us Silas wasn't our natural father. Till the *Tribune* let the truth slip, all the wonderful citizens of Oak Creek had gone along with Silas' secret. What kind of town tells a lie that big? A shitfuck town. And that was why a long time ago, Em and me swore we'd never go back.

And the date of the murder, July 15. That's the day when every year Uncle Silas bought me a cake, stuck candles on it, said to make a birthday wish and blow.

But it's like Em said, we have our secrets, too. The story we'd told the cops about Silas drowning, they bought it hook, line and sinker. It was an easy sell, because the Tyee drowned swimmers about as often as the woods killed loggers. We'd made it look like a drowning. The crazy thing is I thought he *was* our father, but Em only half-thought it. She'd always had those vague memories of the *tall-as-a-tree man*.

I ripped the article out of the notebook, fisted it into a ball and chucked it in the stove.

That put me in a mood. I ripped out #87 and tossed it to the flames, too. Dr. Lund called it Vitruvian Man: *A big stump sawn flat with growth rings circling out that changes shape into an old man who's spread-eagled and staked down and naked with his cock stiff ... the lower half of a woman gone from the hips up no body or*

Trout Kill

head just a pair of legs and a pussy that straddles the old man who cries "Where's the rest of you at?" and then I woke up sweating.

I'd never burned a nightmare before. Always stored them like whoring lures in a tackle box that might someday help Dr. Lund snag the lunker swimming in the deepest part of me, haul it out into the light of day where I could fry and eat the bastard. Watching #87 burn was like a part of me going up in smoke, about the closest thing to a poem I'd ever felt.

Licker knew. He staggered to his feet beside the stove, nosed my hand and then rubbed his butt against my leg. His nose felt as hot as the stove.

"It's okay," I said. "Life's a big pork chop."

He lay down again and rolled onto his side, panting ragged. I had to do something for him soon. The pills from the vet weren't much help. Skim Woolsey, one of the guys down at Sparky's, said he'd take Licker for a ride into the woods, make it quick and painless, then bury him beside a stream. He'd done other dogs that way. All I had to do was give the word.

I went to the refrigerator and got hamburger, hid another ball of it in the palm of my hand. I knelt by the fridge, held out my two fists and called soft, "Hey, Bud."

He didn't lift an ear.

I said louder, "Licker, come."

He lifted his head slow, looked away toward the living room, then swung his big black snout around toward me. He tried to get up, couldn't. Then he lifted his butt, shifted his hind legs underneath himself and, finally, got his body standing on all fours. He staggered toward me, wagging. He nosed one fist then the other fist, looked confused, and then licked the empty fist. He swung his nose to the other fist, then back to the empty one. I opened it. He kept sniffing it. I opened the meat fist, and he slowly swung his head that way, and then took the meat. It fell from between his slack jaws. He laid down right there, panting, eyes glazing over fast, his chest smashing the burger ball. Through it all, he wagged.

The vet had told me he didn't know what would go first: Licker's vision, smell or his appetite. It was all going to hell at once.

The teakettle whistled. I went back to the stove and pushed it to one side, where it soft-wailed till it got quiet.

At the kitchen table again; tried to write something more about the other rice paddy, the other water buff and the M48, but couldn't summon a single word.

I went to the phone.

I'd call Dr. Lund and tell her I'd just woken up with a hard-on. I'd thank her, say she'd made me ache in a pleasant way that Beth couldn't anymore. Tell her I'd just burned Vitruvian Man, then seen a vision of the M48, was now watching the slow expiration of my dog. And after hearing me out, she'd say something wise that, even though she wouldn't mean it to, would shrink me down to an essence: poetry is therapeutic; nightmares are soul mirrors; dogs are a junkie's best friend. And I'd say mirrors don't work in the dark. That's what shrinks do, they shrink you.

I called Ernst.

Maggie answered.

I said, "Ernst there? It's an emergency. I don't have time for small talk. I know he's there. Put him on now."

She laughed. "Oh, it's you, Eddy. Good morning. Are you back so soon? No! Beth said you'd be gone for three days. Where are you? Glass Point? The Edgecrest?"

Trout Kill

"We're home."

"Oh, dear!"

"Yes, exactly. We hit a deer. Put Ernst on."

"Is everyone okay? Beth?"

"We're fine."

"Thank God! Was it the ice? We have ice. The canes are covered with it; but it's so beautiful, a winter blessing from Mary, I'm sure."

Last summer, Maggie made Ernst erect a statue of the Virgin Mary in their vineyard. Father Mullen was coming out later in the week to bless the ground. Maggie was always feeding me bits of her Catholic bullshit. Not because she was a zealot, I wanted to believe, but just to irk the hell out of me. This time I didn't bite, just said, "The Virgin's icy, too, I bet."

She laughed.

Ernst took the phone. "Rat Dick. How'd your trip go?"

He was wondering if I'd been laid. "It didn't. We hit a deer. You working on the walls today?"

"Yeah, come on out."

I heard the bedroom door open, then Beth's slippers come shuffling down the hallway and into the bathroom. "Can't today. I've gotta take the pickup to Jimmy's. The deer busted up the windshield and the radiator. Then I've got to split some oak for Jimmy."

"Oh, hell."

"Yeah."

"You working tonight?"

"Nah. Sparky gave me a couple of days off. You know, for Glass Point."

"He said he'd taste my wine tonight."

"It's great shit. He'll love it."
"We'll see."
"He will."
"So why'd you call?"

I couldn't think of a good reason. "I'll see you later. Good luck with Sparky." I hung up and went over to the stove.

Beth came out of the bathroom and into the kitchen, sleepy-eyed, her robe tied in a loose knot, her hair pinned up in a loose bun. Licker wagged as she walked around him but he didn't even try to lift his head.

Beth got Jesus down from the hook, dropped in a teabag and came to the stove. She said, "Was that Jimmy?"

She'd heard me on the phone. "I called Ernst."

"Oh?"

"Jimmy doesn't open till later, around nine. He'll get us right in. And don't worry about the money. He'll charge a couple cords of oak, for labor."

She filled the mug with kettle water, steam rising up her arm. "What did Ernst want?"

"Nothing. I called him. You know, about the castle."

Her eyes narrowed, like I'd just said Ernst was building a rocket to the moon and he needed my engineering expertise. I'd been helping him build the castle for months. In the years before the castle, going all the way back to when Maggie and Ernst had bought their farm, I'd lent him a hand with the haying and numberless other odd jobs, like banding the nuts on his young bulls. Four years ago we mapped out the vineyard and planted the pinot noir cuttings, a clone suitable for cool coastal climates. Then the next year we'd set a few hundred pecker poles and strung thousands of feet of wire between the poles. When the cuttings grew taller, we trained them to the lower wires. Since then there'd been pruning to do, using machetes, what with the damn vines growing crazy in the spring and the early summer. About a year ago we'd converted his garage into a winery, a slap-dash of presses, fermenters, casks, corkers, pH testers and oak barrels.

Before the vineyard idea came along, Ernst had had a scheme of growing olive trees. He planted saplings. They froze the first winter and died. A few months later, he'd gotten what he called an *epiphany* about becoming a wine man, and so he'd dove head first into learning how, going to every vintner's workshop and studying oenology, especially as related to cool coastal climates. For all the help I'd lent him over the years, he'd paid me with garden vegetables, apples and pears from his orchards, grass-fed beef and more weed than I could smoke. I thought it was a fair trade, my labor for his farm goods, but Beth didn't think so. She liked real wages, and she didn't know about the weed. Like everyone else along that part of the coast, though, Ernst and Maggie were barely scraping by. They had to be resourceful. Ernst hadn't sold any wine yet, and the castle was a big part of his dream to sell a lot of it. Someday the castle would be a grand venue where wine lovers could enjoy handcrafted, biodynamic pinot noir, get married or have their anniversaries. Like the movie said: Build it and they will come.

Beth said, "Ernst asks for your help and you just give it away."

I shrugged, not rising to the bait.

She dropped a tea bag into Jesus, swirled it. "That man has too many dreams."

"He's in up to his eyeballs."

"I suppose so."

"And Em is, too."

"I've been thinking about her. She needs praying for."

I'd told Beth about Em's arrest, being in jail. Prayers wouldn't spring Em, keep her dry and warm or put food on her plate; she needed a job and a roof over her head. "When she gets out, I told her she's welcome to come and stay here."

"Of course she is. The girls would love to see her again."

"She needs a job. Maybe Sparky has something."

Beth swirled the bag faster, blew the steam off, took a quick sip. Her lips barely grazed the rim. She went over to the phone, sat down on the couch and dialed.

I figured she was calling Maggie to fill her in about the accident, and how disappointed she, Beth, was about missing out on Glass Point, the pillow mints, and how if I hadn't been speeding ....

My ass was hot from the stove. I leaned toward the living room, trying to hear what Beth was saying. She had her back to me. The damned kettle started whistling again. Beth hung up and returned to the stove.

She looked okay, not mad. Her bun had come a little more undone. She said, "At least she was nice about it."

"Oh?"

"She said she understood, even after all this time."

"Yeah, who wouldn't?"

"It completely slipped my mind to cancel them."

"Uh-huh?"

"I told her you were driving too fast and ran over a poor deer."

I just looked at her.

"She completely understood and said she wouldn't charge us anything. She was very Christian about it."

I said, "Maybe we could make reservations again, you know, later, after Christmas when the whales are migrating. In the spring or whenever you say."

"The coupon expires today."

She meant the ten-percent-off deal at the Edgecrest, and that I'd pissed away any chance to save real money. "Oh. Sorry. Are you hungry? I'll make breakfast."

She looked at me through the steam rising from the mug.

"I'll fix a batch of pancakes." I headed for the kitchen.

"I'll do it. You'll burn something." She brushed past me and into the kitchen and got an iron skillet off the wall.

I went over to the table, sat, laid the notebook on my lap, took the pencil in my hand and pretended to think, staring down at the lines on the paper. I preferred wide lines. It seemed nightmares fit easier between them.

She laid out bacon in the skillet, set it on the burner, stood there and watched the strips begin to sizzle, then start to smoke; she got a spatula, poked, scooted, nudged and turned the strips.

I tried to grip the pencil as Ernst did when he scrawled his poems, so it stood alertly upright between my index finger and thumb. My hand cramped.

She set the cooked bacon on paper towels. Then, one at a time, cracking each shell against the rim of the skillet with a single, deft motion of her wrist, she emptied three eggs into the spattering grease. She corralled them with the spatula, salted and peppered them. "Why do you help Ernst so often?"

I thought we'd moved on, but no. She liked Ernst, usually, but believed his moods and dreams sometimes got the better of him. She was right about that. They did. His moods wrestled with his dreams, a back-and-forth with no clear winner. That's why I loved him, his mystifying contrariness. In that way, he was like Em. I said, "You know I like building stuff."

She turned and faced me, shook her head, rolled her eyes, sighed, turned back to the eggs and, even though she knew I liked mine sunny-side up, she flipped them. "You need to say no sometimes. We have dreams, too. What about our dreams?"

She meant the lot across the street, that the blackberries were choking *her dream*, and the rain was drowning it. I laid the pencil down. "We don't have the money ... yet."

That last word hung with the bacon smoke curling up from the skillet. She said, "It's been years."

"Yeah, I know."

She shook her head and her bun came undone; her hair tumbled over the shoulders of her robe. "Dreams need tending to. The very least you could do is cut the blackberries."

If we'd been sitting in the Edgecrest's swanky restaurant and eating waffles with strawberries and whipped cream, rather than in our rented kitchen, Beth wouldn't have been so sore about the dream. Her moods always sprang from what was right in front of her. She lacked imagination that way. "Things are going okay. We'll get there someday. Besides, if I cut the blackberries they'd come right back. You have to poison them."

"Things are not *okay*. Not if you keep having *accidents*." She gathered her hair and pinned it back up, taking her time, letting the yolks harden in the pan. She spatulaed the eggs onto the plates and brought them over to the table.

Trout Kill

I closed the notebook and shoved it aside.

She sat down, picked up her fork and poked her egg. No yolk seeped out.

I said, "If you could live your life all over again, from the beginning, knowing what you know now, and you could change anything at all, anything, what would you change?"

She pulled her robe tight; her hands shook; she shoved them in the pockets of the robe. "Nothing that I can think of. No, nothing at all. Absolutely. Period."

I just looked at her, picked up the ketchup and dumped a red puddle on my eggs.

She said, "I'm a good person."

"Yeah. I didn't mean—"

"I'm happy with my life. Our life." She laid the fork on her plate and her hands got real still. Her eyes seemed to uncenter and unfocus, as if the tea was just now stoning her. "And what about you?"

"I'd have taken Licker to the vet sooner. I'd have slowed down around that corner. I'd have run away from home as soon as my legs were strong enough. I'd have gone to Canada instead of Nam. I'd have read more books to the girls, taken them hiking more, collected more sand dollars. I'd have read about Carl Jung and taken notes in high school. I wouldn't be killing the fir in the back yard. Just a whole damn bunch of little stuff like that, you know?"

Her eyes got more scared. She stood up from the table slow, then stepped to the center of the kitchen floor. She turned around in a slow circle, so slow I could see the frays in the hem of her bathrobe. Then another circle, a little bit faster. She stretched out her arms like Jesus on the cross, threw her head back and spun around again faster, looser, sort of like a rag doll. Again and again, each time faster than before, till her robe billowed out and her bun burst free and her hair fanned out. She stopped so fast her hair whipped her face. Her eyes were dreamy, with no more fear. She panted, out of breath, her chest rising and falling. And then she giggled like a nervous kid and blushed.

I sat there frozen with the ketchup bottle, wondering what was going on.

She pulled the cord on her bathrobe and the robe fell open. Underneath, her pajama top was buttoned all the way up, her nipples hard against the flannel. She shucked off the robe and it fell to the floor, where she kicked it toward the sink. She worked her thumbs inside the waistband of her pajamas, shimmied her hips, slid the bottoms down to the floor. One leg at a time she stepped out of them. Legs white as the sugar bowl, a pair of pink panties. They were the Rudolph the Red-nosed Reindeer panties. Embroidered on the front of them, he flew north from her crotch toward her belly button. She unbuttoned the pajama top, shrugged it off, tossed it aside. Her breasts sagged toward the pale tracks on her stomach. She giggled again and curtsied low, with her breasts dangling and shuddering. She wiggled the panties down her thighs, to her knees, let them drop to her ankles, stepped out of them, bent down, picked them up and folded them into a neat pink square.

I smiled but my lips felt ironed.

She stood there full frontal, her chestnut bush and nipples and eyes. She stepped to the table and handed the panties to me.

They held her warmness, and it ranged up my arm and into my chest and down into my groin and I got the inkling of a hard-on. I unfolded them and laid them on the notebook. Rudolph, I noticed, had a matched, seven-point rack. I said, grinning, "Just like at the Greyhound station?"

Her eyes lost their dreamy look and got resolute. "I am taking that job."

The inkling vanished. I played dumb. "Oh? What job?"

Her hands covered her bush, then she let her arms hang free at her sides. "Trudy is on maternity leave, and Wally asked if I'd like to fill in for her. It's a temporary position, until the end of the school year. I begin the first Monday in January. Trudy is due in two more weeks, but until the baby arrives, she said she'd help me with the curriculum and the lesson planning."

Trudy Simnett was the second-grade teacher at the elementary school. Wally Beech, the principal, had come into Sparky's a few nights ago, had his usual two beers, and let it slip to Sparky about Beth filling Trudy's position. Sparky told me about it, thinking I already knew. Beth hadn't said a word to me, knowing I'd probably say we didn't need the money. Money didn't build dreams, hammers did. Besides, Wally was an asshole. I said, "You told Wally about this yet?"

She stood there naked, her nipples gone soft. "You're okay with this, aren't you? I love teaching kids, and you know we can always use the money. We'll save enough to finish building our new house."

I nodded. "Sure. This is great. I'm happy for you." I picked up the panties from off the notebook and pressed them to my face. I smiled with my eyes. I breathed in the scent of the panties, loud, so Beth could hear, but there was no hint of peaches, just the greasy bacon air.

Chapter 8

Beth's panties lay on the table, where I sat sipping the bad coffee in my frog cup. I stuffed the panties into my pocket, thinking I'd give them back when the time was right. Moving with a bounce in her step, humming a Christmas carol, Beth came into the kitchen from the bedroom, where she'd gone to change out of her pajamas.

 She made a grocery list, said we were out of this and that, especially Hamburger Helper. She got her purse and left, taking the ten-minute walk to the Milo Store for the groceries. And a mocha, too. She loved to sit at the store counter, sip her chocolate-coffee drink and visit with Janette Simpson, who ran the store. Sometimes I'd go with her for a coffee; I drank mine black. Afterwards, we'd take a long walk together along the beach or up into the hills. We'd hold hands, but our differing strides—hers short and jerky, mine longer and smoother—would throw off the natural swing of our arms, so I'd try to shorten my strides, and she'd try to lengthen hers, and after just a short while we'd feel like spastics.

 I dialed Jimmy. He said to bring the pickup right down, he wasn't busy, just sitting there beside his potbellied stove and jerking off with Miss June.

 I was there in five minutes, a junk yard scattered with smashed-in and cut-up heaps, the heaps frost-coated, mostly pickups and later model cars, some old Ramblers and Corvairs. About an acre of rust, rain-streaked glass, dented bodies and

Trout Kill

flat tires. The puddles had frozen over. His dog, a Rottweiler, Bozo, got out from underneath a Studebaker, trotted over to my pickup and sniffed me up and down, smelling Licker on my hands, my pants. When a dog smells another dog on you he has to check you out.

Jimmy's office was a lean-to scabbed against a garage and his singlewide.

Inside, he was dressed as he always dressed: Dickies long-sleeve coveralls, a Detroit Tigers baseball cap, leather boots covered in grease. All of him was greasy. He smiled crooked, a few teeth missing, all the others turned as black as the chew in his cheek. He said to come on in and warm myself. The potbelly's dry heat cut right through me. There was a small stack of split oak against the wall. Jimmy's blind eye was hazy from a welding accident, but his good one sparkled blue and clear. When he looked at you, it would sometimes meander. His beard covered his chest, shoulder to shoulder. The pin-ups hanging around the stove suggested Jimmy was an ass man, which he surely was. We shot the shit for a minute, ate a doughnut, then went outside to my pickup.

His good eye stared and he said, "Deer?"

"No, a kid in a wheel chair."

Jimmy har-harred. He spit brown juice. "He musta shit pellets. So you were doin' about forty, huh? At least forty."

"How long?"

"Depends." He popped the hood, bent low over the engine and breathed in the tonic smell of baked-on anti-freeze. "Got hot, did she?"

"Just fix the radiator and the windshield. I can live with the dents."

"Hotter'n a two-peckered rabbit in a fuckin' contest, was she?" He har-harred again, his jiggling beard polishing the radiator cap. "Hotter'n a fresh-fucked fox in a pepper patch, huh?"

"How much?"

"Headlight, too?"

"Yeah, that too. And the hazard lights don't work."

"Wouldn't think you'd ever need 'em."

"Fuck you."

"Have to order a windshield."

"And?"

"'bout a few days."

"And?"

"Two cords, split and delivered, plus parts."

"Okay."

"You shouldn't drive 'er when she's hot as a two-dollar feudin' pistol."

I walked home fast, wanting to get the wood split and stacked. Two cords would take the whole morning and into the afternoon. Before I got to the chopping block, I felt the old urge to wound something. I hurried across the back yard to a big Doug fir at the edge of the hillside; the tree was about a hundred feet tall and maybe that old.

The hammer was leaning against the fir's thick-barked trunk, beside a can of rusting nails. The hammer was an old, wooden-hafted thing I didn't use for building anymore. I took a nail from the can, set its point against the bark and tapped the head once to set the point, then drew the hammer back and drove the nail half in. Another blow sank the head flush with the bark.

There were other nails, lots of them—a band that girdled the entire trunk and, over the years, had left a black stain in the

Trout Kill

bark. The nails were sixteen-penny, long enough to penetrate the bark into the sapwood and injure the tree. Twenty feet up, the needles on the lowest limbs were turning brown, and the slightest wind would send them raining to the ground.

Dr. Lund might help me figure out why I was punishing the fir, if I ever got up the nerve to tell her about it. All I know for sure is that since I started nailing the tree I haven't been punching as many walls.

I tossed the hammer down and went to the woodpile at the other side of the backyard. It was a jumbled heap of oak rounds, green for easy splitting. I shed my jacket to the frozen ground. The splitting axe was stuck in the chopping block. I yanked it out. It was double-bitted, each blade as honed as its twin. I set a round on the block and hefted the axe, one hand tight on its heel, the other loose at its neck. I took a big swing, aiming for the god dot, figuring to halve the round in a single blow. The bit thunked in and sank to its cheek, cracking the round but not splitting it clean. I worked the axe free and had another go. The halves flew apart. Another swing halved a half into quarters.

I did that again and again, split rounds into halves, then quarters. Jimmy burned quarters. They burned hotter than the halves. Sometimes, if there were knots, it took a few swings to make a quarter. I didn't use the wedge. A quick sweat came. I took my shirt off and felt the chill air burn.

Jimmy said his one eye was good enough to see what he needed to. Under the hood of a wreck, he believed everything it told him. For me, it was hard to believe half of what my two eyes saw. In his world, Jimmy saw twice as clear as I saw in mine.

The axe work, though, cleared my mind. I was sorry about the fir for the thousandth time. My hands felt strong. Sometimes when you bury things so deep the only way to get them out is through your hands and sweat.

When I looked up from the chopping block Beth was waving out the kitchen window. She was back from the store. She mouthed, "Are you hungry?" It was past noon. I'd split about a cord but had another cord to go. My hair was plastered wet and steam was rising off my chest. I waved and shook my head no.

There was a fat blister on my ring finger, from the axe handle rubbing there. The red skin bubbled up against the gold band. Ernst and me were philosophically opposed to wearing gloves. Gloves are for pussies. I slipped the ring off and put it in my pocket with the panties. I worked the blister between my teeth and bit down. The bubble popped and I sucked the fluid out. Then I went inside the house.

Beth was putting up the groceries. She gave me a look. "I thought you weren't hungry."

I shrugged. "Maybe a sandwich and a beer."

"Bologna okay?"

"Yeah, thanks." I went straight to the pantry, got my notebook and took it to the stove. Beth was busy in the kitchen. I ripped out three yellowed sheets of old paper—the cheap kind with wide lines and floating bits of wood. They were filled with a kid's loopy cursive—mine, from the second grade. I told myself not to read it again.

dear teacher!

my report is how i got this crummy blister on my hand. it hurts. im a good speller. dad thinks ems slow in the head because she talks to dolly and doesn't knows how to work a beer opener. dad smells sawdusty and won't let me thwack his suspenders. he said to me and em lets play the guessing game. em doesnt like that game. he said whichever of you guesses gets a quarter. we played on the table. something was inside his lunch pail. we could hear it scratching inside. it had to be a critter. i right away guessed a baby owl and dad said nope. i said a baby rabbit and dad said shut your trap its your sisters turn. em took my hand and squeezed it real hard. dad said guess god damit. she guessed a mouse and he said nope. then it was my turn again and i guessed a baby skunk and dad said nope. em guessed a bunch of silly guesses like a fairy or a witch or a goblin. i laughed and dad thwacked me and he thwacked em harder. i guessed a porcupine and dad said nope. em all of a sudden said a chipmunk and dad said you lucky girl heres your quarter. dad opened the lunch box and sure enough it was a chipmunk curled up in a scared ball. em started bawling like she always does when she wins. dad said for her to quite sniveling and for me to go outside and chop goddamn firewood till goddamn suppertime and thats how i got this crummy blister from the axe.

I wadded up the story, opened the stove and tossed it in. The hungry flames were like the nails in the tree. Somehow they just were.

Beth said, "Your sandwich is ready, but we're out of beer."

"Okay, be there in a sec." I had to watch the flames till they died down and the story was gone, but what Uncle Silas did to Em and me would burn forever.

Then the phone rang. It was Sparky, saying he'd heard I was back in town, and that Billy had a family emergency—his wife had the flu—and so he couldn't come in for his evening shift. "Ooo-ee, Darlin'. Can you cover for Billy's ass tonight?"

Chapter 9

Sparky's was busy, with the usual crowd for Cheeseburger Night.

The bar was a century-old relic with a brass foot rail, cigarette burns and at least one bullet hole. Built of oak, the wood was about the same golden-amber as Yukon Jack.

Molly VanGorder flitted from the kitchen to the tables, between the tables, back to the kitchen. She was twenty-two, spunky and sassy, jewelry hanging everywhere, bracelets jangling, her body parts pierced and, as she liked to brag, loaded for bear. She meant *bare*.

Rex Stuey and Ace Martin were playing eight ball on the new pool table, a seven-footer with solid cabinet grade plywood and triple-plated die-cast top corners. About fifteen hundred bucks, according to Sparky. Rex and Ace had already slotted about five dollars worth of quarters. They were betting a dollar a game. Rex worked at the Milo Store, Ace at the gas station. Ace had lost his wife the year before to Hodgkins and was just now climbing out of his mourning hole. Since five o'clock, when he'd come in and started playing pool, he'd downed six Rogue Irish Lagers. Beer didn't seem to faze him. It was Rex, a three-pint screamer, you had to watch out for.

Rex peered at me over the pool table and nodded once, and I nodded back once. He leaned over his stick, eyed the cue ball and poked it at the five ball, which missed the corner pocket by a foot.

Trout Kill

The other two pool tables were busy, too—more locals, their skills at pool about the same caliber as Rex's—but no one was playing video poker or shuffleboard or darts.

Wally Beech—and a couple of other guys I didn't know—were hunkered in the corner at a table by the Wurlitzer, a '41 Model 750 with twenty-four selections on the playlist. Their three heads together over the table, their faces long and somber, they'd been quietly sipping their beers and talking low. Wally was a principled principal: he never had more than two beers. Three might loosen up his tongue or behavior. He was worried about keeping his reputation intact, which elementary principals have to do, I suppose. Tonight he was drinking the special: Santa's Private Reserve. I almost moseyed over and told him Beth was going to be a great teacher, which he already knew. What he might not know, and what I'd never say, was that teaching might give Beth something to think about besides Jesus and my accidents. I stayed put where I was, behind the bar. The less I said to Wally, the better.

Years before, when Kate and BJ were fourth-graders, and right after Wally took the principal's job at the Milo Elementary School, he'd made a big push to recruit part-time parent volunteers. Beth was interested, and one fall morning she put on her red dress and went to the school to sign up. After an informal interview with Wally and his secretary, Ellen Cranston, Ellen had her fill out a form and told her to report to the office Monday morning for orientation. When Beth left the school, she found a note pinned underneath the windshield wiper of the pickup: *Mrs. Trout, please forgive this brash approach, but during your interview, I thought I sensed in you a distinct note of unhappiness. I am quite attracted to you. If you are interested in a discrete* relationship, perhaps we could meet and have coffee some time. Just to chat. If you are interested, simply wear your lovely red dress again next Monday, when you report to the school.

It was signed *Wally*.

When Beth showed the note to me, we had a good laugh, but my amusement sounded damned thin to my ears, and come Monday morning, I noted she wore a blue dress to the school.

At another table, Fred Tripplehorn, Stan Hagan, Trick Pugsley and Skeet Groff played cribbage and drank Scotch. They were regulars, old loggers on Social Security. They flirted with Betty Wilder and Louise Kindrich, who were sitting at a nearby table eating fish and chips. Betty's husband Joe died years before in a logging accident when a choker cable snapped and broke his neck. Louise had been married to the Postmaster, Wilford Kindrich, for about fifty years. Wilford was still kicking, but confined to a wheelchair.

Their flirting was mostly out of ancient habit, just old men and old women joshing over drinks. Seldom did their teasing heat up to the point where two of them would rendezvous in the parking lot, or beyond.

Skim Woolsey sat at the end of the bar brooding, getting shit-faced, staring into his drink as if lashed to it. His third drink since coming in twenty minutes earlier—all doubles, twelve-year Glenlivet, on the rocks. One drink ago, he'd told me the scariest thing in the world was the rattle of ice cubes in his empty glass. He'd been crying. Something was gutting him alive.

Patsy Cline sang on the Wurlitzer. The playlist was mostly hers, with a few other country-western crooners thrown in the mix. Sparky insisted on country-western exclusively. It fit the place, he said, and was easier to sing along with than the rock I preferred. Loving country music was one of Sparky's few imperfections.

The Blazers on the big screen, losing to Sacramento again. No volume, just the disheartening testimonial of the video.

Sparky was in the kitchen, cooking and singing along with Patsy, his voice booming out through the swinging double doors every time Molly pushed her way out or in. Cooking food, Sparky said, was an art form, and he was damned particular about everything, even the cheeseburgers, choosy right down to the lettuce, which had to be organic—an L.A. thing. *Good food served right* was his motto, and he always sang when he *created*, which is what he called what he did.

I polished hot glasses straight out of the dishwasher behind the bar and watched the Blazers go oh-for-five from inside the paint. Kept scanning the crowd for a lifted finger, a head nod or a hand wave, an eyebrow arched—any of the million ways to ask for another drink.

Skim kept his stare iced in the cubes, then lifted his index finger about an inch above the rim of his glass.

I poured another double Glenlivet, took it down to him, put a fresh napkin underneath the glass, toweled up a puddle that wasn't there. Said just to let him know I cared, "Fucking Blazers."

He looked up from the drink, mumbled something, then dove brain first into the Scotch again.

I took his empty back to the dishwasher.

When Skim was ready to talk, he'd lead and I'd follow.

Ernst came in a little after eight o'clock, just before halftime, the Blazers still down. He stood in the open doorway, his bulk filling it. A salt wind pushed around him and into the bar, stirred the cigarette smoke into a blue swirl, spun the paper Santas that Sparky had hung from the ceiling. Ernst had a case of wine under one arm. He squinted at the TV—a farmer gazing west, reading the weather.

I tapped him a pint of Dead Guy Ale the way he liked it, with a head that barely topped the rim and slopped over.

He came over to the bar, set the box down, seized the pint with his paw and drank it down in a single go. Wiped his drinking hand on his pants, then wiped off his wide mouth set in his square head atop an oaken neck. Took off his John Deere cap, raked his buzz-cut with his fingers, then reset the cap and pulled it down to his ears. "Thought you said you wouldn't be here."

I tapped him another Dead Guy, said I was filling in for Jimmy.

He pulled up a stool, sat and frowned. "Curly's got a stuck swivel. Jesus tits. If it's not one thing it's another."

His ancient track hoe, Curly, was always busting down, usually a hydraulic leak in a worn seal or a hose. The hoe had excavated the pit for the dungeon of the castle, and lately had been hoisting boulders to the top of the tower wall. "We on for tomorrow?"

He nodded. "We'll fix Curly, first thing in the morning."

Sparky poked his head through the swinging doors. He wore a hat with reindeer antlers. "Ooo-ee! Ernst, darlin'. I'll be right out." He disappeared behind the doors, and a second later Molly emerged carrying two cheeseburger baskets. She took the baskets to Bill and Ace, then returned to the kitchen.

Sparky came out wearing that ridiculous hat, his flashy red

suit, his red tie with green mistletoe, a green shirt and black Santa boots. An apron with dancing elves. He stood on his tiptoes and kissed Ernst on his cheek.

Ernst wiped it away. "Knock off the shit, Sparky."

Sparky pointed at the entry, where a sprig of mistletoe hung above the door. "Tis the season to be jolly!"

Ernst pulled his hat lower. Even sitting on the stool, he was a foot taller than Sparky. He said, "You look like Santa's whore."

Big smile, perfect teeth. "Flattery will get you somewhere, darlin'." Sparky lowered his voice. "How's the grow comin' along?"

"Good."

Sparky grinned, then pursed his lips and sucked in air, then blew it out and crossed his eyes.

Ernst yanked two corked bottles from the box. They had long, dark-glassed bodies and tapering necks. He stood one of the bottles on the bar, flourished the other one across his palm. "You need a little more class in this joint, Sparky."

Sparky smiled. "Eddy, he slanders you!"

"Fuck you."

"Promises, promises."

Ernst handed Sparky the bottle. "It's one-eighty for the case. That's fifteen bucks a bottle. You turn it around for, oh, let's say six bucks a glass on your dinner menu. You can pour about five glasses per bottle. That comes to thirty bucks a bottle, about three-sixty for a case. Even you can do the math. It's a sure money-maker."

Now Ernst smiled. He'd practiced his pitch.

Sparky turned the bottle over in his hands. "The price

seems fair. But where's the label? Darlin', I can't sell a wine with no name on it."

"So what? It's primo shit."

"Is that what I call it on the menu, Primo Shit?"

Ernst grabbed the bottle out of Sparky's hands, stabbed the cork with the screw he had in his pocket, twisted down the screw, clamped the bottle with one hand and yanked with the other. When the cork popped Ernst snorted—the joyful glee of his dream drawing near.

But I heard the *pop* of an illumination flare, and saw its phosphorescent sun parachuting down in the inky night sky above the concertina.

"Gimme a damn glass."

I handed Ernst a glass. He filled it with purple to the brim, handed it to Sparky. Sparky held it up to the light above a pool table. Then he nosed it. Then he took a sip and swished it around, making a sloshing sound. He nodded, smiled, spit the wine into another glass. "Ooo-ee! You made this yourself?"

Ernst said, "It's even better after it breathes."

"Aren't we all? Darlin', I'll take half a case. We'll see how she goes."

Ernst looked surprised. Then it turned into a big smile. "Jesus tits! Thanks, Sparky. This officially makes me a wine man."

"But you'll need a label. The OLCC says so."

Ernst kept beaming. He got off the stool, clamped Sparky's shoulders between his massive hands, lifted him off the floor and swung him around and around. "I'm a wine man!"

Sparky squealed, kicked his heels up and planted another kiss on Ernst's neck.

Trout Kill

No one paid much attention.

On their last spin around, either Sparky's hand or Ernst's elbow knocked over the other bottle standing on the bar. It rolled off, fell to the floor and shattered there, splashing wine and shards all the way to the foot of a pool table.

Ernst cussed, set Sparky down on his feet again. "There goes fifteen bucks!"

Sparky ran into the kitchen, came out quick with a mop and bucket, started cleaning up the spill while singing like a happy idiot along with the Wurlitzer; he held the mop like it was his dancing partner. Molly came over and swept up the busted glass, her bracelets jangling. Ernst stood there looking glum at the mess. Sparky said, "Your wine is superb, Ernst! First-class! You should be very proud of it." He fist-bumped Ernst then, mop and bucket in hand, he danced his way back into the kitchen. Molly rolled her eyes, followed after him with the broom.

Ernst's good mood had disappeared. He slumped onto his stool, planted his elbows on the bar. The busted bottle was a bad sign, like coyote tracks around the hen house. He was the smartest man I knew, but he believed that omens, like souls, were a viable part of a mysterious universe. The winds of profit and loss were blowing in contrary ways.

I lifted six of the remaining bottles out of the cardboard box and set them behind the bar, in case an OLCC man should wander in.

Ernst said, "How the hell am I going to sell sixty cases only six bottles at a time?"

"The castle, remember?"

"The goddamned thing will never get built, with just the two of us, and Curly always breaking down."

"So, what label did you settle on?"

"Hell, I can't decide."

"I like Two Dogs Humping, with gothic lettering."

He didn't smile. So far, the name he liked best was Mountaintop Noir. He sat up straight on the stool, squared his shoulders, eyed my left hand, said, "Where's the ring?"

It was still in my pocket, where I'd put it while chopping wood. There was a pale circle on my finger. Ernst's own ring was a gold constriction on his beefy finger; it looked painful. I told him I'd been splitting firewood for Jimmy, showed him the blister from the axe handle. He called me a pussy, said he'd buy me a pair of fur-lined gloves. I suggested Drink Piss and Die for a wine name. He still didn't smile. I pulled the ring from my pocket. He asked if he could see it. I handed it over and he lifted it to his nose and smelled it. He handed it back, and I slid it onto my finger and down to the blister. He looked at his own ring and said, "I'd have to cut mine off."

"It's on there tight."

"Might have to take the finger, too."

At the end of the bar, Skim signaled for another one. I got a fresh glass, iced it and poured the Scotch.

Ernst looked down the bar at Skim. "What's eating him?"

"Hell if I know." I took his drink down to him.

As soon as the glass hit the fresh napkin, Skim picked it up and took a drink. His hand shook. When he set it down, he missed the napkin.

I said again, "Fucking Blazers."

He said, "My dad just died."

I blinked. The air snapped like an AK bullet zipping by. But inside I felt nothing. Absolutely nothing, as if the bullet

Trout Kill

had been addressed To Whom It May Concern. I just nodded at Skim, said I was sorry to hear the bad news. Said something else that I don't remember and that rang just as hollow. I picked up Skim's old napkin, his empty glass. His eyes were bloodshot from booze and crying. I said, "The Blazers need a decent back-up center."

"We did a lot of fishing. He loved to fish."

"A big man, a seven-footer who can block out, grab a rebound every fucking so often."

"He was always telling me this old joke about a one-armed fisherman who bragged to his buddies about a big-assed whopper he caught one day, and when his buddies ask him how big, he holds out his only arm and says, 'Oh, 'bout this big'." Skim sobbed, took another drink.

My eyes welled up.

"A million times he told that same fucking joke, and a million times I laughed." He shoved the drink away. "It's still damned funny, don't you think, Eddy? Ain't it damned funny?"

Skim was a blur behind a skim of tears. I nodded. "Yeah, it's funny."

He laid a fifty-dollar bill on the bar.

I shoved it back at him. "Drinks are on the house tonight, Skim."

"No, goddamn it. They ain't on the house. This ain't my house." He left the money, got off his stool, slapped his car keys down on the bar, steered himself toward the door. He stopped between two of the pool tables, turned around, held up one arm and said, "About this big." His laugh sounded strangled.

"See you around, Skim. Sorry about your dad."

"It don't mean nothing."

"There it is."

"Yeah, there it is. Hey, Eddy, just give me the word, and I'll take care of your dog for you."

I nodded. "Will do."

He left, his legs wobbling but, I figured, steady enough to get him home to his wife and three dogs, his twenty-year-old son who lived in the basement. They lived a mile east, up in the low hills that reminded Skim and me of the Nam, the Central Highlands between An Khe and Pleiku.

Skim's half-full drink sat there. I wanted to pick it up and finish it off so bad my teeth hurt; I wanted to cry for Skim's dead dad even though I'd never met him. I thought *Goddamn, Skim's a lucky man.* I picked up his keys, his fifty-dollar bill, the napkins and the glasses and then wiped the bar down. I walked to the till, dropped the keys in and stuck the fifty underneath the tray. The next time Skim came in, he'd get his keys and the money back.

Ernst had taken the box and the four remaining bottles of wine to the table with the cribbage players. He'd uncorked two of the bottles; they were passing them around, the four old loggers and a rookie wine man.

A guy with a white beard shuffled in the door, faded jeans and work boots, the collar turned up on his red wool coat. He came over to the bar, braced his hand against it, coughed a jagged spat, scooted his ass on a stool. His cap was down to his white eyebrows and a toothpick hung from his lips. "Hennessy, please, if you've got it. No ice."

I poured the cognac and served him.

The Blazers were ahead now, up by five in the fourth quarter.

The old guy nodded thanks, took his hat off, lifted the drink slow to his lips, that toothpick out the side. He sipped and set the drink down. "If you don't mind my asking, Eddy, why didn't you and your missus head on up to Glass Point?"

His eyes were snapping blue, fixed on me. He looked vaguely familiar, like a face from the distant past that the years had worn down to a gray and wrinkled semblance. His dry and gravelly voice, though, I remembered quite well. "Spencer?"

He looked pleased that I'd remembered. "That's right."

"Hey, welcome to Sparky's." We shook hands. His was cold.

"A vacation, wasn't it?"

I shrugged. "We decided to come back home."

"Shame."

"It was probably a good thing we did. The radiator had a leak."

"You made it home okay, I hope."

"Yeah."

"That was a damned heartful thing you did for the doe, laying her out under that cedar."

I thanked him again for stopping that night, for helping me out—just a stranger on a dark highway.

He brushed off the gratitude and looked around. "Real nice place you've got here."

I guessed he meant the hanging Santas, the spray-on snow on the windows and the strings of twinkling lights draped around the walls. A Merle Haggard song played, and from the kitchen Sparky was singing along. Ace and Bill were racking their pool sticks, ready to call it a night. Ernst was pouring shots of wine for the cribbage players. Trick, pushing eighty years old, sniffed the wine in his beer glass, rolled his eyes and moaned loud enough for everyone to hear, pretending ecstasy. I said, "Don't let it fool you."

He laughed, or tried to—more like a grimace. His whole body clenched up like a clam. He pulled out some pills from a pocket and popped them into his mouth, chased them with a drink.

"Hell, to tell you the truth, I'm glad we came back home."

"Oh?"

"I was worried about my dog. He's sick. We'd left him with a neighbor."

"Oh?"

"A damned tumor, the vet says."

"A real shame. There's no need for him to suffer."

I nodded, looked away at nothing, then at the door, then at nothing again. "I'll do what needs done."

"When I was a kid we had a mixed-breed dog, a mutt if ever there was one. She got old and sick, and then one day she wasn't around anymore. When I asked my mother about it, she said Queenie had run off. That was the dog's name, Queenie. I was six, maybe seven years old, but even then, I knew better. Queenie had never run before. Years later, my brother and I are walking in the woods and we find a mound of stones."

He coughed, gasped, took a couple shallow breaths. I caught the fusty stench, like a tree so rotted through-and-through that any breeze would topple it. Then a fit of coughing bent him double and he clung to the bar. When the spasms passed, he wiped his mouth with a handkerchief.

I polished a glass to keep my hands busy.

"Sorry about that. Not feeling myself, lately."

Trout Kill

I nodded.

"We dug into the mound and found her collar. There was a bunch of bones. Sheeit! She'd been shot—right through the top of her skull, between her ears. The odd thing was there was a bone that didn't belong with hers. It was too big, probably the rib of a cow. My brother and I figured our dad had taken Queenie for a last walk in the woods, given her the bone to gnaw on, and then put her down clean."

I scanned the crowd for signs of thirst. Wally and his two friends got up to leave. Wally never waved goodbye. "Your dad did a good thing."

"I suppose so. Both for his sons and the dog." He pointed at my jacket, "You were in the Army, hey?"

"Yeah."

"What'd you do?"

"Nothing much."

"I see you washed her blood out of it."

"Yeah, some of it."

He lifted the cognac like a toast, his hand shaking, his eyes boring into me. "Here's to blood." His lips groped for the lip of the glass, then parted for a trickle. His swallow looked painful. As he lowered the glass, he muttered something.

I looked away at nothing again and thought about sniper school, the Black D.I. telling us privates that *in an ambush sitcheation on a nigga-black night, if ya sorry bad asses hear a slope in the bush don't fuckin' look right at 'im. No sirree! Ya won't see shit. Ya gotta employ yer Army-issued, peripheral-type vision—ya know: out the edges of yer eyeballs—and then ya'll stand a better fuckin' chance of seein' 'im first—and first see is first shoot. Ya'll catchin' my drift?*

Spencer pulled out a hanky, coughed and spit into it, then pushed his Hennessy away. "Guess I'd better be getting on home. The missus is most likely wondering where I'm at."

I said, "Take it easy, Spencer. Drop in again."

"Real nice to see you again."

But he made no move to leave, just sat there and folded the hanky and stuck it back in his pocket.

Merle started skipping on the Wurlitzer. The house groaned and the cribbage players started bitching. I walked around the bar, went over to the corner and kicked the juke. Merle started singing again, as good as he ever did.

At the bar, Spencer got his cap, dropped one leg off the stool, then his other leg. He stood, took an uncertain step, steadied himself, said, "That blood on your jacket—if I was you, I'd let it be."

I shrugged, nodded, glanced down at the stain. "This jacket's been washed one time. That's good enough, I suppose."

He gave me a long look and a wistful smile, turned and shuffled to the door. It took both his hands to pull it open. The wind gusted in and roused his hair. He put his cap on and stepped outside.

Back at the bar, I picked up the twenty he'd left for the drink. He'd written a note on it, the handwriting jerky and frail: *Be seeing you, Eddy.*

Chapter 10

Stripped down to my jeans and boots, holding a bent iron bar, I stood atop a round stone tower. Somewhere above the mist, the sun was heading toward noon.

Ernst sat in the cab of Curly, his track hoe, studying a huge pile of boulders, looking for just the right-sized and -shaped one to grab and set into place on the tower wall.

The mist was a gray soup that hid the distant wooded slopes, the farther valleys and, about two miles west, the broad sweep of the Pacific. It shrouded Ernst and Maggie's house, which stood on the crest of the hill, the barn and the chicken coop, and the lower pasture where the cattle grazed. The six-acre vineyard was mostly invisible, except for the closest rows, where we could see the pruned canes stretching along taut wires between the pecker poles. The canes' trunks looked like gnarly thumbs. The statue of the Virgin, about fifty yards away, was just visible.

The world had shrunk down to our work on the castle tower, to hoisting and correctly positioning each boulder, and to the constant grinding of the cement mixer. All morning long, I'd felt a vague weight inside my chest, a thing so heavy it needed Curly to lift it out, haul it off and set it down somewhere far away.

At the Dumpster the night before, during our first pipe and before we were fully high, Sparky told me again how much he loved *creating* food, and how much he loved Ernst and me, loved Beth and Maggie and Molly, loved Kate and BJ and Licker, and even how much he'd loved moping up the busted wine. He loved to work. He said *workin' hands help you love*. Like when his hands worked that mop handle, pushing and pulling the stringy head back and forth through the spilled wine, his hands loving the mop's work.

When he said that, the weight had settled in my chest.

Later, after we'd smoked another pipe, after Sparky'd talked about how *happy* he was, I went home and went to bed. Beth was asleep. I rolled over next to her and put my hand on her hip. Her back was too me; she lay on her right side. Then I let my hand reach around her belly to the top of her bush. I tried to let my heart follow where my hand led. My heart, though, as far as I could tell, stayed where it was, in my chest. My hand knew the shape of Beth's body, and it knew the feel of my framing hammer right down to the heft of its steel spine. I wanted my hand to *know* Beth like it *knew* the hammer. I wanted her to soothe me like the hammer could. Her thighs came together with the soft swell of pussy. She slept, mindless. I lay there listening to the ticking alarm clock and Beth's soft breathing. I tried to feel *happy*. At the very least, I wanted my hand to be *happy*. But nestled in the cradle of her womanhood, it felt restless.

So I'd slipped out of bed, tiptoed down the hallway to the pantry, got my notebook, sat at the kitchen table and, with Licker at my feet, I wrote till it was time to make breakfast, a little before sunup. Then Ernst swung by, picked me up, and we'd driven out to his farm in the gray, murky dawn.

Ernst worked a lever, moved the joystick, maneuvered Curly's iron boom toward the chosen rock, an oblong boulder. The jaws opened and grabbed it.

Trout Kill

First thing that morning, we'd fixed Curly's stuck bucket—a hydraulic line needed replaced. Then Ernst fired up the beast and we'd set to work building more wall. I'd levered the boulders into place with the iron bar; shoveled sand, gravel and cement; mixed batch after batch of concrete; lifted and dumped bucket after bucket of concrete and troweled smooth the joints between the rocks.

A good thing about cool weather is cement sets slow.

The tower stood ten feet above the ground, was twenty-five feet across and looked like a thick doughnut. A circular formwork of plywood and criss-crossed bracing timbers filled the center. We'd already built up several feet of the inner wall with smaller, smooth-faced stones; and now, boulder by boulder, we were building up the rougher outer wall.

Underneath the tower there was a dungeon or, as Ernst thought of it, a wine cellar. We'd built it the summer before. His plan was to build a tower thirty feet above the cellar. We had about twenty more feet to go. At the top, if we ever got there, he wanted battlements and, just for the hell of it, a catapult for launching pumpkins at his cows. From that height, he said, the wine connoisseurs could gaze out across the countryside and marvel at the vineyard and the farm, the distant hills and the ocean.

Ernst and Maggie had made the farm what it was. They'd started with nothing more than a big garden, fruit orchards and fields of hay; they sold their fruits, vegetables and hay to the locals. They scraped by, bought a Hereford cow and bull, started a small herd and sold the beef in the fall. Every dime they earned they invested back into the farm. They were always flat broke—too broke, Ernst said, to have any kids. Then

Sparky had one of his Big Ideas: grow weed in Ernst's barn loft and smuggle it south to Sparky's old stomping grounds in L.A. Like Beth, Maggie didn't know about the grow operation. Ernst had used the first profits from the weed money to buy the olive trees that the winter killed. The following summer, Ernst was driving the hay baler across a south-facing field when he got his big epiphany: to hell with olives; plant grapes. *Vineyard* had a nice ring to it. *Wine man. Pinot noir.* So he'd bought the track hoe and started clearing the rocks from the pasture.

Getting the castle built was now the key to his wine-selling scheme.

Curly, chugging black smoke, swung the oblong boulder up and over toward the tower.

I motioned—a thumb pointing inward—and Ernst eased the jaws that direction till the rock was in position, about a foot from the inner wall. A thumbs up—and the jaws tilted down and released the boulder into a bed of concrete.

The boom swung away and back toward the boulder pile.

I levered the rock with the iron bar, allowing more space between it and the adjacent rock, about two inches, perfect for a strong joint. When the rock was set proper, I tossed loose rubble in the void between the rock's back face and the inner wall, then slopped in a five-gallon bucket of the wet concrete over the rubble. I mucked the concrete into the cracks and voids with my bare hands. No gloves, wanting to scour that blister raw and burnish my wedding ring till it shined.

Later in the day I'd smooth the joints with a margin trowel, make the gray cream rise and make the seams between the rocks watertight.

Curly shoved out the next boulder from the pile, seized it, swung it up to the top of the tower wall.

We set that boulder, then three more.

Ernst lowered the bucket to the ground, idled the engine, stared straight ahead through the window of the cab. He pulled a pencil out of his shirt pocket, laid a scrap of cardboard on his knee, hunched over it and wrote something. The pencil flew for about a minute. Then he pulled out his jackknife, sharpened the stub and wrote some more.

I stood there on the wall loving his passion and how, like the rocks, his poems helped build the castle.

He climbed down from the cab, walked over to the tower and slipped the scrap in a niche. It stuck out like a sprouting mushroom. There were other poems poking out here and there; some were weather-eaten into nothing, and some had worked free and were blowing around the farm with the winds.

He got back in the cab, swung Curly's open bucket up to the wall. I stepped into the yawning jaws, and then Ernst pulled a lever and lowered the boom to the ground. I jumped off, walked over to the mixer and flipped the switch. The drum began to turn, a steady grinding. I shoveled in the 3/4-rock-and-sand mixture first, then the cement—a three-to-one mix. Added water from a hose till the concrete *glopped* in the drum like heavy pancake batter.

Ernst had idled Curly again; he climbed down from the cab, got a wheelbarrow and rolled it over to the mixer.

I said, "Sparky's full of shit about love!"

Ernst shook his head, disagreeing.

We watched the drum rotate. I added a squirt of water and

the mixture loosened. Ernst released the catch and tipped the drum over the wheelbarrow and the slurry slumped out. He locked the drum upright, then pushed the wheelbarrow over to some plastic five-gallon buckets, where he began shoveling the wet concrete into the buckets.

I shoveled another load into the mixer, hosed it down, yelled above the growl, "He's as full of shit as a Christmas goose!"

Ernst loaded the buckets into Curly's jaws and yelled back, "Love's tricky."

I just looked at him. There was uneven ground between us, chewed by Curly's tracks. I'd told him about what Sparky'd said, and Ernst said if the pot he was growing for Sparky was that fucking mind-bending—good enough to make Sparky *that smart* about love—then why couldn't it do the same for me?

I dumped the next load into a second wheelbarrow, hosed down the empty, spinning drum, wheeled the barrow over to the plastic buckets and shoveled them full of concrete.

Ernst climbed back into Curly.

I stepped into the jaws with the buckets Ernst had set there; the boom rose till my feet were as high as the tower. I set one foot on the tower, kept the other foot set inside the jaws, grabbed a bucket by its wire handle and swung it out and up, dumped its load of concrete on the back side of the oblong rock we'd set an hour earlier. Tossed that empty bucket down and, one by one, lifted the other buckets and dumped them between the outer and inner walls. I stepped fully onto the tower and began working the slop into the cracks and voids, and adding chunks of rubble for backfill and strength.

Ernst had lowered the boom, gotten out of the cab and set

Trout Kill

more buckets full of concrete in the jaws. He got back in the cab and lifted them up to me. I hefted them out, dumped them and tossed them down. Ernst swung the boom over to the rubble pile, got out again, went to the pile and started filling Curly's bucket with more rubble.

I yelled over the noise of the idling track hoe, "It had to be love. What else could it be?" I'd told him about the doe, too, how it felt like I'd fallen in love with her. Actually, I'd told him that several times. I couldn't shake the feeling.

He shouted, "Let's go and see this goddamn doe you're so in love with."

"I already told you what happened. Why do you have to see?"

"Telling isn't seeing."

"Fuck."

"We'll get shit-faced and figure out love."

He filled the jaws full of rubble, while I troweled the joints. I figured Ernst had gone stir-crazy, that he'd been cooped up on the farm too long and needed to get away, a little R-and-R. Or maybe he was on the scent of another poem.

Maggie came walking down the hill, out of the mist.

I stood, grabbed my shirt and put it back on.

She waved, shouted hello. She looked nice, wearing a yellow dress and winter coat, matching gloves and scarf, a yellow hat like the kind you'd see in a church. She carried a wicker basket over to big flat rock, spread out a cloth and set the basket there. "Come and eat, you two."

I scrambled down the inner framework, walked out the opening we'd left for a door and joined Ernst and Maggie at the rock.

Maggie was a good-looking woman, ruddy and fit from all the labors required by her farming life, mostly tending to the garden, orchards, house and the chickens. She seldom ventured to the vineyard or the barn. Dark hair and bright blue eyes, a smile that spread far. She opened the wicker basket, handed us roast-beef sandwiches on homemade bread. She'd brought a bottle of wine. Ernst yanked the cork, poured three glasses. We toasted the day's progress on the castle. After our glasses clinked, Maggie asked me about Beth.

"She's meeting Trudy today. I think they're making lesson plans. At the school."

"Imagine, a roomful of eight-year-olds!" She cut an apple in two and gave me half, Ernst the other half.

I ate my sandwich.

Ernst asked what time Father Mullen was coming out for the blessing, and Maggie said he'd be there in about hour.

Ernst said, "Great."

I ate a wedge of goat cheese. "Yeah, great."

Maggie laughed, made a wisecrack about *Ye of little faith*, then asked Ernst to go, please, after he finished with his lunch, up to the house and change out of his work clothes. "Wear your nice suit for the Father's visit."

Ernst said hell no, he wouldn't. He said Father Mullen was supposed to bless the damned soil, because that's where the wine came from, so that's what needed blessing, and the dirt on his pants was the exact same damned dirt that the grapes grew in—the soul of the vineyard—and he didn't have time to gallivant up to the damned house and change.

Maggie poured him more wine.

I just grinned, proud of him.

Maggie said Father Mullen could bless Ernst's dirty pants, too, just as he would bless the ground, and what a good priest he was, coming all the way out from town on such a chilly winter's day.

Ernst eyed the tower, said maybe it was beginning to cant toward the north a bit.

We finished our lunches. Maggie gathered up the leftovers in the wicker basket, folded the blanket, then walked back up the hill and disappeared into the misty rows of wires and poles, trunks and canes.

Ernst climbed back into Curly's cab, and I climbed onto the wall and began troweling the joints.

Ernst said, "Goddamn it," and jumped down from the cab and began stomping up the hill after Maggie.

I laughed, said he was hen-pecked, that I'd help him tie his tie for the Father. He gave me the finger.

The mist began to lift in a light breeze and the weak sun filtered through the swirling wisps. I worked alone in the quiet, no mixer rumbling, no track hoe growling, just the slick scrape of the trowel's flat steel on the cream.

An hour later Ernst, Maggie and Father Mullen came walking down the south slope between the rows. The mist was rising. They each carried a wine glass, sipping their way toward the statue of the Virgin Mary, now clearly visible from the tower. Father Mullen wore a black cassock, a round black hat, a silver crucifix on a silver chain. Ernst wore his best suit and dress shoes, but no tie.

They waved.

I waved the trowel.

The three of them abreast, Father Mullen centered, Ernst

talking biodynamics, his face radiant, him pointing to the pecker poles, the taut wires and the gnarly canes. Maggie, her voice a light song, thanking the Father for coming, remarking about the peeping sunshine, how it was now chasing away the mist—the sure sign of a blessing from above. Ernst nodding, agreeing with the signs. The Father's banter, his laughter like a bell ringing out.

They stood around the Virgin. Ernst, after having rescued the concrete statue from a second-hand store in Glass Point, erected it in the vineyard on a wooden pedestal. She stood about five feet tall, sad-faced, her arms reaching out as if to embrace.

Ernst and Maggie lowered their heads.

Father Mullen sprinkled holy water, said something I couldn't hear.

Maggie wiped her tears.

Ernst raised his head.

I troweled, working the flat steel blade back and forth along a crisscross seam where four rocks met, smoothing that closure, back and forth and back and forth, pressing the steel right up against the rocks' contours, the steel coaxing the holy cream to rise up and seal.

Father Mullen's voice lifted with the last fingers of the late-afternoon mist:

"O, Mighty Father, we appeal to your generous heart, that You might shower blessings upon this wintering earth, these grape plants. That You will temper the chill winds and storms so, come the warming spring, these plants will bring forth nurturing fruits. And we ask that You fill the good hearts of these good people, Ernst and Maggie, with gratitude, fill them with the glory of Your name. O, Father, we ask these things in Your name, amen."

Maggie held her glass up and poured the remaining wine onto the feet of the Virgin. She said, with her voice full of joy, "This glorious wine is ... is like the velvet pants of baby Jesus."

Chapter 11

Ernst, still wearing his suit and nice shoes, drove me into Milo in Old Blue, his flatbed truck. Dust covered the dashboard. Like the speedometer, the heater didn't work. The cab was cold. A scrap of cardboard was stuck in the ashtray, one of Ernst's old poems scrawled in herky-jerky lines that jibed with the bounce of Blue's broken-down suspension. The poem was about earthworms and quantum uncertainty.

As we rumbled down the hill from Ernst's farm, an egg rolled out between my feet from underneath the seat. I picked it up. The shell was dusty brown with pale speckles and a thin whitish smear of dried crap.

Ernst grabbed it out of my hand, pressed it against his cheek and held it there. "It's cold as hell. Been out of the nest too long." He tossed it onto my lap.

I cupped it between my palms, placed my hands between my warm thighs.

"Toss it out the window."

"I'll warm it up."

"It's dead."

"It's not too dead." The shell had begun to warm up a little.

"Dead is dead."

Behind our seats there was a toolbox, some tangled ropes, a brown tarp, a sledgehammer, a dusty wine bottle and scattered bits of hay. And Myrtle, the hen who'd laid the egg. She was hunkered on her nest, her head tucked so low into her

Trout Kill

speckled feathers she looked headless. The loose egg had rolled out of her nest.

To put the egg back underneath Myrtle, I had to twist around on the seat.

Ernst eyed me. "Rat Dick, not even the Virgin can bring it back to life. It's beyond Last Rites."

Ernst might have believed in souls and other bullshit, but he was also a practical farmer. Dead was dead. I slipped it underneath the mother hen, between her warm breast feathers and the warm hay. There were four other eggs in the nest. Myrtle pulled her head up and clucked, then jabbed the back of my hand, hard, with her sharp orange beak.

I jerked my hand back and a bright drop of blood welled up.

Ernst grinned.

It was dark by the time we got to town and pulled into Jimmy's wrecking yard. The Rottweiler greeted us. My pickup was nowhere in sight. It had been three days since I'd dropped it off. I reminded Ernst I'd pick him up the next morning. Castle building could wait a day. We'd be driving up the coast to see the doe. Ernst was curious. I still thought it was a crazy idea, a waste of time. I got out of Old Blue and Ernst drove home. I headed into Jimmy's office.

Jimmy was tipped back in his greasy chair behind his greasy desk, his beard on his chest, his Detroit cap turned backward, his one good eye admiring Miss February, 1993. The wood stove was popping hot. He said, "Yer radiator's tits up."

"Goddamn it."

"Ordered a new one."

"You can't just go ahead and do that."

"Stop Leak ain't worth a flyin' fuck, and I could use another cord. You shouldn't have drove the son-of-a-bitch wherever you drove it to."

I looked inside the garage. My pickup had its hood raised, and where the radiator should have been there was a hole. The dents were still dents, but the new windshield looked good. The old radiator lay atop a heap of scrap metal.

Jimmy spit his chew on the floor, unfolded the centerfold and held it up. "Legs all the way up to 'er ass!"

He was right about the legs. "How long?"

"Another day ... or two. Depends."

"Goddamn it."

"Can't be helped."

"Your oak is split. Two cords. I'll owe you another one for the radiator."

"I'd eat a yard of 'er shit just to see where it come from."

"Where's your phone?"

He nodded at a heap of *Playboy*s that buried the phone. I called the jail where Em was locked up, said I had a sister who was an inmate and asked to speak with Officer Wallace.

Jimmy cocked his ear and looked up from Miss February.

It took a minute for Officer Wallace to come to the phone. She remembered me. When I asked about Em, Officer Wallace said she'd just come on duty, but she'd heard the arresting officer, Korduski, had decided not to press the assault charge. They'd released Em a few hours earlier.

"Where'd she go?"

"I don't know, Mr. Trout. She didn't say a word to me."

It was mixed news, at best. Em was free, but to do what?

She had no place to go in the city except another bridge. The jail was a safe place, and she'd been getting room and board.

I asked if Dr. Lund had come by. Officer Wallace said yes, she had, but not till after Em had already left. I thanked Officer Wallace, said I still owed her and hung up.

Jimmy raised both eyebrows. His blind and pale eye wandered. "Yer sis in trouble again?"

"Trouble? What's that?"

He snorted, pinched a fresh chew out of the can and folded his lip around it.

I called Ernst and left him a message on the recorder: If he still wanted to traipse after a dead doe, he'd have to do the driving because Jimmy hadn't fixed my pickup yet.

Jimmy har-hared.

I hung up, then walked out of the office and through the yard of rusting wrecks toward home.

The porch light was off, and the kitchen window dark. Beth, I figured, was still at the school making lesson plans. *Or maybe Wally's diddling her in his office.* I knew that wasn't true, hated how the thought had popped up and flooded me with spite. Nothing was going on between Beth and Wally except in my head. Right after she'd showed me Wally's note about the red dress, Beth had thrown the dress away. She'd said, "That man ruined it for me."

I walked around the house and into the back yard. The hillside that loomed above the house was blacker than the sky. I felt my way over to the nailing tree, groped for the hammer and got a nail from the can. I drove the nail in by feel, then gave it an extra three or four whacks for good measure, with no clue as to what I was measuring.

Then I went inside the house and called Dr. Lund. I got her machine. I left Sparky's phone number and said to call me right away—but not at my home—if she heard any news about Em.

Licker was sprawled beside the stove, tail flat on the floor. He hadn't come to greet me. The stove was cold. I said, "Hey, Bud?"

He was breathing, but he didn't lift an ear or raise his head.

I got a wad of hamburger from the fridge, took it over and held it underneath his nose.

His nose didn't twitch, and he never opened an eye.

"I'm sorry, Bud. Shit. I'm sorry."

I ran my hand down his back and he woke up slow, with eyes glazed thick. He lifted his head, set it back down. I got on my hands and knees and put my face right against his face and told him I'd help. His breath smelled like the inside of a cave.

He wagged once and whimpered.

I pulled his jaws open, pushed the burger between his teeth and closed his jaws. "Chew it, Bud. Come on." His mouth fell open and his eyes didn't register. I pulled the burger out and tossed it in the stove.

"You just take 'er easy." I stroked his side and rubbed his ears and belly and he went back to sleep. "I'll build you a nice fire, okay?"

I got up, tossed paper, kindling, and chunks of wood into the stove and got a fire going. Then got my notebook from the pantry, sat down at the kitchen table and wrote—not about the paddies or my dog, but something far worse than either of those things, a shitfuck thing about when Em and me were kids. Wrote till the fire needed more wood.

Licker hadn't moved.

Trout Kill

I got up, locked my notebook in the pantry, then left the house and walked down to the elementary school. Across the street from the school, two cars were in the parking lot. One was Wally's, a blue Chevy Tahoe.

The school was painted bright yellow, but the night gave it a murky cast. One gym wall was muraled over with smiling whales and dolphins, a regular Sea World, and another mural showed a tide pool scene with starfish and urchins. The classroom windows faced the street. They were all dark, except for one. It had a blizzard of paper snowflakes taped up on the inside. I walked over and looked between the flakes.

Inside, Trudy was standing at a table covered with big sheets of colored paper, scissors, glue sticks and rulers. She was big in her belly, her arms and face puffed the way pregnant women sometimes get, the way Beth had gotten. Beth was taking down Christmas decorations, carrying them over to Trudy's table. Before leaving for their winter break, the kids had filled the room with cutouts of elves and snowflakes. Now Trudy and Beth were getting the room ready for after winter break.

I just stood there watching—the way I sometimes liked to watch Beth cooking or making the bed in her casual, unhurried ways that I sometimes envied. The desks, about twenty of them, were in a wide half circle facing the front of the room. An old cast iron radiator stood just inside the window, and its waves of heat were drafting up through the snowflakes, tickling them.

Beth took a green cut-out over to a bulletin board and pinned it up. It was a leprechaun. Trudy said something and Beth laughed. Then Beth said something and they both laughed so free and easy it made me sad. Beth got a chair, stood on it and pinned a big paper star to the ceiling on a string. The star had SALLY printed on it. Trudy handed her other stars with other names. Beth moved the chair from place to place, hanging up the stars. When she stretched her arms to pin the stars, her breasts pressed against her blouse, and the bottom of her blouse pulled free of her jeans, and the cuff of her jeans hiked up and her ankles showed.

I followed the sidewalk around the building to Wally's office. A light was on, but I didn't see him inside. Beyond his office was a lit, covered walkway that led past each of the classrooms. They were on my left, the playground to my right. Shredded tires covered the play area. There was a tall slide, a merry-go-round and monkey bars. The swings hung as still as the night.

Room 8 was at the end of the walkway.

Somebody had covered the whole door with a Big Bird poster, with yellow feathers, goofy orange feet and a dialog bubble: "Learning is fun!" I hadn't been inside a classroom in almost thirty years, except for parent conferences, most of which Beth had attended alone.

I'd go in and say hi to Trudy, then I'd ask Beth to walk home with me. We'd have dinner—spaghetti and meatballs, and we'd share a bottle of Ernst's wine. After the wine made the kitchen glow, and Beth glow, I'd finally tell her about Uncle Silas, and as the full magnitude of that horror was sinking in I'd tell I'd been seeing Dr. Lund. It would be a one-two punch, not a drawn-out agony like the night of the doe. For years, those two secrets had been trying to claw out of my chest.

I heard geese honking overhead, but there was no sky

above, or winging skein of Canadians, but just the painted underside of the walkway roof. The noise faded away, and with it my desire to confess.

I left the school and walked across town toward Sparky's, figuring I'd drown my thoughts or summon courage in a beer.

Billy Waysmith, the other part-time bartender, nodded hello when I walked in. He was a rail-thin guy with short gray hair. I signaled him for a beer—he knew my preference—and I headed over to the corner table by the Wurlitzer.

Billy brought the beer over, a porter nitro with a tight head; we bullshitted a minute. His wife was feeling a little better, he said. I told him my dog was dying. He nodded, asked if there was anything he could do. I said no, thanks, that I had it taken care of. He left and I drank my beer. It was smooth, unlike my tumbling thoughts, which jumped from Em to Licker, to Beth and Nura, from Nam to Oak Creek, and from Silas to Dr. Lund. I tried to figure out how my love for the doe could be so clear, with no hint of fog.

In the kitchen, Sparky was singing along with Mel Tillis on the Wurlitzer.

Harriet Brockton walked in and stood by the door, looking around, fidgeting with the top button of her coat. Her unsmiling face looked tacked on. I hadn't seen her in Sparky's for a while.

She and Beth were friends, and I knew her husband, Troy. He owned a salmon charter business up in Glass Point, and we'd gone fishing together. I waved to her, and she walked over in a straight line between the tables, not looking at anyone except me.

I smiled. "Harriet, it's good to see you again."

"A beer would be nice, I suppose." The button she was fiddling with came undone.

I shoved out a chair for her. She removed her coat, shook out her long blond hair, sat down and folded her hands across her lap. She wore a tight sweater and slacks.

I got the twinge of a hard-on.

Billy came over, and she said, "I'll have a Bud Light, please."

Billy rolled his eyes at me, and said to her as pleasantly as he could, "Sorry, but we don't serve Eastern piss."

I grinned, leaned back in my chair.

Harriet looked confused.

Billy recited the long list of choices, all Northwest brews.

I said, "Bring her a Santa's Special Reserve, if that's okay with you, Harriet."

She looked relieved, said that sounded fine.

Billy returned to the bar, poured the glass of beer, brought it over to her and left.

Harriet reached for it, bumped it with her hand and made the head slosh over the rim. "I'm so dang clumsy." She bit her lip and started blinking hard.

I said, "You know, it's illegal to spill a beer."

She laughed, but it sounded tinny. She pushed the sodden napkin aside, took a long drink of the beer, her throat rippling. She clunked the half-empty glass onto the table. "It's nice to get out again and … and see people."

I nodded, felt the squall in her was about to blow. The twinge disappeared.

She pulled a hanky from her coat pocket, laid it on the table. The veins in her hands were blue threads underneath gauze. Her lower lip twitched and trembled; she pressed the hanky to her mouth and let go with a loud sob. "Forgive me, Eddy. I didn't mean for this ... for you—"

I just kept nodding and hoping the storm would pass quick.

She tried to laugh but almost choked, and then she took a deep breath and lowered the hanky. "I'm so awfully sorry."

"Nothing to be sorry about."

She smiled, sat up straight in her chair and seemed to gather up her nerves. "Do you mind my asking you something personal?"

We'd known each other for years, but from a distance. I would have changed the subject had I known what it was. First her beer, and now her guts were spilling. I just shrugged.

"That scar you have?" She was leaning forward over the table and looking at my forehead. Her eyes were Mason-jar blue. "When you get a scar like that, it's forever a part of you."

"It's a birthmark, not a scar."

The hanky came halfway up and her eyes pinched back tears.

I drank my beer, felt a bad headache coming on.

Harriet's jaw got tight and she muttered, "That goddamned cock-sucking mother-fucker!" Her eyes grew wide; her face turned red and she looked like she wanted to crawl underneath the table and hide.

I finished my beer, waved to Jimmy for another round, stalling, giving Harriet time to mop up whatever mood she was spilling.

She blubbered, "Please, please, I'm so sorry."

When Jimmy brought my second nitro, he glanced down at Harriet, then grinned at me and left.

"Troy, he .... We ...."

I said to myself *Just let her talk it out*, but had to fight from getting up and running for the door. The head of my porter was a bit sloppy, and I made a mental note to give Billy a raft of shit about it.

She said, her voice as empty as her beer glass, "We shared everything, toothbrushes and coffee cups. I'm such a fool."

I figured Troy was at the bottom of her grief, that they'd had an ugly scene and he'd split from her.

"Here you are, Eddy, just enjoying the evening, and then I come in and … you are so kind to … and now this! This is terrible of me—involving you, I mean. It's so unlike me. And what would Beth think? Oh, shit! I'm so sorry." She sobbed into the hanky again.

Troy had always had a roving eye. Maybe Harriet had caught it undressing another woman.

She looked over at the Wurlitzer, with its bright lights and colors, its shiny plastic and chrome. "If you don't mind my asking, how long have you and Beth been married?"

"Almost thirty years."

She flinched, said with a stone tongue, "For us, going on twenty-six."

I didn't know if I should congratulate her or offer condolences.

She kept staring at the jukebox. "Here I am, crying in my … my Santa beer, sharing all my problems. You're such a sweetheart for listening to me blather." She laughed brittle. "But what about yours?"

"Mine?"

"You know, your problems?"

I smiled stiff. "Not a cloud in the sky."

"That bad, huh?"

She laughed at her own offhandedness, and I wondered what else she and Beth had talked about.

Her eyes fixed on me. They were dry now, glowing with false courage. She said, "Troy moved out. And I'm all alone."

It wasn't the most original proposition I'd ever heard, or the most desperate, or the first from one of Beth's friends. I kept waiting for her to wink or make a joke, to let on that she was just kidding around. But she looked dead-serious, even hopeful. It was an authentic Milo moment. I raised an eyebrow and nailed my mouth shut.

She said, "I threw my wedding ring into the ocean, and good riddance."

The first Tuesday of every month was Ladies' Night at Sparky's, and whenever a sloshed, over-friendly patron had slipped her address to me on a napkin, I'd winked and said, "Let's not shit in our own nest." Meaning Milo was a real small town, and word spread fast and spousal vengeance often raged as salty as the sea. I'd always been faithful to Beth, except for that one time. I said, "The ocean's good for what you don't want anymore."

Harriet blushed. Her nerve fled and she grabbed her beer glass with both hands and held it tight. "Forgive me. I'm a wreck." She let go of the glass, stood up and slipped her coat back on.

"There's nothing to forgive." After she'd driven down the same road with Troy for almost twenty-six years, they'd wrecked and it had totaled her. Now she was looking for a different road.

She came around the table and kissed me quick on the cheek. "You seem so awfully sad, Eddy."

"Me?" That stunned me. I was content, or at least felt that way after a couple of beers. What vibe was I giving out that said otherwise? And how'd the black squall of discontent raging over her turn a one-eighty so damn fast and start blowing my direction? I thought *But you're the one who's crying now, not me.*

After she left, I finished my beer, then walked back home and made a pot of Hamburger Helper, heated up a can of green beans and set plates on the table. I wasn't in the mood for spaghetti anymore, or wine. I sat down at the kitchen table and waited for Beth to come home.

Licker lay beside the warm stove and even from the distance—about fifteen feet—I could smell his dog scent rising from him.

I got Jack from the pantry, took it over to the stove and sat down on the floor beside my dog, took a long pull of the sweet booze and let the crystalline-sharp thoughts of Nura cut into me.

I'd met her in Glass Point a few years earlier.

Troy Brockton and an old friend of his had invited me on a fishing trip, a salmon charter out of Glass Point. We fished all day, with no luck. Cliff, Troy's friend, had a place near the beach, and he invited Troy and me to spend the night, enjoy a bonfire and a weenie roast.

It was October. The bonfire was a tall jumble of building debris and old lumber, two-by-sixes mostly, and busted doors and window frames. Sparks shot straight up into the cold fog. Cliff's friends showed up, no one I knew. Couples wrapped themselves in warm blankets, roasted weenies and marshmallows on long sticks over the coals. Their faces shined in the glow of the fire. We drank, ate, smoked weed. A guy with a guitar played "If I Had a Hammer" and people sang along.

Trout Kill

Harriet wasn't there, and Beth wasn't there. I'd called Beth and told her I was spending the night, that I'd be home the next day, and she was fine with it.

I sat on a log, drank Jack, watched the scrap lumber burn down to a bed of coals and glowing iron door hinges. Watched Troy head off into the dark with a woman and a blanket. I remembered thinking about the nailing tree at home, how the needles were dying, and what a shame *that* dying was, and what a nature-killing jerk I was, and I'd sworn when I got home I'd take my cat's paw and pull every last fucking nail out.

A woman came over and sat beside me on the log. She wore a heavy sweatshirt with the hood pulled up. I couldn't see her face. She held her hands out to the fire's warmth; her hands were small, almost childlike, with long, tapering fingers and no rings. Then she pulled out a bag of marshmallows from her sweatshirt. She impaled two on the tip of a willow stick, held them over the coals, turned the stick slow. The marshmallows turned light brown, then blackened and burst into sizzling flames. She pulled the stick close to her face and with a single puff blew the flames out. Her face caught the fire light.

She was beautiful.

The smoke swirled around us and blended with the fog.

She smiled, held the stick out for me. The two marshmallows had melted together into one.

I pulled the glob off and ate it; the black skin crackled and dissolved into sweetness.

She stabbed two more marshmallows with the tip of the stick, roasted them, let them catch fire and then blew the flames out, ate them right off the end of the stick.

Weed came our way. We smoked and made small talk, talk that seemed to flow like a gentle creek. Nura skewered more marshmallows and roasted them. Then two weenies, one for both of us—in the same way she'd roasted the marshmallows, till their skins blackened and burst. We ate, smoked, drank and sang along with the Guitar Man.

Nura slid off the log and down into the sand, and then I slid down and settled beside her.

Jack went around the fire and never came back.

We sat cross-legged with our gazes warming in the dying coals and our knees close while someone told a story about sailing in the San Juans. That story led to other stories. Weed smoke joined the wood smoke. The fire glowed with lots of bent nails. Couples staggered away into the fog, and then no one else was around.

I leaned close to her and she smelled like smoke. Time didn't matter anymore, only place.

She held her hands out to warm them again, and I held mine out beside hers. The coals had died down to dim orange. She shivered and hugged her knees. There was a blanket and I wrapped it around us.

She said, "Ummm."

I asked who she was.

She said she was married, with a teenage son, and that she'd come to Glass Point because she didn't love her banking job or her husband anymore. She felt sealed in an airtight vault, combination unknown, and was looking to bust out. She loved kayaking in Puget Sound, flying kites and reading long novels.

I told her about my life; I talked till a great weariness came over me and I fell asleep. I dreamed Nura was in my arms, and that her sadness ran as deep as mine, and when we kissed, her soft lips melted into mine.

When I woke up, her head was resting on my shoulder, the blanket all around us, our toes buried in the fire-warmed sand. It was too dark to see anything; the night fog had settled wet.

I took her hand and she opened her eyes, smiled. She squirmed her toes deeper into the sand, said, "The heat's still down there. Ummm! Can you feel it?"

I wormed my toes deeper into the warm sand.

She got on her knees and scooped out a shallow nest. I helped her. Then we lay side-by-side in the cozy nest and stared into the black fog. She said, "Hold me tight, just for a little while."

She trembled in my arms. Her eyes were invisible. She took my hand and put it on the mound of her breast. I said, "Hold me tight, too." She moaned and pulled me so close I lost any sense of north or south. I fumbled with the zipper of her jeans.

She helped me.

She rolled aside and, in one shadowy move, she arched her butt off the sand and pulled her pants down and off.

It seemed the bravest thing in the world.

I took my jacket off and slipped it underneath her ass.

My own zipper was eager but clumsy. Halfway down, it stuck. I shoved my pants down to my knees. She pulled me down and onto her.

Her skin was warm, her belly and lips and breath, all warm. My knees and toes pushed against the sand between her legs. She said, "Let's love each other for tonight."

"Yes, for tonight."

The sand shifted beneath my knees and her ass, my elbows and her back. My pants choked my knees. I kissed her. She was yielding and clovey. She helped me enter her. We moaned. She arched upwards, and I thrust and my toes slipped. She helped me find a rhythm. She laughed—a short burst of joy that erupted and tightened her around me. It felt strange, her joy enfolding me like that.

I said, "Laugh again."

She did.

Then our bodies found their pace till we surrendered and exploded.

We lay there for a long while afterwards. Our breathing eased and was as steady as the ocean's growl. Then she began to wiggle and squirm, said, "Things are getting hot. My butt."

I laughed.

"No, seriously."

I rolled off her. She sat up, scooted off my jacket and rubbed her butt. I pulled my pants up. "Feel here," she said, and held my jacket out to me. I felt where her hand was. The fabric was hot, charred. Our joined bodies had pressed the jacket against an ember from the bonfire that, evidently during our lovemaking, had found air and kindled back to fuller life. It had scorched the cuff of the jacket sleeve.

She said there was sand in her teeth, her ears, her butt and armpits and hair. I tackled her and we rolled across the wet sand laughing. Then we stood and shook the sand off. The grit had sifted into every part of us.

Wrapped in that blanket, we walked hand-in-hand along the beach. The fog had lifted. Beneath the handful of stars, the rolling surf glowed. We found our way across the beach to a

Trout Kill

street that led to her cottage. She'd parked her VW bug there. We stood beside it, not saying anything. Words, I figured, were just zippers to fumble with. We kissed. She whispered goodnight and went inside. There were no goodbyes, just understood ones. I stood there and felt euphoria slipping away, guilt slipping in.

I went back down to the beach and walked a long way south, a couple of miles, till I came to a rocky headland and couldn't go any farther, couldn't see a way around guilt, then turned around and ran all the way back to Glass Point. Found a phone booth underneath a streetlight beside the Chamber of Commerce. It was late, almost four o'clock. I dropped in the quarters and stood there staring at the numbers, trying to remember which ones to push.

Eighty miles down the coastline, our phone rang. Beth would have been asleep, buried in the covers of our bed. Kate and BJ were spending the night with friends. Licker, healthy then and dozing underneath the bed, would have cocked an ear at the first ring, looked toward the crack underneath the hallway door. He might have sensed it was me calling, and he might have whimpered.

I thought *Ten rings. That should be enough.* I figured the first several wouldn't rouse Beth, but the fifth or sixth ring might penetrate her dreamless head and wake her. I counted the rings. *Ten seems more than fair.* If she answered, I'd say I was sorry and weep my guilt. I'd say I needed help. I'd say there were too many sharp corners and I'd wrecked. I'd say I was wrong: I did love her. I did. *I do.*

I thought about the depth of her sleep, and the length of that hallway, and *How loud is a ring and how deep is her sleep?*

and I calculated the moments of her lying there before waking up and then her muddled wondering *Who in heaven's name could be calling at this time of night?*, and then her throwing back the blankets, her feet hunting for her slippers before shuffling down the hall and crossing through the kitchen to the phone where she'd pick me up.

Chapter 12

Old Blue chugged along, Ernst steering with one hand, his fingers thick as sausages, a bottle of wine clamped between his legs like a green dick. His poem in the ashtray was gone; maybe he'd stuck it in the castle wall. Up ahead, beyond the span of the hood of the flatbed, the white lines stitched their way north up the coast highway. The more Ernst drank, the slower he drove—just the opposite of me.

Myrtle was still camped on her nest behind the seat, being a good hen. The peck she'd given me had left a scab and a round bruise. Ernst thought the good eggs were near to hatching, and when I'd asked him how he knew, he said he could tell by the hints of relief in Myrtle's clucks.

I said, again, "I don't know why I love her. I just do."

Ernst tipped the bottle to his mouth, swished the wine, swallowed it and breathed in through his nose. "Ahh! Subtle notes of dewy clover, black currants and … fecund summer breezes. All in all, pinot as smooth as Cupid's thigh."

The morning sky was bitter-clear. A thin frost had veneered the deep shadows of the shore pines, the sand hummocks and foredunes.

Working the tower wall with no gloves and handling the rough iron bar had torn the flap of skin off the blister on my finger, and the concrete I'd mucked with my hands had cracked the newly grown circle of pink skin.

A scrap of plain white paper lay on the seat. Ernst had

sketched out another tentative illustration for his wine label. Among his other talents, Ernst was a fair artist. The drawing showed a cone-shaped mountain and four cherubs. The cherubs were winged, sweet-faced boys with little dicks. They were flying around the mountain, which looked like Mt. Hood. When he'd asked me my opinion of it, I'd told him the cherubs look like buzzards circling a tit. He'd written down a list of possible names for the wine: Noir Dew, Coastal Chateau, Bad Ass Noir, Castle Wine, Hereford Pinot Noir, Frog Spit Noir, and Mountaintop Noir.

Ernst nodded at the road ahead. "Is this the place?"

Seeing the yellow warning sign again, the bent black arrow, then going around that same corner, the curve of it unfolding to the exact spot where she'd been standing those days ago—I heard the tires screech, felt her thud against the fender and the pickup's queasy skid across the blacktop. It had been dark then. Now, in the bright light of day things looked sharp but felt menacing, like I had twenty-twenty vision while sinking deeper in a bog. I'd loved Beth. Then the doe happened. I was sorry. The doe was a mother and Beth was a mother. They were both beautiful. I loved the doe and Beth. I'd killed the doe. Her fawns had been hiding in the tall grass, and that's why she'd bolted—to go to them. Her love for them killed her. To her I'd been nothing, not even her killer. *I am nothing to her even now. How could I not love her? Beth?*

I blinked fast and turned my head so Ernst wouldn't see.

He pulled off the highway, stopped just short of where Spencer had handed me the gun, then backed Blue into the shoulder and cut the engine. He got out, stood in the gravel with his bottle in his hand, looked around. A crow flew off, a

Trout Kill

black hole winging in the sky. Frost covered everything. The woods were thick between the ocean and us.

I got out and stood beside Ernst, our two streaming breaths merging in the cold and making one cloud.

A pair of earmuffs lay in the ditch, probably thrown from a passing car by some kid.

Ernst studied the land like farmers do, with knowing squints, then turned and looked down the highway, toward the corner. I'd told him the full story, and maybe right then he was feeling what I was feeling, the sense of being in a place where pain and love had crashed into each other and gotten mixed up.

I walked to the place on the highway where she'd been thrown by the impact, where I'd shot at her and missed, where she'd died, where some part of me had begun to die, too, it now seemed, and another part come alive. Ernst followed. The recent rains had washed the blood away, but where the .45 slug had pitted the blacktop, a tiny black pond had frozen there. There were washed-out chunks of lasagna puke, and a piece of bone. I picked it up, a whitish shard, from her busted front leg that had absorbed the brunt of my carelessness. I showed it to Ernst.

His shoulders slumped and he nodded. He toed the pit. "You're a lousy shot, Rat Dick."

"The dark was in my eyes."

"Maybe it was love."

He said that with a straight face, no irony. The blue in his eyes was deep. I said, "The dark was real dark."

He stared off into the woods. "When you hit a deer with a car, your soul sneers."

I just looked at him. The bottle in his hand hung limp.

A car came around the corner and we moved off the highway into the ditch. The car sped past, accelerating. Three more cars followed, bumpers chasing bumpers, the drivers gawking at us standing there. The sounds of their engines and tires faded away, and the distant ocean leaked through the trees again.

I walked to the edge of the woods, to a big patch of dead grass and began looking around. Ernst followed. The frost on the grass coated our boots, which left dark prints in the white. Ernst found the place, a flattened circle in the grass, just inside the margin of the woods, between a clump of azaleas and ferns, where the two fawns had lain and hidden.

"Like Myrtle's nest," I said.

"But without the eggs," he said. He knelt down, ran his hand over the grass, stood, pointed off toward the south and began walking that way. He didn't go far, then knelt in the grass again. "Looks like coyotes."

I walked over. A dead fawn lay there, a blacktail, just a chewed heap of hide and bones with toothpick legs, big ears and a black nose. Its open eyes were thick-fogged. All around, the grass was crushed and bloody, with scattered bits of hair. The coyotes had gone in through the stomach, then gnawed into the rib cage. The signs were fresh.

Ernst stood and looked around. "Maybe the other fawn got away."

"Goddamn it." The odds of that were thin as the frost.

"That's the way it goes. A butterfly flaps its wings …."

"This time, I'm the fucking butterfly."

We went to the big cedar tree, shouldered through the

Trout Kill

frosty bottom branches. Inside the cathedral of boughs, the light sifted with the shadows.

The doe—what was left of her—was still there, next to the trunk. The coyotes had found her, too. They'd gotten to her insides, her throat and haunches. Her eyes were gone—to the crows, by the look of it, a surgical job.

I felt okay about the coyotes and the crows, for the way the dead belong to the living, and the same sweet nausea I'd felt before came rushing back, what I'd called love. It enfolded me, as the boughs of the cedar did. I dropped the shard of bone beside her carcass, then raised my bottle and offered up a silent toast to her and her fawns. I drank.

Ernst said, "She's a part of the wondrous universe, just as cherubs and quarks are. Yin and Yang, crows and cars and coyotes. Propensities are infinite and collapse into singularity through consciousness."

I had no idea what he meant. "Why do I love her?"

"She is beautiful."

"Yes, she is. Even now."

"Especially now." He knelt down into the thick cedar duff, grabbed a handful and sprinkled it over the doe. "There's a poem about this guy. He's driving one night along the Wilson River and finds a doe in the road."

"That poem Mr. Willis made us study?"

"From Stafford."

It surprised me that a poem from Senior English almost thirty years ago could just pop into my head again, or at least a few echoing impressions.

"She'd just been hit by a car. Remember?"

"Yeah. And this guy happens along and stops to check her

out. But she's dead, right?" I looked up through the cedar maze for a sliver of the sky.

"She's big in her belly."

"Yeah. And so ... he puts his hand there and feels the fawn kick inside of her. Goddamn!"

"So now the guy has to think about what to do."

"He can't just leave the doe on the road. Other drivers might come along and ...."

Ernst looked up at me. "Swerve."

"Yeah, right. They'd have to swerve to miss her in the road, and that might kill someone. So, the guy ... he ... he shoves the doe off the road and into the river."

Ernst nodded. He stood up, had to keep his head ducked beneath a thick branch. "I'd have cut the fawn out of her with my jack knife."

"But it would just die anyway."

"It would see the stars first."

I just looked at him. He'd lost me. I almost wished we'd stayed home and worked on the castle, because it's easier to work with your hands than your head.

"Then, after the stars, I'd have shoved them both into the river."

I tried to see what he was getting at. Sometimes, even Ernst didn't know what he meant. He knew most of my secrets—even those about the rice paddies and the red dress. But his knowing didn't stop their festering. I lifted the bottle up into the branches and drank the wine straight down, glugging it, the way Ernst said was all wrong for the wine's soul—a vulgar rush down a dissing throat.

He knelt, scattered another few handfuls of duff on the

doe, then turned and made his way out between the swooping branches.

I followed him back to the road, where we climbed in the flatbed. Ernst turned around in the middle of the highway and we headed back. He drove slower than before and didn't say anything. We passed a long strand of beach, and the morning's high tide had left driftwood scattered north and south as far as we could see.

Ernst said, "You love the doe because you love her."

As smart as he was, that sound like a half-assed explanation.

"Love is a singularity."

"She was a beauty beyond my reach."

A couple of miles farther on, Ernst pulled over, parked at the top of a rocky headland, sat stone-faced behind the wheel and stared out at the gray ocean. Some mood had him by the throat again. Just beyond the guardrail, a steep cliff plunged to the rocky surf below. The swells rolled through beds of kelp. About a mile out, an abrupt wall of fog hid everything that was beyond.

Myrtle clucked.

Ernst kept staring.

Beside the flatbed, a trail led down to the beach. A sign at the head of the trail said Beware of Sneaker Waves. In the distance the wind had cut the dunes into weird-shaped sculptures, yardangs.

Ernst said, "Right here at this place, right now, I can feel my soul."

"Is it sneering?"

"It's contemplative."

I took another drink, swallowed it with a lot of air. All

morning long the wine had tasted like grapes, but now black cherries came to mind. Then a hint of chocolate, the dark kind that Beth loved: sweet first—then a stab of bitter, lingering. It was hard to sort between the sweet and the bitter.

Ernst looked at me. "What's yours feel like?"

I pulled a baggie out of the glove box and rolled a joint. I told him my soul was real worried about Em. I didn't know what to do for her. We smoked. The cab got hazy like the ocean air. I said I hoped Em would come and live awhile with Beth and me. He doubted that would happen and said Em had a mind of her own, one contrary to almost everything. I told him Beth got a job at the elementary school. He didn't ask about Wally. When I held up the wine bottle and peered through the glass the sky was darkly green. Things looked warped. I said, "What's it like to have a father and a mother?"

He shook his head slow and didn't say a word.

His own parents were dead and buried in a cemetery with headstones with engraved names. They'd lived tough lives and they'd raised Ernst, and they'd given him lots of memories, some good and some of bad, but memories.

"Tell me."

"It's like having roots."

"Deep ones?"

"Yes."

"Goddamn, you're a lucky man."

He nodded, took another hit of weed.

Ernst had a way of growing things on his farm that didn't mess with the dirt, helped the dirt be itself. He mixed witchy, mystical brews during certain phases of the moon and sprayed them on the vineyard, believing the earth and grapes would welcome the concoctions. *Wellness is good dirt* he liked to say. No pesticides or herbicides to fuck with the microbes. He read the dirt on his farm like weathermen do the sky.

I said, "Why is Maggie so goddamned happy all the time?"

"The dirt."

I laughed.

He didn't.

We got back on the highway and Ernst drove slower than before, being stoned now as well as drunk. We crested a hill, and ahead we could see the miles stretching to the south where the Tyee Bridge crossed the mouth of the river. A thin sea mist filtered the sun. Beyond the bridge in Milo, the sun winked off the tin roof that covered the grange hall at the south end of town.

When we came to the bridge, Ernst mashed the gas peddle down and Old Blue stuttered forward at a faster clip. Ernst knew that about me, too, how what lurked in the wide mouth of the river—the lunker that was Uncle Silas—had its own mouth that scared me shitless. What he didn't know was that I'd put the lunker there.

Chapter 13

The blue sky made me flinch and squint, and turned the ocean indigo, and the sunlight caught the frosty Virgin and made her glitter. The mixer growled away.

I stood on the castle wall, bare-chested and sweating, packing stone rubble in the voids. Ernst sat inside Curly's cab, his hands on the controls; he swung the boom toward the boulder pile, and the jaws of the hoe grappled with another big rock. Then a black cloud belched from Curly's exhaust pipe, and the machine coughed, sputtered.

Ernst, cussing, shut it down. He jumped from the cab, picked up a rock and hurled it at Curly. It struck the track and glanced off. He shook his fist. "You god-damned monster!" Then he picked up another rock, spun around and threw it hard at the Virgin. He threw like a farmer does, stiff-armed, with no follow through. The rock fell short among the canes.

I picked up a chunk of stone, reared back and threw it. My arm and aim were better. It missed, barely, sailing just past the Virgin's head.

"What the hell're you doing?"

I shrugged. "Rocking Mary."

He glared at me, turned and started trudging up the hill toward the barn. I scrambled down from the tower and followed him, hurrying past row after row of the wintering plants that stretched around the hillside. The trunks and canes were stunted, and it was hard to imagine that the coming spring would bud them back to life, that the vines would once again leaf green along the wires.

    The doors of the barn were wide open, the barn half full of hay bales, wintering feed for the cattle. The tractor was parked inside, an old John Deere, its wheels caked with dried mud and cow shit. I loved the smell of last summer's sun-cured hay, the cobwebs and the chicken crap. We climbed the stairs to the loft, where Ernst unlocked a door to the earthy fragrance of cannabis.

    There were two doors along each side of a central corridor. The doors entered into heated, insulated rooms with plywood walls. The first door on the left was the seedling room where a bank of T5 fluorescents germinated seeds, helped them grow into tall seedlings that would show their sex. Sparky got the seeds from Mexico. When we could tell them apart, we'd cull the males and toss them in with the cattle feed, then transplant the females into bigger pots in the main grow room.

    The grow room was wrapped with five-mil plastic; small fans kept the air moving to reduce the chance of mildew. Flex ducts brought in fresh air, and out-vented the stale air through carbon filters. The maturing plants grew on racks festooned with drip hoses, and each day they got twenty hours of T5 light. Later on, to induce their flowering, we'd cut the top from each plant, stress them and starve them for light. Females made the best quality shit, and Sparky's L.A. connection demanded the best.

    Another room was light tight, where we'd eventually move the mature, flowered plants to spend their dark phase. It was also the drying room.

    We entered the first door on the right. The room was long

and narrow, with a big table for processing and packaging. A panel of switches and timers controlled the fans, humidifiers, heaters, pumps and lighting. Biodynamic, nutrient-rich soup filled big plastic drums. Immersible pumps hummed.

Ernst went over to a shelf against the wall, got a dried bud out of a coffee can, stuffed it in a pipe, struck a match against his jeans, stuck the stem between his teeth, held the match to the bowl, puffed, then sucked in a lungful of smoke. On the exhale, the cords in his neck flattened. He said, "That goddamn castle."

"It's a beautiful dream." And it was. From time to time, Ernst just forgot.

He shook his head. "Curly's always breaking down."

A cardboard poem was stuck in the wall. I pulled it out: five lines about a murder of crows. I said, "Yeah, it's always some damned thing costing you money." I put the poem back in the wall.

He handed me the pipe. It pleasured my hand, the feel of the warm bowl nesting. Drawing in the smoke and holding it helped time to slow down, and when I released and drew a breath of clean air it seemed I'd forgotten what I wanted to know, and that was all right, and the castle would someday get built, and someday Ernst and me would catapult pumpkins.

We talked about Curly, how much the busted seal—Ernst was sure it was an oil seal—would cost, and how many days it would take to fix it. The castle would have to wait.

He said, "Fuck it. Let's go work on the door."

Ernst locked up, and we left the barn. The two of us walking side-by-side back down the hill, the rows of canes stretching below us, I said, "Remember that day I told you about, when Em and me were at the Tyee with Uncle Silas?"

He nodded, his big shoulders rolling with every step. He eyed the nearest canes and headed toward them.

"I wrote about it again last night."

"Couldn't sleep, huh?"

"Shit was running through my head, shit I never told you."

"Oh?"

"The worst shit."

He stopped and knelt beside a cane that branched left and right along the lowest wire. "You were ... what? About five years old?"

I stood behind him. "Yeah, and Em was eight. There was a path on a hillside above the swimming hole."

"Path?"

"An old deer trail. Em and me were, uh, playing there. The river was running low and warm, like it does in late summer, and we could smell the stink of the spawned-out shad. We'd been swimming; my cut-offs were still wet."

Ernst pulled a weed out of the ground and looked close at its roots. He smelled them.

I said, talking faster, feeling the pot take ahold, "*Dad.* That's what we called him then."

"Your uncle?"

"Yeah."

Ernst shook the weed, and dirt from its roots sprinkled in his palm; he tongued a small clod into his mouth, let it dissolve, swirled it around and then spit the brown out. He nodded, pleased.

"That day, he was swimming up the rapids in that narrow chute of fast water. Remember?"

Ernst nodded, tossed the weed aside.

"Those trunks of his, orange as an orange. You could see them a mile away. He was a damned strong swimmer, from slinging two-bys on the green chain for all those years. His arms just kept knifing into the current. But like it always did, after awhile the river whipped him and he turned onto his back and let the river carry him."

Ernst stood and we continued down the hillside toward the castle site, nearly fifty yards away. Curly looked like a sullen yellow beast eating away at the pile of rocks; the growl of the mixer drifted up to us.

"Uncle Silas drifted down to the shallows, below the rapids, then swam over to the shore. He'd told us not to wander off, to stay at the sandbar. He yelled, "Emmie! Emmie!" We never answered, just stayed hidden there in the trees along the path. We could see the river dripping off him. He looked mad, not worried. He never called my name, just Em's."

"This is what you wrote last night?"

"For three, four hours."

Ernst stomped a molehill and kept walking. "Where's this going, Rat Dick?"

"We kept heading up the path, deeper into the woods, till we could hardly hear Silas calling out. There were sword ferns, a lot of them. We came to a big madrone, and Em wanted to hug it. We held hands, but our arms couldn't reach around it."

The morning sun was at our backs, and it threw our side-by-side shadows long across the thawing ground of the vineyard. The mixer got louder, its growling motor, and the glopping tumble of the wet concrete seemed to match the throbbing in my head. I'd never felt such a stoned urgency

Trout Kill

to reveal a truth. I stopped walking. After a few more paces, Ernst stopped, too, and turned and looked at me.

"You know that kind of slick bark a madrone has, like bone, and how it's darkish red? I told Em the tree was pretty, like she was. I told her to turn her back, and she did, and I got out my pocketknife and started carving her name into the bark. I wanted to surprise her. Before she looked, I'd carved the first two letters. When she saw them, she got so mad at me her fists balled up, said I was hurting the tree. I told her trees are tough. She pointed to where I'd peeled away the dry, outer bark. Underneath, it was white and wet. 'It's crying,' she said, 'and from now on you can just call me Em.'"

Ernst was staring at me, his blue eyes keen, like they got when he wrote poems. He knew better than to say anything, that if he just didn't say a fucking word, then the whole story would come tumbling out this time. He turned and started down the hill again, slower, with none of his usual hurry, walking closer so he could hear me over the rumbling mixer.

"I put my knife away, said I was sorry, and something else about owing the tree. Uncle Silas was calling out for Em again, louder than before, like maybe he'd left the river and was coming after us. Em and me stood there, at the madrone, wondering what to do. The trees ... we couldn't see the river anymore."

I paused, the thump of the mixer exploding in my skull, wondering how to put the rest of the story, how to say it, wanting Ernst to understand. The sky seemed to help—no clouds or fog, no ocean haze, just clear and blue.

"Then, from farther up the hill, we heard a soft noise. It sickened me, made me freeze and sweat at the same time.

God-fucking-damn, Ernst! Em looked so fucking scared and hugged herself and shook her head no, no. I was so stupid, just a fucking little kid, wanting not to know what the hell was going on, but still knowing. Shit! I don't know, even now. It's fucking weird, thinking back on it. But I told Em I had to go and see, and she begged me not to, 'No, please, don't!' I said I had to, had to, had to. She grabbed my arm, but I pulled away and ran up the path and left her alone at the goddamned crying tree."

At the mixer, Ernst added a squirt of water, to wet the load. We walked past the bags of cement, the boulder pile and the track hoe to the tower wall. We'd left a rough opening for a doorway, facing due west, where during the spring solstice the sun sank into the ocean—a pagan thing of Ernst's. A two-foot-thick lintel stone lay across the top of the opening. An oak frame for the door leaned against the tower, and my tool belt lay on the ground, along with some wooden stakes and lumber.

"On the path, I tried to be quiet, you know, and avoid the dried leaves and ... keep myself a secret."

Ernst looked at me again—probably wondering if I'd smoked too much pot, or if he had. But I just grabbed the frame, and he took the other side and we lifted it toward the opening.

"Funny, what I remember about that path. Shit like how the sun was boring straight down between the trees, and in the shadeless places how the tips of the ferns were curled brown. But mostly it was that noise, a soft moaning, almost like a breeze through the leaves. Shitfuck!"

We set the frame into the opening.

"The noise was closer, coming from just ahead on the path. But it wasn't the wind, or the river. It was …."

Ernst glanced at me, then away, and still he didn't say a word. His hands were brown against the oak frame.

"It was whimpering, a kid's whimpering."

Ernst shifted his side of the frame, aligning it with the wall, and I shifted mine.

"I tiptoed up the path, sneaking closer, hardly breathing, wanting to see the secret—that's how I thought of it, what was happening. A big secret. So I couldn't let him see me sneaking up on him … Uncle Silas."

Ernst's eyes were full of questions that he dared not ask, not right then. He had to be wondering how in the hell I could have been sneaking up the path to find Silas. Wasn't he down by the river, looking for Em and me? But it was the only crazy way I could think of to tell the story.

I said, "When you were a kid, you ever hold your breath so no one would hear you?"

Ernst shrugged.

"I was hoping he couldn't see me."

We held the frame steady. The top of it was just below the lintel stone, its two sides in line with the walls.

"I wanted to be invisible … so he wouldn't see me … and to catch Em. She was the one moaning, not the wind. She was the one. She needed caught. She was in his bedroom with the door closed and needed caught. His lunch pail was back at the Whetstone house, where he'd left it, open, on the kitchen floor. He'd made her—us—play the guessing game. She won. He gave her a quarter."

Ernst's eyes got more puzzled. He hadn't caught on yet:

Em was me, and I was Em, and Uncle Silas was a lunker who'd swallowed both of us.

"I snuck up the path to a small clearing in the ferns. That's where they were, Silas and Em … and me. The sun beat down. It was the two of them, and me, and the tree and the river, just her and him … and me. She—I—was down on her knees in front of him, her knees—mine—pressing into the fir needles, his orange trunks around his ankles, him standing over her—me—and him looking up at the trees, moaning. And she—I—whimpering."

I punched the castle wall, but had to say the rest of it, had to get the full, sorry, goddamned story into the open air and sunshine. "I was thinking *Poor Em, and poor Me.* I could feel her knees pressing, and my knees pressing, the two of us, our measly small knees, the sun boring down on our red, skinny shoulders, our eyes clamped shut around our puny whimpers, and his smells pushing into us, his stink of dead shad."

I stood there, white-knuckled.

Ernst held the frame steady.

I backed away, crying.

Ernst said, "The braces."

I nodded, buckled on my tool belt, fumbling with it. I pounded two wooden stakes into the ground, one to each side of the frame, and then got a couple two-bys, for bracing. I nailed one end of them to the stakes. The hammer felt clumsy, its swing awkward, as if the punch had battered grace, me just banging away with no tempo, getting madder at the nails … that old saying, if all you've got is a hammer, then every problem looks like a nail.

Ernst grabbed a level and plumbed the frame till the bubble was centered. I nailed off the braces to the frame, securing it. I pounded in another nail, and another and another, and then Ernst grabbed my hand.

He said, "Let's fill the void."

I sagged; he let go of my hand.

I took scraps of plywood and nailed one to the back edge of the frame, then across the top and down both sides, covering the narrow spaces between the frame and rocks. Then the same thing for the front, leaving an opening at the top.

Ernst went over to the wheelbarrow, shoved it to the mixer and dumped in the fresh load. He hosed off the drum, then shut down the mixer. The sudden quiet hurt. He wheeled the barrow over to the door frame.

I stood there trembling, scared and weak, feeling like all the years hadn't really passed, and I was a kid again.

Ernst began shoveling the cement into the opening at the top of the frame, and it glopped down between the forms, sealing the frame to the tower wall. I tapped the forms with my hammer, jostling the wet concrete into the pockets of air.

I said, "Afterwards, Uncle Silas walked down the path to the river. Em and me, we brushed the needles off each other's knees. We cried. We walked back down the path, and when we got to the madrone tree Em said, 'When we're older, let's someday kill him.' I said, 'Okay, Em'—the first time I ever called her that."

Ernst set the level to the frame, double-checking. "Jesus Christ, Eddy, you do have a soul." He set the level down, got a scrap of cardboard and began scribbling out another poem. When he finished, he handed it to me. I read it, cried more, then I stuck it in the wall.

Chapter 14

Em showed up the next day, late in the afternoon, out of the clear blue, didn't even knock, just threw the front door open and shouted, "Brother, here I am!"

I was watching TV; Beth wasn't home. I ran to the door to see Em dropping her backpack on the porch, grinning like a big shit-bird.

She jumped into my open arms, and I spun her in circles. She talked a mile a minute, saying the cop had dropped the charges, that she'd spent a night at a friend's house, that the friend lent her money for a bus ticket, and that the bus took forever and ever to reach Milo, stopping in every Podunk town along the way. Her butt was sore from sitting.

I grabbed her backpack, and we went into the house.

Except for her tired eyes, Em looked great. Hair clean and shiny, skin scrubbed; no holes in the knees of her jeans, no patches on her shirt. A decent winter coat that she kept zipped up, saying she felt cold. Em's clothes, I figured, had come from her friend, too, who must have been about the same elfin size as Em was.

She went right over to the refrigerator, where little magnets held photos, a calendar and a grocery list. There was a picture of Kate and BJ, with their college friends in a dorm room. She stared at it, touched it with a finger, asked how the girls were. I said they were doing great, and coming home in a couple of days for Christmas. On the side of the fridge, BJ had put a jumble of magnetized words. Laughing, being silly-assed, Em shoved them around and said, "Street queen seeks lizard boy."

I asked if she was hungry.

"I ate a sandwich on the bus. It was real good, bologna, with mayonnaise and mustard, tomato and lettuce." She arranged more of the words on the fridge. "And a Coke. Did I tell you about the Coke? No thanks, Brother. I'm not hungry now. Maybe later, okay? Yes, later."

She went over to the table, picked up the salt shaker, shook some on her palm, licked it off, plunked the shaker back down. She walked around smiling, touching things: Beth's apron hanging on a nail, the canister of sugar, a bowl of apples sitting on the counter. I told her Beth had landed a temp teaching job at the elementary school and was there getting ready.

"That's so nice, yes, nice. Beth will be happy about that, won't she? Real happy. Those little kids are gonna just love her to death, don't you think?"

She kept one hand clenched in a fist—just like the fist in her cell—and I kept waiting for her to spring something about Dad, but she never did.

She said, "Licker-boo!" and hurried over to the stove, where he was slumped on his side, tongue panting. She knelt down to him, ran her hand back and forth along his black coat. "Licker-boo, it's me!"

He didn't lift his head—then gave her a single wag of his tail, her stroking him, his eyes blank, her seeing how sick he was and her eyes misting up, his black nose dry and hot as the stove, hers red and running snot.

"What's wrong with him?"

I said, "He's getting better."

She put her face down next his face, eye to eye, so her nose was right against the gray hairs on his muzzle. "Don't lie to me."

I hadn't told her about Licker dying for the same reason I hadn't told her about the doe. She loved animals. I said, "The vet gave me pills. They kill the pain. There's nothing I can do for him right now."

"There's always, always, always something you can do." She looked up at me ... past me and through me. Her eyes were red and flitting everywhere.

"Look, I've got to go to work. Why don't you come down and see Sparky about a job?"

"A job?"

"I told him you might be coming by." That was another lie. There'd been no need to tell Sparky about Em. He'd give her a job even if he had no real work for her. His heart was that big.

She stood up, brushed the hair out of her face. "That's it! I'll get a job and save money. I'll buy a place all my own. It'll have big, big windows. And a garden. A dog, cat, canary. It won't take long. A year? Yes, about a year, then I'll have my own place. Don't you worry, Brother. I won't hang here for long, maybe for just a couple of nights, okay? I mean, if it's okay with Beth. You know me. I'll find a place." She laughed, brittle. "But no more bridges. I've had enough of them. I've got a little money. Did I tell you? One of Vaughn's old friends, you know, came by and saw me. He owed Vaughn some money, but Vaughn's ... you know. Of course you know. So, uh, he, uh, gave it to me. Some money."

I figured she was cooking up another fantasy, one with

no concrete to give it real shape or strength, and that in fact she didn't have a clue about tomorrow. She was probably off her meds again and too broke to put herself up at the Good 'Nough Inn—if it was even open for guests. Still, I wanted so bad to see a bare glimmer of what she was seeing and believe in her dream of a house. I said, chipper, "Okay, let's go and see Sparky."

She turned back to the dog, bent down and stroked him again from his head to his tail. "Can't we help him? He needs help."

"Yeah, okay. I'll take him back to the vet tomorrow and—"

She fixed me with a look that was somewhere between sorrow and understanding. "No, not that. I mean real help that ends his suffering now."

She knew Licker would die soon—days, not weeks. She knew the vet would give him a shot and that would be it. They'd incinerate him. She wouldn't allow that, and neither would I. I'd do it myself—put Licker down. I'd shoot him. I'd bury him in the back yard, as far away from the nailing tree as I could, at the edge of the woods where the ferns and azaleas grew thick. I nodded. "Yeah, I'll take care of him."

"Promise?"

"Sure, I promise."

"When?"

"Now. Okay? Is that what you want to see? I'll get the damn gun and shoot him, okay? Is that what you came here for?"

She stroked Licker one last time, rubbed his ears. "No, Brother, not right-this-minute now. Let's go and see Sparky."

We went into the girls' bedroom, where I tossed Em's backpack onto the bed with my old baseball glove I'd left there.

"You can sleep here tonight. Tomorrow, I'll see about getting you a room at the Good 'Nough. You can save your money, till you get on your feet. Okay?" She nodded her agreement. I said that after the girls went back to school in early January, she'd be welcome to use their room again till she found a permanent place of her own.

She stood between the twin beds, looking around, and picked up the glove, slipped her hand into the leather fingers, smacked the pocket with her tiny fist. "I can't wait to see BJ and Kate again. We'll play some catch. It'll be fun."

I pulled open Kate's dresser drawer, got a softball and tossed it to Em. It nestled into the webbing. She stood there, the glove on one hand, her other hand still curled in a fist. She clamped the fielder's glove between her arm and chest, pulled her hand out and laid the glove and ball on a dresser. She stepped in front of the dresser mirror. Her eyes had a thousand-yard stare, as if her reflection had shell-shocked her. I took her fisted hand; she tried to pull away but I held it tight. She said, "Don't, Brother."

I peeled her little finger back and, sure enough, the tip of the butterfly's blue wing was sticking out from underneath her ring finger. I said, "Open up."

"I'm afraid to."

"Why?"

"I'll lose it."

"Let's put it in your hair."

"It'll fall out."

"No it won't."

"It'll get lost."

"Open."

She uncurled her fingers.

I took the barrette. She'd been holding it so tight there was an impression in her palm. I turned it over, inspected the wire clasp, worked it back and forth, snapped it shut and then opened it again. "It's strong. See? It won't fall out."

She nodded, just kept staring into the reflection of her own eyes.

"Left side or right side?"

"Left."

She stood there. I gathered her hair in a loose bunch above her left ear, slipped the clasp underneath the bunch and snapped it shut.

She raised her hand and touched it. It was lopsided. "Is it pretty?"

"Its wings are drying in the sun."

"That's goofy." She turned her head sideways, looked at the butterfly in the mirror, smiled like a shy kid, reached up and twisted the barrette so the butterfly was flying straight ahead.

I said it was time for me to go to work, that we'd have to walk to Sparky's because the pickup was at Jimmy's getting fixed. She said she felt like walking, anything but taking another bus. On our way out of the house, I turned the porch light on.

Outside, the sun had just set and the air was cold and the sky streaked with purple. Across the street, the blackberry vines were almost invisible. We walked fast to keep warm. Em talked about when Licker was a puppy, how the girls had named him because he was always licking their faces. As we approached the elementary school, I asked if she wanted to stop in and see Beth. The lights in Room 8 were on. Em just shook her head and walked faster. When we got to Sparky's the purple sky had turned to black. The sign in front of the bar and grill said "Steak Night! $9.95!"

The place was pretty quiet, with Johnny Cash on the Wurlitzer, with Sparky in the kitchen singing along. Molly came through the swinging doors carrying a plate with a steak, baked potato and green beans. She didn't see us. A hockey game was mute on the big screen. The new pool table already had a brown stain on the green felt.

Skim was perched on the same stool as before, nursing a beer. He smiled when he saw us, waved. Em waved back.

I kissed her on the cheek, showed her the mistletoe above the door. She giggled, stood on her tiptoes and pecked my chin with her dry lips. "Almost merry Christmas," she said.

We walked toward the swinging kitchen door, but she veered away toward Skim, saying over her shoulder. "I'll have what Skim's having." She sat on the stool next to him.

He smiled large. "How you doing, Em?"

She smiled large back. "I'm really, really good. You?"

I just looked at her. Since Vaughn's death she'd supposedly given up booze of any sort. Alcohol and meds don't mix, she'd heard a hundred times, and will fuck with your brain. And since Vaughn died she'd been funny around men, skittish one minute and brassy the next. More than once, especially in the months after Vaughn killed himself, when her moods had ranged between dark and darker, I told her she had to forget about Vaughn, move on, find another man and get a job. Now she was flirting up Skim, an old friend of hers, and married, and whose father had just died. With her, there was just no telling.

Trout Kill

I went behind the bar, tapped a pint of Shakespeare Stout—no head, just pond-flat—and took it down to her.

Skim nodded hello, then grinned and stretched out one arm. "It was this big."

Em looked puzzled. "What's that all about?"

"Nothing. Just a fish story."

I went into the kitchen, where Molly was forking raw T-bones onto a big platter. The steaks had come from Gertrude, one of Ernst's grass-fed heifers that we'd butchered a month ago. Sparky stood at a long table, whisking something in a deep bowl and singing along with Merle Haggard. He wore a green suit and a red apron, his Christmas get-up. I told him Em was at the bar.

He grinned, his white teeth in perfect rows. "Ooo-ee!" He kept whisking as he turned a knob on the gas grill and a blue flame whooshed alive. "Is she stayin' for a while this time, darlin'?"

"Who's Em?" Molly asked.

"My sister. She's looking for a job."

Molly's eyebrows went up.

Sparky put the whisk down. "Tomorrow's Taco Night. Tell her to be here at four o'clock sharp. And, Molly, darlin', you can show her around the kitchen and whatnot."

Molly's pierced lips grinned. "I'll start her with the lettuce." She went to the sink and, bracelets jangling, started peeling potatoes.

I wanted to hug Sparky for his kindness, but just thanked the hell out of him.

"Think nothin' of it, darlin'."

"I owe you."

"Nonsense."

I asked if I could take home a steak after work, for dinner the next day, and he said to help myself. I went into the walk-in cooler, picked out a single fat steak with no bone; wrapped it up in wax paper and slipped it inside my jacket. I went back to the bar.

Em was shoulder to shoulder with Skim, talking quiet with him, looking happy, and her beer was half-gone. They'd dated once, years before Em had ever met Vaughn. Probably they'd done more than just date. Em had gone out with a lot of guys in high school, including Ernst, but they were always short-lived flings. For her, *happy* had always been a fleeting thing, here one moment and gone the next, like sea foam scattering in a gust. A job was what she really needed, not a married guy like Skim, and especially not another loser like Vaughn. Skim was okay, but he was dealing with serious Nam issues, and he couldn't give her what she needed most—peaceful sanity—and most likely he didn't even have an interest; he was just being friendly. She needed a job to anchor her, like working at the grill, where she'd make good food with good smells, where she'd have to follow strict recipes with their regimen of ingredients, their cumin and sea-salt, their olive oil and pepper. The grill would keep her hands busy with rolling pins and cleavers, spatulas and ladles. The work would keep her head on straight.

I set my elbows on the bar, looked right at her and told her about the job Sparky was giving her. Molly would show her the ropes, and she'd begin working the next day at four-o'clock sharp—and don't be late!—and the pay wasn't great, but she could eat all the free tacos she wanted.

Trout Kill

She lit up and her eyes shined. "Oh, that's so wonderful! Thank you, Brother! I love Sparky! Thank you, thank you!" She slid off the stool, ran through the swinging doors and into the kitchen.

Skim shrugged.

For a minute the kitchen sounded like a regular love fest, Sparky *Ooo-ee*ing, Em laughing, pots banging, both of them singing along out of tune with the Wurlitzer. Sparky kept shouting, "Rematch! Rematch!" Meaning the last time Em had stayed in Milo—just passing through on her way to Reno to visit with Vaughn's sister—she'd whipped Sparky in five straight games of cribbage, skunking him three times.

Skim smiled at the hubbub, said Em was looking good, that she'd said she was sticking around for a while. He asked for another beer. I got it, set it right in front of him on a fresh napkin. I said, "That offer still stand?"

He nodded, leaned in closer.

I said, "He hardly knows who I am anymore."

Skim shook his head. "Christ, Eddy."

"You remember the place, right?" I'd told him about my back yard, the place at the edge of the woods.

"Sure. It's a real great spot. And don't worry: I'll make the hole deep."

"Cover it with big rocks."

"Sure thing."

I slipped the steak from inside my jacket, set it on the bar in front of him. "He's got no appetite anymore. But just put this with him."

He gave me an understanding look. "When's a good time?"

"Tomorrow, around six o'clock. Beth'll be at the school. Em and me will be here, working. Just go on in the house and get him. He can't walk anymore, so you'll have to carry him. After it's done, drop by and let me know."

He nodded, drank his beer.

"Thanks a million. I owe you. You like wine?"

"Look, there's no damned need for you—"

"I'll see about a case of Ernst's pinot, for you and the wife."

Em came back out of the kitchen, hurried over and sat next to Skim again. She was all perky and upbeat, said it'd be great fun to work with Sparky and Molly.

The barrette held her hair behind her ear in a way that, somehow, made her look younger, almost girlish.

Skim congratulated her about the job, said he'd like to buy her a beer, and another for himself, too.

Then, just that quick, her eyes went blank like someone had turned off a switch. She said she didn't want another beer. She reached up, unclasped the barrette and pulled it out. Her hair fell back into its old habit of hiding her face. She handed the barrette to me. "Here," she said, "before I lose it."

I shook my head. "You keep it. It's yours."

"No, it's not mine anymore." She laid it on the bar.

Skim was looking back and forth between Em and me and the barrette.

I slipped it into my pants pocket where Beth's panties were still wadded in a ball, walked down to the tap and got Skim's beer, took it down to him, shot Em a hard look that said *What the hell's going on?*

She spun around on her stool and watched the two guys shooting pool.

I went to the dishwasher, started removing the clean pint glasses and setting them bottoms-up on a towel.

Trout Kill

The place had gotten busy. The regulars were ordering steaks, settling into their pool or shuffleboard games, cribbage or pinochle games, their flirting and swapping lies, and the video poker machine had Gladys Millton's full attention and a big chunk of her monthly pension.

Skim slid off his stool, hugged Em goodbye, said he'd be seeing her around, he hoped. Her arms hung at her sides and she never hugged him back.

After he left, she watched Molly wait the tables, and then she stared into her empty beer glass and picked at her fingernails. Then she wandered over to the Wurlitzer and stood there looking at it, sort of mesmerized, like its bright lights and colors had kidnapped her brain. Her fingers played with the buttons. Never, ever would she dare to hold a quarter long enough to drop it in the slot to spin a song. For her, quarters held the same terror as the Tyee Bridge did for me.

I walked over to the juke, pulled a quarter out of my pocket and dropped it in, punched the buttons of her favorite song, Patsy Cline's "Crazy," about a woman being crazy over her man, her feeling so lonely and blue, her wondering and worrying.

Em put her arm around me, said, "Thank you, Brother." Then she leaned down and rested her forehead on the juke glass and closed her eyes and, seemingly rapt, swaying with the music, let the song flow over her.

I felt her own special craziness come creeping into me, and mine go seeping into her. Patsy's broken heart welled me up, how she sang with a woman's pain that seemed infinitely more reflective than a man's could ever be, that Em's kind of crazy was far worse than mine, and her loneliness.

I kissed the top of Em's head, then left her at the juke, went back to the bar, took two beers over to Fred and Skeet. They were playing cribbage, using matchsticks for pegs. We bullshitted for a minute. When I turned around, Em wasn't at the Wurlitzer. The song had ended. She wasn't in the kitchen, either. I watched the door of the women's bathroom, but she never came out.

Maybe she'd set up a covert rendezvous with Skim in the parking lot. I checked outside. His pickup was gone, and no sign of Em.

Goddamn.

Maybe she'd simply decided to walk back to the house, take a hot shower, slip into bed and take a nice long snooze. In the morning, I'd make her a spud and bacon breakfast. That was wishful thinking, and more than likely she'd hooked up with Skim for the night.

Around one o'clock the placed emptied and Molly went home. I set all the chairs up on the tables, filled the dishwasher with glasses and plates; Sparky swept and mopped the floors. I counted the till, gave the money pouch to Sparky. He kept the money in a safe in his trailer. We locked up, then went outside to the Dumpster for our smoke. Sparky packed his pipe and when he fired it up the wind blew the smoke away fast. I told him Em had disappeared. He said not to worry, that she was a big girl, that she'd be a big help in the kitchen. For some reason stupid got its fingers down my throat faster than usual, after only one hit, and I felt real good: Em had a job; Beth had a job; Skim would take care of Licker for me; the girls were coming home and it was almost Christmas.

After the second pipe, I told Sparky I was going home and making mad, passionate love to Beth.

He laughed and said, heading off toward his trailer, "Ooo-ee! You lucky bastard."

I walked home. The porch light was still on, and a note was stuck in the screen door—from Beth, I figured, saying she was working late at the school; or from Em, letting me know what in the hell was up. A dark shape was lying on the porch.

For a moment, I thought it was Licker—that he'd somehow gotten himself up from beside the stove, staggered out the front door and collapsed. Or maybe Beth had come home from the school, put him outside for his nightly piss, then forgot and shut him outside. Or maybe he'd died and she'd laid him on the porch for me to take care of.

It was the black-tail fawn Ernst had found, and that the coyotes had killed.

Goddamn.

I looked around, up and down the street and in the darker places, figuring I'd see a pranking kid running away and laughing his ass off. The neighborhood was quiet, nothing stirring, the moon a bright sliver above the blackberry patch. Maybe the fawn was Jimmy's sick idea of a joke, or Ernst's.

The coyotes had done more work, gnawing into the haunches, the ribcage. Underneath the porch light, the bone was yellow, the flesh almost burgundy. One eye was gone, the other thickly chowdered.

I grabbed its legs and picked it up. Its head swinging at the end of a long neck, the carcass weighed nothing. I carried it around to the side of the garage, laid it on the stack of lumber. I thought again about the fawn's mother, how I'd snuffed her life, how the coyotes and crows had come for her, found her, cared for her. Her fawn seemed far removed from where it ought to be, with her, and putting what I'd killed in a good place was what I had to do. In the morning, I'd dig a hole for Licker, so it'd be ready when the time came. I'd make it deep and wide enough for two, and save Skim the trouble.

Back at the front porch, I got the note out of the screen door. The words were so faintly scrawled I had to hold them up to the light above the door:

Son, I am your father, Pence Trout. Like Emily, you do not believe this to be true. It is. You know me as Spencer. I have a story to tell you. My home is not far. Please come tonight, as my time is running short.

I spun around and scanned the shadows of the night again, the same shabby neighborhood underneath the curved moon. I made a fist and punched my open hand, a quick, smacking jab. "Shitfuck!" Now the crazy old guy was fucking with me, and being cleverly nasty about it: Pence Trout was the same name mentioned in the *Oak Creek Tribune* of the man wanted by the cops in 1950 for shooting a doctor named Redbow.

"You mind fucker—Pence or Spencer ... whoever the hell you are."

On the back of the note were directions to his home: follow the coast highway about thirty miles north of Milo to milepost 198. That was very near to where I'd hit the doe.

Spencer was the nutcase claiming fatherhood; he'd had the guts to ambush Em, and who now had me zeroed in his sights. The fawn was his whacko remembrance of the night I'd first met him. He'd called me *Son* then, too. How could he have known about the *Tribune* story? I'd burned it. Maybe when he'd seen Em she'd let something slip, a name or date.

I tore up the note, punched my hand again, stood there

Trout Kill

on the porch shaking mad. Then suddenly afraid: Had a murderer come to my home? If he was Pence Trout, then he was a murderer. The front door was unlocked, like it always was, like every other trusting door in Milo. I ran inside the house, down the hallway to the bedroom. Beth was sound asleep, the blankets snugged up to her chin, her chestnut hair beautiful, her soft snore a fine-toothed saw cutting pine.

In the girls' room, the beds were still neat and tucked, the baseball glove still lying on the dresser, where Em had set it. Her backpack was gone, so she'd returned and got it before hooking up with Skim.

I went to the pantry, got Jack and drank deep, then deeper.

Stepped over to the fridge and saw a new message Em had arranged with the magnets: *thank you for trying brother.*

And a word she'd made by cutting out the individual letters from a bunch of other words: *v-a-u-g-h-n.*

Goddamn.

I went over to the stove. It was still warm. I stood there shivering, wondering *What the hell's going on?* I figured Spencer had made it a point to come into Sparky's and cozy up to his latest fantasy: me, his "son." When I'd met him that night on the highway he'd put up a nice-guy front, mentioning Glass Point and the fawns, and then at Sparky's he'd told me his sad story about his boyhood dog and the steak bone. I'd swallowed it all.

And as far as Em went, I tried not to be scared for her anymore. She had flitted into Milo and flitted out. She could handle herself. She was a turtle and shit bounced off her. Her bus ticket, I figured, had been round-trip. She'd just popped in to say hi, get a glimpse of her brother's dull life, get laid by the first dick she met, and then hit the road again.

And Licker?

He wasn't crapped out beside the stove. I hurried back into the bedroom, got down on my hands and knees and checked underneath the bed.

No dog.

I punched the floor hard, busting open my knuckles, and all the while Beth never stirred.

Chapter 15

I felt sick at heart and needed fresh air. I paced from the kitchen to the stove, worried about whether to call Sparky, Ernst, Jimmy, Skim, the Fish and Game Commission. I got my notebook, yanked out #23, struck a match and burned it. It didn't help.

I left the house, walked across the street, circled around the tangle of wild blackberries that had grown around the foundation. Beyond the lot, I crossed the coast highway, climbed up the foredunes, then dropped down the other side to a path. A raft of clouds had blown in and the moon was gone. I walked to the beach, no destination in mind, just walking. A southwest wind carried rain. Far out in the black sea, a single light winked—maybe a deck lantern on a trawler.

Then found myself standing at the edge of the surf and staring at the dark hulk of the Avian Wing, grounded about a hundred yards out. The stern of the wrecked ship was gone, torn away by an offshore reef.

I felt a giant fist clench my heart and rip it out.

I stripped off my clothes and started wading out in the cold surf. It broke low against my shins. The tide was coming in. I dove, and the black cold squeezed my breath out. I surfaced, stroking hard, angling toward the north side of the prow. The swells pushed me toward the steel hull. At the ship's stern, the sea churned white against the jagged metal and broken cables.

The tide carried me shoreward along the ship's starboard side. My feet touched bottom and I tried to stand on numb legs. A wave knocked me down, tumbling me along the sandy bottom. I came up sputtering, stood and braced myself against the next wave.

Back on the beach, I dressed quick, shivering, teeth clicking, fingers numb. I stretched out on the sand, burrowed down till I was covered, a periwinkle in its thin shell. Above, no stars or moon; the wind howled and the rain slanted.

Son, I am your father.

I stood, shook some sand off, started sprinting north with the wind. I yelled, "You can't touch me, motherfucker!" I collapsed, gasping, and threw up. A wave scudded up the beach, and its wash trickled the sand from underneath me, and the backwash, and I was sinking, a sense of vertigo. I staggered to my feet, ran full-out till a familiar beach house told me where I was, back at the path leading to my home.

At the house, I got a short rope, lashed the fawn's four feet together and slung the animal across my back. I got a shovel and started walking. The rain fell harder and the wind blew harder. The fawn's head bumped against the back of my calf. I kept an eye peeled for Spencer's black Ford.

At the elementary school, I went to the playground where, at the foot of the slide, I dropped the fawn to the ground. I scraped away the shredded tires and began digging. The kids' feet had packed the sand hard. The rain stopped, but the wind cut cold. My old blister heated up and my knuckles bled. I made the hole deep. The moon raced through the clouds. I removed the rope and laid the fawn in the hole. I thought *I'm reckless and I'm sorry.*

When I filled the hole, the blister broke open and the pain felt good. I tamped the dirt firm, then spread the rubber shreds back over the ground. It rained again, a downpour, and beads of water skittered down the slide and cascaded off. Soon enough, after their winter break ended, the kids would come laughing down the slide, and their happy feet would tend the grave.

I ran home, tossed the shovel in the yard and went inside. I called Skim and got his answering machine. It was the dead of night, nearly four-thirty. Mindful of his wife, I told Skim to forget about the job we'd talked about, and to call me back. I wanted to ask him about Em.

I hung up the phone, ran into the bathroom and threw up again. The toilet ran. I let it. I got my notebook, two joints and a bottle of Jack. At the kitchen table, still feeling queasy, I wrote. Outside, the wind whistled through the nailing tree, and I just kept putting down the words till the pencil got dull and I had to sharpen it with a paring knife, and still the words kept tumbling out, a mad, fevered rush of them, mixed with smoke and Jack.

"Eddy, what in God's name?"

Startled, I looked up from the tip of my pencil, still pouring forth. Beth was standing by the refrigerator in her bathrobe and slippers, hands on her hips, her eyes pinched and suspicious. For a moment, I didn't know who she was, this stranger who'd suddenly stepped into the middle of my unfolding tale, distracting and inquisitive, rudely so.

I closed the notebook. "I couldn't sleep."

"You never even came to bed." She stared at the clock on the wall. It was pushing five-thirty. "All the night long."

"Yeah, like I said."

Beth cinched her bathrobe tighter. The Jack was empty. A half-smoked joint lay beside it. My clothes were still rain-soaked. The fire was long out and the house gone cold. Out the kitchen window, just darkness, no hint of daylight. Beth eyed the Jack bottle as she had the clock, with stern judgment, as a cop might examine a spent casing at a murder scene, and then she went to the stove to build a fire.

I said, "Em's gone."

She threw in paper and kindling and put a match to it. "What on earth are you talking about?"

Then I remembered: I hadn't told Beth about Em showing up. I filled her in, said Sparky had offered her a job but then she disappeared. "Maybe she took the bus back to the city." I didn't tell her about Skim.

Beth said, "Honestly. That woman cannot afford to throw away her blessings."

I had no idea what she meant. I said, "She's trying. It's hard for her."

Beth nodded. "I know she is, Eddy. But sometimes she's her own worst friend."

She was right: When it came to shooting herself in the foot, Em seldom missed. But sometimes, for Em and for me, the easiest thing to do was throw away our so-called blessings and march on, beholden to no one, trapped in a state of *owing*. I had to change the subject. "Have you seen Licker around?"

She frowned. "When I came home last night, he wouldn't get up from beside the stove, not even to go potty. Are you taking him to the vet today?"

"He's gone. I've looked for him everywhere."

"Did he run away?"

She said that as if he was capable, like he was a wayward pup. "He's never run off before. And he's too damn sick, and even if he could run, he wouldn't."

She went over to the Christmas tree, where she reached up and straightened the angel on top, one of those plastic jobs that glowed whenever it was plugged in. "Maybe Emily took him to the vet. You know how she loves that dog."

I said yeah, maybe. But Em knew Licker was too far gone for the vet. After she'd left Sparky's and got her backpack, she could've walked to the Good 'Nough Inn, which I'd mentioned to her. More than likely, though, Skim had given her a lift somewhere or she'd just made up her mind to hitchhike, which she'd done plenty of times before. And it had crossed my mind that Spencer might have taken Licker. I'd already pegged him like Em, a dog lover, and I'd told him how sick Licker was. Maybe he thought he'd be doing me a big favor by shooting my dog for me. The thought made me mad as hell.

I went to the phone and called Jimmy, an early-riser so he could beat off a few times, I figured, before he ambled off to work, if work is what it was. I asked him when the hell my pickup was going to be ready. I spoke loud and firmly, mostly for Beth's benefit. The new radiator was due for delivery by noon, he said, then it'd take a couple hours to install. It should be ready by three or four o'clock. I said, "It damn well better be." He said, "Don't get yer friggin' panties in a bunch," and hung up.

Beth said, "You know, come to think of it ... it just crossed my mind that maybe Emily may not have wanted to spend the night here, with us and the girls. You know how she is about imposing. She's awfully sensitive that way."

I just looked at her.

"And you know as well as I do that she flies around from here to there, willy-nilly, her whims taking her God knows where."

The kettle on the stove started whistling. Beth walked over, filled her cup with steaming water and put the kettle down. She swirled a teabag around and around by its string.

I got the phone book, but could find no listing for the Good 'Nough. Maybe Denis hadn't gotten around to placing the listing. I told Beth I was going to shower and shave, then head over to the inn and see if Em was there.

She said, "Good for you. I know you will not sleep a wink until you find her. Such a lost soul, that woman."

Chapter 16

Just beyond the elementary school, the street narrowed, wound up a hill to the top of a bluff and dead-ended at The Good 'Nough Inn. Painted a bright orange with white trim, the old two-story structure stood out against the gray backdrop of sky. Gulls festooned its gabled, red-shingled roof. Thick rhododendrons, planted about a half-century ago by Oscar Milo, the town's founder, crowded the walls and reached to the second-story eaves. A sparse lawn sloped down the bluff to the foredunes.

The front door swung open into what Denis called the drawing room; it was crowded with dark-upholstered chairs, crown moldings, massive built-in bookcases crammed full of books, and built-in cabinets filled with curios and antiques. Denis loved collecting junk. Worn rugs covered the oak floor. An iron chandelier hung above a long table, where an aquarium sat. Leaded glass windows lined the right side of the room, and at the far end, a big picture window looked toward the ocean.

Denis was in the kitchen. He was wearing an apron over his worn, blue-striped bathrobe, and his hands were immersed in a pan of brown liquid. He lifted a dripping oyster from the pan and smiled. "To put more lead in your pencil. Ha-ha!"

"I could use more lead."

He washed his hands at the sink, came over and hugged me. His belly was a lump of soft dough. He was gray-whiskered, balding, with a blighted-pear nose, a flushed face and three quivering chins. He said, "You've got sand in your ear."

I fingered it out, from the beach, dull, ashen grains. "What smells so damned good?"

He nodded toward the oven. "Cinnamon rolls, my man. Hungry?"

I said I was, and that I was looking for Em, my sister, wondering if she might have checked in the night before.

"No, she hasn't been here. And we're not quite ready for paying guests. We hope to open next week." He frowned. "She's not in any trouble, I hope."

I told him about Em showing up, then her disappearance.

"Well, that's a trifle unusual."

"Not for her."

"She's certainly welcome here, anytime." He opened the oven door and pulled out the rolls, browned and gooey.

From the bedroom off the kitchen, a man emerged wearing a blue-striped bathrobe that matched Denis' robe. He, too, had pasty skin, a sagging belly and a wide ass.

Denis grinned slyly, winked, said, "Eddy, I'd like you to meet my dear friend and, uh, pelvic associate, Robert. Ha-ha!"

Robert waved hello, scratched his butt. "So, you're the electrician, Eddy?"

"And the plumber, the roofer, et cetera," Denis said. "Eddy is a man of many skills, and he's simply gorgeous in his tool belt. It seems, however, that he's recently misplaced his dear sister, Emily."

"Oh?"

"Eddy assures me it's nothing to be alarmed about. Evidently, he's misplaced her before, like a pair of slippers."

Robert said, "A man can't find his dick until he's had his morning coffee." He got a sack of coffee beans off the counter, opened it and stuck his nose inside. "Ah! The Guatemalan highlands!"

Denis pulled a pack of cigarettes from his bathrobe, tapped one out, lit it, took a deep drag that firmed his jowls and his chins. He handed the cigarette over to Robert, who inhaled in the same fashion. They stood there together by the marinating oysters, sharing puffs on the cigarette, and then in coinciding orchestration they nonchalantly reached around and scratched their own asses. I felt privileged, somehow, to witness this private familiarity.

Robert held up the sack of beans. "Cuppa hot joe, Eddy?"

I shrugged. "Coffee never tastes as good as it smells."

They both shook their heads. Denis said, "See, Robert, what I have to cope with in this backwater town? Savages!"

"He simply lacks the proper edification."

Denis got a coffee grinder, the old-fashioned kind with a wooden bin and a handle to crank. Robert poured the beans in the bin and slid it shut. Denis eyed Robert, winked, turned the crank once and stopped. Robert snapped his fingers. Denis cranked again; Robert snapped again, this time thrusting out his hip. Denis turned faster, and Robert snapped his fingers and swiveled his hips like a hula-hooper. Denis laughed and danced around the table with the grinder, cranking away, grinding the beans, and Robert shimmed after him. They made hot eyes at one another, coy and full of what looked like teasing love. They bellowed out a song, maybe a rumba, maybe something Cuban, and Denis shook the sack of beans like a maracas.

The two men, panting and sweating, collapsed heavily against one another, shoulder to shoulder, grinning like kids.

Denis pulled out the grinder drawer and thrust it under my nose. "What does it smell like? And, please, don't say *coffee*."

I breathed in deep. The black heap of fresh grounds smelled like … what? "It's like black licorice and dirt."

"Wonderful!"

Robert shrugged. "Sure, licorice and dirt. Why not?"

Robert dropped a paper filter into the top of a coffeemaker, an hourglass-shaped vessel with a wooden girdle around its waist. Denis measured out a black mound of grounds into the filter, then slowly poured steaming water from a kettle over them. Deep-black liquid dribbled from the bottom of the filter into the hourglass. He poured a cupful and handed it to me. "First, you taste with your eyes, and then with your nose, and then your tongue, and last of all with your soul. Allow the flavors to take your soul places it's never been before."

I lifted the cup to my nose, breathed the steam in deep, let my breath slowly out and then took a sip.

Denis and Robert looked expectant.

The coffee tasted rich and strong, surprisingly so, and fertile, like you could grow something in it, and not at all like the swill Mr. Coffee made. "So this is what I've been missing." Denis and Robert beamed, and I swore I'd buy my own grinder and hourglass and Guatemalan beans. I'd learn to sing the rumba, too, if that's what it took for a decent cup of coffee.

Robert said, "Maybe *now* you'll find your sister."

They belly laughed, poured themselves a hot cupful of the dark brew, grabbed cinnamon rolls and handed one to me. I washed the roll down with coffee, and they talked about going on a trip to France to hunt truffles with pigs, and I felt so fucking good right then … in the company of those two men,

Trout Kill

just letting my worries slip away for that brief time, listening to them dream about truffles. I didn't ever want to leave, and more than anything else I wished Em were there to feel what I did. I said, "I need a room. For tonight, and maybe longer."

Denis arched a caterpillar brow.

"For Em, for when she shows up. I'll pay." I reached for my wallet.

He held up his hand. "Don't be ridiculous. You won't pay a single solitary cent."

"But it could be a week, or longer."

"It's yours, for as long as you need."

"It's for Em."

"Yes, so you say, so you say." He glanced at Robert, who shrugged and smiled. "That's fine. She can have the suite. The trim still needs a bit of touching up. She'll enjoy the lovely king bed, with its grand ocean view. And, please, don't insult me with your offers of filthy lucre. Your construction prowess has whipped this old dame into shape, Eddy. So, please! Tonight, we're dining on oysters, roasted vegetables and sweet potatoes. I insist that you and Beth join Robert and me. You simply must ... and Emily, too, if—"

"No. Beth can't make it. And Em won't need the suite. The Chanterelle Room is fine."

Denis and Robert looked at me and their smiles faded. I didn't say another word. Robert lit another cigarette. I sipped the last of my coffee and set the cup down. Grains of sand lay in the bottom of the cup; they'd fallen out of my hair.

Denis said, "Very well, Eddy. Come with me." He led the way out of the kitchen, past the den and up the stairs. At the top there was a dim hallway, with four different colored doors down the length of it; they each led into a bedroom; and, at the far end of the hall, a fifth door entered a shared bathroom. A brass placard above the nearest door said CHANTERELLE ROOM. We entered. A narrow bed stood by the window. There was a tiny desk, a dresser, and a Morris chair that reminded me of Dr. Lund's office. Denis said the extra linens were in a bottom drawer.

"Thanks, Denis. I owe you. And Em does, too."

"Balderdash!"

From downstairs, voices seeped up through the floor vent. Robert had turned on the radio.

Denis said, "This is the very least I can do." He left, closing the door behind him.

I sat on the bed, emptied of the joy I'd felt downstairs in the kitchen. *What am I doing here? Why did I lie about Beth and dinner and the room?* I got up and went to the window.

The glass pane was old, wavy, and distorted the view outside. Dull morning light bathed me. Outside, new shingles covered the steeply pitched roof. I'd reroofed last fall, before the rains came. In the back corner of the yard, the garden shed leaned eastward, as if some strong onshore gust had shoved it that way. Denis had told me to leave it that way. It was charming, he said. Now the winds were calm again, and the whitecaps that had dotted the ocean earlier in the day were gone. The ocean is like that, tossed one minute and flat the next.

I pulled Beth's pink nylon Rudolph panties out of my pants pocket. The butterfly barrette was snagged it them. I freed it, slipped it back into my pocket. I stretched the panties wide between my thumbs and held them up to the window, hoping the day's early light might shine through them and illuminate a feeling close to what I felt for the doe, but all I felt was the drifting, and all I saw was a prancing Rudolph, his absurd nose.

I pressed them to my face, again, like I had in our kitchen, and breathed deep to inhale Beth's scent, her shit and sweat, the wet of her pussy, her bloody menstrual flow, her guts and brains and heat—any solid vestige might have worked. There was not a trace of her.

The window was the single-hung kind, with cast iron weights and ropes and pulleys hidden inside the jambs. Denis had painted it shut. I had to bang the frame hard to crack the paint, then I jimmied the lower sash up till I could get my fingers underneath and lift.

I squeezed the panties into a soft ball and threw them out the open window. They flew above the roof, then fluttered open and fell like a shot flamingo to a loose gutter spike, where they snagged and hung.

Exhausted, wanting sleep and not to dream, I closed the window, stripped naked and slipped between the freshly laundered bed sheets.

Chapter 17

I woke up groggy, threw the blankets back and raked my fingers through my hair, loosing a trickle of sand onto the sheets and into a fold of the pillowcase. My clothes lay jumbled on the floor. I got up, dressed, stepped over to the window and pulled it up. The late afternoon was growing dark, thickening with fog that hid the low foredunes and muffled the surf. The long sleep had done me good: I felt rested, and remembered no dreams.

I crawled out the window and onto the roof, where I braced my feet and hands against the steep pitch. Above me, a gull sat on the ridge of the gable. I scooted down the slope on my ass, about ten feet, and set my heels against the outer lip of the gutter. The panties hung on the loose spike. The other spikes were spaced about five feet apart and looked solid. I leaned forward between my knees, reaching for the panties. They were just beyond my fingertips. I inched closer, grabbed them and leaned back, trying to shift my weight off my heels. The loose spike shot into space. My feet followed, and I hurtled off the edge into a blurry uprush of rhody leaves and branches, of flailing arms and legs.

I hung upside down, entangled among the branches of the rhodies, clutching the panties in my hand. The crumpled section of gutter dangled from the eave. Nothing felt broken, just a few scratches; blood was rushing to my head. I twisted myself around till I was upright among the stiff, lower branches, and my feet found the ground. I'd come to rest a few feet from the picture window that looked out from the drawing room. Beneath it, the pruned branches allowed for a view, and looked like the sharp stakes in a punji pit. Had I fallen there, I'd have been skewered. I felt lucky, almost.

Denis and Robert came running to the window. Open-mouthed, they stared down at me. Denis yelled, "Are you okay?" I gave him a thumbs-up. He turned and hurried away. Robert looked like he was about to cry. "Hold on!" he shouted.

Ernst appeared beside Robert; he grinned and shook his head, as if to say *Look at you, Rat Dick.* He raised his wine glass and mock-toasted me.

I waved the panties at him, as if they'd explain everything.

He pressed his lips to the window and kissed the glass, fogging it.

I looked around for a way to extricate myself.

"Eddy! Are you hurt? Speak to me!"

It was Denis, standing on the lawn, wheezing from the short sprint he'd just taken from the drawing room, looking pale, his three chins quaking.

I said I was fine, just a few scratches.

"My goodness! My goodness!"

I stuffed the panties into my pocket, then weaved my out of the branchy maze to the lawn, where Denis began pulling leaves from my hair, out of my collar. He peered at my neck. "You've got a nasty scratch there. I'll tend to it. Come inside and I'll get the iodine."

I followed him. Old Blue was parked in the driveway. Ernst, I figured, had dropped by to sell Denis wine, or try to. Inside the drawing room, Ernst was still standing at the picture window. He looked smashed, with his head drooping and his shoulders slumped, feet turned outward for improved stability. He lifted his wine glass. "Here's to women's underwear."

Robert hurried over and asked if I was okay. He looked half-drunk.

"He's got a nasty scratch," Denis said, pulling down my collar and showing Robert. They both smelled like wine and cigarettes. They rushed off together to get the iodine.

Ernst said, "What the hell you doing here? Where's Em … and whose panties are those?"

I ignored him. In the aquarium on the table, a lone fish was swimming laps around the graveled bottom. I stepped closer. It was a goldfish, the kind with the fancy, frilly tail. For all the weeks I'd worked on the inn, the aquarium had sat empty. The fish finned to the top and blew a bubble that burst, rippling the surface. A little net and a box of fish food were on the table. I sprinkled in a few flakes.

Ernst said, "They gotta be Beth's, right?"

His tongue was thick and slow.

The goldfish darted to a flake, gobbled it.

I said, "You get Curly fixed yet?"

"Right?"

I dumped in a big heap of flakes. They dispersed and started sinking. The fish zipped back and forth, sucking in one after another after another. Its mouth was an O. Then it shit a dark cloud and circled back through it. A fish with too much food, I knew, might glut itself to death. I got the net and scooped up a few flakes.

"Beth's, right?"

"Fuck off, Ernst."

Trout Kill

Denis and Robert came hurrying back from the bathroom. "Remove your jacket, Mr. Trout, and let us tend your grievous wound."

I took the jacket off; it had, I figured, saved me from the worst of the fall. I hung it on the back of a chair. Denis tucked my shirt collar down; Robert opened the iodine and pulled the dauber out. They inspected the scratch, fussing. The iodine smelled like weak chlorine, and it didn't sting.

Ernst staggered a step closer. "What the hell're you doing up on the roof, huh?"

Denis clucked his tongue. "Very, very nasty." Robert opened a Band-Aid and peeled off the strips.

Ernst said, eyeing my jacket, "Lemme see 'em. Come on, lemme see 'em."

Robert pressed on the Band-Aid.

I said, "Myrtle's eggs hatch yet?"

"Come on. Lemme."

He reached for the jacket, and I slapped his hand away. He scowled.

Denis capped the iodine. "What on earth are you two fussing about?"

Ernst had fixed on the jacket like a setter on a grouse. His eyebrows were up by the chandelier, his eyes shining with purpose. "I just wanna hold them, okay?" He grabbed for the jacket, lost his balance and bumped into the table. "Lemme hold 'em. That's all ... just lemme hold 'em."

I stood between him and the jacket. He was in the grip of another vortex spiraling him deeper into self-pity, seeing *only* those panties, a sort of pink fantasy that he *had* to get his hands on and his nose into, *had* to kiss like he'd kissed the window.

He ached for what I wouldn't let him near. First, I'd thrown the panties into a gutter, then risked my neck to retrieve them, and was now defending them. That day when I was eighteen and left on the bus for basic training, Beth had done the smartest thing she could've done: given me her panties. She knew they'd keep me loving her. She knew how love worked. Ernst and me had been friends a long, long time; we'd gotten stoned and rambled on for hours about love, brain-addled discourses that aimed to forge a nail we could hang our hats on. But our dissertations always circled back upon our simple mindedness. And, now, I was shielding the panties from Ernst because Beth was all I knew about love.

Facing Ernst, him drunk and me sober, I got jealous, a green jolt that clenched my hands into fists. What I felt for Beth had to be love. I stepped toward him and raised those fists.

Denis moved between us, smiled, put his pudgy hand on Ernst's chest and said real loud, "I'd like two—no, three—cases of your Purgatorio! Ha-ha! Purgatorio! A stroke of genius, Ernst. A name like that will expiate our sins."

Ernst swayed, grinned and seemed oblivious of my anger. "Goddamn, boys, I'm a wine man."

I lowered my hands.

"Robert, my love, please fetch us a bottle, a corkscrew and four fresh glasses."

Robert hustled into the kitchen, his wide ass a sway. The goldfish swam a slow lap through another swirl of watery shit. Ernst collapsed backward onto the couch. Denis rechecked the Band-Aid on my neck. Robert returned with a fresh bottle and four clean glasses. The bottle had a taped-on label, the drawing Ernst had made of the mountain and the flying cher-

Trout Kill

ubs. Robert, who'd returned from the kitchen, said, "If you'll do the honors, Ernst."

Ernst rolled off the couch, stood, seized the bottle and the corkscrew and stabbed it into the cork. He yanked the cork out and, almost magically, his drooping head lifted and he squared his shoulders back. His eyes focused.

The glasses were long-stemmed and big-bowled. With a flourish, Ernst splashed a purple stream into each of them. He held the wine bottle up to the chandelier and shouted, "We christen thee, Purgatorio!"

Denis and Robert shouted, "Purgatorio! Here, here!"

Ernst beamed and we all drank.

Denis said, "Ah, ah! Fruity essence is an absolute imperative. Shouts of joyous *Prunus serotina* and, if I'm not mistaken, an undertone of roasted cacao seeds."

Ernst spun around and banged into the aquarium, sloshing water over the side and onto the floor. The fish was a gold streak darting in the choppy sea.

Robert ran to get a towel.

Denis said not to worry about the fish, and asked if we'd like to join him and Robert for an oyster dinner, and Ernst said he was starved and could eat a horse. I was hungry, too, but had to get out of there. The green spite I'd felt toward Ernst hadn't vanished, and Em was lost somewhere, and Licker was gone, and I'd buried a dead fawn where children played, and Spencer was a nail that needed pounded down, and it all seemed as if I were still tumbling through the air and the ground was rushing up fast. I set my wine glass down on the table. "I've gotta see about my pickup." I walked to the door, opened it, and started running from the inn, down the bluff and into the fog.

Chapter 18

Jimmy, his cap turned backwards, was working in his excuse for a mechanic's garage, bent over the gaping hole in my pickup where a newly installed radiator should have been. Wrenches, ratchets and screwdrivers were scattered across the engine. Jimmy muttered, "They sent the wrong friggin' part."

"Goddamn. You said—"

"Wanna hand me that screwdriver?" He pointed.

"Then I'll need the loaner."

He pulled his head from underneath the hood. "What's yer hurry? It'll only be another day, maybe two."

"I've got to find my sister."

"How'd you lose 'er?"

"Any gas in the loaner?"

"Maybe. How'd you get that hickey? She's a real beaut."

He meant the scratch on my neck from the rhodies. I'd pulled off the Band-Aid when I left the inn. I ignored the question. "Keys?"

"Hangin' on the door aside Miss October."

I got the keys, hustled outside and jumped into the loaner, a maroon, '93 Dodge Intrepid. The interior smelled like a barroom floor, the front seat had a rip, and the gas gauge read empty. The starter whined, caught ahold and the engine started. The radio lit up but didn't work. I left Jimmy's and drove toward home, less than a mile. The wipers' back-and-forth just made blurry streaks.

Trout Kill

When I walked into the house, no one was home, no dog, Em or Beth. The fridge didn't hum and the fire didn't crackle. Just an uneasy stillness and the queasy sense that I was still falling, tumbling and falling. I had to get out of there, away from the angel on the tree, the Jesus mug and my baseball glove. For the first time since finding the fawn on my porch, I *knew* where I had to go.

I went into the bedroom and packed a change of clothes into a travel bag. Got my notebook and stuffed it in the bag, left the house, tossed the bag into the Intrepid and drove to the elementary school. I parked next to Wally's Tahoe where, across the street from the school, I had a view of Classroom 8.

The paper snowflakes were gone from the windows. Inside, Beth was visible from the waist up. She was arranging the desks. Trudy wasn't there. I got out of the car and walked across the street to the sidewalk. I stood there and watched. Beth moved from desk to desk with sure steps, nudging them one by one into a row. She was on the last row, the one closest to the door. She stood back, folded her arms and checked the row for straightness. Each desk sat directly underneath a big star hanging from the ceiling. The stars had kid's names. Beth reached up, spun a star and smiled.

I remembered Mr. Willis' Senior English class at Oak Creek High. One day he asked the class about a scene in a story when, on a hot summer day at some beach—somewhere in Africa, I think—this French guy shoots an Arab. He'd had some sort of run-in with the Arab earlier, and the Arab had a knife. The funny thing was, the first shot drops the Arab, and he's lying there defenseless, and then the guy pauses, his finger still on the trigger, and he could have just walked away, no problem, a justifiable case of self-defense. But he goes ahead and plugs the Arab three or four more times, a cold-blooded murder. Mr. Willis asked the class *Why the pause? Why the needless extra shots?* I didn't pretend to know the answer, and kept my mouth shut. No one did, it seemed, not even Beth or Ernst, not even after hashing it out for most of the period. And, it seemed, not even Mr. Willis knew, or if he did he wouldn't explain in a way that made any sense, just something ridiculous about the sun. The fucking sun! I remember getting mad at Mr. Willis, thinking he was holding back, wasn't being fair, but most of all because he was asking the wrong damn questions, that we should've been talking more about the Arab, not the French guy. I wanted to know what the Arab might have felt when he pulled a knife against a stranger and his gun that don't give a shit.

Standing there watching Beth in the classroom, I got mad. I didn't have a good reason to, just a feeling that boiled up, and I got mad for being mad. What made it worse was she looked so damned happy doing what she was doing, being a teacher, organizing and getting ready for the kids, and smiling like I'd seldom seen before, with her whole face. Her happy in the classroom, me mad outside—she seemed a stranger, beyond my ability to understand. I felt helpless, like the Arab. And sad, too, for not knowing what questions I should ask.

I walked down the sidewalk, turned a corner and passed by Wally's office. He was sitting at his desk talking on the phone. He looked up, saw me and nodded. I nodded back and kept walking.

The fog made the playground hard to see. I walked closer. Moisture had condensed into beads on the monkey bars and the teeter-totter, and the biggest beads slid down the shiny pole where the kids played tetherball. Where I'd buried the fawn at the foot of the slide, the shredded tires looked undisturbed. I could do that well, bury things to hide them.

At the door of Classroom 8, the old poster with Big Bird was gone, replaced with a new one that said *Let all the children come unto me*. The verse pissed me off even more, because little kids had enough shit to deal with—Santa Claus and the Easter Bunny—and what parts of the Bible I'd read never asked questions, just pretended to have all the answers.

I stood there till my anger faded, then went inside the classroom.

Beth was sitting at her desk, reading some sort of booklet. Her Jesus mug sat there. She never heard me enter. She looked like a teacher: red pantsuit, crisp collar, no jewelry, reading glasses perched on her nose. The fluorescent lights made her chestnut hair brassy.

Twenty small desks faced the front whiteboard; Beth had written MRS. TROUT in the upper corner. There were five rows of four desks each. The floor was carpeted blue; the beige walls had stenciled eagles and cougars, whales and dolphins. A bulletin board had drawings and art projects; another board had a list of names with gold stars pasted after them. Beth was only filling in for Trudy, but she'd made the room her own.

Somewhere in the basement of the school the old boiler kicked on, sent a surge of hot water through the pipes and into the cast iron coils of the radiator standing by the windows. The coils groaned and threw off waves of heat that floated up to the ceiling and made the paper stars twirl on their strings.

I said, "Beth."

Her head jerked up and her hands flew apart. The booklet dropped onto her desk. She gasped, blinked, took off her reading glasses and set them down on the desk. Her face creased with a frown. "What on earth?"

"Sorry. Didn't mean to startle you." I walked down an aisle of desks. They came to my knees and looked fragile. I bumped one with my knee, accidentally. The star above it said JUSTIN.

She leaned forward in her chair as if to rise and rush to the desk's defense. But then she settled back again, turned her head away and looked out the window. She said, scanning the parking lot across the street, seeing only the Intrepid, "Did Jimmy make the repairs yet?"

I told her no, not yet, there'd been a mix-up with the parts.

She shook her head. "He's such a hopeless man."

"What's that you're reading?"

She picked up the booklet, showed me the cover. "It's the student-parent handbook. Policies and procedures and guidelines."

"Wally's rules?"

She brushed the hair out of her face, primped it behind her ear. "There's so darn many to remember. Attendance policies and so forth. But I don't mind. It's comforting to have things set down in black and white." She frowned, laid the booklet on her desk. "Jimmy probably has another excuse, I suppose. What is it this time?"

I told her about the mix-up with the radiator, how it's easy for someone to confuse one part number with another part number, then send the wrong part.

"He should be more careful."

I shrugged. "I'm leaving for a while."

"Emily wasn't at the inn, I take it. That woman! Running off and not letting anyone know. Where will you look for her?"

"This isn't about Em, okay."

"What on earth do you mean?"

"It's about ... us. I have to go away for a ... for a time."

"Us?" She straightened a pile of papers lying on the desk, then looked up and right at me. "Eddy? What are you trying to tell me?"

"It's just for a couple of days." I sounded like Jimmy, making a lame promise about how long it'd take to fix something.

She stood, walked around her desk and down the aisle next to mine. She stopped at the desk I'd bumped out of kilter, and she nudged it back an inch and into its proper place, aligned beneath the ceiling star above, and with the entire galaxy. She said, again, "Us?"

I nodded. "Yeah, us."

"What on earth for?"

"I have to go and see."

"See?"

"If ... I love you."

She blinked fast. "See?"

I nodded, swallowed, and started blinking as fast as she was.

Her eyes brimmed up. She stepped toward me and her leg bumped into Justin's desk and knocked it out of place again. Her face was pale, like her legs had been when she'd danced in the kitchen. "I don't understand. What is happening here? Now? What is happening, Eddy? Please, tell me."

"I don't know. It's important. Things have been .... I don't know."

"Is this about ... what?"

"Love."

"Our love?"

"Yeah."

"Oh, Eddy." She bent over Justin's desk and put her palms flat on its laminated top. Her head hung down, and her hair almost touched the desk. "What about the girls? And Christmas? What about ... everything?"

"Everything is going to be okay. Tell the girls I've gone looking for their Aunt Em."

She stood up straight, pulled her shoulders back. Her eyes were as wet as they could be without a tear escaping. She said, "Are you okay?"

"Yes. No. Maybe." I shrugged, half-grinned.

A tear spilled out, ran down her cheek to her jaw, vanished underneath her chin. Then she hurried back to her desk and grabbed a tissue and began dabbing at her eyes.

My eyes were wet, too. Everything looked blurry. "I have to go and see, about us."

"How do you do that? See?" She blew her nose into the tissue.

"I don't know. I have to see how to see." I was making no sense, not even to myself.

"You don't *see* love. You *feel* it." She pulled another tissue out and blew her nose again. Her shoulders trembled.

"Yeah. I guess that's right. I don't know."

"I'm here, right in front of you. You see me now, don't you?"

"Yes, I see you." I felt awful, a cold-blooded sniper who'd just shot his wife through her heart. And shot his own heart, too. She was trying to regroup, fighting off the panic that had to be rising up in her. And, I hoped, she was summoning outrage. I deserved an onslaught of her wrath, and I wanted her to scream in my face, pound my chest with her fists and call me *bastard*.

She said, sobbing, "Where will you go?"
"Not far. I'll call. I promise."
"The inn?"
"No, not there."
"And for how long?"
"Not long."
"A day, two?"
"Not long."
Then she did the worst thing she could've done. She clenched the tissue in a fist and said so soft and full of hurt that the radiator almost drowned her out, "Go, then, Eddy. See if you can see."

Chapter 19

I left the school and drove to Sparky's. It was Taco Night. The parking lot was packed. I cruised through the lot, keeping my eyes peeled for a black, four-door Ford, wire holding its trunk shut and an old man behind the wheel. The Ford wasn't in the lot. But if he was in Sparky's I'd walk up and jab my finger in his chest and call him a sick fraud; I'd spit in his face and say, like Em had, *Why don't you just hurry up and die?*

I parked the Intrepid, hurried into Sparky's and checked every face in the bar. It was the usual crowd, and no Spencer. The patrons sat at tables eating two-for-a-buck tacos, or they ate tacos and played shuffleboard, cribbage, pinochle, video poker, pool, or they ate tacos, watched the big screen and swapped lies.

Skim was sitting at the end of the bar on his favorite stool. He saw me and nodded.

I could tell at a glance that he'd gotten my phone message, and that he hadn't seen Em and was now curious as hell about what was going on. I wasn't in the mood to fill him in.

I walked to the bar, where Billy was already tapping out a porter for me. Sparky was in the kitchen, singing along with Waylon Jennings on the juke. Billy sat the beer down and said, "Look what the cat drug in."

I pushed away the glass and asked if an old man with a bad cough had been in.

"Don't believe so." He eyed me. Like many old bartenders, his sixth sense had been honed by a million stories, and it was telling him something was up, along with my refusal of the beer.

I asked him if he could cover for me for the next couple of days. He said no problem. He tapped another beer, took it over to a guy playing shuffleboard, then he sauntered over to Skim and began bullshitting with him.

I sat on a stool and stared straight ahead at the glass shelf behind the bar where the booze was lined up. I had to tell Sparky that Em wasn't coming in. She'd betrayed his blessing, just as Beth said she had. Sparky's kitchen would have been so damned good for her. I just sat there staring at a gin bottle, listening to "I'm a Ramblin' Man" and the clatter of pool balls, the laughter and cussing and flirting.

Go then. See if you can see. When Beth had said that, I'd just leaned over Justin's little desk and hugged her goodbye. My embrace was awkward, all arms, and hers hung slack at her sides. Her shoulders trembled, and her hairspray smelled like citrus. I left, being extra careful not to bump another desk out of place, and just as I opened the door I heard Beth sob, and it tore at me.

Molly came rushing out of the swinging doors with a platter full of tacos, hustled them over to the cribbage players. She was dressed like a forest elf, with green tights and a pointed hat. They joshed her. She joshed them right back and shook her bracelets at them. Hustling back to the kitchen, she gave me her evil eye—her pierced-eyelid evil eye—and flung her arms out in a silent question: *How come that sister of yours isn't humping these darn tacos?*

I said, "Em's sick tonight. Tomorrow, maybe."

She shook her head and disappeared through the swinging doors.

Sparky came out before the doors had stopped moving; he was dressed in his red Santa suit, a fake beard, black shiny boots and belt, a stocking cap. He yelled out to the crowd, "Ho, ho, ho! Merry syphilis and a clappy new year!" No one paid much attention. He came over and sat beside me.

I said, "You look fucking ridiculous. Have you seen Em around?"

"And bah, humbug, to you, darlin'. Sorry, but it's just me and the one elf."

I told him about her disappearance, that her backpack was gone and no one had seen her around. "I was half hoping she'd be here."

"We surely could've used an extra elf tonight."

I said, "Yeah, sorry about that. The job was exactly what she needed."

He pulled at his beard.

"I've been a bad little boy, Santa."

"Ooo-ee! Santa will forgive you, if it's not too bad. And what would this bad little boy like for Christmas?"

"My sister. And my dog. And my wife."

His black hands folded a white napkin and he hummed along with Willie Nelson, and my white hands just laid there with a blister, a wedding ring and a busted knuckle.

"Little boy, what can Santa do to help?"

"There was an old guy who came in a couple of nights ago—sickly looking, real weak and frail. Wore a red shirt and a pair of leather work boots; he ordered cognac, no ice, talked about his dog dying when he was a kid. His name's Spencer."

He took off his Santa cap and scratched his head. "Sorry, darlin', but that doesn't ring a bell."

"It's funny how right after that old man shows up, Em disappears."

Sparky looked worried. "Maybe you should call the police."

"And tell them what, that some whacko is claiming he's our father?"

"Father?"

"Yeah."

He pulled at his beard again. "Yesterday, when she came into the kitchen about the job, we both got to laughin' and gigglin', and she was givin' me big hugs and kisses, actin' happy as a lark. But there was somethin' else about her that kind of got me to worrin'. She seemed awfully, oh, brittle, you know, like she was a thin plate that any little bump will break apart?"

"She's probably off of her meds again. They help keep her on an even keel."

He cinched his belt up a notch. "Maybe you should call that doctor you've been seein'."

"Yeah, maybe."

"All of us could use a little help sometimes, and for your sister this is lookin' more and more like one of those times."

"I told Beth I was leaving her ... for a while ... to see about things ... to see about Em and things."

His shoulders slumped; he pulled at his beard again. "Oh, darlin', darlin', darlin'."

I felt like running back to the school and pleading with Beth to forgive me. I said, "I've got to work things out in my head."

"Your heart, too?"

I just looked at him. "Can you advance me a hundred?"

He fished his wallet out of the suit and gave me the money.

"Em usually fills me in, you know? She tells me what in the hell's going on, but not this time. She's shutting me out. All I've got to go on is a hunch."

"For a bartender, that's somethin'."

"It's just a shot in the dark." I slid off the stool to leave. "Thanks, Sparky. I'll be out of town for a couple of days. Billy says he can cover."

Sparky nodded, pulled the Santa cap lower on his head, and his dark eyes filled with worry. "You be careful, hear?"

Outside in the parking lot, the Intrepid's starter growled and clicked. The engine didn't start. I turned the key again and got weaker growls and clicks. "Shitfuck!" I wanted to strangle Jimmy.

I grabbed my travel bag, got out and started walking down the foggy highway. The on-coming headlights were faint orbs that grew brighter as they approached, and then after they whooshed past they became red taillights that vanished in the soup. I walked to the school. The lights were off in Classroom 8, and Wally's Tahoe was gone. Maybe he'd given Beth a lift home. *Go then. See if you can see.* The fog seemed to fill my head. I walked up the bluff to the Good 'Nough Inn. Old Blue was still parked outside. I opened the door of the cab, threw the travel bag onto the seat. Behind the seat, Myrtle clucked a warning to stay clear of her nest. I could hear faint peeps; her chicks had hatched.

Inside the inn, booming out from the kitchen, an opera greeted me, a woman's high, wavering voice. It sounded like a radio. The second thing I noticed was the goldfish, floating belly-up against the glass wall of the aquarium. Goddamn. I walked over. It wasn't moving. I poked its whitish belly, submerging it, and it bobbed right back up, as dead as ever. Its belly looked like a marshmallow. I'd accidentally dumped in too much food and the fish had gorged itself to death. I was beginning to feel like the fish, as if Spencer and Em had dumped a load into my little world, and I had gobbled it up and now I couldn't crap it out fast enough. I got the net, scooped out the fish, and took it to the toilet and flushed it down.

In the kitchen, an old record player was spinning, belting out the opera, something in Italian, I guessed. The record had bad scratches, but Ernst, Denis and Robert didn't seem to notice. When I entered, they all turned their heads and stared at me. They looked uncomfortably awestruck, slow-eyed and -witted, their movements sluggish, as if begrudging my interruption of their musical interlude. Denis stood over a pan of oysters sizzling in olive oil, and savory smells filled the air.

I said to him, "The fish is dead."

He lifted a spatula from the pan. "Irony?"

"What?" Ernst said.

Denis flipped an oyster. "The fish."

"The fish," Robert repeated, as if it were obvious.

"Who?" Ernst asked.

"That's the fish's name: Irony."

I said, "Oh."

"Dead, you say?"

"It ate too much. I'm sorry. I flushed it."

"The loss of any life diminishes me."

"A tragedy."

"A fish story."

"There's more fish in the sea."

"That's a fine kettle of fish."

"I'm sorry. I'll get you a new one. I owe you, Denis. I gave it too much food."

Robert said, "Too much of a good thing isn't good."

Ernst said, "Where's the panties? Let's all have a look at them."

I grinned.

Ernst frowned.

Denis shrugged. "How're you doing, Eddy, the fallen-roof man? Ha-ha!"

I said, "Ha-ha."

"The sins of fallen men are purged with Purgatorio!" Denis poured a glass of wine and handed it to me. I set it down on the counter.

Ernst eyed me sideways and cradled a bottle of his newly christened Purgatorio like a baby in his arms. As drunk as he was, he knew something was up. He was leery.

Robert's eyes were as red as the wine. He leaned close to me. "My goodness, the Band-Aid? It's gone!" He rushed off to get another one.

Denis laid a baguette on the table, cut it down the middle, splayed the halves face-up and began to layer them with mayonnaise.

Robert came back, waving two new Band-Aids.

Ernst was now studying the makeshift label that he'd taped onto the bottle of wine. "Are they're too fucking small?"

"What?"

"The cherub wings."

"They need more feathers."

"Just bigger ones, like eagle feathers."

"Fish feathers."

"Horsefeathers."

Trout Kill

Robert peeled the strips off the Band-Aids and stuck one, then the other on my neck. "Eddy, there's sand in your ear!"

"Sand?"

"What sand?"

Denis laid fried oysters onto the halved baguette, added slices of cheese, herbs and mushrooms. His pudgy hands moved sure and quick and his belly jiggled. "Would you please fetch the flame, Love."

Robert got a butane torch sitting on the counter, lit it, adjusted the hissing flame to a sharp blue point, then began sweeping it back and forth over the sandwiches. The cheese bubbled and began to turn brown. Robert turned off the torch. Denis cut the baguette halves into segments, each with its own oyster. He gave me one. It was hot and delicious. We stood there and ate till the sandwiches were gone, lips smacking, moaning our pleasures.

Ernst said, "Where'd the sand come from, huh?"

"The fucking beach."

Denis went to the refrigerator, got out a big silver tray with three goblets, each filled with fancy ice-cream sundaes with a cherry on top.

"You've outdone yourself," Robert said, stroking Denis on his arm, bumping his hip into Denis' hip.

Denis said, "The richest Tahitian vanilla bean ice cream, dappled with twenty-three-karat gold leaf, drizzled with Amedi Poceleana, the world's best chocolate. A smattering of candied fruits, and so forth and so on. And the *coup de grace*, a smattering of Grand Passion Caviar."

The sundaes were piled high in the goblets and looked sculpted, like yardangs.

I said, "You can eat gold?"

Denis and Robert laughed, as if eating gold were something they did every day. Denis said, "We're celebrating the Inn's grand opening in grand style. Ha-ha!"

I ate mine straight down, and it was sickening sweet. The cold numbed the back of my throat, gave me a headache. Things swirled. It got hard to breathe, and I thought *I'm going belly-up.*

Ernst turned his big head toward me. It lumbered from side to side, like he was sniffing the wind for a human scent. His feet were splayed outward, for balance.

I said, "They sent Jimmy the wrong damned radiator, and his loaner just died on me. I need to get somewhere tonight."

Ernst said, "Where the hell to?"

I ripped the Band-Aids off. "Milepost 198."

Chapter 20

Ernst, iron-faced, one hand rigid on the floor shift, the other clamped on the steering wheel, drove Old Blue down the fog-shrouded hill from the inn. He was so mad at me he'd forgotten how drunk he was. We passed by the elementary school, which was hard to see through the murk, then came to the coast highway and turned onto it, heading north. Behind the seat, Myrtle clucked real soft ... and then came a cheeping chorus of soft peeps. I tried to count the different sounding peeps—impossible, like counting notes in a song.

Ernst said, "Don't fucking tell me. It's your own damned business. I don't want to know."

Heading over the Tyee Bridge, tires droning over the steel grates, Ernst didn't speed up. Always before, he had. Always before, he'd remembered that the bridge made my spine go slack, bowels loosen, chest tighten. Maybe he was hoping Uncle Silas would leap up from the river and snatch me from the cab, a lunker gulping a mayfly. I couldn't see the river below, and through the thick fog Blue's one headlight could barely see the iron girders and the white lines ahead. The bridge, I knew, was at milepost 228, so Spencer's place was thirty miles farther north.

At the end of the bridge I breathed easier. The fog became a chowder that obscured the mileposts.

Ernst was doing me a blind favor. He didn't know what Spencer'd done, or that he was driving me to Spencer's place on the vague hunch Em might be there, or so I was telling myself. And he didn't know I'd thrown the panties out the window, and that I'd gone to see Beth and told her I needed to go away for a while. *Isolated myself from, become disengaged and detached from, to go and see.* Telling him all that, it seemed, would dilute what remained of my clarity of purpose.

I said, trying to break the icy silence, "Did you count them?"

Ernst just drove and stared ahead into the fog.

"I'm guessing, oh, maybe five."

A halo of white light approached from behind, followed us close for about a mile, then passed in a rush on a straightaway; its taillights vanished in the fog. The chicks kept peeping. I turned around in the seat and reached back into the nest.

"What the hell're you doing?"

"There were five eggs."

"So?"

"I want to count how many hatched."

"You'll fuck up the nest."

"There should be five chicks."

"There's just four, damn it."

He meant the cold egg hadn't hatched, and that he was a farmer, and farmers knew a dead egg from a live one, and who the fuck was a part-time bartender to question that. I slid my hand underneath Myrtle and into her nest. It was warm there, between her smooth feathers and the hay, in with the downy chicks. Myrtle clucked and fussed and beaked my hand, again, sharply. I tried to count the chicks, but they were an elusive, feathery cloud. "Five. There's definitely five." I grabbed one, pulled it out from the nest and cupped it between my hands in my lap.

"Trout! Goddamn it!"

I stroked the chick's bony breast and it settled right down, its heart beating against my thumb. I said, "This is the one."

"One what?"

"The one you said was dead."

"Bullshit."

"No, it is."

"Put the damned thing back in the nest right now." Ernst scowled; his big fingers choked the wheel. He flipped the wipers on to clear the beaded moisture off the windshield; they swished halfway up and stuck. He slapped the wheel so hard the truck shimmied.

He'd been this angry the summer before, too. We were butchering Sally, a heifer, out behind his barn. Her skinned carcass hung from a beam, and her guts were heaped on a sheet of black plastic. We were smoking joints; I tossed the butt of mine away, toward the hen house against the barn. A high fence and tin roof enclosed the hen house, to keep out the coyotes, raccoons, skunks, hawks, possums and stray dogs. We'd just cut away a hind quarter, our arms bloody to our elbows, when Ernst said he smelled smoke—not weed smoke. Thick yellow curls were rising from the dry hay where I'd tossed the butt. Flames shot up. He cussed and ran around the corner of the barn for the garden hose while I tried to stomp the fire out. The embers just scattered. By the time Ernst hosed down the flames, they'd scorched the side of the barn. The hens were clucking mad and thrashing their clipped wings against the wire. For about a week afterwards, they never laid a single egg.

I slipped the chick back in the nest, and Myrtle pecked my hand—again. I sucked the wounds, got the iron taste of blood and told myself *She's a good, good mother, fierce with her love.*

Ernst said, "How's it taste, Rat Dick, your own damned blood? What the hell's wrong with you?"

"There're definitely five chicks."

"Fuck you."

"Definitely." I got the weed out of the glove box and rolled one. The match flared.

Ernst snatched the smoking joint out of my mouth, took a long drag and then blew the cab full of smoke. "Like I said, I don't want to fucking know any of it. I'll just drive. I'll just be your fucking toady chauffeur."

I stared into the fog and forgot about the mileposts. Blue labored up a hill, engine groaning, and Ernst shifted to a lower gear; then we headed down the other side, gaining speed—but impossible to know exactly how fast, with the busted speedometer. We were flying blind through soup.

I said, "Something happened when I was fifteen."

Ernst peered ahead, trying to see the white lines and hold back his anger.

"And when Em was eighteen."

Ernst leaned forward till his face was over the steering wheel and close to the windshield.

"And one day when Uncle Silas came home from the mill, a damn-hot evening, when the heat pours into you. Em was in her swimsuit, cut-offs for me. Silas said to hop in, that he'd got a watermelon at Olney's. Just three cents a pound, he said. We jumped in the back. He cut us each a big wedge and handed them out the window to us. The melon was ice-cold—funny that I remember that. He took off down Whetstone road, and Em and me sat against the rear of the cab. We ate melon and spit the seeds and ... and talked about what we had to do."

My hands gripped my knees, and my jaw was too tight, hurting, so I took a deep breath, and it helped.

Ernst leaned closer to the windshield. "I can't see shit in this soup."

"Yeah, it's pretty bad."

He grunted.

"We parked underneath a cottonwood tree, and Silas changed out of his work clothes and into his trunks. The river was running low, had the same old smell of dry moss and dead shad. He yelled at her, 'Ain't you gonna first take off your damned shoes, Emmie?' She said she'd cut her foot and didn't want to get sand in the cut, then dove in and swam out. He headed up river to the chute. I was just standing there barefooted on the shore, poking a dead shad, pretending interest. There was a baseball-sized rock, half buried in the sand; I toed it loose.

"He played his old swimming game, his battle against the rapids and, like his arms always did, they got tired, and he flipped over and the current took him downriver, toward the slower water where Em was."

I took the joint from Ernst and puffed on it, rolled the window down and blew the smoke out. Cold air swirled in. "Do you know what the bastard said to me that morning, before he went to work?"

Ernst stared ahead.

"'You love your sister, don't you? Love her more than anything else in this whole world. You'd hate for anything bad to happen, wouldn't you?'"

Ernst almost had his nose pressed against the windshield. "Can't see the goddamn mileposts."

I rolled my window up. "Where Em was, it was about fifteen feet deep. I waved to her, and she waved back. She saw him drifting toward her. She started thrashing around, you know, like she was drowning, and yelled out for help. He heard, and started swimming fast for her. She went under and came up, sputtering, and yelled out, 'Cramp!'

"I kept working that rock with my toes till it lay free in the wet sand.

"He screamed out for her to float on her back ... and she went under again ... and he dove down for her.

"I jumped in and swam out fast. Em was still under, and she'd been down too long, and we hadn't talked about being down that long. The Tyee was bloomed with algae, the water green. I dove, and all I saw was green ... then a flash of orange—his trunks. He'd reached her. She was caught in something ... a sunken tree ... a forking limb. She was limp, her hair floating, and he was pulling at her foot. I panicked, couldn't hold my air, and my vision closed down to a tiny green circle. But, goddamn, Silas was a fucking fish, like he had gills and could've stayed down there all day long. I had to swim up for air and—"

My voice broke. I rolled the window down again and gulped in the fresh air, tossed the joint into the night.

Ernst slowed Blue to a crawl; he steered off the highway and into the shoulder. "You said 198? That's where we're going?"

"Yeah."

We crept along, looking for the next milepost. Ernst said, "The next one's some-damn-where." And then, "I'm still listening."

"Yeah, okay." I rolled the window up again.

Trout Kill

"He hauled Em up by her hair. She looked dead, with blue lips. I grabbed her arm and tried to help pull her ashore, but he snarled, 'Don't touch her. I've got her.' I let go. God-fucking-damn it, I let go of her."

"Easy, easy," Ernst said.

"He pulled her in, laid her down in the sand and fell over her, bent over her .... He clamped his mouth over hers and ...."

"Easy, easy."

"Fuck, fuck, fuck!"

Ernst stared into the fog again.

"... and he breathed into her. And her chest rose once. He kept doing that, and her chest kept rising and falling. He kept saying, 'Emmie! Oh, Emmie!' He kept breathing into her and her chest lifted each time and I was just standing there, my knees jelly, me thinking she was dead. She wasn't supposed to drown. He'd breathe into her, and he'd breathe into her. But then Em's eyes rolled open and she coughed and sputtered and—Fuck! What scared me right then was how her eyes locked onto me, and how calm they were, with no fear in them at all. None."

Ernst pulled Blue up to a milepost and centered it in the headlight. He said, "There's two-seventeen." Then he steered Blue off the shoulder and back onto the highway.

"When she was staring up at me, I remembered the rock. I got it. It was hot from the sun. I stepped behind Silas. He was still over her, his face close to hers, and he was brushing the wet hair from her face, and the sand, and that's when I bashed his head with the rock."

Ernst said, "Jesus-fucking tits."

"He grunted and crumpled and pinned Em with his chest across her chest. She screamed, 'Get him off of me! Get him off of me!' I dropped the rock and ... puked up watermelon, and it just kept coming up and coming up. Em's kicking and screaming and pushing at him. His head was bleeding all over her. I finally grabbed his arm and dragged him off. Em scrambled to her feet and started bawling. His head had a dent. I stood there ... stupid in my own goddamn puke. The next thing I remember was pulling him toward the river, and how his heels left trails in the sand. Em just stood there crying and freaking out. I got him to the river and—fuck!—that's when he groaned. What a shitfuck! I just turned him face down in the water and held his head down till the bubbles stopped."

Ernst looked at me, his face gone slack.

"I floated him out to the deeper water and dove, dragging him down to that tree. Some flood had probably put it there. Em's tennis shoe was caught in the fork. It seemed a good place to put Silas. I wedged him in, and the slow current bent him at the waist ... and it seemed I could've held my breath for-goddamned-ever."

I lit a new joint, took a deep hit, passed it over to Ernst. He shook his head and drove. He steered off the pavement again so he could read another milepost. "Two-oh-two."

For the next four miles we didn't talk, just counted the mileposts. The fog got worse. It was four solid walls and a ceiling. I wondered what Ernst was thinking, his friend a murderer, and if he'd ever thought of killing someone. *Sure*, I figured, *who hasn't?* We came to the corner where I'd hit the doe, where Ernst and me had stood over her underneath the cedar, and where, I hoped, the duff would someday get deep

Trout Kill

enough to cover her bones. I loved her fiercely—if it was love that I felt: a tight chest, a sweet lump I couldn't swallow down, and the sureness she could never love me back.

If I asked him to, Ernst would turn right around and take me back home. I'd walk in the house and BJ and Kate would rush over and give me big hugs. They'd ask me about Em, if I'd found her yet, and about Licker, their old pal who they'd miss terribly. Beth, though, would coolly retreat behind her high stone wall, and I couldn't blame her for that, and I'd try to bust it down.

The fog lifted a bit, enough to read the mileposts. We passed three more, and then came to 198.

"There's got to be a turn-off up ahead, on the right. Keep going."

About a hundred yards farther, we came to a gravel road that disappeared up the hill and into the fog and dark. It was steep, pot-holed, and it switchbacked through dense stands of spruce, scatterings of mossy cedar and white-barked alders. In a grove of spruce, the road forked. Ernst slowed. "Which way?"

To the right, the road crossed a small wooden bridge. To the left, a set of fresh tire tracks in the frosty gravel disappeared around a turn. I pointed left.

Ernst drove on, following the switchbacks. We emerged from the woods and entered a meadow. Then, a short distance farther, we drove out of the fog. The stars were keen, the bright moon a sliver, about a third full, and the hilltop seemed adrift on a cotton sea. Ahead, the road crossed the meadow toward a lone house, about a quarter mile away.

I asked Ernst to pull over and killed the headlight. In

the sudden quiet, the cooling engine pinged. The house was ablaze—every window luminous. The surrounding meadow was frosted white.

I said, "That poem, the one about the doe? You said you'd cut her open and let the fawn see a light."

Ernst nodded.

"The fawn, it didn't get to have a say, did it? I mean, about being born? It knew nothing about … anything. It didn't even know it had a mother."

"No one has a say. We're just born."

"Right. No one. We're all born out of nothing."

He nodded. "Every living thing wants to feel something before it dies, a faint touch, a breeze, even pain. Something from this world, so it'd know it was here. That's why I'd shine a light into that fawn's eyes, and the brighter the better. To make it blink, or maybe turn its head away. Then I'd shove it into the damned river."

I told Ernst what was going on, explained everything I knew about Spencer, lifting each of the heavy truths into place one after another. I said Spencer wasn't my father. That was the heaviest truth. I said Em was crazy to think it so. That was big, too. But, still, I couldn't find a way to tell him what I'd said to Beth, about me having to see if I loved her.

He kept looking up the road at the house and listening to me. And then, "Fuck, Trout. I hope you know what you're doing."

I opened the door and got out. "Wait here. I'll go check it out."

"Don't get shot."

"If he's there, I'll …" I shrugged, shut the door and started jogging up the road, following the tire tracks. The icy gravel crunched underneath my boots. The meadow was big, covering the top of the hill. Nearing the house, I slowed to a walk. From the road, a long graveled driveway led to an outbuilding. A dark car was parked there. I remembered the car that had sped past Ernst and me, just this side of the Tyee Bridge. I didn't get a good look at it, but it must have been Spencer's Ford. He'd probably shadowed me around Milo as I got the loaner from Jimmy, then heading to Sparky's place, my walk from there to the inn, and then leaving there with Ernst.

The house stood just off the road, a few yards north of the driveway. It was a log-built A-frame, and its front face came to a point like a ship's prow and had nine big windows. The roof was cedar-shaked, with three glowing skylights. The white plume from the chimney drifted north.

The house struck me like a cold fist: It was the Whetstone house—the logs, the prow, and even the hydrangea-lined path leading from the road to the porch.

Goddamn.

Except the Whetstone house had fewer, smaller windows, and no skylights or porch trellis, and no rocking chairs—two of them—sitting on the porch.

I approached along the path. The cold had stunted the hydrangeas, and the roses climbing the trellis were winter-bitten. The rocking chairs looked hand-built from alder limbs. The porch appeared to slant northward, toward the trellis. I climbed the three steps, crossed the porch to the nearest bright window. Inside, the living room was woodsy, with fir floors and rustic furniture. Every light was on, no shadows anywhere. A big stone fireplace with a raised hearth; a staircase leading up to a loft; a colorful painting on a wall. No movement, voices, radio or TV—just the shallow huffs of my breath clouding the glass pane.

I stepped off the porch, went around to the rear of the place. The windows were curtained; bedrooms, I figured, like at the Whetstone house. The one-third moon threw shadows between the humps of the wall logs. Behind the house, a good-sized garden with a tall deer fence. Old corn stalks pointed at the stars. There was a scarecrow. Just beyond the garden, the car and the outbuilding, a tin-roofed structure with a wide sliding door.

I returned to the porch. The front door was built with thick planks and iron hinges. I took a deep breath and knocked. Nothing. I knocked again, louder, my fist a hammer. "Spencer! Goddamn you! Open up!" If he answered, I'd knock him on his ass and ask point-blank about the sick game he was playing, fucking with Em and me. I'd say the same thing Em did: *Why don't you just hurry up and die?*

The house was silent.

I tried the door. It opened inward to a rush of warm air. In the living room, the ceiling was vaulted, cedar-clad. I yelled out his name again. The fireplace snapped. I backed out the door to the porch, leaving the door open, retreated to the path, and then sprinted to the road and down it, toward Old Blue.

Standing beside the flatbed, Ernst was tossing an egg into the air, catching it in his big paw, tossing it up again.

I said, "His car's there, but no one's home."

"Then let's get the hell out of here."

"What's with the egg?"

He tossed it up again. "It didn't hatch, Rat Dick. It's dead, like I told you it was." He let it drop and it cracked open between my boots. "There's four chicks, not five."

I shook my head. "Okay, but you didn't know for sure. It could've lived."

"Why'd you lie?"

"Did you hear what I said about Spencer?"

"This is a wild fucking goose chase. What are you going to do if you find the old coot, club him with a rock, too?"

"Not a bad idea." I turned away from Ernst, stepped to the truck and got my travel bag out from behind the seat. "I'm staying here. Thanks for the ride."

"What the fuck for? You said he's not here, and Em's not either."

"I'm going to settle things, once and for all."

Ernst threw his hands up. "You're the one who's crazy."

I turned and started walking up the road.

Ernst got in the flatbed, started it and pulled it up beside me. I kept walking. He leaned across the seat and opened the door on my side. "Get in, damn it."

I did. He drove up the road to the house. I kept watching the windows and the doorway for Spencer to appear, but the only thing moving was the chimney smoke. Ernst eyed the place, wary. "Shit," he said, "it looks like your old Oak Creek place." He parked by the path. "That's a clue, don't you think, about the father thing."

"No, I don't think."

"This cool reception is no way for a father to greet his long-lost son."

"Fuck you."

I climbed out, and then Ernst got out and came around to my side. Our moon shadows stretched side-by-side across the gravel, westward. He half-grinned, and for a moment I thought he might hog-tie me, toss me on the flatbed and take me back to Milo. He said, "How are you going to know if he's crazy or not? It's a hard thing to prove. It's quantum, like love is. Might be a particle, might be a wave."

It seemed obvious to me. I'd just look him straight in the eye until he blinked and then I'd know he wasn't my father. No one can hide a lie about blood that big. I said, "I'll just know."

"Rat Dick, this might not be your brightest idea."

"I don't love Beth anymore ... I think."

He got a puzzled, worried look. "Where the hell did that come from?"

"I need to figure things out. Us. I need to figure us out."

"Here?"

"Yeah, why not?"

"I thought this was about a crazy man."

"It is."

"Shit, this is quantum."

"Maybe worse."

"You don't love Beth? Exactly when did you figure out this little nugget? Jesus tits! You keep saying you don't know what the hell love is, and now you're saying you're 'out of it.'"

"I'm the crazy one."

"No shit." He swept his arms out wide and turned in a circle. "Hell, Eddy, this isn't the place to figure anything out."

He was sober now, calling me Eddy, wondering what was going on, reminding me how love had always dodged the weak-assed arrows from our weak-assed bows, trying to bring it down to earth, trying to understand it, but those arrows had missed by miles. We'd never come close to winging love. And, I figured, he had his own doubts about loving Maggie. He'd never said so directly, which made me suspect so all the more. I said, "I've got to try again, and I'm here now, so this is the place."

His shoulders slumped. "Christ. Does Beth even know you're here, or what you're up to?"

"She doesn't know I'm here. I told her I had to go away for a while."

"Damn it. Then Maggie will know about it, soon enough."

"Probably."

"Hell, then I'd better stick around for a while—at least for tonight. Alone and on your own, you'll fuck this up, whatever it is you're trying to do."

"No."

He looked hard at me.

"You had parents. They loved you. Maggie loves you. That makes you different from me. Maybe that's why the two of us can't figure out love."

He looked hurt, and he was. I was telling him there were times when a friend couldn't help. But he never said another word about it, just shrugged and stepped over and hugged me. It surprised the hell out of me; he'd never done that before. I stood there, with his farmer's arms squeezing me, his warm shirt pressing against my cheek. He said, "When you're ready to come home, call me."

"Yeah, okay, thanks."

"The castle needs you."

"Right. And don't tell Beth where I'm at."

He released me, then stepped away and over to the truck, where he reached behind the seat and pulled out two bottles of wine. "Here," he said, handing them to me, "you're in purgatorio now."

Paul Dage

I nodded thanks, slipped them in my bag.

He climbed back behind the wheel, turned Old Blue around, drove down the hill through the frosty meadow and disappeared into the wall of fog.

Chapter 21

The living room so nearly matched the Whetstone house that it could have sprung from the same blueprint. Broad fir planks spanned the floor; the walls were stout spruce logs, honey-colored, with knobby branch collars and adz scars. The chinking between the logs was white, not gray.

I stood just inside the front door, where I'd dropped my bag beside the hall tree, fashioned with hand-planed wood and dovetailed joints.

The night of the accident, and again when he'd come into Sparky's place, Spencer had struck me as a friendly guy. He had trolled his congeniality like a lure, tempting me to bite. For me, he was just another customer, though one who'd lent me his gun. But Em had swallowed his lure: She wanted and needed to believe he was "dad," and because she did she'd gotten pissed—maybe at herself as much as him—and told him he could do her a "big favor and die."

It occurred to me I didn't know Spencer's last name or, for that matter, my own father's.

There was an oil painting hanging on the wall beside the hall tree: thin pale arms twisting upward into a yellow sky like weird, sickly branches with busted fingers.

The couch and chairs were woodsy, hand-fashioned out of alder, upholstered with dark brown leather; their dovetails were identical to those of the hall tree. I crossed the room to an empty bookcase, its shelves wiped clean. On the opposite wall, a second bookcase was empty, too.

The wooden staircase led up to a closed loft door.

The kitchen was adjacent to the living room. Black pots and pans hung on the walls; two full cups of cocoa sat on the counter. The cups felt warm. Hanging beside the refrigerator, another oil painting: a young man dressed like a logger and a pregnant woman.

What does a house reveal about a man, the walls and floors and ceilings, the wood- and stonework, the furniture and the paintings? Was Spencer an artist?

I walked past the fireplace to a hallway. There were three doors. The one on the right led to an empty bedroom with no bed or dresser, a clean-swept floor and bare walls. At the Whetstone house, when Em and me were growing up, we'd shared this room. It had bunk beds. Later, it was the bedroom Beth and me used after we got married.

The door across the hallway opened into a bathroom.

At the end of the hall, the third door led into a larger bedroom. The bed was unmade, the covers rumpled. Clothes lay in heaps on the floor; a shirt hung on the chair by the window; on the bedside dresser, empty bottles of ibuprofen and Percocet; the stale smell of old cigarettes. The log walls had a dark yellow cast. On Whetstone Road, Silas had slept in this bedroom. It was where he took Em after she "won" the lunch pail guessing games—to save me, her little brother, from him. Sometimes, though, I won.

Back in the living room, the fireplace spit a bright orange ember that turned slowly black on the hearth. A pair of black-sooted owls—forged andirons—stood inside the firebox.

Trout Kill

They had big, wise eyes. The mantel was a thick slab of polished walnut.

A doll sat there.

She had blond, shoulder-length hair, a round face, a pink mouth and staring green eyes. She wore a red-and-white gingham dress, a dark smudge on the front of it. One foot had a white sock; the other foot was bare and pink. Her arms were outstretched, and her bent legs dangled over the mantel. Her hair was straight, flipped up on the ends. It fell easily over her right ear, but was gathered behind her other ear in a sort of pleat with a crimp.

Goddamn.

I got the barrette from my pocket, took the doll down and sat on the hearth. On my lap, she faced me with her arms reaching out. The heat from the fire warmed my back. I opened the metal clasp and slid it into the crimp—a flawless fit, right down to the tiny rust stains in her hair. I snapped the clasp shut. It looked like a blue butterfly had landed there.

Goddamn, Em.

I swallowed hard. I saw that snowy winter day, Em and me at the loft window, the red bird landing in the white snow, Em smiling with her licorice teeth, Dolly's red hair and a whitefish barrette. Everything I saw was clear and stark: white snow, red feathers, red hair, white barrette.

White fish and blue butterflies?

A crimp that fits?

There was only one way to figure it: Em had had two different dolls, a blond-haired one—the one in my lap—and a redheaded one—the one I remembered.

I stood, put the doll back up on the mantel, pushed her

arms down to her sides and turned her head so she looked away.

I yelled out, "Spencer!"

The empty house never yelled back.

I yelled out, "Em!"

Two leather chairs sat in front of the fireplace. There was a small side table, a telephone and a brandy snifter. A dusky liquid filled the snifter. I picked it up and held it to my nose.

Hints of oak and clovered honey ... cognac ... probably Hennessy.

I threw the glass into the fireplace, shattering it against an owl, and boozy flames roared up the chimney.

Spencer had messed with Em's head—saying he was sorry for what he'd done, saying he understood our hatred. He was dead right about our hating him, but had no idea how much. I wanted him in the flesh, so I could see him bleed.

I crossed the living room and ran up the stairs to the loft, where a small open area overlooked the living room, the dining and kitchen areas. The door into the loft was padlocked. I turned and, three at a time, leapt down the stairs. I went to the front door, threw it open and stepped outside onto the porch. The slap of cold air felt good; my breath shot out white. To the west, the low-lying sea of fog spread as far as the moon glowed. Hidden beneath the fog were the woods and, about a mile away and down the hill from Spencer's porch, the unseen ocean. I ran around the corner of the house and down the driveway, following the tire tracks. Between them, coming from around the corner of the house, there was a faint set of waffled boot prints. I bent down close to examine them. The imprints were small, probably left by a child or a woman. Had

Em been wearing boots? I followed them to the car, a black Ford with the trunk wired shut. A larger set of prints led from the driver's door to the trunk, where they got muddled with the waffle prints. A shovel lay in the gravel. The two sets of prints went from the rear of the car to the corner of the outbuilding where, side-by-side, they headed down the hill and into the meadow.

I swung the driver's door open. The dome light didn't work, and the interior felt warmer than the chill night air. Warm cocoa, warm car. The keys were in it. A plastic bottle of Percocet, empty, lay on the seat.

I walked around to the trunk, twisted the wire free and opened the lid. A dark shape lay inside, wrapped in a blanket. For an iced moment, I thought it was Em. From underneath the blanket, a black paw was sticking out, motionless. I lifted the blanket. It was Licker, curled up as if asleep.

Goddamn you, Spencer!

I grabbed the shovel off the gravel and swung it at the rear window like a Louisville Slugger. The glass caved, crystallized. I swung it again, and again, busting every window. I stood there trembling. What kind of man steals another man's dead or dying dog? I threw the shovel down, stepped through the sliding door and fumbled on the wall for a light switch.

It was a woodworker's shop, with shavings strewn across a dirt floor, with muted woodsy scents, especially the sweeter tones of cedar. There was a table saw and lathe and planer, a drill press and sander. Work benches. Coffee cans filled with nails and screws, bolts and nuts and washers. A pair of worn overalls hanging on a nail. Harness buckles and wood chisels. A roto-tiller, the tines caked with dried mud.

Spencer was a crafty man, handy with the tools, a front-door maker, a hall tree maker, a couch and chair maker. He measured and remeasured, sawed and pounded the wood he loved. When he'd lent me the .45—another tool?—I took a shot at what I loved and missed.

I returned to the car, got behind the wheel and started the engine. The heater gushed warm air and the radio blared a Christmas song. I shut the music off. Christmas was impossible, a misty illusion. Through the windshield, the moon was splintered. I pulled the car into the workshop and parked it between a workbench and the table saw. I got out and wired the trunk shut. Come morning, Licker would be frozen. I left the workshop and slid the door shut.

Now, there was no thought of going home.

Where the car had been, a cap lay on the ground. I hadn't seen it before. It was beat up, the brim worn. I pounded it against my knee and it took the shape of Spencer's head. In no hurry, I walked up the driveway. The stars seemed brighter than before, sharp gleaming points against the black sky, like the embers from a wigwam burner. I tried on the hat. It fit, perfectly.

I hung the cap on the hall tree, and then went looking through the hand-built, finely mitered cupboards for the Hennessy.

Chapter 22

What woke me up from the depths of a dreamless sleep was a loud woodpecker thunking on the front door.

Thunk, thunk, thunk!

I was lying in the leather chair, a recliner, no blanket or pillow. Both the fireplace and my feet were cold. Last night, I'd found the Hennessy and drunk it straight, all the while pacing back and forth through the house, all the while wondering *what the hell do I do now?* Call Ernst to come and get me? Call Dr. Lund and ask where Em might be? Go home and beg Beth to … what? Call the cops and tell them Spencer was a dognapper?

The empty cognac bottle lay on the floor, and the morning light speared through the skylights and into my skull.

And what about Em? She was in a ragged state and liable to hurt herself. This time it'd be pills, I figured, rather than a knife. She'd probably gone back to the Big City and was camping underneath another bridge. I'd find her. I'd make her see Dr. Lund and we'd all three have a sit-down and get Em thinking straight, find her a job and help her past her morbid thing with Vaughn.

Thunk, thunk, thunk!

And then: "Mr. Gatz, Bucky's really hungry!"

It sounded like a kid. The morning was gray, my head was killing me and the kid was yelling at the wrong house.

"Mr. Gatz, you home yet!"

I roused myself, planted my stocking feet on the floor and sat up, groggy.

At the window beside the door, the boy's face appeared. He was eight or nine years old, I guessed, and wearing earmuffs. He pressed his face against the glass, fogging it, looking toward the kitchen. He didn't see me. Then he disappeared from the window and, a moment later, the door inched open. He stuck his head into the room, yelled, "Bucky's really, really hungry!" He cocked his head sideways, lifted one muff off an ear and seemed to listen harder. He eased the door fully open, stepped into the living room and shut the door. He glanced down the hall toward the bedrooms, then tiptoed to the landing at the foot of the stairs. He grabbed the newel post, stared up the stairs toward the loft, and then began climbing the stairs.

Goddamn.

I stood—too quick—and the fog in my head began to spin. I staggered, grabbed the mantel to brace myself.

The kid whirled around and spotted me. His eyes got wide, then narrowed with suspicion. He leapt down to the landing and began backing away toward the door, ready to turn and bolt. He was tall and whip-skinny, wearing blue jeans and a brown corduroy coat. The muffs stood out on his head like halved cauliflowers.

He said, "You ain't Mr. Gatz."

"You're in the wrong house, kid."

"Huh?" He slipped the muffs off and hung them around his neck. "Huh?"

I waved at the door. "Go on home."

"But it's milk time."

"Gatz doesn't live here."

Trout Kill

"Huh?" He looked dumbfounded. "He does too! That's his hat right there!" He pointed at the cap—Spencer's—that I'd hung on the hall tree the night before.

"Do you mean Spencer?"

"Uh-huh."

"Spencer Gatz?"

"Uh-huh."

"Well, he's not here."

He glanced down the hall. "Maybe he's resting up. He's been resting up a lot."

"He's not here. Go on home."

The kid looked disappointed. "Shoot. When's he gonna be back?"

"How the hell should I know?"

"But it's almost Christmas. He's gotta be here."

I scratched my head, yawned, rubbed my eyes. The damned kid was grilling me. I had to come up with a story. If he told his parents about me—a grouchy stranger in Spencer's house—they might come around and start asking sticky questions. "Look, kid, I'm Spencer's friend, okay?"

He smiled—a flat wrinkle. "Oh. How come I ain't seen you around before?"

I had to piss bad and needed coffee—gallons of Denis' hand-ground Guatemalan—to wash out the cobwebs and help me figure out what to do next. I wanted to build a rip-snorting fire and felt ravenous, the fumes of that oyster sandwich near gone. But, first, the kid had to go. "I've got a lot of important work to do. Go on home, kid."

"But what about Bucky?"

"He's not here either."

"He is so!" He ran to the door, threw it open and pointed. "He's right over there." He ran outside and, a moment later, flashed past the porch window.

"Shit!" I went to the door.

Outside, there was no wind and the fog hadn't budged. The hilltop was still an island, and the rocking chairs sat motionless.

The kid was standing by the rose trellis at the end of the porch. A blacktail fawn was there, a rope around its neck, nibbling on the roses. The fawn had dun-colored hide, spindly legs, tall ears and saucer eyes.

I said, "I'll be goddamned."

The kid untied the rope from the trellis. "Grandmom says you shouldn't cuss about stuff."

"So, this is Bucky?"

"Uh-huh. I've got to feed him, otherwise he might get really sick like his brother got and, and … you know …?"

The fawn was thin and looked like it needed a good meal. "Yeah, go ahead and feed him."

The kid sprinted toward me down the length of the porch and disappeared into the house. The fawn kept nibbling.

I went inside and over to the landing. A counter separated the kitchen from the dining table; two paintings hung on the walls, one by the table and the other, which I'd noticed earlier, was in the kitchen. The kid had gotten a pan down from a wall rack and set it on the stove. He jerked open the refrigerator, grabbed a carton of milk, opened it and poured some in the pan. "Ain't it too close to Christmas for you to do work? Ain't it supposed to be vacation, like from school?"

"It's a thinking kind of work, and that's the hardest kind."

"But thinking ain't work."

"Kid, you need to hurry up and——"

He stuck his finger in the pan of milk. "But the milk's gotta get mukewarm 'cause Bucky likes it that way."

I muttered and headed for the bathroom; it was different from the Whetstone house, with a shower instead of a bathtub. I pissed. After I flushed, the toilet ran. I let it.

Back in the kitchen, the kid was dunking his finger into the milk again. "Just a sec ... it's almost mukewarm."

"Luke."

He licked his finger, frowned, then ran into the bathroom, where I heard him jiggling the toilet handle. He sprinted back to the kitchen and checked the milk again. "It's almost warm enough. Bucky likes it warm like his mom's milk is ... was."

"What's your name, kid?"

"Raymond G. Samples the Third." He wiped his running nose with the sleeve of his coat.

"You live around here?"

He nodded vaguely. "Uh-huh."

"You're Mr. Gatz's neighbor?"

He looked at me like I had a nut loose. "Uh-huh."

I walked over to him and stuck my hand out, acting friendly. The kid might know something worth knowing about Spencer. "It's nice to meet you, Raymond. I'm Eddy."

We shook. His grip was strong. His blue eyes were as round as the fawn's. He said, sounding rote, "It's a pleasure to make your acquaintance, Eddy."

Someone had taught the kid manners.

He turned back to the stove and checked the milk again. "Are you and Mr. Gatz real good friends?"

"Let's call him Spencer, okay?"

"Okay. When's he coming home?"

"I couldn't say."

"The last time he was at the hospital it was for a long time, but maybe this time it won't be so long."

"Oh? Sick, is he?"

"I hope he gets better real soon."

The hospital didn't make sense. Spencer had lured me to his home; his car was here, my dead dog in the trunk. I went to the fireplace, got the doll off the mantel, slipped it into my jacket and then walked to the open counter between the kitchen and the dining room. There was an oak dining table and four sturdy chairs. A plastic baby bottle stood on the counter, the nipple off. Raymond brought the warm milk to the counter, filled the bottle and screwed the nipple on. He took the bottle, tipped it upside down over his wrist and squeezed a few drops out. He nodded, licked off his wrist.

I said, "Who showed you how to do that?"

"Do what?"

"The wrist thing."

"Grandmom did." He frowned. "I have to live with her now."

"Oh?"

"Uh-huh." He clutched the bottle.

"Raymond, come here a sec, would you? I want to show you something."

Curious, he came around the counter and looked up at me. I pulled the doll out. "You know anything about this?"

He looked away and began drilling the toe of his sneaker into the floor. "I didn't mean to."

Trout Kill

"Tell me about the doll, okay?"

He turned and bolted to the front door, threw it open, dashed outside and sprinted across the porch.

"Goddamn it."

I left the doll on the counter and followed him outside. At the rose trellis, he had untied the fawn and was leading it toward the porch steps. He sat on the bottom step, his back to me, facing the fawn. He had a cowlick in his brown hair, and his muffless ears were already turning red in the biting chill. He held the bottle out. Bucky seized the nipple between his black lips and began to suckle.

Raymond said, "Neato! Wizard!"

Something warm and sharp tore at me. I tried to blink it back, but it resisted. The boy loved the fawn. The fawn trusted him. The hydrangeas and the road were frosted white. The meadow was white. The sky was gray and heavy, and the sea of fog had drifted higher up the hill. The island was smaller now.

Raymond held the bottle up and Bucky suckled it.

"Wizard!"

A small breeze stirred, tipping the two rocking chairs forward, then back.

Raymond set the empty bottle down. The fawn nosed his coat pocket; the kid reached in and pulled out an apple, then a jackknife from his trouser pocket. Bucky's tail twitched. Raymond quartered the apple and held out a slice of it. The fawn seized it; his lower jaw worked sideways, the apple crunching.

I said, "Bucky: That's a damn good name."

Raymond puffed out his chest a bit. "I got to name him. Spencer said a man-deer is a buck. Buck and Bucky, get it?"

241

"Clever."

"I helped to catch him."

"Oh? Where'd you catch him at?"

He sleeved his nose again. "Bucky's mom, she's .... She had a accident."

"Down on the highway?" I pointed down the foggy hill, southerly, in the direction I'd hit the doe.

He nodded. "How'd you know that?"

"Roads and deer don't get along sometimes. And Spencer took you there?"

"Uh-huh. It was maybe three days ago, something like that. Bucky had a brother. He's, uh ...."

The kid couldn't say the word *dead*. His sensitivities had been tactfully informed. "And you found Bucky's brother by the road, too?"

He twisted around on the steps and looked up at me. "How'd you know about that?"

"Like I said, me and Spencer are friends."

"Oh, yeah."

The way I figured it, sometime after I'd met Spencer on the highway that night, he'd taken Raymond to the site of the accident to help find the twin fawns. Spencer knew they wouldn't live long. They'd found one of them—Bucky—still alive; the coyotes hadn't gotten him. Spencer took Bucky to his home. Then, shortly afterwards, Spencer returned for the dead fawn. He took it—his lure—into Milo, dropped it on my porch, left the note and, for a second lure, he stole Licker.

Raymond fed the fawn another apple slice.

I stepped off the porch, walked along the path between the stunted hydrangeas. At the road, I turned and faced the house.

Trout Kill

At the porch, Raymond was feeding Bucky the remainder of the apple, holding it high. Bucky reared up on his hind legs and snatched it from Raymond's hand. The kid ran to the road and stood at my side. The fawn followed, sniffing at his pocket, the rope trailing behind. Raymond grabbed the rope. "Grandmom said I'm supposed to make darn sure Bucky gets his milk two times every day. And Spencer said he might run off someday, you know, to the forest."

I studied the house, searching for the defects that I knew how to fix. It seemed older, more run-down than it had the night before. The salt air had bubbled loose the paint on the window frames, and the weed-filled flowerboxes were rotting. The porch sagged. Birds, probably flickers, had bored holes in the eaves. Thick scabs of moss had blighted the cedar shakes, and several of the shakes were gone, blown away by Pacific storms. A leak, it seemed, was just another storm down the road. I said, thinking aloud, eyeing the roof and estimating the square footage, "It'd take about twenty-five squares, give or take." I pointed. "See there, where the shingles are blown off?"

Raymond looked up at the roof. "What squares?"

"And about twenty-five rolls of thirty-pound felt."

"Felt what?"

"And jacks for the pipes."

"Who's Jack?"

I looked at him. "What do you know about the doll?"

He frowned, tugged on the rope and drew Bucky closer, scratched the fawn behind its ears. "I found it. It was in a old box. I was supposed to take all the boxes out and burn 'em. You know, in the garden. Spencer was cleaning the house real good. He said it was important. The boxes had old stuff in 'em. There was lots of old junk up in the loft." He glanced up at the loft window; it reflected the sky. "I carried lots of books up there too. He paid me five whole dollars. But I didn't want to burn the doll. You know? I almost took it to the garden but then I didn't. So I left it in the box."

"And Spencer found it there?"

"Uh-huh."

"What'd he say?"

"He said he should be mad at me."

"But he wasn't, was he?"

He nodded, looked at me like I might know a thing or two. "He said he'd forgot all about the doll."

"Where's your house at, Raymond?"

He waved toward the southwest. I walked over to that corner of the house. Raymond towed the fawn along. From the driveway by the corner of the house, a well-worn path meandered down the hill and through the meadow. I hadn't noticed it the night before. It disappeared into a stand of bare-limbed alders. Beyond the alders, about a half-mile away, a thread of smoke lazed into the sky. I said, "That smoke yours?"

"Uh-huh. Grandmom's baking Christmas stuff. You know, cookies and stuff."

"What about your parents?"

He twisted his sneaker into the ground—what I might have done, even now, even being forty-seven years old—if someone had asked me that same question. I picked up a piece of gravel and heaved it as far as I could down the hill toward the alders. "How long you lived with your grandmom?"

Raymond got a rock and chucked it. "Since last summer I have."

Trout Kill

I threw another rock. "Just the two of you together?"

Raymond threw another. "Uh-huh."

I turned, stepped off the driveway and knelt at the corner of the house. The foundation was rough fieldstones and mortar. There were finger-wide cracks in the mortar, a crumbling mix of too much sand and too little cement. The corner stones had worked loose, and the entire foundation was eroding. Spencer knew wood, but not rock. I said, "A guy'd have to jack up the house and bust out the old foundation; he'd have to dig a new footing and use re-bar."

Raymond said, "Who the heck's Jack?"

"This jack, he lifts heavy things."

"Oh."

"And shims. A guy can never have enough shims."

"What's shims?"

"They tighten loose things up."

"Oh."

"Your grandmom? Is she good friends with Spencer?"

Raymond's face lit up. "Uh-huh. She brings him lots of chicken soup. They take real long naps. They sit on the porch and rock and talk about stuff and they used to walk down to the ocean and show me the star fish and stuff." He frowned. "Then he got sicker so he can't hardly walk anymore."

I scraped the mortar between two stones with my thumbnail. It was chalky. I pried out a loose stone. *Chicken soup and long naps.* I stood, turned and threw the stone as far as I could down the hill.

Raymond watched it bounce down the slope of the meadow.

"And sometimes, even if you have all the right tools, and

even if you know exactly what you have to do, even if you take your sweet time and measure twice and cut once—even then you can still fuck it up."

Raymond pulled Bucky closer. "You talk like Spencer talks."

"Oh? How's that?"

"Sort of mean, sort of nice." He turned to leave. "I got some chores."

"Do me a favor, okay, Raymond? I want you to take something home to your grandmom, okay?"

He shrugged, nodded.

I ran back inside the house, pulled one of Ernst's bottles of wine from my bag, took it outside and handed it to Raymond.

He studied Ernst's hand-drawn cherubs flying around the mountain with their tiny wings; he read the label and his face bent into a question. "Purr-gah-tore-ee-oh?"

"Tell her it's from me, Eddy Trout, Spencer's friend."

"Trout, like the fish?"

"Yeah, like the fish."

He ran down the path and through the meadow, his feet squirrel-quick, his muffs bouncing around his neck, Bucky trotting along side, the rope between them hanging slack. They both disappeared into the alders, toward the rising smoke.

Chapter 23

Spencer's kitchen was like the Whetstone house: the counters and cupboards, the fridge and the stove, the silverware drawer with its forks on the left-hand side, then the spoons and the butter knives, the worn floor in front of the sink. In the fridge, a stack of t-bone steaks, a bowl of chicken soup, the milk, a bag of coffee beans in the door. I got out a steak and the coffee, organic and grown in Guatemala.

Goddamn, Spencer drinks good coffee.

I threw the steak in a hot skillet, set the kettle on to boil and then milled the beans to a black heap. The ground coffee reminded me of Denis' kitchen, of him and Robert dancing the rumba and their loving laughter.

I forked the sizzling steak over, cracked four brown-shelled eggs into the pan. Their yokes were orange-yellow suns. The kettle whistled, reminding me of Beth's morning routine, her slippers shuffling to the stove, getting the fire going, setting the kettle on, making tea in her Jesus mug. She'd let the girls sleep in. When BJ and Kate were little, they sometimes had scary dreams. Beth soothed them. I told them the dream pixie had sprinkled too much dream dust up their noses, making the dreams scary. In all our years together, Beth had never once shared a dream of hers with me. Maybe she never had them.

I poured a stream of hot water over the grounds and it seeped through a paper filter into a white mug.

I ate at the dining table. A window looked north. The fog

had lifted, clearing the near fringe of the woods and, farther north, I could see the coast highway. Beyond a yet farther rise of hills, the white surf divorced the poker-faced ocean from the land. The distant horizon was a blur.

I broke a yolk. It pooled around the steak. I cut a piece. It was marbled and tender, nearly raw in the middle. The meat juices pooled with the yolk. I chewed slowly, savoring. A tear came, swelled, rolled down my cheek and fell to the table. I wolfed the food, stuffing steak and eggs, hardly chewing, washing down the lumps with the coffee.

I got up, stood there trembling. The plate was empty and I was hungry, and the coffee was gone. I got the doll off the counter, walked it over to the fireplace and set it back on the mantel.

Then I went outside to the road. A hawk flew past, low, its shadow a blur on the frosty meadow. I walked down the road and into the woods; it was coldest in the shadows, warmer where the sun slanted through the trees. Walking felt good. At the highway, I stood on the shoulder and watched the traffic go by. I'd hitch a ride to the Big City and find Em. Maybe she was underneath another bridge, and maybe I could save her. A car came, northbound, and I stuck my thumb out and it never slowed. *Goddamn.* I turned and started walking back up the road, then cut away into the dank woods and followed a deer trail. It switch-backed and crossed the same shallow creek three times. Wading through the creek, I scared a murder of crows in a tree. They flew off, cawing.

At the house, I took a long nap in the chair by the fire.

Sometime later that afternoon Raymond dropped by again—he just thunked on the door and barged in, slammed the door behind him, ran over to the foot of the stairs and yelled toward the loft, "Mr. Gatz, you up there yet?" He took off the cauliflower muffs and listened for an answer.

I sat up in the chair. "Raymond, what the hell?"

"Ain't Mr. Gatz home from the hospital yet?"

"Spencer, remember?"

"Ain't he ever coming home?"

"Yeah, he'll come home."

"I gotta feed Bucky because he's gotta have milk two times." He dashed into the kitchen and set the milk pan on the stove.

"Okay, but make it quick." I got up and went to the dining table where my dirty breakfast plate sat.

Raymond was dunking his finger into the warming milk. "That's getting to be about *luke*warm." He smiled at me. Then he filled the bottle, screwed the nipple on and dribbled two drops of milk on his wrist. He nodded. "Spencer ain't home yet, but he promised me."

"Oh? What promise?"

"The Undergood ... for Christmas. He said I could have it."

"Is Christmas today?"

He gave me a look.

"What the hell's an *undergood*?"

His look turned to puzzlement. "You know, for making up stories."

"Oh, yeah. Of course. Guess I'm a little sleepy-headed yet, got to clear the cobwebs out." I had no idea what he meant.

"You got spiders?"

"Never mind."

"Uh, I almost forgot. Grandmom said to say thank you."

"Oh, yeah, the wine. Well, that's just great, Raymond. Did she like it?"

"Uh-huh. She liked lots of it. She ain't laughed like that in a long time. She's, uh, gonna bring you a surprise present."

"Oh? Well, that's just perfect."

"I ain't supposed to say what it is, but you're gonna like it." He ran out the door and slammed it shut.

I poured a cup of cold coffee, sipped it, wondered when Raymond's grandmom might show up with her "surprise." Sooner rather than later, I hoped.

I got up from the table, walked over to the stairs. There were fourteen steps, same as the Whetstone house. I climbed to the loft, went to the door and rattled the lock. Inside, I pictured the Whetstone loft, with its one small window, a sleeping cot, a small desk where Em and me, when we were little, kept our crayons and, later, where we'd done our homework. Silas seldom went there.

I went down the stairs, got the notebook out of my travel bag and took it to the kitchen table. Shoved my breakfast plate aside, sat down, opened the notebook and stared out the window. No words came to mind, not a one, as if the Silas stories I'd told to Ernst had drained some stale reservoir of words out of me. I felt muddled, wondered *What in the hell am I doing here?*

I went over to my travel bag, stashed the notebook, then to the fireplace chair where I reclined and stared at the skylights till I drifted off to sleep.

Got up many hours later, went outside and pissed off the porch on a frozen hydrangea. Bucky had shit there, black pellets on the white frost. The morning had broken clear, cold and windless; the bald sun turned the ocean into iron. On the top porch step, the feeding bottle sat empty.

From a distance, coming from somewhere to the southeast, Raymond's frantic cry: "Bucky! Dang it! Stop!"

I hustled to the driveway. At the bottom of the meadow, Bucky was trotting toward the alder woods, the rope trailing. Raymond was in hot pursuit, his frantic cries ringing in the crisp air.

I turned, walked northwest, entered the meadow and made my way down the hill to the margin of the spruce and cedar woods. The sun, rising low behind, threw my shadow long. At the margin, I turned north, sticking close to the woods. The ground was rough, uneven, covered with rotting leaves and needles. Above and to my right, the house stood at the crown of the hill. I shoved my hand into my pants pocket. Beth's panties were there, warmed by my body's heat. It was almost like touching her. I circled the hilltop and, after about half an hour, heading south now, I came to the alder woods. Farther on, I found a dirt path disappearing into the gray-boled trees. Imprinted in the path, Bucky's tracks looked like matched garlic cloves. And beside them, a print of Raymond's tennis shoe.

Coming slowly up the path through the alders, a tiny, gray-haired woman approached. She wore a plaid, long-sleeved shirt, baggy overalls, boots and a floppy yellow hat. A hodge-podge of dried, spattered paint covered her overalls. She had a brown shawl draped around her thin shoulders.

She saw me, smiled and quickened her pace. Her face glowed; she carried something covered with a checkered towel. As she approached, the bells on the flouncing brim of her hat jingled. She stuck out her free hand. "Hello, Eddy. It is a pleasure to make your acquaintance. I'm Doris Henquist, Raymond's grandmother."

I nodded, kept my hands at my side.

Her smile faded; she lowered her hand. Her eyes had the odd coloring of a daffodil just before it blooms: yellow-green, almost reptilian. She said, "I wanted to stop by and thank you for the wine. Thank you. It's quite lovely."

"You're welcome."

"I enjoyed a glass with my dinner last night—well, two glasses." She laughed, and it sounded like the bells tinkling on her hat.

"It's a good wine."

"I know very little about wine, I'm afraid, except for what I like."

"That's all you need to know."

"The label is ... a sort of prototype, I gather."

"Yeah, a work in progress."

"Well, it's simply lovely—the wine, I mean. Did you make it?"

"No. Making good wine takes a good soul."

"Yes, I imagine it does." She looked up the hill toward the house. "Have you seen Raymond this morning?"

"No." It was a lie, a sort of warm-up for those that might follow. Raymond and the fawn were probably nearby, somewhere in the alders.

"If you see him this morning, just shoo him home. He can be a pest, I know. And that darn fawn. He's grown so awfully fond of it. Raymond can be a handful, at times, so full of vinegar. He's such—"

"A boy."

Trout Kill

She smiled again, faintly. "Yes. He's such a *boy*."

"He needs a dog. Dogs make better pets. A dog is a friend for life."

She nodded, as if the advice was friendly and she was considering the possibility of a dog, and like my blunt words had simply bounced off her. She didn't know, it seemed, that Spencer had stolen Licker, so he probably hadn't told her about the dead fawn he'd left on my porch. I said, almost sneering, "I'm Spencer's very good *friend*."

Her eyes tightened and her ruddy face paled. She knew I was lying, as I wanted her to know. She held out the towel-covered thing. "I hope you like rhubarb pie."

I didn't reach for it, and she kept holding it there, suspended between us in her weathered hands, waiting for me to take it. She said, "Spencer is very ill. Very."

I took the pie. The dish was warm. For a moment, the fingers of her empty hands stayed bent from their memory of the dish, and then she snugged the shawl across her breasts. I said, "Thank you."

"The rhubarb is quite tart, so I added extra sugar."

"I like tart."

She nodded. "The rhubarb is from my garden. Last fall, I froze several bags. I'm afraid Spencer's garden is ...." Her voice trailed off.

"Dead."

She blinked. "He planted it last spring, but he never got the chance to tend it." A gray curl fell from beneath her hat. "If you do find the pie a bit tart, try topping it with fresh cream."

She knew things about Spencer, this woman who'd napped with him, strolled with him along the beach and rocked side by side with him on the porch. "Tart is good. I used to eat sour apples when I was a kid."

"Funny that you should mention apples: Spencer won't touch an apple pie."

I knelt down on the path. Bucky's tracks were spaced wide apart, more toe than heel, and set deep in the dirt. He'd been running. Raymond had been running, too, chasing after. The kid loved the fawn the way a boy should, with a wide-open heart that's plain for everyone to see. I looked up at Doris. "Raymond and Bucky went this way." I pointed up the hill toward the house. "Will you join me for some pie? I'll make coffee." I stood and stepped off the path, inviting her to lead the way.

The healthy color had returned to her cheeks. "That's very kind of you. Yes, I'd love to, but I can't stay too long." She glanced down the path, the way she had come, and then her gaze returned and held me steady.

"Where is he? The Glass Point hospital?"

She half-smiled, then looked away and wrapped her hands in the shawl. "I see Raymond has spoken to you." She pulled her shoulders back. "Spencer would like you to wait at his home, perhaps for another day or so, until he's a bit stronger."

"I've waited forty-seven years."

She stiffened. "I know you have, Eddy. Please, he has so much to tell you."

"Where is he?"

She stepped past me and began walking up the path toward the house.

Carrying the pie, I followed her. The sun was fully up and had a thin, luminous halo—a sundog—surrounding it.

Trout Kill

Sunlight slanted through the alders, throwing branchy shadows across the frosty meadow. Doris, who had to be pushing seventy, walked with easy-swinging arms and a gliding stride that made her hat chime like a splashing creek. Her gray hair, I guessed, had once been raven black. In the frost, her boots left small waffle tracks that matched those on the driveway.

She seemed an honest woman, and I liked her, but none of that would stand in my way.

At the top of the meadow, we came to the driveway, where the tire tracks and her own boot prints, still distinct in the frosty gravel, led to the workshop. Crossing the driveway, she seemed not to notice them and went directly to the gate of the garden. We stood there, our breaths shooting through the chicken wire.

The garden was good-sized, about a hundred feet square. There were black rows of moldering tomato vines. The corn lay flattened, with some few stalks still erect, defiant of the winter winds. Rotted heaps of zucchini and squash and pumpkins. Among the rotting tomatoes, a scarecrow stood on a pole, outfitted with a faded red shirt and suspenders, tattered blue jeans and an ancient pair of caulk boots. A tin hat sat on its pillow head.

Just beyond the gate, the ground was charred black where, I guessed, Raymond had burned the junk from the loft. Were it not for Raymond's prudence, Em's doll would have perished in the flames.

Doris was staring at the scarecrow. "Last spring, despite the doctor's advice about avoiding hard labor, he insisted on putting in his garden. They had removed a lung. It was in January. Cancer."

She left the word hanging in the chicken wire, as if I'd see it there and feel something. I twined my fingers into the wire and squeezed hard, crimping it.

"I helped him with the tilling and the planting, but it was entirely too soon after his operation. This garden nearly killed him."

I remembered what Spencer said that night on the highway when he handed me the .45—that things needed taken care of. He'd meant the doe was suffering and need shot, and that I should use his gun to do it. And perhaps he'd been thinking that his garden, too, was suffering. It was Em, though, whose garden was in the worst shape, most needed the thistles yanked out, its soil amended and then replanted with hearty seeds. When Spencer went to the city and spooked her with his claim of fatherhood, she cursed him but hadn't denied his claim. For her, he was a bad seed. Then he found me in Milo and, on the night of the accident, he must have tailed Beth and me out of town. When he came around that corner, what a big surprise we must've been. But he'd played it cool. When he handed me the gun, he was trying to plant another bad seed.

Doris said, "And then Raymond came along and ...." Her half smile faded away. "I'm sorry, Eddy, to be rambling on and on this way."

"You can till this one under, let the dead stuff compost."

"Yes, that would be the best thing to do."

I turned from the gate and walked toward the house. Doris followed.

Raymond came running up the hill from the woods. Bucky pranced along beside him, the rope trailing from his neck. The kid ran full out, arms thrashing, his gawky legs out of kilter.

Trout Kill

As he and the fawn passed by, racing for the house, he yelled, "Yahoo! Pie!"

Doris shouted, "Raymond, wash your hands first."

The kid and the fawn disappeared around the corner of the house.

The feeding bottle sat on the porch steps. The front door was wide open. Bucky, the untied rope hanging from his neck, had wandered over to the trellis and was nibbling rose stems. I went inside the house, while Doris scraped the mud off her boots. Inside, Raymond was standing at the landing, looking up at the loft door.

Doris entered. "Young man, you go look after Bucky. Tie him up, as I've told you a hundred times. Do you want him running off again? Then you can wash your hands."

"But he's supposed to run off, remember?"

"When it's his time, he will. But he's not quite old enough yet."

"But, dang it, how am I supposed to know when he's old enough?"

Doris sighed. "When he's ready, he'll tell you so."

"If he's all the time tied up, how's he supposed to tell me anything?"

Doris shook her head, giving up, and followed me into the kitchen, where I set the pie on the counter. At the sink, Raymond trickled water on his hands and wiped them on his pants. Doris laid her hat on the counter and told Raymond to get three saucers from the cupboard.

He hustled over to the cupboard, got the saucers and set them on the counter. "When do I get to open my Christmas presents?"

"I've told you: this evening after dinner." She got the coffee cups from the cupboard, then stepped to the drawers for the tableware. She got three forks and two spoons, and she didn't even have to glance down: her hands knew where to go.

I put the kettle on to boil, then ground the coffee.

She cleared the table of my breakfast dishes, set the pie on the table and cut it into wedges. She plated one big piece and two smaller ones. "Raymond, please bring the cream."

He ran to the fridge, got the cream and hustled it over to the table. He eyed his piece of pie, poked the filling and licked off his finger.

"Young man!"

I stood at the counter and wished the water would hurry up and boil.

She sat down at the table and stared out the window, toward the ocean. She said, "Raymond, come here this instant."

Raymond frowned, stepped over and stood beside her.

She pointed out the window—a grandmother's imperative. "Look there!"

Bucky was trotting off down the hill toward the woods.

Raymond's eyes got as big as the saucers. "Holy cow!"

She said nothing; her eyes had brimmed up and she wiped them with the hem of her shawl.

Raymond looked longingly at his pie, then in confusion at his grandmother, and then he spun away from the window and ran toward the door. "Bucky ain't ready enough yet!"

I yelled after him, "Raymond, take the bottle. You left it on the porch."

He slammed the door shut behind him. Doris watched

Trout Kill

him sprint down the hill after Bucky, waving the bottle, waving an apple.

I went to the fireplace, threw more wood onto the embers. The wood was pitchy fir. It caught fast and snapping flames roared up the chimney.

At the table, Doris said, "Pence wasn't sure you'd come."

I faced the kitchen and yelled, "I don't know any-damned-body named Pence." I crossed the living room to the front window. In the meadow, Raymond and the fawn were dancing together: Raymond held the bottle high, making Bucky rear up and reach for the nipple, and then Raymond would prance away, teasing and laughing.

The kettle whistled. I returned to the kitchen, filtered the hot water through the coffee grounds, and took two brimming cups to the table. Doris, hands in her lap, hadn't touched her pie. I placed her coffee down, then sat across from her.

She picked up her spoon and stirred with lazy swirls.

I grabbed my fork.

She sipped her coffee.

I sipped mine.

She cut off the tip of her pie and forked it to her mouth. She chewed mindfully—a chef grading her creation. "Still too darn tart." She poured some cream on it.

I poked at my crust. The filling looked like pale jam.

She let out a long sigh, as one who is facing an unpleasant and monumental task, and looked right at me with her yellowish eyes. Her gray hair spread across the shoulders of the brown shawl. "You were born, I believe, the sixteenth of July, 1950."

"No. That's not right. It was July fifteenth." I cut off a big bite and stuffed it into my mouth. The pie was sweet, not tart like I'd been hoping for. I wanted bitterness. And then I shoved in another bite, cramming it in with the first. I chewed loud, lips smacking, and I swallowed loud. "So, you're Spencer's lover."

She laughed soft, blushed, looked out the window. "Come the spring, usually in mid-March, the meadow all around the house bursts with purple lupine. And iris, too. Everywhere you look, it's a lovely purple." She ran her finger along the windowsill. "Years ago, this hilltop was covered with the forest. When Pence—Spencer—moved here, he cut the trees down to build this place." She touched a branch collar on a log in the wall and traced it with her fingertip. "Before, when he was a much younger man, he was a logger, but he seldom, if ever, speaks to me of those years. But he told me once that he owed something back to the forest. I think he'd cut down many trees, and wanted to make amends." She looked out the window again. "Come the spring, usually about the middle of March, when the meadow is bursting with lovely purple, it reminds me that he planted them, the flowers, in the same ground where the trees had once stood."

I held my fork like a pitchfork. "He doesn't owe Em and me one goddamn thing. Nothing. Absolutely nothing."

Her hands stiffened; she folded them into her shawl. "I bought my home when the lupines were blooming. I was looking for a big house in the country, one with a small guesthouse, for when my daughter and her husband and Raymond came for visits. After I moved here, the very first thing I did, even before I had unpacked all my paints and palettes, was clean the guesthouse. Then, because it was springtime and I had the itch,

Trout Kill

I planted a garden, mostly lettuce and other greens. Raymond was just a baby. Those were good days." Her voice faltered. "And then, last summer it all changed, and Raymond came to live with me .... He loves it here, on this hill by the sea."

"What happened to his mother, father?"

She lifted a hand as if to adjust her hat on her head—a hat that was on the counter. "It was a ... car accident." She lowered her hand to the table and it floundered there.

"That's tough on a kid."

"He was riding in the backseat—buckled up, thank God. The nightmares are still plaguing him and—it just now dawned on me—he has not mentioned having a bad dream since Bucky came."

I wished I had my own curative amulet, one I could romp with in the woods.

"When the fawn goes away, as it will soon, do you think a dog might help?"

"Yeah, I think so, and make it a big one like a shepherd or a Lab—not a pissy runt that wears sweaters."

"Spencer is ... making final arrangements."

I leaned forward, my elbows on the table, the fork tight in my fist. "For his dying?"

She nodded twice. She picked at a dried scab of red paint on the thigh of her overalls.

"How'd you meet him?"

"It was in the fall, nearly ten years ago. I was gathering chanterelles in the forest, down on my hands and knees, grubbing about beneath a fir. In November, the chanties are plentiful, and so delicious. It was raining. He was out taking a walk, smoking a cigarette, and he heard the bells on my hat ringing. He said, 'You must be the belle of the woods, I presume.'"

"Charming."

"He ... he fell in love with my hat. It was ... the hat ...." She glanced at the hat and her eyes filled with pain.

"You paint? You're an artist?"

"I am."

The nearest painting was hanging on the wall behind Doris, on the right-hand side of the window. It showed the wrinkled hands of a woman, holding a broken sand dollar. "You painted this?"

She nodded, didn't bother to turn around to look at it. "I could never get her hands just right. Hands are so ... difficult."

She reached inside her shawl and pulled something from a pocket of her overalls. It was a photograph. She placed it on the table and slid it across to me. "Your mother knew her way around a paint brush, too."

A moment ago, the fork in my hand had felt like a weapon. My hand went numb; the fork clattered to the table. *How can you have a mother if you've never had a mother?* My eyes fought to look at her, but I forced them to stare at Doris. The photo was another one of Spencer's whoring lures. "She's not my mother. I don't have one."

She spoke soft. "Her name was Rose. She died young, very young. I have always loved that name: Rose. It's so beautiful and filled with promise."

I banged my fists on the table and shoved up from my chair. Doris jerked her hands back to her lap. The chair toppled back and fell to the floor. I stepped over to the counter and grabbed Doris' hat, a shapeless felt thing, paint-spattered like her overalls, and the hue of an autumn leaf. The bells, tarnished, were clasp to the brim by their crowns. I shook them at her and they rang, tinny. "Didn't you hear me? No mother!"

She flinched. "It's ... it's Rose's hat." She was staring at the photograph.

I threw the hat down on the table. "That's crazy!"

"No ... I mean ... he always thought of it as so, of me ... as her."

Doris' eyes filled with tears. She turned away and stared out the window.

I picked up the photo.

It was an old black and white Kodak, the kind forgotten in an attic shoebox. A young man and woman were hugging, leaning in close for a kiss. She was pregnant, her belly like a watermelon. He was dressed like the scarecrow in the garden, with a patched shirt and rough jeans and caulk boots, with a tin hat set square atop his head. She wore a flower-patterned dress and a floppy hat with brim bells that sparked in the sun.

Doris vaguely resembled the youthful woman in the photo, who appeared to be about twenty. Both women were petite, with thin faces and small noses, but Doris had a sharper chin and more hawk-like eyes, while the younger woman evoked a feline semblance. Doris' hat and the one in the photo looked identical.

Doris said, "Eddy, she is your mother."

I shook my head, denying it, and stepped away from the table, went around the counter to where the oil painting hung in the kitchen, the one I'd noticed when I first entered the house. I held the photo up to it. The two images nearly matched— a logger and a pregnant woman, hugging and about to kiss. In the background, a forested mix of firs and oaks. The years had dulled the photo, but the newer paints glowed: her white dress filled with blue flowers, her long hair carrot-red, and her cat-like eyes. In their two profiles, his eye was bluish-green, the color of the sea, and hers a vivid green, like Em's eyes. *Could she be our mother?* Always before, a rose was just a flower.

In the lower right corner of the painting, the initials DH—Doris Henquist. I said, "You painted this?"

"Yes, a few years ago."

"Why?"

"Spencer …." She faltered.

"He asked you to?"

She sobbed.

I dropped the photo to the floor, grabbed the painting off the wall. It was a parody, a forgery of love. The canvas on the square frame was a taut drum. "He loves Rose, and your shadow of her!"

Doris' face pinched, and the tears fell from the point of her chin.

"You're nothing but a memory of her!"

She groaned, laid her head on her arms and wept.

I ran from the kitchen with the painting and threw it into the fireplace. Red tongues licked at the frame; they had an appetite; they grew and snapped. The doll sat on the mantel, mocking. I punched the stones, cracking open the fresh scab on my knuckle. The frame sagged and twisted out of square, and dark spots appeared on the face of the canvas. His tin hat turned black and her dress burst into flames, and then their reaching lips exploded. The whoosh of heat pushed out past the andirons and stirred the doll's dress.

Doris had gotten up from the table and walked to the landing of the staircase. She had the hat in her hand, bunched and folded so the bells couldn't chime. She braced herself against the newel post, as if gathering her strength, then walked toward me, touching things—the arm of the couch, the back of a chair. She halted beside me. Already, the flames were settling into an ember bed. She lifted down the doll from the mantel. Her eyes were dry now, almost fierce. She wet her finger on her tongue and began rubbing the dress. She rubbed hard. The spot of grease smeared. She sighed, brought the doll to her breasts, wrapped it in her shawl and said, "You love being held, don't you, Dolly?"

Was there nothing this woman didn't know? No nerve she couldn't fray? I walked away, over to a window. Across the meadow, the hawk had returned. It soared low above the frozen grass, hunting. Raymond and the fawn had disappeared. I turned and faced Doris. "Where is Em? Do you know?"

She shook her head as if she hadn't understood me, then walked to the landing of the staircase.

I shouted, "Who the hell are you?"

"I am Pence's lover."

"Goddamn him!"

"Please. Come, you need to see for yourself." She pointed up the staircase.

I shook my head, turned away from her to watch the flames. I pulled the panties out of my pocket. When Beth gave them to me that morning in the kitchen—her standing there naked, me at the table with my bacon and eggs—we hadn't made love for months. I remembered seeing the fear in her eyes, and then their dreaminess, and how she'd roused my inkling of a hard-on. The dance, I realized, had been a gambit to win me over to her teaching job.

I tossed the panties to the embers and they melted.

I walked over to Doris. Her eyes were as sparkling as the doll's in her arms. She now seemed liberated from the narrow instructions Spencer may have given her. She reached inside her shawl, withdrew something and handed it to me. It was a key. "Here. Take this. Go and see your mother."

Chapter 24

The fourteen fir treads leading up to the loft were foot-worn. At the top of the staircase, I turned and looked back down at Doris. She said, "Take a few minutes. Alone."

I turned to the door, keyed the lock and swung the door open. Deep shadows laced the long, narrow, log-walled space. I flipped the switch beside the door, but no lights flickered on.

Knee-high stacks of books covered the floor. Along the walls, the shelves sagged with more books. At the far end of the room, a gabled window allowed in the day's feeble light. Beneath the window sat a wide desk and a swivel chair. A typewriter squatted on the desk.

Between the stacks of books, a narrow aisle led toward the desk. Midway along the aisle, I stopped and picked up a book. It was a novel, a sea adventure, and its jacket was dust-covered. When I flipped it open, a toothpick fell from between the pages to the floor. I closed the book and set it down, and when I thumbed through several of the other books, more toothpicks—their ends chewed to a frazzle—slid from between their pages. The books were novels and, it appeared, so too were the hundreds of others—a lifetime of fictions, mostly crime thrillers and voyaging stories. The room was a mausoleum for mannish fictions, with no apparent regard for the motherly.

Overhead, a stout spruce beam ran the length of the loft vault. *How many books*, I wondered, *are contained in that beam?*

A long time ago, Pence Trout had left his home on Whetstone Road and come here, to this hilltop, his sanctuary from fatherhood, where he'd cut down a small forest, built a log house, changed his name, made a flower-filled meadow, planted a garden, chewed toothpicks and read novels.

I walked to the window. Looking north, beyond the near meadow and the woods, I could see in the distance the coast highway disappear around the shoulder of a hill, then emerge into view again. A lone blue car moved south. Far out in the wind-capped sea, a crab boat was a black dot.

The sound of Doris' footsteps came scuffing up the stairs. I turned and faced the door. Cradling the doll, she entered the room. Shadows hid her face; her shawl hung loose. She reached for the light switch.

"Don't bother. The lights don't work."

She glanced up at a bare-bulb fixture.

"There's a lot around here that's falling apart."

She stepped farther into the room. "Yes, I suppose so. But it's only a light bulb."

"What is it you wanted me to see?"

"The books, first. How much he loves them."

"Loves?"

"Yes."

"Squirreling them here like this, it seems pretty damned crazy."

"You don't understand." She pointed into the shadows. "The painting there, it's your mother's."

On the south wall, half hidden in the gloom, a dark square hung beside a shelf packed with books. I hadn't noticed it.

"Rose was a talented and wonderful painter."

I walked down the aisle. The shadows masked the painting, and its features were impossible to discern. Stacks of books stood in my way. I crawled over them and they wobbled, and the books shifted underneath my hands and knees ... a sense of vertigo, of moving over unstable ground. I stood on my knees and lifted the painting off a hook. It had a black wooden frame. I passed it back to Doris, returned to the aisle and took the painting to the window.

It was an underwater seascape, as viewed from beneath the water. At the top of the canvas, a murkish globe of yellow seemed both immersed in the watery grays and undulating blues, and floating above them. Rising from the bottom, a mass of greenish tendrils twisted upward toward the yellow.

I turned it over. Hand written in pencil was the word *Kelp* and the date 3/11/50. A scrawling signature said Rose T.

A seizure chilled me, as if a cellar web had grazed my neck and I snatched for it and touched nothing.

Doris said, "Everything will be just fine, Eddy. You just need more time to understand, that's all."

I turned the painting over again and held it at arm's length. The green forest of kelp, stretching upward toward the sun, seemed to sway back and forth. "Why is it here?"

"He lives here, near the ocean, because he loves it so."

I shook the painting at her. "Talk straight, goddamn it!"

In Doris' arms, the doll's blond hair lay against the brown shawl. She spoke dreamily. "When he's gone, I'll strew his ashes in the sea he loves."

I snorted my disgust. "Monsters can't love."

"There is a place, not far from here. It's all been arranged."

"We'll see about that."

She came down the aisle to the desk, rested her hand on the back of the chair. "Years ago, there were many other paintings—dozens of them. Except for this one, they were all ... lost."

"How? What happened to Rose?"

She took a faltering breath and looked away.

I set the painting on the desk, leaning it against the window. Spencer was using Doris, I figured, for another lure to draw me out and soften my rage. The more she spoke, though, the angrier I got. "Spencer doesn't love you. He never has. He's always loved Rose."

She moaned; the room seemed to swallow it. She leaned against the chair and steadied herself. "Please, Eddy ...."

"His dying gladdens me; it damn near makes me giddy."

She wiped her eyes with the shawl. "He's close by."

"If I see him, I'll shoot him down like a sick dog."

"No, I don't think you'll do that. There's too much you need to understand."

"Where is he?"

"Will you agree to see him, and listen to him?"

I turned and stared out the window. "How long has he got?"

She sobbed once. "Not long. He's being well cared for."

"And when he's dead, because you think he loves you, you'll *strew* him in the kelp? Strew, strew, strew!"

"Please, Eddy. Is nothing sacred to you?"

"No, absolutely nothing."

She flinched. "What kind of son are you?"

I grunted scorn. "No kind at all."

"What of Emily? She has a say in this, too."

"Why'd he track her down, and me, and then stalk us with

his fucking crazy lies, our so-called father? Our god-damned, so-called father?"

She collapsed into the chair, and seemed as shrunken as the doll, her eyes flat and void, as if my sneering ridicule had drained her.

I picked up a book and threw it at the ceiling, and when its pages fluttered open it dove into the stacks, skidded off and fell between them.

Doris startled. "Please ...."

"Why did he abandon us to Silas?"

Her hand groped for the arm of the chair. "As a young man, Spencer felt he was not a good father for Emily; his mind was too much in the clouds, in his imaginary stories. Silas took her swimming and bought her gifts. He believed Silas was a good man, a mostly good man better grounded in the real world. You must believe that."

"Silas was a monster."

"He didn't know about Silas' ... fondnesses, not until much later, after Silas' death. When he found out, it stunned him."

"How could he not have known? Goddamn it, they were twin brothers living in the same house for years." I wished I hadn't burned the old article from the *Oak Creek Tribune*, so I could throw it in her face.

"Silas hid what he was. No one saw it."

"A town full of blind people?"

"It was 1950, and things were very different then."

"And my so-called mother? Where the hell was she in all of this?"

"She raised Emily and painted and was a housewife." Her

head nodded forward as if she were praying. "I'm sorry, but I can't say any more about her."

"Goddamn it."

"Look around you." She waved an arm at the books, and then spun the chair around and faced the desk and the typewriter.

"You're in this with him, aren't you?"

"Whatever do you mean?"

I didn't know what I meant. I just stared at her, this old woman who I'd known for about an hour. The puzzle pieces flew around in my head, and the more pieces she added, the more they changed shape.

"Please, Eddy, if you believe just one thing believe this: It was not until many years after you were born that Spencer learned he had a son."

I grabbed another book and threw it against the wall. "How the hell could he not know that?"

"Please—"

"It's just another fat lie."

"Emily, she was only three years old when...." She stroked the doll's hair.

"What happened?"

She flinched, turned away in the chair and reached toward a shelf beside the desk. There were several identical, green-jacketed books. She pulled one out and handed it to me. "Here, this will tell you everything."

I took it. It was *Night Drives,* a novel by Spencer Gatz.

"Goddamn."

"Rose ... and the horror of what happened ...."

The jacket showed an ocean highway winding through the night. In the front of the book, there was a toothpick sticking up, marking a place. I opened to it, and the paper's stale mustiness spoke of years past. The toothpick was whole, intact, and the epigraph said, "Regret deeply, and live afresh."

"It's all there, the story and the horror."

I turned to the first chapter and read aloud, "'Jeremiah stood at the top of it.'"

"He was Spencer's father ...."

I snapped the book shut and threw it on the desk. "So he wrote a goddamn story."

Doris raised a hand to her throat. "Years ago, after your father and I became ... dear friends, I discovered that nearly every night he went for a drive. He would be gone for about an hour, and then return here, to the loft, where he'd write into the small hours of the new day. He would not tell me where he went, so one night I followed him. I was curious, not distrustful. He drove to the ocean, an overlook a few miles from here, where he stood in the dark for a few minutes. One day I asked him about it, and he said the drives made him feel more alive, and the ocean, too."

I shook my head. "Spencer Gatz—a pen name and a smokescreen."

Doris got the novel off the desk and slipped it inside her shawl. "I'll keep it for you."

"Don't bother. He murdered a man, a doctor. Whatever he calls himself, he's a murderer."

She groaned and shook her head.

"That's why he ran away from Oak Creek, to hide from the law. Spencer hid Pence, and Gatz hid Trout."

She turned and looked across the expanse of the loft, the multitude of books. "He cannot bear to throw away a single one. These are his truest love."

"Where is he?"

She sagged deeper into the chair, raised one hand to the typewriter and rested her fingers on the keys.

I wanted rid of Spencer. I kicked over a stack and the books scattered in the aisle, the motes rising in a storm.

Doris yanked her hand off the keys. She groaned, "Oh, no! How could he? How could he?"

She was staring at the typewriter, an old Underwood model, black and ponderous. The rubber platen had a puckered hole. I looked closer. The hole had a powder burn. I grabbed the machine, spun it around. The rear panel had a jagged exit wound. In the wall directly behind the desk, there was a gash where the mushroomed slug had embedded.

She looked up at me, her eyes grieving. "He promised it, for Christmas. Raymond loves this old thing."

When he shot it, Spencer must have been sitting where Doris was, in the chair, and he'd put the muzzle right up against the platen.

"What will I tell him?"

I pressed on a key and the thin steel arm swung partway up and jammed. I pushed down another and another. They all jammed together, a tangle of arms. A level tipped inside of me, and the bubble slid from rage toward ... joy. Yes, joy. Spencer had shot what Raymond most loved. I imagined the boy's pain, and it gladdened me.

"I ... don't understand."

I pulled a desk drawer out. The gun was there, the Browning .45 that I'd shot the road with, missing point blank what I loved.

We both heard the door bang open downstairs, and then a

moment later Raymond shouted, "Hey, where's everybody at?" Doris' face went white.

"Hey, where'd you guys go to?" The quick patter of Raymond's feet racing around downstairs, looking for us.

She stood quickly and her shawl snagged on an arm of the chair. She yanked it free; the chair swiveled. The doll slipped and she caught it by a leg. The book fell from beneath the shawl to the chair. She grabbed it up, turned to the aisle and froze, staring at the books scattered on the floor. She stepped carefully, avoiding each book as if it was a trip-wired mine, a bouncing Betty.

Raymond's feet came thumping up the stairs.

Midway along the aisle, Doris halted to gather up her shawl, the book, the doll.

Raymond raced into the room and halted by the door. His coat hung open, muffs gone and ears red. He gawked around, like he'd just entered a church, wide-eyed and slack mouthed. He spotted the typewriter. "Neato! The Undergood!" He started down the aisle.

Doris spread her arms and the shawl unfolded like wings. The doll fell to the floor. "Raymond, now is not a good time. Let's go home."

He advanced, stopping a few steps from her. "But it's Christmas. The Undergood." He leaned around her, trying to see. The stacks came to his waist.

She leaned with him, used the shawl as a screen. "Come, now. I will make a nice batch of chocolate chip cookies. They're your very favorite." She stepped toward him.

He backed away. "But I ain't even had my pie yet."

I said, "Damn it, Raymond. It's busted."

"Huh?"

She said, "Chocolate chip. Chocolate chip!"

I said, "It's shot right through the heart."

"Huh? What heart?"

"Raymond, you simply cannot play with it today. Maybe in a few days you can. Yes, a few more days."

I said, "He shot the goddamned thing."

"Huh?"

"It's nothing, Raymond. The typewriter is just a little, little bit broken. We can fix it. Spencer will."

"Broken? I didn't do it. Honest!"

"Of course not. Spencer will mend it as good as new."

"But it's mine! For Christmas! Mr. Gatz promised it."

"You cannot play with it now. Not today. Please, come along. We will take home your piece of the pie, and we'll bake a lovely batch of cookies. Yes, pie and cookies." She tried to shoo him back toward the door.

He scrambled out of the aisle and onto the stacks; he scooted toward the wall, a skipper legging across pond scum. She reached for him. Beyond her grasp, he stood on his knees and peered at the typewriter. "How come the letters are messed up like that?"

Doris pulled the shawl tight again. "You can't play with it now, Raymond."

"It ain't play. It's stories."

"Yes, of course it is." She held out her hand to Raymond. "You can make all sorts of wonderful stories about wizards and dragons, but not today."

"But it's mine now."

"Of course it is."

Trout Kill

"But it's Christmas."

"Raymond, please. Spencer is not here. He's in the hospital, remember? When he comes home, he'll give it to you then."

I liked Raymond. A lot. His heartbreak was plain to see, and I felt it, and I could also see him sitting at the typewriter and plinking away, thrilled by the dragons flying in his head and the keys' fatty smacks. He was a damn good kid, and he needed to see the monster Spencer was.

I grabbed the gun out of the drawer, pointed it up at the spruce beam that spanned the length of the room. "The damned Underwood's got a fucking hole in it. It's dead, no good anymore for your stories. Spencer shot it, okay?"

Raymond's eyes seemed to gather up the dim light; they glowed fierce. Then his whole face blinked. His shoulders bunched and his hands made fists. "You did it! You ain't no friend!" He scrambled off the books and returned to the aisle. Doris lunged for him and missed. He spun away and bolted out the door.

Doris stood with her back to me. Her gray hair fell on the brown shawl. When she turned and faced me, her daffodil eyes fixed on me. I lowered the gun. She said, "He's just a boy! He loves an old, sick man who, who …." She turned, hurried out of the room and then down the stairs.

My joy swelled and curdled.

I turned to the window. Raymond was kneeling on the road, gathering up a handful of gravel; and nearby, Bucky was nosing grass in the meadow. The muffs were looped around the fawn's neck. Raymond stood, one hand fisted, and reached into his coat pocket with his other hand. He pulled out an apple. Bucky's head came up; his ears pointed at Raymond, and he trotted forward, the muffs bouncing against his front quarters. Raymond jerked his arm back and hurled the rocks so hard his coat collar slipped up past his ear. The rocks fanned out and pelted Bucky; he sprang straight up, twisted in mid-flight and landed on four frantic legs. He sprinted down the meadow, toward the woods. Raymond yelled something. Then he dropped to his knees, shrank inside his coat and began crying.

Doris appeared, running out from underneath the porch roof. She hurried down the hydrangea path. At the road, she knelt beside Raymond and wrapped him in the shawl. She held him. After awhile, together, they stood up. She brushed off his knees and wiped his nose.

When Raymond looked up and saw me standing at the loft window, his whole face said he wanted me dead.

They walked together to the driveway, and then they disappeared around the corner of the house.

Chapter 25

I stood in the loft with the gun.

There was the shot Underwood, and Rose T.'s painting, *Kelp*. And Dolly, the barrette clipped in her hair, still lying in the book-strewn aisle where, a few minutes before, Doris had dropped her. The loft door stood wide open. Downstairs in the kitchen, the rhubarb pie sat on the counter, and the old black-and-white photograph lay on the floor. The ashes of Doris' painting were still cooling in the fireplace. My dog needed buried.

I had a fair idea where Em might have gone, and I had a damned good notion where Spencer was.

It was Christmas morning. My house in Milo seemed a thousand miles away, as if it belonged to another man in another life, but I could clearly picture Beth and the girls, still wearing their pajamas, gathered around the Christmas tree. Despite my absence, Beth would insist they open the presents. The girls would smile and they'd pretend everything was okay, for their mother's sake, and they'd keep glancing at the front door, hoping for me and Licker, and they'd set my gifts aside— a college sweatshirt, or maybe a fifth of Jack that they'd got an older friend to buy.

I set the gun on the desk, picked the doll up from the floor and cradled her in the crook of my arm. Em needed her. I went downstairs. My travel bag sat by the hall tree: Spencer's book, *Night Drives*, lay atop the bag. Doris must have dropped it there on her way from the loft to comfort Raymond. The spiteful joy I'd felt when I'd upset the kid had vanished, replaced with a festering regret. I kicked the book off the bag; it banged against the hall tree and fell to the floor. I put the doll in the bag, zipped it shut and went outside, where I leapt down from the porch and hustled to the corner of the house.

At the bottom of the meadow path, walking slowly together, the shawl draping their shoulders, Doris and Raymond were approaching the alder woods. Raymond kept glancing back up the hill, probably searching for Bucky. They walked into the trees, heading along the path and then disappearing toward the distant column of chimney smoke from Doris' home. A short distance from that smoke a second, thinner plume scarcely rose above the tops of the alders.

I ran down the hill and through the meadow to the woods, where I halted and stood behind a tree. Up ahead on the path, the brown shawl moved between the white-barked alders. I followed it, keeping my distance. About a quarter mile farther, Doris and Raymond emerged from the woods at the edge of a large garden. It was strewn with straw mulch, with two clown scarecrows wearing red polka dot pants and yellow raincoats. They walked to a large, clapboard-sided white house, flower boxes hanging from the windows, and went inside.

The second plume was rising from the chimney of the smaller guesthouse. Nestled in a small grove of alders and rhodies, it stood about fifty yards from the big house.

I circled around the garden, keeping hidden among the trees, the wild rhodies and the underbrush. I crossed the driveway, then made for the rear of the guesthouse. There was a small window, the curtain halfway open. I crept up and looked inside.

Trout Kill

A small sink, an electric range and counter cabinets. A wood box stacked full with alder and a potbelly wood stove. A tiny bathroom. Near the only door, a small bunk with a dinosaur bedspread.

A bed sat directly beneath the window where I stood. Wearing pale green pajamas, with the blue quilt and a white sheet pulled to his chin, with his eyes closed and his arms folded across his chest, Spencer lay there. Bottles of pills sat on a bedside table.

The waffle prints and tire tracks that Spencer and Doris had left on the frosty driveway told the story of that night: After Spencer stole Licker and left the note for me in Milo, he'd sped home, parked at the workshop and got a shovel—the one I'd found beside his car. He intended to bury the dog, most likely, and knew he had to work fast, since Ernst and me were on our way. Doris was waiting for his return; she'd made him a cup of hot cocoa. When he didn't come to the house, she got worried, walked to the workshop and found him lying at the rear of the Ford, where their prints got muddled up. She'd probably insisted they call an ambulance, but he'd said no. He had to hide somewhere close by and regain his strength. So Doris helped him walk to her guesthouse, where she could care for him—no car ride there, not with a dead dog in the trunk. Doris had most likely concocted the hospital story for Raymond's benefit, so he wouldn't see the full extent of "Mr. Gatz's" illness.

I ducked away from the window, retraced the path through the alder woods and sprinted back up the hill to Spencer's workshop. I slid the door fully open. Inside, the Ford had a flat front tire—a nail, probably one that had been lying on the sawdust floor.

I unwired the trunk and opened it. My dog lay there. I removed his collar, dropped it in a pocket of my field jacket, then lifted him out. His body was frozen stiff, legs tucked close, tail between his legs, and weighed almost nothing, like the dead fawn. My white breath shot over his black coat.

I carried him outside and over to the garden gate. I nudged through, went over to a bare patch of ground and laid my dog down. Spencer had said that places are important. They are. Underneath the cedar, where the coyotes could find her—that had been a good place to put the doe. Gardens, too, are good places.

First, I'd bury my anger, and then my dog.

I ran back to the workshop, got the shovel and hustled back to the garden. Where the scarecrow stood would be a good place. I stabbed the shovel into the frozen ground, then shoved the scarecrow over. A lumberjack with black button eyes in a pillow head, it toppled and lay among the moldering tomato vines. I tossed it aside, scraped a clearing in the vines and began digging, levering out the frozen lumps and throwing them aside. Underneath the icy crust, the ground was soft, dark and rich. I shaped a good-sized pit, roughly seven feet long and three feet wide. The blister on my hand turned raw, and the pile of loose dirt grew. I shed my jacket and shirt, and my steam lifted into the cool evening air.

Fat worms glistened, and the blade cut many in two. The hole got waist-deep and, later, the feeble sun fast sinking toward the ocean, it got as deep as I was tall. Still, I kept digging, wanting it deep and wide enough to bury forty-seven years. Every blade full I tossed up and out showered dirt till my sweat ran brown.

Trout Kill

Exhausted, arm-weary and thirsty, I sat at the bottom and rested. The earth, cool against my back, smelled like an old shoe in a fusty closet. Above, the rectangle sky was gunmetal blue. I stood and began scraping at the uneven walls, blading them smooth and plumb, crisping the corners and flattening the bottom. I wanted his last home built sounder than his first.

Finished, I laid the shovel crosswise across the top sides of the hole, grabbed the handle, chinned myself up and scrambled out. I ran back to the house, got a blanket from the bedroom and a steak from the fridge, and then returned to the garden.

Where I'd laid my dog, I began digging again, making a grave for what I loved, not a hole for what I didn't. I shaped it just wide and deep enough. I set Licker on the blanket, put the steak underneath his nose, wrapped him tight and laid him to rest. "You're a good ol' boy." I scooped up the loose dirt in handfuls and buried him, many handfuls, tamping careful as I filled, leaving a perfect mound that by winter's end would settle flat and become just another part of the garden.

I got my shirt and jacket and jogged back to the house. At the kitchen sink, I drank deeply, then stuck my head underneath the faucet and rinsed the dirt from my hair, washed off my shoulders and chest. The water ran brown. I toweled dry and put my shirt and jacket on.

On the floor where I'd dropped it, lay the photograph of Pence and Rose. I picked it up. He was my father; she was my mother. I craved to forgive someone. But how ... and why? I dropped the photo in my pocket, for Em: She'd want to see their faces, maybe liken them to those in her dreams: the red-haired woman, the man tall as a tree.

Hungry, I got a steak from the fridge and ripped off a raw

mouthful. I chewed quick and swallowed. For Licker—because of what I should have done for him, but didn't—I bolted down the rest of it.

The rhubarb pie sat on the counter. I clawed out a handful and it was galling sweet.

I went to the loft and, from the desk where I'd put it, got the pistol. The clip was two rounds short of full—from when I'd shot the highway and Spencer shot the Underwood. I held my arm straight out, elbow not quite locked, and sighted over the stacks of books at the door. My hand shook and the gun shook. I did a slow pivot, aiming here and there, the room ripe with targets, wanting to shoot *something* ... a book, the desk or chair, the painting, a log through its god dot. I jerked my arm straight up and pulled the trigger; a neat hole appeared in the spruce beam. It did not bleed.

I dropped the gun into a jacket pocket and turned to the Underwood. Raymond's Christmas present, ungiven. I lifted it off the desk; it weighed about as much as an armload of firewood. *Why had Spencer shot it?* I stepped over to the window. *Maybe for the same reason he'd taken my dog.* I heaved the machine. It shattered the bottom pane of glass, tumbled down the porch roof, leapt over the gutter and disappeared, thudding on the ground below.

I turned to the shelf beside the desk, where Doris had gotten the copy of *Night Drives*. There were other copies, ten or so, all inscribed with his message of deep regret.

Regret for what?

I took the books to the busted window and, one by one, threw them out. Some sailed beyond the gutter like Frisbees, and some flapped open and dove for the ground.

Trout Kill

Back outside the house, I stood on the porch. My knees were trembling. The typewriter had landed in a hydrangea, crushing it. The novels were scattered, one sailing as far as the road. I pulled the typewriter out of the bush and carried it around the house to the garden, where I dropped it in the hole. It landed exit wound up, jammed keys down.

I went back and gathered all the novels on the ground, brought them back to the hole and dumped them in.

Hungry still, I went back to the house, the kitchen. The plank floor in front of the sink was stained and foot-worn, the nail heads shiny. Over their years together, I imagined, Doris and Spencer had stood there countless times and washed the dirty dishes, her washing, him rinsing, the two of them happy. I got a fork, sat at the table and ate the last of the rhubarb pie. Doris had been right: the pie was tart, and how could I have ever thought it sweet? I cried, sobbing. It seemed Something Big wanted to bust out of me, and Something Bigger wanted in.

The sun was setting, its light streaming through the windows of the living room. I went to a window. On the porch, the arms of the rocking chairs were touching. Raymond must have knocked them together, or maybe it had been a gust of wind. At the horizon, the sun was an inch above the ocean. Three distant boats were specks moving north together, side-by-side.

At the bottom of the meadow, a small white pickup emerged from the woods and came toward the house. It slalomed back and forth around the potholes. The glare off the brand new windshield hid Beth. Even at a distance, I could see the damage to the right-front fender, still stove in by what I loved.

My stomach flipped. I ran back to the kitchen sink, where I heaved up the pie and steak.

Chapter 26

I had returned to the window and was watching her as the sun sank into the ocean. Ernst, I figured, must have told her where I was, as I'd somehow known he would, and I wasn't mad at him, just resigned to what, at last, I had to face.

She had parked my pickup, and was now standing behind the cab, peering warily over it at the house.

I'd rinsed out my mouth, but the sour bile lingered.

She walked to the front of the pickup where, facing the house, she raised a hand to shield her eyes from the glare off the windows. She squinted, gave no sign of having seen me. She wore a red, Christmasy dress, knee-length, and a green coat with black buttons. The dress looked new, and her chestnut hair looked different, cut shorter. She fiddled with the buttons of her coat.

The pickup idled, its exhaust drifting. Apparently, Jimmy had finally gotten around to replacing the radiator, too; and like I'd told him not to, he hadn't touched the dented fender. Someone had hosed the doe's blood off the hood.

She hugged her arms against the evening chill, and seemed to be staring at the porch rockers. Against the green coat, her hands were paper white.

Where my heart used to be, I half hoped that place would feel the old squeezing ache—the gentle hurt that I'd once called love. Always before, it had cast Beth in the wistful light of our history. I felt nothing. Then something sharp broke inside of me, like the first thrust of Something Big busting out.

Trout Kill

I went outside to the porch and waved to her.

She smiled, tight, and stayed rooted by the pickup.

She'd either have a lot of pointed questions, or she'd retreat behind her cold stone wall. Her questions, if she chose to go that way, would be confident and merciless, and they'd show she still loved me, and that her new dress and styled hair were aimed at me, to strike a blow at my foolishness, and not meant to catch the eye of Wally Beech, which had always been a half-wishful figment of my imagination.

I stepped down to the hydrangea path. "Hi, Beth."

She vaguely primped her hair, a flapping sort of gesture, her hand touching nothing. The wind, smelling of salt, kicked up from the west and flattened her dress against her knees. "Hello, Eddy."

I walked right up to her. Her eyes held neither judgment nor query, just hurt. I hugged her. Her shoulders were stiff; they yielded, then braced again. Her coat pressed against my field jacket, and the gun in my pocket. Her hair had been long, cascading down her shoulders, but it now came to her jawline, a severe cut. It smelled of lilacs.

"You look good, the new dress. And I like your hair."

She stepped back. Her eyes changed, from hurt toward doubt. "God, Eddy. You just sweet-talk and pretend everything is okay? After what you've done?"

"Yeah, sorry."

"You left. You never told me where you were." She looked all around, then at the house. "Where are we?"

The sun had set, and the fading dusky light lent the log walls of the house a gilded patina. "This is Spencer's Gatz's place. He's a friend of mine."

"Eddy, what is happening? Here and now, what is happening?"

"I met him just the other day."

"I'm frightened, for us."

Her fear was plainly in her hands, how they clutched at the buttons of her coat. No actress, she had never been one to wear a mask. She would say directly what was on her mind: What am I doing? What do I want? Will I come home, and when?

I said, "Let's go inside? There's a fire. It's warm."

She shook her head. "Just tell me what is going on."

I nodded. "I'm trying to."

"You look ... tired. Do you feel okay?"

I shrugged. In fact, my knees were weak and my gut twisting. I needed Jack. I missed her long hair.

"Where are we?"

"I told you: It's Spencer Gatz's place."

"Not that, Eddy. I mean *us*: Where are *we* at?"

"I ... I don't know."

"At the school, when you told me you were going away for a while, do you have any idea how much that hurt?"

"I know, I know. I was looking for Em. I thought she might be here."

"Does she know this man, Spencer?"

"Yes, she knows him."

She glanced at the front door, as if daring Em to open it and step outside. "But she's not here, is she?"

"I don't know where she is."

"And I suppose you told Spencer all about us, that we are having ... difficulties."

"No. It's none of his business."

"Thank God for that."

The pickup idled quiet, purring, inviting me to get in and drive home with Beth, to BJ and Kate and the ham dinner. I kept waiting for the old ache to swell up, that old velvet-toothed trap baited with alluring, soothing words like *almost* and *still* and *maybe*: I *still almost* loved Beth *maybe*. *Maybe* things could *almost* be okay, and we could *still* make a go of it.

I could have come clean about the bonfire fling I'd had with Nura two years ago, and say that sometimes I could smell her in my dreams, and her smell was like certain subtle roses are. I could have confessed to killing Silas when I was fifteen and, if she didn't fully believe I'd been justified, I could have drawn her an exact picture of his cock, its peculiar, monstrous canting to the right. I could have confessed my fantasies of Dr. Lund, Patricia. Confess that my heart had never been in the building of the blackberry house, and that every swing of my hammer had been false, and how the foundation was built on sand, not solid ground. Confess that the man she'd married was planning patricide, and soon.

I just jammed my hands into my pockets.

She looked hopeful—maybe thinking I was reaching for her panties, and that their spell over me still held like when I'd gone to the Nam. She said, "You wanted to go away and think, and now you have had some time to think, and that's why I'm here."

I looked away, down the hill and across the meadow to the dark wall of the woods. "Spencer came into Sparky's the other night. He told me a story about when he was a kid, about how his father took their old, sick dog to the woods and shot it."

"Eddy, what on earth are you saying?"

"Killing things, it sort of runs in the family, I guess."

She put her hand on my arm. "Where is Licker? Is he okay?"

"He died and I buried him."

She squeezed my arm. "I know how much you loved that dog. God bless him."

"He's in a good place now."

"I'm still confused about ... everything. What about Emily? Have you heard anything?"

"No, nothing."

She nodded, bit her lip. "I'm sorry for her, too, Eddy. I think I see what is happening. Lord knows, you have never been one to spill your feelings out for the world to see. I know you are upset about Emily. You two have always been so very close."

"Licker was a good dog."

She let go of my arm. "Did you hear what I said, about Emily?"

"Yeah, I heard."

Her gaze drifted up to the loft window. She pointed. "What happened?"

"Nothing, just an accident."

That word had always put her on edge, how I was so quick to attribute events to a benign fate that belied God's will. Her face was red, from the wind and, I knew, her growing frustration. She backed away another step, set her voice so firm it cracked. "God, Eddy. Are you seeing someone else? Is she here now?"

She was asking about the two rockers on the porch, if I'd sat there with a lover and held her hand as we watched the sun set. Goddamn. I'd been all wrong about her new dress, that she'd intended it for me. It wasn't. It was for her Jesus, to honor His so-called day of birth. And her hair fashion was meant to impress the folks at the elementary school, and the bunch of second-graders she'd be teaching. I said, "Beth, there's nobody else."

"Do you love me?"

We stood face-to-face, three paces apart. Her eyes stared into mine. I felt no need to blink. She did blink, pushing out a tear. She had summoned all the nerve she could muster, and her question deserved a straight answer. I remembered Mr. Willis' Senior English class, the exact moment I thought I fell in love with Beth. It was how her chestnut hair spilled down the back of her gauzy blouse, and underneath the blouse, faintly visible, how the marvel of her bra strap excited me. Since then, I'd told her a million times I loved her; sometimes the words flowed out of me, and other times I'd had to think to say them. Now, all those times added up to nothing. I said, "I almost love you."

She looked stunned, mystified. "What in God's name do you mean?"

"I loved you once, then I thought I loved you, and now I almost do." It was a half-truth or, depending, a half-lie.

She gasped, as if the twilight's chill had suddenly pierced her. "Almost?"

"That's not good enough, I know."

"The girls ... they're asking where you are."

"Yeah."

"They're making your favorite dinner, ham and scalloped potatoes. Oh, God, Eddy. They want to play catch with you and field grounders and catch flies. We can get another dog. The girls bought you a brand new fishing pole."

The sky was mostly black and, except for the thin orange line of the sunset, it had merged with the sea. The boats I'd seen earlier were invisible.

She clutched my warm hands in her cold hands. She leaned so close our faces almost touched. Lilacs bloomed in her hair. Worry and fear and sorrow swam in her eyes.

My next breath failed me. I said, choking it out, "Beth, I don't love you."

She dropped my hands and pulled back, bumping against the pickup. Her eyes turned hard and filled with distance, and the quickness of their change gladdened me. She'd be all right. She steadied herself against the hood. "So, there is another woman. Oh, God, Eddy. You bastard."

Chapter 27

When Beth sped down the hill in the pickup, she plowed right through the potholes and the taillights bounced crazily till they disappeared into the woods.

I stood there, feeling that giant fist reach into my chest again and start probing around. I cried and my guilt grew, as if my tears were feeding it.

Goddamn shitfuck.

The air tasted saltier than it had in recent days, and somewhere in my head it meant the weather was about to change. I went back inside the house and, cold to the bone, stood so close to the fireplace the sleeves of my jacket steamed.

Restless, I paced the room, weaving between the couch, the chairs and the end tables. The furniture was sturdy, built stouter than the house, with its crafted dovetails, its alder joints and fir joints and oak joints. I found another bottle of Scotch and started drinking.

The novel lay beside the hall tree where I'd kicked it, with its black-lettered *Night Drives* and *Spencer Gatz*. I opened it. Spencer had pounded out the first drafts of the story on his Underwood. *The story will help you understand*, Doris had said. *Understand what?* I snapped the book shut and heaved it across the room, aiming for the fireplace. It fluttered like a knuckleball, tailed off, bounced off an owl andiron and fell to the hearth. The book laid there, its spine bent.

I drank more, got a flashlight and went outside. The driveway leading to the garden was black, like my mood, but my feet knew the way to the garden gate and over to the hole. I stood at its edge, a pit blacker than the night. I switched on the flashlight.

The typewriter looked like a rock, and the books like forest leaves.

I tipped the Scotch up and drank deep and looked up at the keen stars till the bottle was empty. Into the hole it went.

I switched the light off, set it down beside the hole and went to the workshop where the car sat, with its flat tire and shovel-smashed windows. I got behind the wheel, started the engine, backed out, drove to the road and headed down it. The wheel pulled hard to the right and one headlight aimed acutely down. Through the fractured windshield, it was hard to see clear. Where the road forked, I turned left over the small wooden bridge and headed up the driveway. After about a hundred yards, I turned the headlights off. There was moon enough and stars enough to see by and I drove slow. I crested a small rise, put the car in neutral and coasted. At the guesthouse, the porch light was on.

The main house was lit up, all the curtains glowing. Doris and Raymond, I imagined, were just now sitting down to their Christmas dinner.

I pulled off the driveway, parked behind a clump of rhodies and turned the engine off. I got out, unwired the trunk and opened it. The blanket Spencer had used for Licker lay there. I circled through the woods, retraced the path to the back window of the guesthouse, and peeked inside.

A bedside lamp lit the room. Doris, the shawl around her shoulders, was sitting next to Spencer on the bed, holding one of his hands atop the blue quilt. He looked asleep. She brushed his white hair across his forehead with her fingers. He moaned, opened his eyes. She leaned over and kissed him gently on the forehead. He said something, too muffled and faint for me to discern. She pulled back, shook her head. He spoke again, waved a finger in the direction of the bedside table. She glanced at the table, nodded once, then squeezed his hand and kissed him again.

I ducked down and stood beside the window. Doris was saying her consoling goodbyes, and all I could do was wait there with my hands trembling and hope he wouldn't die before I could kill him. The night was calm. Somewhere in the dark woods an owl hooted, sounding like the far-away barks of a dog—*whoo ... whoo ... whoo-uh*. A northern spotted owl, I figured, with keen eyesight in the darkness. And my eyes, too, could see clearly that Spencer was my father. I listened hard for the owl to call again, but only heard the wood stove door creak open, then close shut again. It was Doris feeding alder to the fire, to keep Spencer warm through the night. Then a moment later, the window went dark; she had turned off the bedside light. The front door opened. Standing at the back corner of the guesthouse, I watched Doris walk slowly across the yard and to her brightly lit front door, where she turned, looked back for a moment, and then went inside.

The owl hooted again.

I pulled the .45 from my jacket and unsafetied it, then went around the guesthouse to the door, entered, and shut the door behind me.

The room was dark and warm, filled with the gravelly, uneven rasping of Spencer's snoring. Each labored gasp seemed as if it might be his last, and then another breath would stutter forth. The stove popped. I stepped over to the bed and turned on the lamp.

His long-whiskered face was washed-out yellow, with pallorous undertones. His closed, sunken eyes rolled and shimmied, as if he were in the midst of a dream, and in that dream death was an inch away and closing fast.

Doris had tucked the quilt around him, swaddling him; a toothpick lay in a fold of the pillowcase. On a bedside table, there were pills and medicines, a half-full water glass, a dull pencil and a notepad. I picked the pad up, flipped it open. The scrawls were faint, something about *settling up*, and *the woman, the boy*. I set the pad down.

I raised the gun—it was surer than a rock—and my trembling hand stilled. *You want to be my father, Spencer? Okay, you're it!* My finger curled around the tine of the trigger, and I told myself if I can manage this, then Something Big will flood out of me, a torrent of rage. And I told myself after he is gone, Something Bigger, a sort of calmness, will surely flow into me.

I shoved the gun into the quilt, point-blank against his chest.

His eyes twitched open, shut and then opened again. He croaked, "So, you did come."

It would be better this way—with him seeing me.

His eyes were filmy blue, hazed over. He wiped his gray tongue across his dry lips, lifted his head a bit, blinked away the haze till his eyes sparked. He said, "That gun, it belonged to your grandfather."

I twisted the gun and the quilt wound around the barrel.

"There're things you need to hear."

"You've said too damned much already."

Trout Kill

He coughed; red spittle flecked his chin. "Then go ahead, chop my rope." He winced, but his eyes still blazed. "One way or another, I'm soon enough dead."

"Soon enough isn't soon enough."

"I'm inclined to agree."

"There'll be no ocean for you, and no kelp."

His head sank back into the pillow. "Sheeit. What else did Doris jabber about?"

Seeing him weak and helpless brought a joy I hadn't counted on. Every breath he took was a shaking death rattle. I pulled the gun back. "No use wasting a bullet."

He pulled an arm from beneath the quilt, then pointed a shaking finger at the bedside table. "In the drawer, there."

"Why'd you leave Em and me?"

"No time for that." He pointed again. "A will ... you and Emily."

I laughed. "Nothing of yours is ours. Nothing."

"What about Emily?"

"Remember what she told you, underneath that bridge?"

He grimaced. "I do ... and I am." The spark in his eyes had grown fainter. He waved the finger again, this time at the gun. "Your grandfather's name was Jeremiah."

I remembered the name—Jeremiah—from the first sentence of the novel.

"He was a Bible-thumping cuss ...."

"I don't have a grandfather."

"And the Underwood, too ...."

"Raymond's Christmas present?"

He looked away. "It was time for me to shoot the damned thing."

"Raymond knows you did."

He nodded. "I'll make it up to the boy."

"It busted him up, how you broke your promise."

"I never should have promised. I regret it."

"Yeah, so you can 'live afresh.'"

He half smiled. "Susanna, your grandmother, she ran off with Harold Weeb. After your grandfather found out, he got roaring drunk. He told me, 'Never let a woman chop your rope.' Then he went out to the woods, roped and spurred up a spar tree, maybe a hundred-fifty feet or so, did a handstand on top, and then he let himself fall. A goddamned handstand! A goddamned madness!" He coughed again and red dots sprinkled the sheet.

He meant Susanna's infidelity was the axe that had chopped Jeremiah's rope. "Is that the 'horror' Doris meant?"

"No, not hardly. She meant your brother."

I shook my head. "What the hell?"

"Your twin, he died when you were born." He reached for me, trying to touch my hand, but I pulled it away.

"You're crazy. I don't have a brother."

"Doris gave you the book. It's all in there."

"In your goddamned story?"

He nodded and stayed silent. I paced to the stove and back. "Fucking crazy … fucking crazy."

"I'm real sorry about your dog."

"No ocean for you, no kelp."

"He was dead, lying on your porch. I took him, trying to spare you the grief."

I laughed, bitterly. "You spared me nothing. I buried him, and now it's your turn."

"Sometimes a man has to bury what he loves."

My eyes almost welled up with rage but I blinked them dry.

"I'm sorry."

"Another regret? You just keep racking them up."

"Son, a life without regret is a life unlived."

I turned away, stepped to a window that looked across the yard at the main house. Doris was standing at the kitchen window and, it appeared, doing something over the sink. No sign of Raymond. She glanced toward the guesthouse, and I ducked out of sight.

Spencer said, "No need for you to worry about the missus."

When I peeked again, she was still standing at the sink, looking down at her work. Then she stepped away and disappeared. Spencer was right about regrets. Life was full of them. Doris had them; Raymond had them; I had too many to count and, given the chance, I'd go back in my life and overhaul my fuckups. Beth, though, said she wouldn't change a single thing. She was a different sort of creature, one who lacked the imagination for fucking up.

"Son, before I go, I'd like a chance to settle up."

I stepped away from the window and over to the bed. Spencer had shoved the quilt and the sheet down to his waist. The slight rising of his chest did not show beneath his pajama shirt. I raised the gun again. "That's what I'm here for."

"Please, son ...."

Now there was fear in his eyes, but not of death. He needed more time, to say the things he needed to.

I lowered the gun, then pulled the drawer of the bedside table open. There was a legal-looking envelope with a lawyer's name. I got it and shook it in his face. "Your will means nothing. You hear me? Nothing."

Blood trickled from his nose. His hands clasped the quilt.

I took the envelope to the stove, opened the door and tossed it to the flames.

He whispered, "You and Emily ...." His body went rigid and his jaws clamped shut—a convulsion. His eyes rolled up, and all but the whites disappeared.

I stepped back to the bed and pointed the gun between his unseeing eyes.

His body spasmed; his hands clenched the quilt and bunched it. He moaned, and a fading sigh escaped his lips. Then the creases in his face went slack, and his hands let go and were still.

"Why now, after forty-seven years?"

He said nothing, and there was some small dignity in that, and then it hit me that his face and the face of Silas I remembered were the same face. They were twin brothers, just like the article in the *Oak Creek Tribune* said. Why hadn't I seen it in Spencer's face before?

I pulled the trigger and my hand bucked. Explosion filled the room. He never moved, except for a tuft of hair over his left ear, which fluttered at the passing slug. Inches from that ear, a neat hole appeared in the pillowcase, and the toothpick lying there leapt off the pillow to the floor.

I stood there shaking. I dropped the gun to the floor and felt rage take a firmer hold on me. *You died too soon!*

I kicked the bed and his arm flopped over the edge. I grabbed a bottle of his pills and poured them over him; they hopped like pelting hail. "Goddamn you, Spencer." I yanked away the bedding and threw it to the floor; the pills scattered and rolled. He laid there, a shrunken old man in green pajamas, dead.

Nothing else seemed to have died, only him.

I grabbed his arms and pulled him up, so he was sitting. I knelt down beside the bed, then slung his torso over my shoulder. I stood. He was a sack of hollow bones, no meat. I turned toward the door. His smell filled me—an old man's stale sweat, and the sour stink of his regret. For a moment, I lost my bearings. The door was gone, the windows gone, the ceiling and the floor. I was floating; he weighed nothing, and was nothing, and together we were nothing. I stepped forward ... toward something ... the door. Outside, the chill air swept away his smell. I breathed deep and my head cleared. With spring in my steps, I carried him to the car, his arms flopping, his head bouncing, and rolled him off my shoulder into the open trunk. He lay curled on the blanket like my dog had, a sort of comma. I laughed—a mocking snort that sounded strangely like the owl's hoot. I got in and started the car. The radio played that rat-a-tat song about the drummer boy—and I couldn't remember ever turning it on. I spun the dial, found a crackling hiss of static and cranked the volume high.

I drove back to the workshop, the flat tire flapping, the hiss screeching, the windshield hiding the road. I pulled inside the shop and parked.

A rusted wheelbarrow stood in the corner by the garden tools. I wheeled it over to the trunk of the car and hauled Spencer out by his pajamas. For the first time, the full weight of his body registered. He seemed to weigh twice as much as before. He slumped into the tray of the barrow, a curled-tight ball, with his knees pressing to his chest, his feet tucked under his butt and his arms crossed. I wheeled the barrow outside, over to the gate, through it and shoved toward the hole. Spencer's head thumped against the tray. The barrow screeched, the wheel begging oil. At the edge of the hole, I pulled the handles up and the tray tipped forward. Spencer sloughed out and disappeared into the black hollow. I let the barrow tumble down. Dirt showered, drumming loud on the metal tray, but soft on his pajamas.

"There's your ocean, Father."

I got the flashlight off the ground, where I'd left it. At the bottom of the hole, Spencer was a crumpled heap, his face planted in the dirt, his ass lifted at the moon. The barrow shrouded the Underwood. Dirt trickled on a book. I let the flashlight fall. It tumbled down, the yellow beam slashing here and there. It struck a book, winked out and blackness filled the hole. There were memories, too, that I wanted to wink out, go black.

I looked up at the one-third moon. Was it waxing or waning? I felt sick; was it waxing or waning? And joy, too; was it waxing or waning?

I grabbed the shovel, stabbed it into the loose mound of excavated dirt, lifted out a heaping blade full and pitched it in. Filling holes is easier than digging them. I shoveled fast and thought about the twin fawns: the one killed by the coyotes, the other very much alive. Coyotes are more akin to cedar trees than playground slides. And then in my head I saw a sick, double-trunked tree: Jeremiah and Susanna were the far-reaching roots; Pence made one of the two boles, and Silas the other; Em and me were limbs that forked off Pence; and the two smallest branches—BJ and Kate—split away from me. Like my nailing tree, this tree was shedding dead needles.

I filled the hole and then, sweating and tired, sucking juice from a blister, I leaned on the shovel. I hadn't tamped the hole, and a body displaces dirt. The coming rains, I figured, would settle the loose ground and, come spring, there'd be a pond about a foot deep, Spencer's ocean.

I got the scarecrow and shoved its pole so deep into the ground the caulk boots touched. There were two different moons: the bright one in the sky, and its dull twin mirrored on the scarecrow's tin hat.

I howled at both of them.

Chapter 28

The next morning, I dropped my travel bag on the front porch and then stood there drinking the last of Spencer's Scotch. I'd developed a taste for it. The distant ocean was flat gray; a dark bank of clouds obscured the horizon. A change in the weather was coming. It looked like rain.

Nearer, at the western fringe of the meadow, against the backdrop of the dark tree line, a gauzy mist hugged the ground. It was a white pond. A doe's head popped up above the ground fog, looked up the hill toward me, then dropped back into the mist. A short distance away, another doe raised her head. Then another and another, four in all. They'd lift their heads, flick their ears, munch their mouthfuls of grass, and then their heads would sink beneath the white gauze and vanish.

It was spooky, their heads popping up and down in the white pond, and the dark tree line, and remembering the water buff.

In the rice paddy that hot morning, till the buff raised its head above the ground mist, I couldn't see it. When I did, I knelt on one knee, brought my rifle to my shoulder, flipped off the covers and focused the scope. The buff was thick-horned and gentle-eyed. Its mouth worked a cud. Behind me, crapped out on a berm at the edge of the paddies, bug-bit after humping through the bush all night long, my LRRP team was taking a break. The LT was squatting behind a date palm, taking a dump. About eighty yards away, an M48 tank, heavy-tracked

Trout Kill

and long-barreled, was idling on a dirt road. I swung my scope that way. The gunner behind the 50-cal was eyeing the buff, too. He opened up, the 50' spitting red tracers. The first burst sailed high, a whipping red rope that cut into the tree line. The buff just stood there. The gunner adjusted. The second rope cut the buff from neck to brisket. It dropped beneath the mist. The 50' clatter stopped; the gunner hooted a rebel yell. The tank belched oily smoke and lumbered off the road and into the paddy, a black dragon floating through a misty white sea. Where the buff had dropped, the tank churned back and forth, back and forth, shambling and roaring, its treads throwing brown water, the gunner pumping his fist.

    I dropped to a prone position and shouldered my rifle. I adjusted the scope's zoom ring, drew a bead and cross-haired the gunner's nose. He was pimple-faced, about nineteen, with a bad excuse for a mustache. The chinstrap on his helmet dangled; there was a bottle of mosquito repellant tucked underneath the rim band. I centered the god dot—that point where the crosshairs intersect—and squeezed. The bottle of repellant exploded; the helmet spun halfway around the gunner's head. He yanked it off, pointed off into the bush and yelled something. I rolled over onto my back, pulled out a joint from my shirt pocket, lit up and smoked till I got stoned and the LT finished his shit.

    After about ten minutes, the four does floated off through the mist and disappeared into the tree line.

    I tossed away the empty Scotch bottle, stepped off the porch and went to the workshop. I got a can of gasoline sitting by the door, and a pair of pruning shears hanging above the bench. I was heading back to the house when Raymond came walking—not running—up the path through the meadow. He was wearing a new brown coat—a Christmas gift from Doris, I supposed. He saw me, scowled, kept his distance, jammed his hands deep into the pockets of the coat. "You seen Bucky?"

I kept walking, hoping he'd go away, knowing he was mad as hell at me, and for damned good reasons, I had to admit. He tagged along, wary of me, ready to bolt as the day we'd met. I nodded toward the lower meadow where the does had been grazing. "He was down there this morning." It was a lie. I hadn't seen the fawn that morning.

He ran up beside me. "You think he'll maybe stick around, you know, for a little while more?"

"Probably not."

He shoved his hands deeper.

"But, yeah, maybe he'll hang around a little longer."

He brightened, pulled his hands out of the pockets and eyed the gas and the clippers. "What's those for?"

"The gas is for cars. They run on the stuff." I waved the clippers. "And I've got some pruning to do."

"Pruning?"

"Cutting out the dead parts so a rose can get stronger."

"Oh, yeah. Grandmom does that, too." He turned and looked back down the driveway at the garden, frowned. "How'd it get backwards?"

"What?"

"The scaregrow. It used to look that way"—he pointed east—"but now it looks that way." He pointed north.

I stopped and looked back. The scarecrow stood where I'd planted it, beside the hole, next to the shovel that was stuck upright in the dirt. "The wind must've turned it."

Trout Kill

"Oh."

"Does your grandmother know you're here?"

He looked down at his feet.

"Hey, don't sweat it. I won't tell her."

"Thanks, Mr. Trout."

The kid had a memory for names. "That new coat looks good on you."

"Grandmom got it for me for Christmas. And some neat games and stuff."

"Uh-huh. What did you get for her?"

"I wrote her a special story ... on the Undergood ... before ... you know ... when it still worked okay." He frowned and stared at the scarecrow again.

"I'll bet she really liked it."

"Maybe she will, whenever she gets around to reading it. She was acting really funny last night, after she came back from a walk, and after we ate and had dessert, and when we opened presents, and then later on."

"Oh?"

"Right when I was getting my pajamas on, she said she wanted to go for another walk, a short one, and she did—a real short one—and when she got home she was kind of upset, like she'd been crying or something. She started drinking that—how do you say it, Pur-ga-tore-ee-oh? She drank the whole rest of the bottle, and then she made me go to bed. And then, really early this morning, even before breakfast, she got the broom and a pail and a mop and some other stuff and went out to the little house and started, you know, sweeping the floor. Like I said, she's acting really funny. Nobody does boring stuff like that the day after Christmas."

"Yeah, I guess not." Last evening, before going to bed, Doris had checked on Spencer and discovered he was missing. At first glance, maybe she'd thought he'd managed to crawl out of bed and, delusional, wander off into the woods, or back home. But then she'd probably seen the gun I'd dropped on the floor, and the hole in the pillow, but no blood. She'd panicked, perhaps, and thought about calling the cops—but something told me no, she hadn't called anyone. I figured Spencer had made her understand whatever happened between him and me, she shouldn't interfere. What could she do, other than hold her sorrow in check and hope for the best? This morning, she'd begun cleaning the guesthouse, and maybe sweeping the memory of me into the trashcan.

We started walking up the driveway again. Raymond was searching the hilltop for Bucky. "You think Bucky's big enough to, you know, be okay all by himself?"

"He'll be just fine."

Raymond sidled closer. "Do you think I should warm up some more milk?"

"No."

"I guess when fawns grow up, they eat apples, huh?"

"Look, Raymond, I'm sorry for what I said about the Undergood. Okay? It was wrong. I owe you one. And your grandmom, too. I owe her more than one."

He looked at me. "Grandmom said it ain't your fault for getting mad."

"She's a little bit wrong about that."

"I shouldn't've thrown the rocks." He studied his hand, the one that had done the deed. "It ain't Bucky's fault either. I gotta find him. I gotta make it up to him."

At the crest of the driveway, where it met the road, I pointed down the slope of the meadow toward the spruce woods, where the mist still obscured the ground. "See that tall spruce? He was there, earlier, eating grass."

Raymond started down the hill, stopped and turned around. "I was wondering something."

"Yeah?"

"About the Undergood."

"It can't be fixed."

The kid's face bunched up, looked like he was going to cry. He raised the sleeve of his new coat toward his running nose, hesitated, and then lowered his arm. "But why did he break it?"

"Because ... he loved it too damned much."

"That don't make any sense."

"I know."

"But he said it was mine."

"Sometimes you make a promise you can't keep."

"But it writes good stories."

"Use a pencil." I pulled one from my jacket, walked over and handed it to him.

He shook his head, as if to say the pencil was dumb, but he slipped it into his pocket. Then he pointed at my jacket. "You got something on the back of it."

"Oh?" I pulled the bottom of it around, so I could see the back. There was a small dark stain. It was dried blood, from Spencer's nose when I'd carried him to the car. "Yeah, I guess so."

"You need to wash it good."

"No, I don't think so."

He gave me another look, then shrugged and took off running down the hill toward the woods, his arms pumping crazy, his legs scattered crazy, crying out, "Bucky! Bucky!" His legs disappeared into the low-hanging fog, and he headed toward the tall spruce.

I went to the rose trellis, made of cedar lattice and as tall as the porch roof. I set the gas down and studied the roses. They were scraggly, thick-caned and big-thorned; the rambling stems were mildewed and frostbitten. Bucky had browsed off the tips.

I had only a vague idea of how to prune. You lop the canes shorter, cut out the weaker ones that rub against the stronger ones, remove the damaged wood, and open up the middle so air flows better. You make angle cuts, not horizontal cuts.

The clippers felt dumb in my hands, so I was careful. A thorn got me. And then another and another, making red beads pop on my arms and hands. After lopping off a few of the blackened canes, the clippers got smarter. It took awhile and that was okay, and the thorns were okay.

Standing back, I checked my work. I'd cut off more than I'd left. The canes were short, the deadwood gone. Come spring, new, healthy shoots would sprout from the canes, I hoped, and they'd grow strong, and then about June the buds would bust open. The roses, I imagined, would be sweet-scented and white.

I dropped the clippers, got the can of gas and took it to the porch. I got my bag, then walked to the corner of the house, where the foundation was crumbling. Spencer hadn't known a god-damned thing about making strong mortar. I took my notebook out of the bag—I'd almost forgotten it was in there—snapped the three rings open and yanked the sheets of paper out, a ream two inches thick.

I crumpled the paper into tight balls, about a dozen wads, and stacked them against the stone foundation. They made a small white mountain, its peak just beneath the bottommost

Trout Kill

log of the wall. I screwed the cap off the gas can, held the can over the balls of paper and ... hesitated. Doubt crumbled my certainty. When she'd burned down the Whetstone house, Em had used gasoline. Gasoline is certain.

I flung the gas can away, across the driveway, and it landed in the meadow.

Down the hill toward Doris' house, above the alders, one smoke rose, drifting north toward me.

I struck a match on my jeans, held the tiny flame beneath one of my old nightmares—or maybe it was the drawing of the periwinkle house. The fire spread up the mountain fast, and the flames licked at the bottom log.

I got my travel bag, went to the road and headed down through the misty meadow, into the dark spruce and cedar woods, past the fork and the wooden bridge. I never looked back, was tired of doing that. There was a fair chance the flames would catch hold of the logs and burn the house down, and a fair chance they wouldn't.

At the coast highway, the mist was all gone. A car approached, heading north. I stuck my thumb out. The driver never slowed, just sped past as if she hadn't seen me. The whisper of the distant surf sifted through the woods. A truck came along, and I stuck my thumb out again and it pulled over, a rusted-out Chevy.

The driver leaned across the bench seat and shoved the door open. "Where you headed, bud?" He was nineteen, or thereabouts, the sleeves of his t-shirt rolled up, his black hair slicked down, smoking a cigarette.

"North, then east."

"Jump in."

I threw my bag in the back. It had Em's doll, Licker's collar and my last bottle of Purgatorio. I missed Ernst, wished we were tooling down the highway in Old Blue and philosophizing. And I'd brought *Night Drives*. I figured reading the story might help unbury some part of me. And I'd tucked the old photograph of mom and dad in my shirt pocket.

The guy's name was Tony. He was a crabber heading up to Glass Point, where the tourists paid good money to eat "bugs from the sea." We shook hands. He laughed and nodded toward the big cooler in the back, the kind campers use for their beer. "Got a big-assed load of fresh bugs."

I said, "How much for one?"

He shrugged. "Five bucks sound okay?"

I pulled my wallet out and slipped a fiver in the ashtray. He grinned, said I could have my pick.

I jumped out of the cab and opened the cooler. The Dungeness, packed in ice, had fat claws. I grabbed one with an eight-inch carapace and jumped back in the cab. Tony drove. I snapped off the two claws, cracked open their tough shells between my teeth.

Tony eyed me. "You are one hungry man."

I tore into the claws with my fingers, pulling out the fleshy strings of white meat, licking the juices.

"There's a hammer in the glove box, man."

I got it out and smashed the carapace, my knee the anvil. Stuffing crabmeat in my mouth, tasting nothing but sweet, I eyed the road ahead. "How fast will this piece of shit go?"

"Let's fuckin' see." Tony stomped the pedal down and the pickup groaned. We gained speed and the speed felt good, putting healing distance between Spencer and me.

Trout Kill

To my left, through the blur of passing trees, I caught glimpses of the beach, the white surf and the ocean's broad gray. Up ahead, the green coastal hills sloped down to the shoulder of the highway. A corner loomed, and we sped toward it.

Somewhere beyond that corner, centered in my crosshairs, was Em. She was camped underneath a bridge in the Big City, the river flowing by. Silas, too, was there, lurking in the deeper water. It was a clear morning, the sun rising above the skyscrapers. Em, sleepy-eyed, her hair messed up, was just now crawling out of her sleeping bag. A boat cruised underneath the bridge, and a car sped over it. Em smiled large when she saw me, and larger yet when I held the doll out for her. Her street-rough hands held it tight to her breasts, and she said, "Welcome home, Dolly. I've missed you."

I gave her the old black and white photo, and after she studied it for a long time I said, "Are they the faces in your dreams?"

She nodded, and then we hugged each other and began to cry.

CPSIA information can be obtained at www.ICGtesting.com
Printed in the USA
BVOW070404060213

312496BV00001B/2/P